D0180652

Theodore Sturgeon was born in New York City and has spent much of his life on the West Coast. Author of hundreds of short stories and a half-dozen novels, Sturgeon has won the Hugo Award for his novel, *More than Human*, and the International Fantasy Award for his novel, *The Dreaming Jewels* (known for many years under the title, *The Synthetic Man*). He has also received the Nebula Award for his story "Slow Sculpture."

His death in May 1985 was mourned by lovers of fiction everywhere.

"The magic of Theodore Sturgeon's writing lies in his understanding of the many ways there are to be human."
>—Larry Niven, author of *The Integral Trees*

"The Sturgeon magic does not diminish with the years. His stories have a timeless quality and a universality which is beyond fantasy and science fiction and yet is always found in the best of those genres."
>—Madeleine L'Engle, author of *A Wrinkle in Time*

"Theodore Sturgeon is one of the finest writers alive, by any standards whatsoever."
>—Poul Anderson, author of *Orion Shall Rise*

Bluejay Special Editions
Each Bluejay Special Edition is printed on acid-free paper and bound in a durable trade paperback format. Authors whose works have already been published in the series include Philip K. Dick, Harlan Ellison, Edgar Pangborn and Theodore Sturgeon.

Books by Theodore Sturgeon

*Denotes a Bluejay Book

ALIEN CARGO

Theodore Sturgeon

BLUEJAY BOOKS INC.

A Bluejay Book, published by arrangement with the Author.

Copyright © 1984 by Theodore Sturgeon
Jacket art by Rowena Morrill
Book design by Joann Hill Willig

All rights reserved. No part of this book may be reproduced or transmitted in any form or by any means, electronic or mechanical, including photocopying, recording, or by any information storage or retrieval
system, without the express written permission of the Publisher, except
where permitted by law. For information, contact Bluejay Books, Inc.,
1123 Broadway, Suite 306, New York, New York 10010

Manufactured in the United States of America
First Bluejay printing: June 1984
First paperback edition: April 1986

Library of Congress Cataloging in Publication Data

Sturgeon, Theodore.
  Alien cargo.

  1. Science fiction, American. I. Title.
PS3569.T875A79   813′.64   84-12302
ISBN 0-312-94007-6

This book is printed on acid-free paper. The paper in this book meets the
guidelines for permanence and durability of the Committee on Production
Guidelines for Book Longevity of the Council on Library Resources.

To
Lady Jayne
who has at last taught me
this unthinkable arrogance:
I deserve her!

INTRODUCTION

The volume you hold in your hands is what it is—a package of self-evidences, to your liking or not, memorable or not. I do hope you like them.

To me they are, perforce, a great deal more than that. I wish devoutly that I could share with you the spaces between them, filled with what each has meant to me, and, for that matter, also the spaces between the lines.

Someone—maybe me—wrote about music that the spaces between the notes made the music as much as the notes themselves. This is certainly true for me, because "I was there." You can only surmise, intuit, guess what is in the spaces between the words and the lines and the stories. The spaces here are filled with the memories they have invoked as I arranged the stories in the order you see—a chronological order which, when set out in a table of contents, looks so neat and consistent. It was neither as I lived in these spaces, and I am astonished at their wealth and detail, amazed that I could have lived through some of them, yearn to revisit the scenes and feelings and attitudes which I held as I wrote them; I do truly wish I could share it all with you, the loves and losses, the delights and dangers, and above all the learnings. The learnings. Living a life is a very educational experience, one very much worth doing.

In the spaces between the black marks on these pages are wars, oceans, sunsets, miseries, laughter, loss and loneliness; fury and puzzlement; rewards denied, rewards—so many—rich and unexpected. How can you know the space between words that was seven months long; how can you know how hard it is to be breezy and light sometimes, how joyful it is to hear your own words singing back to you some song you never knew you knew?

But you know, the same is true of you when we meet (should we meet) and the spaces between your words and your breaths and the beats of your heart are as full as the spaces in this book, as full of memories and learnings as anything here, anything I can ever do. Which is why I have come to the understanding that when we meet I am face to face with hints and silent miracles, learning which you have and I have not. I look at my words and see clearly the metaphor: on each page there is far more blank space than markings. So we each are to each other; all we can do, all we must do, all over the world, is to come to a realization that we must accept and honor that which seems at first like blankness; it is, in you, a far richer treasure than any of our words and gestures.

I extend herewith these markings. I would like you to enjoy them.

Theodore Sturgeon
Oregon, 1984

CONTENTS

IT

In 1975 I accepted an invitation to the San Diego Comic Convention, all expenses. I thought it kind of them, but was mystified, for though I had written instructional comics just before this country entered WW II, and a couple of issues of something called *Iron Monroe,* derived from a John Campbell series back in the 'thirties, I had no track record in the comics; nor was a fan or collector. I went, I met some wonderful people whom I still regard as "family," and at the banquet, where Ray Bradbury was giving out awards and uttering verbal bouquets about the recipients (in one case gracefully calling another writer "teacher," and telling how for two years before he sold a story he used to anatomize every one of this writer's stories, until he jealously hated him) I suddenly realized, with a sweet and shocking clutch of the gut, that he was talking about *me.* And when I rose to go up front and accept it—it was the Convention's highest, the Golden Ink Pot—the same award they gave Seigel and Schuster for Superman. And for the first time in my life I faced an audience and couldn't think of anything to say beyond two words; one was "thank" and the other was "you."

Subsequently I learned for the very first time that my story "It" is seminal; that it is the great granddaddy of *The Swamp Thing, The Hulk, The Man Thing,* and I don't know how many other celebrated graphics.

There's no romance within this story, but a lot surrounds it. I wrote it, of all times and places, in 1939, on my first honeymoon when, barely out of my 'teens, and very immature, I had no business having honeymoons. And it was at this same Convention that in 1976, I met my present wife, the incomparable Reverend Lady Jayne.

It walked in the woods.

It was never born. It existed. Under the pine needles the fires burn, deep and smokeless in the mold. In heat and in darkness and decay there is growth. There is life and there is growth. It grew, but it was not alive. It walked unbreathing through the woods, and thought and saw and was hideous and strong, and it was not born and it did not live. It grew and moved about without living.

It crawled out of the darkness and hot damp mold into the cool of a morning. It was huge. It was lumped and crusted with its own hateful substances, and pieces of it dropped off as it went its way, dropped off and lay writhing, and stilled, and sank putrescent into the forest loam.

It had no mercy, no laughter, no beauty. It had strength and great intelligence. And—perhaps it could not be destroyed. It crawled out of its mound in the wood and lay pulsing in the sunlight for a long moment. Patches of it shone wetly in the golden glow, parts of it were nubbled and flaked. And whose dead bones had given it the form of a man?

It scrabbled painfully with its half-formed hands, beating the ground and the bole of a tree. It rolled and lifted itself up on its crumbling elbows, and it tore up a great handful of herbs and shredded them against its chest, and it paused and gazed at the gray-green juices with intelligent calm. It wavered to its feet, and seized a young sapling and destroyed it, folding the slender trunk back on itself again and again, watching attentively the useless, fibered splinters. And it snatched up a fear-frozen field creature, crushing it slowly, letting blood and pulpy flesh and fur ooze from between its fingers, run down and rot on the forearms.

It began searching.

Kimbo drifted through the tall grasses like a puff of dust, his bushy tail curled tightly over his back and his long jaws agape. He ran with an easy lope, loving his freedom and the power of his flanks and furry shoulders. His tongue lolled listlessly over his lips. His lips were black and serrated, and each tiny pointed liplet swayed with his doggy gallop. Kimbo was all dog, all healthy animal.

He leaped high over a boulder and landed with a startled yelp as a longeared cony shot from its hiding place under the rock. Kimbo hurtled after it, grunting with each great thrust of his legs. The rabbit bounced just ahead of him, keeping its distance, its ears flattened on its curving back and its little legs nibbling away at distance hungrily. It stopped, and Kimbo pounced, and the rabbit shot away at a tangent and popped into a hollow log. Kimbo yelped again and rushed snuffling at the log, and knowing his failure, curvetted but once around the stump and ran on into the forest. The thing that watched from the wood raised its crusted arms and waited for Kimbo.

Kimbo sensed it there, standing dead-still by the path. To him it was a bulk which smelled of carrion not fit to roll in, and he snuffled distastefully and ran to pass it.

The thing let him come abreast and dropped a heavy twisted fist on him. Kimbo saw it coming and curled up tight as he ran, and the hand clipped stunningly on his rump, sending him rolling and yipping down the slope. Kimbo straddled to his feet, shook his head, shook his body with a deep growl, came back to the silent thing with green murder in his eyes. He walked stiffly, straight-legged, his tail as low as his lowered head and a ruff of fury round his neck. The thing raised its arms again, waited.

Kimbo slowed, then flipped himself through the air at the monster's throat. His jaws closed on it; his teeth clicked together through a mass of filth, and he fell choking and snarling at its feet. The thing leaned down and struck twice, and after the dog's back was broken, it sat beside him and began to tear him apart.

"Be back in an hour or so," said Alton Drew, picking up his rifle from the corner behind the wood box. His brother laughed.

"Old Kimbo 'bout runs your life, Alton," he said.

"Ah, I know the ol' devil," said Alton. "When I whistle for him for half an hour and he don't show up, he's in a jam or he's treed something wuth shootin' at. The ol' son of a gun calls me by not answerin'."

Cory Drew shoved a full glass of milk over to his nine-year-old daughter and smiled. "You think as much o' that houn' dog o' yours as I do of Babe here."

Babe slid off her chair and ran to her uncle. "Gonna catch me the bad fella, Uncle Alton?" she shrilled. The "bad fella" was Cory's invention—the one who lurked in corners ready to pounce on little girls who chased the chickens and played around mowing machines and hurled green apples with a powerful young arm at the sides of the hogs to hear the synchronized thud and grunt; little girls who swore with an Austrian accent like an ex-hired man they had had; who dug caves in haystacks till they tipped over, and kept pet crawfish in tomorrow's milk cans, and rode work horses to a lather in the night pasture.

"Get back here and keep away from Uncle Alton's gun!" said Cory. "If you see the bad fella, Alton, chase him back here. He has a date with Babe here for that stunt of hers last night." The preceding evening, Babe had kind-heartedly poured pepper on the cows' salt block.

"Don't worry, kiddo," grinned her uncle, "I'll bring you the bad fella's hide if he don't get me first."

Alton Drew walked up the path toward the wood, thinking about Babe. She was a phenomenon—a pampered farm child. Ah well—she had to be. They'd both loved Clissa Drew, and she'd married Cory, and they had to love Clissa's child. Funny thing, love. Alton was a man's man, and thought things out that way; and his reaction to love was a strong and frightened one. He knew what love was because he felt it still for his brother's wife and would feel it as long as he lived for Babe. It led him through his life, and yet he embarrassed himself by thinking of it. Loving a dog was an easy thing, because you and the old devil could love one another completely without talking about it. The smell of gun smoke and wet fur in the rain were perfume enough for Alton Drew, a grunt of satisfaction and the scream of something hunted and hit were poetry enough. They weren't like love for a human, that choked his throat so he could not say words he could not have thought of anyway. So Alton loved his dog Kimbo and his Winchester for all to see, and let his love for his brother's women, Clissa and Babe, eat at him quietly and unmentioned.

His quick eyes saw the fresh indentations in the soft earth behind the boulder, which showed where Kimbo had turned and leaped with a single surge, chasing the rabbit. Ignoring the tracks, he looked for the nearest place where a rabbit might hide, and strolled over to the stump. Kimbo had been there, he saw, and had been there too late. "You're an ol' fool," muttered Alton. "Y' can't catch a cony by chasin' it. You want to cross him up some way." He gave a peculiar trilling whistle, sure that Kimbo was digging frantically under some nearby stump for a rabbit that was three counties away by now. No answer. A little puzzled, Alton went back to the path. "He never done this before," he said softly.

He cocked his .32-40 and cradled it. At the county fair someone had once said of Alton Drew that he could shoot at a handful of corn and peas thrown in the air and hit only the corn. Once he split a bullet on the blade of a knife and put two candles out. He had no need to fear anything that could be shot at. That's what he believed.

The thing in the woods looked curiously down at what it had done to Kimbo, and tried to moan the way Kimbo had before he died. It stood a minute storing away facts in its foul, unemotional mind. Blood was warm. The sunlight was warm. Things that moved and bore fur had a muscle to force the thick liquid through tiny tubes in their bodies. The liquid coagulated after a time. The liquid on rooted green things was thinner and the loss of a limb did not mean loss of life. It was very interesting, but the thing, the mold with a mind was not pleased. Neither was it displeased. Its accidental urge was a thirst for knowledge, and it was only—interested.

It was growing late, and the sun reddened and rested awhile on the hilly horizon, teaching the clouds to be inverted flames. The thing threw up its head suddenly, noticing the dusk. Night was ever a strange thing, even for those of us who have known it in life. It would have been frightening for the monster had it been capable of fright, but it could only be curious; it could only reason from what it had observed.

What was happening? It was getting harder to see. Why? It threw its shapeless head from side to side. It was true—things were dim, and growing dimmer. Things were changing shape, taking on a new and darker color. What did the creatures it had crushed and torn apart see? How did they see? The larger one, the one that had attacked, had used two organs in its head. That must have been it, because after the thing had torn off two of the dog's legs it had struck at the hairy muzzle; and the dog, seeing the blow coming, had dropped folds of skin over the organs—closed its eyes. Ergo, the dog saw with its eyes. But then after the dog was dead, and its body still, repeated blows had had no effect on the eyes. They remained open and staring. The logical conclusion was, then, that a being that had ceased to live and breathe and move about lost the use of its eyes. It must be that to lose sight was, conversely, to die. Dead things did not walk about. They lay down and did not move. Therefore the thing in the wood concluded that it must be dead, and so it lay down by the path, not far away from Kimbo's scattered body, lay down and believed itself dead.

Alton Drew came up through the dusk to the wood. He was frankly worried. He whistled again, and then called, and there was still no response, and he said again, "The ol' flea-bus never done this before," and shook his heavy head. It was past milking time, and Cory would need him. "Kimbo!" he roared. The cry echoed through the shadows, and Alton flipped on the safety catch of his rifle and put the butt on the ground beside the path. Leaning on it, he took off his cap and scratched the back of his head, wondering. The rifle butt sank into what he thought was soft earth; he staggered and stepped into the chest of the thing that lay beside the path. His foot went up to the ankle in its yielding rottenness, and he swore and jumped back.

"Whew! Somp'n sure dead as hell there! Ugh!" He swabbed at his boot with a handful of leaves while the monster lay in the growing blackness with the edges of the deep footprint in its chest sliding into it, filling it up. It lay there regarding him dimly out of its muddy eyes, thinking it was dead because of the darkness, watching the articulation of Alton Drew's joints, wondering at this new uncautious creature.

Alton cleaned the butt of his gun with more leaves and went on up the path, whistling anxiously for Kimbo.

Clissa Drew stood in the door of the milk shed, very lovely in red-checked gingham and a blue apron. Her hair was clean, yellow, parted in the middle and stretched tautly back to a heavy braided knot. "Cory! Alton!" she called a little sharply.

"Well?" Cory responded gruffly from the barn, where he was stripping off the Ayrshire. The dwindling streams of milk plopped pleasantly into the froth of a full pail.

"I've called and called," said Clissa. "Supper's cold, and Babe won't eat until you come. Why—where's Alton?"

Cory grunted, heaved the stool out of the way, threw over the stanchion lock and slapped the Ayrshire on the rump. The cow backed and filled like a towboat, clattered down the line and out into the barn-yard. "Ain't back yet."

"Not back?" Clissa came in and stood beside him as he sat by the next cow, put his forehead against the warm flank. "But, Cory, he said he'd—"

"Yeh, yeh, I know. He said he'd be back for the milkin'. I heard him. Well, he ain't."

"And you have to— Oh, Cory, I'll help you finish up. Alton would be back if he could. Maybe he's—"

"Maybe he's treed a blue jay," snapped her husband. "Him an' that damn dog," He gestured hugely with one hand while the other went on milking. "I got twenty-six head o' cows to milk. I got pigs to feed an' chickens to put to bed. I got to toss hay for the mare and turn the team out. I got harness to mend and a wire down in the night pasture. I got wood to split an' carry." He milked for a moment in silence, chewing on his lip. Clissa stood twisting her hands together, trying to think of something to stem the tide. It wasn't the first time Alton's hunting had interfered with the chores. "So I got to go ahead with it. I can't interfere with Alton's spoorin'. Every damn time that hound o' his smells out a squirrel I go without my supper. I'm gettin' sick and—"

"Oh, I'll help you!" said Clissa. She was thinking of the spring when Kimbo had held four hundred pounds of ragging black bear at bay until Alton could put a bullet in its brain, the time Babe had found a bearcub and started to carry it home, and had fallen into a freshet, cutting her head. You can't hate a dog that has saved your child for you, she thought.

"You'll do nothin' of the kind!" Cory growled. "Get back to the house. You'll find work enough there. I'll be along when I can. Dammit, Clissa, don't cry! I didn't mean to—Oh, shucks!" He got up and put his arms around her. "I'm wrought up," he said. "Go on now. I'd no call to speak that way to you. I'm sorry. Go back to Babe. I'll put a stop to this for good tonight. I've had enough. There's work here for four farmers an' all we've got is me an' that . . . that huntsman.

"Go on now, Clissa."

"All right," she said into his shoulder. "But, Cory, hear him out first when he comes back. He might be unable to come back. He might be unable to come back this time. Maybe he . . . he——"

"Ain't nothin' kin hurt my brother that a bullet will hit. He can take care of himself. He's got no excuse good enough this time. Go on, now. Make the kid eat."

Clissa went back to the house, her young face furrowed. If Cory quarreled with Alton now and drove him away, what with the drought and the creamery about to close and all, they just couldn't manage. Hiring a man was out of the question. Cory'd have to work himself to death, and he just wouldn't be able to make it. No one man could. She sighed and went into the house. It was seven o'clock, and the milking not done yet. Oh, why did Alton have to——

Babe was in bed at nine when Clissa heard Cory in the shed, slinging the wire cutters into a corner. "Alton back yet?" they both said at once as Cory stepped into the kitchen; and as she shook her head he clumped over to the stove, and lifting a lid, spat into the coals. "Come to bed," he said.

She laid down her stitching and looked at his broad back. He was twenty-eight, and he walked and acted like a man ten years older, and looked like a man five years younger. "I'll be up in a while," Clissa said.

Cory glanced at the corner behind the wood box where Alton's rifle usually stood, then made an unspellable, disgusted sound and sat down to take off his heavy muddy shoes.

"It's after nine," Clissa volunteered timidly. Cory said nothing, reaching for house slippers.

"Cory, you're not going to——"

"Not going to what?"

"Oh, nothing. I just thought that maybe Alton——"

"Alton," Cory flared. "The dog goes hunting field mice. Alton goes hunting the dog. Now you want me to go hunting Alton. That's what you want?"

"I just—He was never this late before."

"I won't do it! Go out lookin' for him at nine o'clock in the night? I'll be damned! He has no call to use us so, Clissa."

Clissa said nothing. She went to the stove, peered into the wash boiler set aside at the back of the range. When she turned around, Cory had his shoes and coat on again.

"I knew you'd go," she said. Her voice smiled though she did not.

"I'll be back durned soon," said Cory. "I don't reckon he's strayed far. It is late. I ain't feared for him, but——" He broke his 12-gauge shotgun, looked through the barrels, slipped two shells in the breech and a box of them into his pocket. "Don't wait up," he said over his shoulder as he went out.

"I won't," Clissa replied to the closed door, and went back to her stitching by the lamp.

The path up the slope to the wood was very dark when Cory went up it, peering and calling. The air was chill and quiet, and a fetid odor of mold hung in it. Cory blew the taste of it out through impatient nostrils, drew it in again with the next breath, and swore. "Nonsense," he muttered. "Houn' dawg. Huntin', at ten in th' night, too. Alton!" he bellowed. "Alton Drew!" Echoes answered him, and he entered the wood. The huddled thing he passed in the dark heard him and felt the vibrations of his footsteps and did not move because it thought it was dead.

Cory strode on, looking around and ahead and not down since his feet knew the path.

"Alton!"

"That you, Cory?"

Cory Drew froze. That corner of the wood was thickly set and as dark as a burial vault. The voice he heard was choked, quiet, penetrating.

"Alton?"

"I found Kimbo, Cory."

"Where the hell have you been?" shouted Cory furiously. He disliked this pitch-darkness; he was afraid at the tense hopelessness of Alton's voice, and he mistrusted his ability to stay angry at his brother.

"I called him, Cory. I whistled at him, an' the ol' devil didn't answer."

"I can say the same for you, you . . . you louse. Why weren't you to milkin'? Where are you? You caught in a trap?"

"The houn' never missed answerin' me before, you know," said the tight, monotonous voice from the darkness.

"Alton! What the devil's the matter with you? What do I care if your mutt didn't answer? Where—"

"I guess because he ain't never died before," said Alton, refusing to be interrupted.

"You *what?*" Cory clicked his lips together twice and then said, "Alton, you turned crazy? What's that you say?"

"Kimbo's dead."

"Kim . . . oh! Oh!" Cory was seeing that picture again in his mind— Babe sprawled unconscious in the freshet, and Kimbo raging and snapping against a monster bear, holding her back until Alton could get there. "What happened, Alton?" he asked more quietly.

"I aim to find out. Someone tore him up."

"Tore him up?"

"There ain't a bit of him left tacked together, Cory. Every damn joint in his body tore apart. Guts out of him."

"Good God! Bear, you reckon?"

"No bear, nor nothin' on four legs. He's all here. None of him's been et. Whoever done it just killed him an'—tore him up."

"Good God!" Cory said again. "Who could've—" There was a long silence, then. "Come 'long home," he said almost gently. "There's no call for you to set up by him all night."

"I'll set. I aim to be here at sunup, an' I'm going to start trackin', an' I'm goin' to keep trackin' till I find the one done this job on Kimbo."

"You're drunk or crazy, Alton."

"I ain't drunk. You can think what you like about the rest of it. I'm stickin' here."

"We got a farm back yonder. Remember? I ain't going to milk twenty-six head o' cows again in the mornin' like I did jest now, Alton."

"Somebody's got to. I can't be there. I guess you'll just have to, Cory."

"You dirty scum!" Cory screamed. "You'll come back with me now or I'll know why!"

Alton's voice was still tight, half-sleepy. "Don't you come no nearer, bud."

Cory kept moving toward Alton's voice.

"I said"—the voice was very quiet now—*"stop where you are."* Cory kept coming. A sharp click told of the release of the .32-40's safety. Cory stopped.

"You got your gun on me, Alton?" Cory whispered.

"Thass right, bud. You ain't a-trompin' up these tracks for me. I need 'em at sunup."

A full minute passed, and the only sound in the blackness was that of Cory's pained breathing. Finally:

"I got my gun, too, Alton. Come home."

"You can't see to shoot me."

"We're even on that."

"We ain't. I know just where you stand, Cory. I been here four hours."

"My gun scatters."

"My gun kills."

Without another word Cory Drew turned on his heel and stamped back to the farm.

Black and liquidescent it lay in the blackness, not alive, not understanding death, believing itself dead. Things that were alive saw and moved about. Things that were not alive could do neither. It rested its muddy gaze on the line of trees at the crest of the rise, and deep within it thoughts trickled wetly. It lay huddled, dividing its newfound facts, dissecting them as it had dissected live things when there was light, comparing, concluding, pigeonholing.

The trees at the top of the slope could just be seen, as their trunks were a fraction of a shade lighter than the dark sky behind them. At length they, too, disappeared, and for a moment sky and trees were a monotone. The thing knew it was dead now, and like many a being before it, it wondered how long it must stay like this. And then the sky beyond the trees grew a little lighter. That was a manifestly impossible occurrence, thought the thing, but it could see it and it must be so. Did dead things live again? That was curious. What about dismembered dead things? It would wait and see.

The sun came hand over hand up a beam of light. A bird somewhere made a high yawning peep, and as an owl killed a shrew, a skunk pounced on another, so that the night shift deaths and those of the day could go on without cessation. Two flowers nodded archly to each other, comparing their pretty clothes. A dragonfly nymph decided it was tired of looking serious and cracked its back open, to crawl out and dry gauzily. The first golden ray sheared down between the trees, through the grasses, passed over the mass in the shadowed bushes. "I am alive again," thought the thing that could not possibly live. "I am alive, for I see clearly." It stood up on its thick legs, up into the golden glow. In a little while the wet flakes that had grown during the night dried in the sun, and when it took its first steps, they cracked off and a small shower of them fell away. It walked up the slope to find Kimbo, to see if he, too, were alive again.

Babe let the sun come into her room by opening her eyes. Uncle Alton was gone—that was the first thing that ran through her head. Dad had come home last night and had shouted at mother for an hour. Alton was plumb crazy. He'd turned a gun on his own brother. If Alton ever came ten feet into Cory's land, Cory would fill him so full of holes, he'd look like a tumbleweed. Alton was lazy, shiftless, selfish, and one or two other things of questionable taste but undoubted vividness. Babe knew her father. Uncle Alton would never be safe in this county.

She bounced out of bed in the enviable way of the very young, and ran to the window. Cory was trudging down to the night pasture with two bridles over his arm, to get the team. There were kitchen noises from downstairs.

Babe ducked her head in the washbowl and shook off the water like a terrier before she toweled. Trailing clean shirt and dungarees, she went to the head of the stairs, slid into the shirt, and began her morning ritual with the trousers. One step down was a step through the right leg. One more, and she was into the left. Then, bouncing step by step on both feet, buttoning one button per step, she reached the bottom fully dressed and ran into the kitchen.

"Didn't Uncle Alton come back a-tall, Mum?"

"Morning, Babe. No, dear." Clissa was too quiet, smiling too much, Babe thought shrewdly. Wasn't happy.

"Where'd he go, Mum?"

"We don't know, Babe. Sit down and eat your breakfast."

"What's misbegotten, Mum?" Babe asked suddenly. Her mother nearly dropped the dish she was drying. "Babe! You must never say that again!"

"Oh. Well, why is Uncle Alton, then?"

"Why is he what?"

Babe's mouth muscled around an outsize spoonful of oatmeal. "A misbe—"

"Babe!"

"All right, Mum," said Babe with her mouth full. "Well, why?"

"I told Cory not to shout last night," Clisssa said half to herself.

"Well, whatever it means, he isn't," said Babe with finality. "Did he go hunting again?"

"He went to look for Kimbo, darling."

"Kimbo? Oh Mummy, is Kimbo gone, too? Didn't he come back either?"

"No dear. Oh, please, Babe, stop asking questions!"

"All right. Where do you think they went?"

"Into the north woods. Be quiet."

Babe gulped away at her breakfast. An idea struck her; and as she thought of it she ate slower and slower, and cast more and more glances at her mother from under the lashes of her tilted eyes. It would be awful if daddy did anything to Uncle Alton. Someone ought to warn him.

Babe was halfway to the woods when Alton's .32-40 sent echoes giggling up and down the valley.

Cory was in the south thirty, riding a cultivator and cussing at the team of grays when he heard the gun. "Hoa," he called to the horses, and sat a moment to listen to the sound. "One-two-three. Four," he counted. "Saw someone, blasted away at him. Had a chance to take aim and give him another, careful. My God!" He threw up the cultivator points and steered the team into the shade of three oaks. He hobbled the gelding with swift tosses of a spare strap, and headed for the woods. "Alton a killer," he murmured, and doubled back to the house for his gun. Clissa was standing just outside the door.

"Get shells!" he snapped and flung into the house. Clissa followed him. He was strapping his hunting knife on before she could get a box off the shelf. "Cory—"

"Hear that gun, did you? Alton's off his nut. He don't waste lead. He shot at someone just then, and he wasn't fixin' to shoot pa'tridges when I saw him last. He was out to get a man. Gimmie my gun."

"Cory, Babe—"

"You keep her here. Oh, God, this is a helluva mess. I can't stand much more." Cory ran out the door.

Clissa caught his arm: "Cory I'm trying to tell you. Babe isn't here. I've called, and she isn't here."

Cory's heavy, young-old face tautened. "Babe—Where did you last see her?"

"Breakfast." Clissa was crying now.

"She say where she was going?"

"No. She asked a lot of questions about Alton and where he'd gone."

"Did you say?"

Clissa's eyes widened, and she nodded, biting the back of her hand.

"You shouldn't ha' done that, Clissa," he gritted, and ran toward the woods, Clissa looking after him, and in that moment she could have killed herself.

Cory ran with his head up, straining with his legs and lungs and eyes at the long path. He puffed up the slope to the woods, agonized for breath after the forty-five minutes' heavy going. He couldn't even notice the damp smell of mold in the air.

He caught a movement in a thicket to his right, and dropped. Struggling to keep his breath, he crept forward until he could see clearly. There was something in there, all right. Something black, keeping still. Cory relaxed his legs and torso completely to make it easier for his heart to pump some strength back into them, and slowly raised the 12-gauge until it bore on the thing hidden in the thicket.

"Come out!" Cory said when he could speak.

Nothing happened.

"Come out or by God I'll shoot!" rasped Cory.

There was a long moment of silence, and his finger tightened on the trigger.

"You asked for it," he said, and as he fired, the thing leaped sideways into the open, screaming.

It was a thin little man dressed in sepulchral black, and bearing the rosiest baby-face Cory had ever seen. The face was twisted with fright and pain. The man scrambled to his feet and hopped up and down saying over and over, "Oh, my hand. Don't shoot again! Oh, my hand. Don't shoot again!" He stopped after a bit, when Cory had climbed to his feet, and he regarded the farmer out of sad china-blue eyes. "You shot me," he said reproachfully, holding up a little bloody hand. "Oh, my goodness."

Cory said, "Now, who the hell are you?"

The man immediately became hysterical, mouthing such a flood of broken sentences that Cory stepped back a pace and half-raised his gun in self-defense. It seemed to consist mostly of "I lost my papers," and "I didn't do it," and "It was horrible. Horrible. Horrible," and "The dead man," and "Oh, don't shoot again."

Cory tried twice to ask him a question, and then he stepped over and knocked the man down. He lay on the ground writhing and moaning and blubbering and putting his bloody hand to his mouth where Cory had hit him.

"Now what's going on around here?"

The man rolled over and sat up. "I didn't do it!" he sobbed. "I didn't. I was walking along and I heard the gun and I heard some swearing and an awful scream and I went over there and peeped and I saw the dead man and I ran away and you came and I hid and you shot me and—"

"Shut up!" The man did, as if a switch has been thrown. "Now," said Cory, pointing along the path, "you say there's a dead man up there?"

The man nodded and began crying in earnest. Cory helped him up. "Follow this path back to my farmhouse," he said. "Tell my wife to fix up your hand. *Don't* tell her anything else. And wait there until I come. Hear?"

"Yes. Thank you. Oh, thank you. *Snff.*"

"Go on now." Cory gave him a gentle shove in the right direction and went alone, in cold fear, up the path to the spot where he had found Alton the night before.

He found him there now, too, and Kimbo. Kimbo and Alton had spent several years together in the deepest friendship; they had hunted and fought and slept together, and the lives they owed each other were finished now. They were dead together.

It was terrible that they died the same way. Cory Drew was a strong man, but he gasped and fainted dead away when he saw what the thing of the mold had done to his brother and his brother's dog.

The little man in black hurried down the path, whimpering and holding his injured hand as if he rather wished he could limp with it. After a while the whimper faded away, and the hurried stride changed to a walk as the gibbering terror of the last hour receded. He drew two deep breaths, said: "My goodness!" and felt almost normal. He bound a linen handkerchief around his wrist, but the hand kept bleeding. He tried the elbow, and that made it hurt. So he stuffed the handkerchief back in his pocket and simply waved the hand stupidly in the air until the blood clotted. He did not see the great moist horror that clumped along behind him, although his nostrils crinkled with its foulness.

The monster had three holes close together on its chest, and one hole in the middle of its slimy forehead. It had three close-set pits in its back and one on the back of its head. These marks were where Alton Drew's bullets had struck and passed through. Half of the monster's shapeless face was sloughed away, and there was a deep indentation on its shoulder. This was what Alton Drew's gun butt had done after he clubbed it and struck at the thing that would not lie down after he put his four bullets through it. When these things happened the monster was not hurt or angry. It only wondered why Alton Drew acted that way. Now it followed the little man without hurrying at all, matching his stride step by step and dropping little particles of muck behind it.

The little man went on out of the wood and stood with his back against a big tree at the forest's edge, and he thought. Enough had happened to him here. What good would it do to stay and face a horrible murder inquest, just to continue this silly, vague search? There was supposed to be the ruin of an old,

old hunting lodge deep in this wood somewhere, and perhaps it would hold the evidence he wanted. But it was a vague report—vague enough to be forgotten without regret. It would be the height of foolishness to stay for all the hick-town red tape that would follow that ghastly affair back in the wood. Ergo, it would be ridiculous to follow that farmer's advice, to go to his house and wait for him. He would go back to town.

The monster was leaning against the other side of the big tree.

The little man snuffled disgustedly at a sudden overpowering odor of rot. He reached for his handkerchief, fumbled and dropped it. As he bent to pick it up, the monster's arm *whuffed* heavily in the air where his head had been—a blow that would certainly have removed that baby-face protuberance. The man stood up and would have put the handkerchief to his nose had it not been so bloody. The creature behind the tree lifted its arm again just as the little man tossed the handkerchief away and stepped out into the field, heading across country to the distant highway that would take him back to town. The monster pounced on the handkerchief, picked it up, studied it, tore it across several times and inspected the tattered edges. Then it gazed vacantly at the disappearing figure of the little man, and finding him no longer interesting, turned back into the woods.

Babe broke into a trot at the sound of the shots. It was important to warn Uncle Alton about what her father had said, but it was more interesting to find out what he had bagged. Oh, he'd bagged it, all right. Uncle Alton never fired without killing. This was about the first time she had ever heard him blast away like that. Must be a bear, she thought excitedly, tripping over a root, sprawling, rolling to her feet again, without noticing the tumble. She'd love to have another bearskin in her room. Where would she put it? Maybe they could line it and she could have it for a blanket. Uncle Alton could sit on it and read to her in the evening—Oh, no. No. Not with this trouble between him and dad. Oh, if she could only do something! She tried to run faster, worried and anticipating, but she was out of breath and went more slowly instead.

At the top of the rise by the edge of the woods, she stopped and looked back. Far down in the valley lay the south thirty. She scanned it carefully, looking for her father. The new furrows and the old were sharply defined, and her keen eyes saw immediately that Cory had left the line with the cultivator and had angled the team over to the shade trees without finishing his row. That wasn't like him. She could see the team now, and Cory's pale-blue denim was nowhere in sight. She giggled lightly to herself as she thought of the way she would fool her father. And the little sound of laughter drowned out, for her, the sound of Alton's hoarse dying scream.

She reached and crossed the path and slid through the brush beside it. The shots came from up around here somewhere. She stopped and listened several times, and then suddenly heard something coming toward her, fast. She ducked under cover, terrified, and a little baby-faced man in black, his blue eyes wide with horror, crashed blindly past her, the leather case he carried catching on the branches. It spun a moment and then fell right in front of her. The man never missed it.

Babe lay there for a long moment and then picked up the case and faded into the woods. Things were happening too fast for her. She wanted Uncle Alton, but she dared not call. She stopped again and strained her ears. Back toward the edge of the wood she heard her father's voice, and another's— probably the man who had dropped the brief case. She dared not go over there. Filled with enjoyable terror, she thought hard, then snapped her fingers in triumph. She and Alton had played Injun many times up here; they had a whole repertoire of secret signals. She had practiced birdcalls until she knew them better than the birds themselves. What would it be? Ah—blue jay. She threw back her head and by some youthful alchemy produced a nerve-shattering screech that would have done justice to any jay that ever flew. She repeated it, and then twice more.

The response was immediate—the call of a blue jay, four times, spaced two and two. Babe nodded to herself happily. That was the signal that they were to meet immediately at The Place. The Place was a hide-out that he had discovered and shared with her, and not another soul knew of it; an angle of rock beside a stream not far away. It wasn't exactly a cave, but almost. Enough so to be entrancing. Babe trotted happily away toward the brook. She had just known that Uncle Alton would remember the call of the blue jay, and what it meant.

In the tree that arched over Alton's scattered body perched a large jay bird, preening itself and shining in the sun. Quite unconscious of the presence of death, hardly noticing Babe's realistic cry, it screamed again four times, two and two.

It took Cory more than a moment to recover himself from what he had seen. He turned away from it and leaned weakly against a pine, panting. Alton. That was Alton lying there, in—parts.

"God! God, God, God—"

Gradually his strength returned, and he forced himself to turn again. Stepping carefully, he bent and picked up the .32-40. Its barrel was bright and clean, but the butt and stock were smeared with some kind of stinking rottenness. Where had he seen the stuff before? Somewhere—no matter. He cleaned it off absently, throwing the befouled bandanna away afterward. Through his mind ran Alton's words—was that only last night? — *"I'm goin' to start trackin'. An' I'm goin' to keep trackin' till I find the one done this job on Kimbo."*

Cory searched shrinkingly until he found Alton's box of shells. The box was wet and sticky. That made it—better, somehow. A bullet wet with Alton's blood was the right thing to use. He went away a short distance, circled around till he found heavy footprints, then came back.

"I'm a-trackin' for you, bud," he whispered thickly, and began. Through the brush he followed its wavering spoor, amazed at the amount of filthy mold about, gradually associating it with the thing that had killed his brother. There was nothing in the world for him anymore but hate and doggedness. Cursing himself for not getting Alton home last night, he followed the tracks to the edge of the woods. They led him to a big tree there, and there he saw something else—the footprints of the little city man. Nearby lay some tattered scraps of linen, and—what was that?

Another set of prints—small ones. Small, stub-toed ones.

"Babe!"

No answer. The wind sighed. Somewhere a blue jay called.

Babe stopped and turned when she heard her father's voice, faint with distance, piercing.

"Listen at him holler," she crooned delightedly. "Gee, he sounds mad." She sent a jay bird's call disrespectfully back to him and hurried to The Place.

It consisted of a mammoth boulder beside the brook. Some upheaval in the glacial age had cleft it, cutting out a huge V-shaped chunk. The widest part of the cleft was at the water's edge, and the narrowest was hidden by bushes. It made a little ceilingless room, rough and uneven and full of pot-holes and cavelets inside, and yet with quite a level floor. The open end was at the water's edge.

Babe parted the bushes and peered down the cleft.

"Uncle Alton!" she called softly. There was no answer. Oh, well, he'd be along. She scrambled in and slid down to the floor.

She loved it here. It was shaded and cool, and the chattering stream filled it with shifting golden lights and laughing gurgles. She called again, on principle, and then perched on an outcropping to wait. It was only then she realized that she still carried the little man's brief case.

She turned it over a couple of times and then opened it. It was divided in the middle by a leather wall. On one side were a few papers in a large yellow envelope, and on the other some sandwiches, a candy bar, and an apple. With a youngster's complacent acceptance of manna from heaven, Babe fell to. She saved one sandwich for Alton, mainly because she didn't like its highly spiced bologna. The rest made quite a feast.

She was a little worried when Alton hadn't arrived, even after she had consumed the apple core. She got up and tried to skim some flat pebbles across the roiling brook, and she stood on her hands, and she tried to think of a story to tell herself, and she tried just waiting. Finally, in desperation, she turned again to the brief case, took out the papers, curled up by the rocky wall and began to read them. It was something to do, anyway.

There was an old newspaper clipping that told about strange wills that people had left. An old lady had once left a lot of money to whoever would make the trip from the Earth to the Moon and back. Another had financed a home for cats whose masters and mistresses had died. A man left thousands of dollars to the first person who could solve a certain mathematical problem and prove his solution. But one item was blue-penciled. It was:

> One of the strangest of wills still in force is that of Thaddeus M. Kirk, who died in 1920. It appears that he built an elaborate mausoleum with burial vaults for all the remains of his family. He collected and removed caskets from all over the country to fill the designated niches. Kirk was the last of his line; there were no relatives when he died. His will stated that the mausoleum was to be kept in repair permanently, and that a certain sum was to be set aside as a reward for whoever could produce the body of his grandfather, Roger Kirk, whose niche is still empty. Anyone finding this body is eligible to receive a substantial fortune.

Babe yawned vaguely over this, but kept on reading because there was nothing else to do. Next was a thick sheet of business correspondence, bearing the letterhead of a firm of lawyers. The body of it ran:

> In regard to your query regarding the will of Thaddeus Kirk, we are authorized to state that his grandfather was a man about five feet, five inches, whose left arm had been broken and who had a triangular silver plate set into his skull. There is no information as to the whereabouts of his death. He disappeared and was declared legally dead after the lapse of fourteen years.
>
> The amount of the reward as stated in the will, plus accrued interest, now amounts to a fraction over sixty-two thousand dollars. This will be paid to anyone who produces the remains, providing that said remains answer descriptions kept in our private files.

There was more, but Babe was bored. She went on to the little black notebook. There was nothing in it but penciled and highly abbreviated records of visits to libraries; quotations from books with titles like "History of Angelina and Tyler Counties" and "Kirk Family History." Babe threw that aside, too. Where could Uncle Alton be?

She began to sing tunelessly, "Tumalumalum tum, ta ta ta," pretending to dance a minuet with flowing skirts like a girl she had seen in the movies. A rustle of the bushes at the entrance to The Place stopped her. She peeped upward, saw them being thrust aside. Quickly she ran to a tiny cul-de-sac in the rock wall, just big enough for her to hide in. She giggled at the thought of how surprised Uncle Alton would be when she jumped out at him.

She heard the newcomer come shuffling down the steep slope of the crevice and land heavily on the floor. There was something about the sound—What was it? It occurred to her that though it was a hard job for a big man like Uncle Alton to get through the little opening in the bushes, she could hear no heavy breathing. She heard no breathing at all!

Babe peeped out into the main cave and squealed in utmost horror. Standing there was, not Uncle Alton, but a massive caricature of a man: a huge thing like an irregular mud doll, clumsily made. It quivered and parts of it glistened and parts of it were dried and crumbly. Half of the lower left part of its face was gone, giving it a lopsided look. It had no perceptible mouth or nose, and its eyes were crooked, one higher than the other, both a dingy brown with no whites at all. It stood quite still looking at her, its only movement a steady unalive quivering.

It wondered about the queer little noise Babe had made.

Babe crept far back against a little pocket of stone, her brain running round and round in tiny circles of agony. She opened her mouth to cry out, and could not. Her eyes bulged and her face flamed with the strangling effort, and the two golden ropes of her braided hair twitched and twitched as she hunted hopelessly for a way out. If only she were out in the open—or in the wedge-shaped half-cave where the thing was—or home in bed!

The thing clumped toward her, expressionless, moving with a slow inevitability that was the sheer crux of horror. Babe lay wide-eyed and frozen, mounting pressure of terror stilling her lungs, making her heart shake the whole world. The monster came to the mouth of the little pocket, tried to walk to her and was stopped by the sides. It was such a narrow little fissure, and it was all Babe could do to get in. The thing from the wood stood straining against the rock at its shoulders, pressing harder and harder to get to Babe. She sat up slowly, so near to the thing that its odor was almost thick enough to see, and a wild hope burst through her voiceless fear. It couldn't get in! It couldn't get in because it was too big!

The substance of its feet spread slowly under the tremendous strain and at its shoulder appeared a slight crack. It widened as the monster unfeelingly crushed itself against the rock, and suddenly a large piece of the shoulder came away and the being twisted slushily three feet farther in. It lay quietly with its muddy eyes fixed on her, and then brought one thick arm up over its head and reached.

Babe scrambled in the inch farther she had believed impossible, and the filthy clubbed hand stroked down her back, leaving a trail of muck on the blue denim of the shirt she wore. The monster surged suddenly and, lying full length now, gained that last precious inch. A black hand seized one of her braids, and for Babe the lights went out.

When she came to, she was dangling by her hair from that same crusted paw. The thing held her high, so that her face and its featureless head were not more than a foot apart. It gazed at her with a mild curiosity in its eyes, and it swung her slowly back and forth. The agony of her pulled hair did what fear could not do—gave her a voice. She screamed. She opened her mouth and puffed up her powerful young lungs, and she sounded off. She held her throat in the position of the first scream, and her chest labored and pumped more air through the frozen throat. Shrill and monotonous and infinitely piercing, her screams.

The thing did not mind. It held her as she was, and watched. When it had learned all it could from this phenomenon, it dropped her jarringly, and looked around the half-cave, ignoring the stunned and huddled Babe. It reached over and picked up the leather brief case and tore it twice across as if it were tissue. It saw the sandwich Babe had left, picked it up, crushed it, dropped it.

Babe opened her eyes, saw that she was free, and just as the thing turned back to her she dove between its legs and out into the shallow pool in front of the rock, paddled across and hit the other bank screaming. A vicious little light of fury burned in her; she picked up a grapefruit-sized stone and hurled it with all her frenzied might. It flew low and fast, and struck squashily on the monster's ankle. The thing was just taking a step toward the water; the stone caught it off balance, and its unpracticed equilibrium could not save it. It tottered for a long, silent moment at the edge and then splashed into the stream. Without a second look Babe ran shrieking away.

Cory Drew was following the little gobs of mold that somehow indicated the path of the murderer, and he was nearby when he first heard her scream. He broke into a run, dropping his shotgun and holding the .32-40 ready to fire. He ran with such deadly panic in his heart that he ran right past the huge cleft rock and was a hundred yards past it before she burst out through the pool and ran up the bank. He had to run hard and fast to catch her, because anything behind her was that faceless horror in the cave, and she was living for the one idea of getting away from there. He caught her in his arms and swung her to him, and she screamed on and on and on.

Babe didn't see Cory at all, even when he held her and quieted her.

The monster lay in the water. It neither liked nor disliked this new element. It rested on the bottom, its massive head a foot beneath the surface, and it curiously considered the facts that it had garnered. There was the little humming noise of Babe's voice that sent the monster questing into the cave. There was the black material of the brief case that resisted so much more than green things when he tore it. There was the little two-legged one who sang and brought him near, and who screamed when he came. There was this new cold moving thing he had fallen into. It was washing his body away. That had never happened before. That was interesting. The monster decided to stay and observe this new thing. It felt no urge to save itself; it could only be curious.

The brook came laughing down out of its spring, ran down from its source beckoning to the sunbeams and embracing freshets and helpful brooklets. It shouted and played with streaming little roots, and nudged the minnows and pollywogs about in its tiny backwaters. It was a happy brook. When it came to the pool by the cloven rock it found the monster there, and plucked at it. It soaked the foul substances and smoothed and melted the molds, and the waters below the thing eddied darkly with its diluted matter. It was a thorough brook. It washed all it touched, persistently. Where it found filth, it removed filth; and if there were layer on layer of foulness, then layer by foul layer it was removed. It was a good brook. It did not mind the poison of the monster, but took it up and thinned it and spread it in little rings round rocks downstream, and let it drift to the rootlets of water plants, that they might grow greener and lovelier. And the monster melted.

"I am smaller," the thing thought. "That is interesting. I could not move now. And now this part of me which thinks is going, too. It will stop in just a moment, and drift away with the rest of the body. It will stop thinking and I will stop being, and that, too, is a very interesting thing."

So the monster melted and dirtied the water, and the water was clean again, washing and washing the skeleton that the monster had left. It was not very big, and there was a badly-healed knot on the left arm. The sunlight flickered on the triangular silver plate set into the pale skull, and the skeleton was very clean now. The brook laughed about it for an age.

They found the skeleton, six grim-lipped men who came to find a killer. No one had believed Babe, when she told her story days later. It had to be days later because Babe had screamed for seven hours without stopping, and had lain like a dead child for a day. No one believed her at all, because her story was all about the bad fella, and they knew that the bad fella was simply a thing that her father had made up to frighten her with. But it was through her that the skeleton was found, and so the men at the bank sent a check to the Drews for more money than they had ever dreamed about. It was old Roger Kirk, sure enough, that skeleton, though it was found five miles from where he had died and sank into the forest floor where the hot molds builded around his skeleton and emerged—a monster.

So the Drews had a new barn and fine new livestock and they hired four men. But they didn't have Alton. And they didn't have Kimbo. And Babe screams at night and has grown very thin.

CARGO

—either alien, or very definitely not alien, just different. Depends on how you use the word. Also written in '39 or early '40; England was at war, and I wrote out of my experience in the Merchant Marine. Also, it was a fun story. Later on, I stopped writing fun stories for a very long time. I got pretty grim, I did . . .

I heard somebody say she was haunted. She wasn't haunted. There's another name for what ailed her, and I'll tell you about it if you like. I was aboard her when it started, and before. I knew every sheared rivet on her. I knew her when she was honest, a drab and prosaic member of our merchant marine. I saw what happened to her.

She was one of those broad-shouldered old hulks built by the dozen during War I. Her sisters lay rotting and rusting and waiting for a national emergency to prove their unseaworthiness. O.K. They make good shrapnel. Her name was *Dawnlight,* she was seven thousand tons, a black oil tanker, limped like a three-legged dog, and was as beautiful as a wart. She could do nine knots downhill with a fair wind and an impossible current. When she was loaded she steered well until the loss of weight from burned fuel in the after bunkers threw her down by the head, and then she proceeded as will any tanker with a loss back aft; when she was light she drew seventeen feet aft and nothing forward, so that when the wind blew abeam she spun on her tail like a canoe.

Yes, I knew her of old. She used to carry casing-head. That's airplane gas that makes explosive vapors at around 40°F. So one day a fireman found casing-head seeping through the seams of No. 9 tank into the fireroom and evaporating there. He fainted dead away, and the crew took to the boats during the night. The Old Man woke up at noon the next day screaming for his coffee, put two and two together, and with the help of two engineers and a messman, worked her into a cove in a small island off Cuba.

It so happened that a very wealthy gentleman thereabouts turned up with a nice offer, with the result that the Old Man and his three finks made for Havana in a lifeboat with their pockets full of large bills and the ship's log, which contained an entry describing her explosion and sinking. After that she carried crude oil for the wealthy gentleman to war zones. Great sport.

What made it such great sport was that not only did the *Dawnlight* have no business being afloat, but she had no business being in her particular business. Her nationality was determined by the contents of the flag locker, and her current log looked like a set of the Encyclopædia Britannica. They'd run up one flag or another, and pick a log to suit.

But she paid well and she fed well, and if you could keep away from the ocean floor and the concentration camps, you'd find her good shipping. If you must commit suicide, you might as well get rich doing it.

I caught her in a certain drydock that makes a good thing out of doing quick work and asking few questions. Her skipper was a leathery old squarehead whose viscera must have been a little brown jug. Salt cracked off his joints when he moved. He was all man back aft and all devil on the bridge, and he owned our souls. Not that that was much of a possession. The crew matched the ship, and they were the crummiest, crustiest, hardbitten bunch of has-been human beings ever to bless the land by going to sea. Had to be that way.

Any tanker is a five-hundred-foot stick of dynamite, even if she isn't an outlaw. If she's loaded, she'll burn forever and a week; and if she's light she'll go sky-high and never come down. All she needs is a spark from somewhere. That can happen easily enough any time; but imagine dodging subs and pocket battleships on both sides of the martial fence—swift, deadly back-stabbers, carrying many and many a spark for our cargoes. We had nothing for protection but luck and the Old Man. We stuck to him.

The *Dawnlight* was the only ship I'd have taken, feeling the way I was. Once in a while the world gangs up on a guy, and he wants an out. The *Dawnlight* was mine—she'd pulled me through a couple of dark spots in the past—once when a certain dope fell and cracked his silly skull in a brawl over a girl, and I had to disappear for a while, and once when I married the girl and she took to blackmailing me for a living. Aside from all this, though, the *Dawnlight* was the only ship I *could* get aboard. I carried an ordinary seaman's certificate, indorsed for wiper. The Department of Commerce was very lenient with me and let me keep those ratings after I ran a naval auxiliary tanker on the rocks. Passed out drunk on watch. Anyhow, the Old Man gave me the eight-to-twelve watch as third mate, papers or no papers. It was that kind of a ship. He was that kind of a skipper. He had the idea I was that kind of a sailor.

We left the drydock (it's up North somewhere—that'll do!) and headed east and south. We were in ballast, carrying only two hundred big cases of farm machinery in the two dry cargo holds. Farm machinery with steel-jacketed noses and percussion caps. Nice chunky crates of tractors with rifled barrels. We followed the coastline pretty much, but stayed far off, out of the south-bound steamer lanes. This wasn't long after the beginning of the war, when all hands ashore and afloat were excited about neutrality zones, so we wanted to keep our noses clean. However, we weren't too worried. We weren't the only gray-painted, unidentified hulk at sea by any means, and anyway, we had the skipper.

We dropped down to about 33° and headed due east. It was early fall—the hurricane season—but the weather was fine and mellow. We kept the morning sun a point off the starboard bow, and in the evening we tore up the base of the shadow we threw ahead. The black gang talked of an unheard-of sixty-three revolutions per minute from the engine, when she hadn't done better than fifty-seven in the last twelve years. Every time I shot the sun or a star on my watch, the ship stood still and waited for me to get it, and I navigated as if I had a radio beam in my pocket. It didn't seem like the old *Dawnlight* anymore, with her rotten gear and her chewing-gum calking. It was a pleasure to work her. Even Cajun Joe's sea bread stopped giving me heartburn.

Yes, it was too good to be true, so in the long run it didn't turn out to be true. After we reached longtitude 30° everything about that ship went haywire. Nothing was really wrong, only—well, there was the matter of the sextants, for instance. Four of them—mine, and the first's, and the second's, but worst of all, the Old Man's ancient binocular-type monster. They all went just a little bit off—enough to throw us eight or ten degrees off course. You see, after we passed 30, we changed course a shade north to head us up toward Gibralter; and no sooner had we done that than clouds popped up from nowhere and the weather got really thick.

Nights we sailed in a black soup, and days we sailed in a white one, and the compass was the only thing that would even admit where we might be. Things got screwy. The revolution counter said we were making a wabbly seven point two knots. The patent log claimed an even six. But it wasn't until the third day of fog, about five bells on my morning watch, that we really found out that we were being led astray. About the sextants, I mean.

There was a hole in the clouds, high on the starboard beam; I saw it coming up, figured it would show the sun, and whistled up the Old Man and the mate. I was right; it was a small hole, and as the three of us lined up on the wing of the bridge with our sextants, the second came bumbling sleepily up with his.

Old Johnny Weiss was at the wheel, steadying the lubberline onto the compass card the only way an old shellback trained in sail can steer a ship.

"Watch the clock, Johnny," I said and got the image of that cloud hole on my mirror.

"Hi," he said, which was the nearest any of us came to "Aye-aye, sir," on that scow.

We froze there, the four of us, each sextant steady as a rock, waiting for the gleam. It came, and the Old Man said "Hup!" and we fixed our arcs.

We got the time from Johnny—the old clock in the wheelhouse was chronometer enough for us—and we broke out our tables. Our four sights came out close enough. Position, 31° 17′ N, 33° 9′ 40″ W—which landed us about four hundred miles due east of the Madeiras. We found that if we split the difference between the distance-run given by the deck and engine logs, we'd reach that position by dead reckoning. It looked good—too good. The *Dawnlight* was balky steering, what with her outmoded hydraulic telemotor and her screw-type steering engine. She'd never performed that way.

As soon as I was alone in the chart house I went over my figures. Everything was jake, but—the primary mirror on my sextant was askew. Slipped down a bit in its frame. Why, a thing like that could prove us a hundred and fifty miles off course! It had never happened before—it was a new sextant, and I took care of it. Now how in—

I slipped down to the Old Man's office and went in. He and the mate were bent over the desk. They straightened as I came in.

"Cap'n I—"

"Vot reading dit you get on your sun gun?" he asked me before I could finish my speech. I told him. He scratched his head and looked at the mate.

The mate said: "Yeah, me, too." He was a Boston Irishman named Toole; four foot eleven in his shoes. He was wanted for four very elaborate murders. He collected seventeenth-century miniatures. "I got the same thing, only my sextant's on the bum. That couldn't be right. Look—the eyepiece on the 'scope is off center."

"Look now here," The Old Man took down his behemoth, and showed me a gradation plate sliding around loosely over its pulled rivets. "Yust py accident I gat the same."

"My gosh! That's what I came down to tell you, skipper. Look at this." I showed him the loose mirror on my instrument.

Just then Harry, the second mate, edged into the room. He always edged through doors on the mistaken assumption that he was thinner fore and aft than he was across the beam. It was hard to tell. Harry saw everything and said nothing, and if he was as innocent as he hugely looked, he would not have been aboard the *Dawnlight*. He said:

"Cap, m' readin' on that sight was off. My sextant—"

"—has gone gebrochen. Don't tell me dis too."

"Why . . . yeh. Yeh."

"Four sextants go exactly the same amount off at the same time for four different reasons," said Toole, examining a bent arc track on Harry's sun gun. The captain sighed.

No one said anything for a minute, and we hardly noticed it when the captain's deck lamp winked off. The engine room speaking tube shrieked and I answered it because I was nearest, I heard:

"Skipper?"

"Third mate."

"Tell the Old Man that No. 2 generator just threw its armature. Cracked the casing all to hell."

"What's the matter with No. 1?"

"Damfino. Fused solid two hours ago. And no spares for anything, and no cable to wind a new armature."

"O.K." I turned and told the skipper.

He almost laughed. "I vas yust going to say dot ve'd haf to take a radio bearing on Gibraltar and Feisal. Heh. Didn't y'u tell me, 'Arry, dot dere vas no acid for the batteries on the radio?"

"I did."

"Heh." The skipper drummed for a moment on his desk, looking at me without seeing me. Then he saw me. "Vot de dirty hell are y'u duing down here ven y'u're on vatch? Gat up dere!"

I got—there were times when you couldn't play around with the old boy.

Up on deck the weather looked the same. The sea was slick and the air was warm, and I had to fumble around to locate the bridge ladder. Johnny was steering steadily, easily, a couple of spokes each way every couple of minutes. He was the only man aboard that had the feel of that crazy ship, with her warped keel and her scored and twisted propeller. He looked up at me as I stepped into the wheelhouse and grunted.

"What's up, Johnny?"

" Reckon you know where we are, huh?"

"I reckon."

No sense in getting the crew talking. Sailors gossip like a bridge club, and for the same reason—grouped people with the same basic interests. I've seen three quarters of a crew packed up and ready to leave because some wiseacre started the rumor that a ship was going to be sold for scrap at the next port.

Johnny grunted, and I went into the chart room to monkey with that slipped glass in my sextant. The way the weather looked, I'd never have a chance to use it again, but then you can't tell about an African coastwise fog. What had made Johnny so quizzical? The more I tried to think of something else, the more that bothered me. About ten minutes later, working on the theory that the last word said before a long pause is the one that sticks, I went back into the wheelhouse and asked:

"Why do you want to know?"

"Oh, nothin'." He spat, and the tobacco juice rang a knell on the cuspidor. "Jest thinkin'."

"Come on—give."

"Waal—seems to me we been steerin' east b' nor'east about two days—right?"

"So?"

"Youse guys was so busy peekin' through yer sextants at the Big Light that you didn't see it was in the wrong place."

"The sun? In the wrong place?"

"Yep. Steerin' east b' nor'east this time o' year, hereabouts, seems to me the sun'd show about broad on the bow at ten thirty in th' mornin'."

"Well?"

"So it shows up high an' dead abeam. Don't seem right, somehow."

He was right. I went and sat down on the pilot's stool. Radio dead, sextants haywire; all we have is the compass and gold old Bowditch's dead-reckoning tables. And now—the compass?

"Johnny, are you sure you were on course when we took that sight?"

His silence was eloquent. Old Johnny Weiss could steer anything with a rudder unless it had a steering oar, and then he was better than most. If we had a radio, we could check the compass. We had no radio. If we could get a sun sight, we wouldn't need the radio. We couldn't get a sun sight. We were lost—lost as hell. We were steering a rock-steady compass course on a ship that was pounding the miles away under her counter as she had never done before, and she was heading bravely into nowhere.

An ordinary seaman popped in. "Lost the patent log, sir!"

Before I could say, "Oh, well, it didn't work, anyway," the engine-room tube piped up.

"Well?" I said into it, in the tone that means "Now what?"

It was the third engineer again. "Is the skipper up there?"

"No. What is it?"

"A lot of things happen," wailed the third. "Why do they all have to happen to *me?*"

"You don't know, shipmate, you don't know! What's up?"

"The rev-counter arm worked loose and fell into the crank pit. The I.P. piston grabbed it and hauled counter and all in. Goddlemighty, what goes on here? We jinxed?"

"Seems as though," I said, and whistled down the captain's tube to report the latest.

Everything depended on our getting a sun sight now. We might have calculated our speed at least from the revolution readings, a tide chart and propslip table. The admiralty charts don't give a damn about this particular section of sea water. Why should they? There's supposed to be a deep around the Madeiras somewhere, but then again there's flat sand aplenty off Africa. Even the skipper's luck wouldn't pull us out of this. I had a feeling. Damn it, we couldn't even hail a ship, if we met one. It would be bound to turn out a q-ship or a sub-chaser, tickled to death to pinch our cargo. Farm machinery. Phooey!

The saloon messman came up carrying clean sheets for the chart-room cot. I knew what that meant. The bridge was going to be the skipper's little home until we got out of this—if we did. I was dead beat. Things like this couldn't happen—they *couldn't!*

We had a council of war that night, right after I came on watch, the captain and I. Nothing had happened all day; the sun came out only once, on the twelve to four, and ducked in again so quickly that Harry couldn't get to his sextant. He did set the pelorus on it, but the ship rolled violently because of some freak current just as he sighted, and the altitude he got was all off. There'd been nothing else—Oh, yes; we'd lost three heaving lines over the side, trying to gauge our speed with a chip. The darnedest thing about it was that everything else was going as well as it possibly could.

The cook had found nine crates of really fancy canned goods in the linen locker—Lord knows how long they'd been there. It was just as if they'd been dropped out of nowhere. The engines ran without a hitch. The low-pressure cylinder lost its wheeze, and in the washrooms we got hot water when we wanted it instead of cold water or steam. Even the mattresses seemed softer. Only we just didn't know where we were.

The Old Man put his hand on my shoulder and startled me, coming up behind me in the darkness that way. I was standing out on the wing of the bridge.

"Vot's de matter; vorried about de veather?" he asked me. He was funny that way, keeping us on our toes with his furies and his—what was it?—kindnesses.

"Well, yes, cap'n I don't like the looks of this."

He put his elbows on the coaming. "I tell y'u boy, ve ain't got nodding to fret about."

"Oh, I guess not, but I don't go for this hide-'n'-go-seek business." I could feel him regarding me carefully out of the corners of his eyes.

"I vant to tell y'u something. If I said dis to de mate, or Harry, or vun of de black gang, dey vould say: 'I t'ink de ol' squarehead is suckin' vind. He must be gettin' old.' But I tell y'u."

I was flattered.

"Dis is a old ship but she is good. I am going to be sorry to turn her over to sumvun else."

"What are you talking about, skipper? You're not quitting when we get back?"

"No; before dat. Dass all I vorry about, y'u see. Dis vill be de first command I lost half a trip out. I vas master of thirty-two ships, but I always left dem in der home port. It von't be like dat now."

I was more than a little taken aback. I'd never seen the stringy old gun runner sentimental about his ship before. This was the first time I'd ever heard him mention it in printable terms. But what was all this about losing his command?

"What's the matter, cap'n—think we'll go to camp?" That was a *Dawnlight* idiom and meant being picked up by a warship of some kind.

"No boy—nodding like dat. Dey can't touch us. Nobody can touch us now. Ah—hear dat?"

He pointed far out to port. The night was very still, with hardly a sound but the continual seethe of millions of bursting bubbles slithering past the ship's side. But far out in the fog was an insistent splashing—that heavy smacking splash that every seaman knows.

"Porpoise," I said.

The skipper tugged at my elbow and led me through the wheelhouse to the other wing. "Listen."

There it was again, on the starboard side. "Must be quite a few of 'em," I said laconically, a little annoyed that he should change the subject that way.

"Dere is plenty, but dey are not porpoises."

"Blackfish?"

"Dey is not fish, too. Dey is somet'ing y'u have seen in books. Dey is vimmin with tails on."

"What?"

"O.K., I vas kidding. Call me ven y'u are relieved."

In the green glow from the starboard running light I saw him hand me a piercing gaze; then he shambled back to the chart room. A little bit short of breath, I went into the wheelhouse and lit a cigarette.

The cuspidor rang out, and I waited for Johnny to speak.

"The skipper ain't nuts," he said casually.

"Somebody is," I returned. "You heard him, then."

"Listen—if the skipper told me the devil himself was firing on the twelve to four, then the devil it would be." Johnny was fiercely loyal under that armor of easy talk. "I've heard them 'porpoises' of yours for three days now. Porpoises don't follow a ship two hundred yards off. They'll jump the bow wave fer a few minutes an' then high-tail, or they'll cross yer bow an' play away. These is different. I've gone five degrees off to port an' then to starboard to see if I could draw 'em. Nope they keep their distance." Johnny curled some shag under his lip.

"Aw, that's . . . that's screwy, Johnny."

He shrugged. "You've shipped with the Old Man before. He sees more than most of us." And that's all he'd say.

It was about two days later that we began to load. Yeah, that's what I said. We didn't dock, and we didn't discharge our farm machinery. We took on—whatever it was our cargo turned out to be. It was on the four to eight in the evening when the white fog was just getting muddy in the dusk. I was dead asleep when the ship sat down on her tail, stuck her bow up and heeled over. The engines stopped, and I got up from the corner of my room where the impact had flung me.

She lay still on her side, and hell was breaking loose. Toole had apparently fallen up against the fire-alarm button, and the lookout forward was panicky and ringing a swing symphony on the bell. A broken steam line was roaring bloody murder, and so was the second mate. The whistle, at least, was quiet—it had fallen with a crash from the "Pat Finnegan" pipe.

I leaned against the wall and crouched into a pair of pants and staggered out on deck. I couldn't see a blasted thing. If the fog had been thick before, it was twenty times as thick now.

Someone ran into me, and we both went skittering into the scuppers. It was the mate on his way down to the captain's room. Why the Old Man wasn't on the bridge, I couldn't savvy, unless it had to do with that peculiar attitude of resignation about his imagined loss of command.

"What the hell?" I wanted to know.

Toole said: "Who is that—third mate? Oh. I don't know. We've hit something. We're right up on top of it. Ain't rocks; didn't hear any plates go. Isn't sand; no sand bank this size could stay this far from land."

"Where's the skipper?"

"In his room, far as I know. C'mon, let's roll him out."

We groped our way to the alleyway door and into the midship house. Light was streaming from the skipper's room, and as we approached the door we heard the rare, drawn-out chuckle. I'll never forget the shock of seeing this best of captains, a man who had never dented a bilge plate in his life, sprawled back in his tilted swivel chair with his feet on a tilted desk, chuckling into a tilted bottle of Scotch.

Toole squawked: "Cap'n! We've struck something!"

The skipper giggled. He had a terrific load on. I leaned past Toole and shook him. "Skipper! We've struck!"

He looked at us blearily. "Heh. Sid-down, boyss, de trip iss over. Ve have not struck. Ve is yust finished. Heh!"

"Clear the boats," Toole said aside to me.

The skipper heard him. "Vait!" he said furiously, and lurched to his feet. "I am still in command here! Don't lower no boats. Ve are not in distress, y'u hear? Heh! Ve are loading. I know all about it. Go an' see for y'uselfs, so y'u don't belief me!"

Toole stared at the captain for a moment. I stood by. If Toole decided the Old Man was nuts, he'd take over. If not, then the squarehead was still running the show. Suddenly Toole leaned over and cut the master switch on the alarm system. It had a separate little battery circuit of its own, and was the only thing electrical aboard that still operated. The silence was deafening as the alarm bells throughout the ship stilled, and we could hear a bumble of voices from back aft as the crew milled about. They were a steady bunch; there would be no panic. Toole beckoned me out of the room and left. Once we were outside he said:

"What do you think?"

"I think he's— I dunno, Toole. He's a seaman first and a human being afterward. If he says we're not in distress, it's likely true. Course, he's drunk."

Toole snorted. "He thinks better when he's drunk. Come on, let's look around."

We dropped down the ladder. The ship lay still. She was careened, probably with her starboard side under water and the starboard rail awash.

Toole said: "Let's go to port. Maybe we can see what it is we've hit."

We had to go on all fours to get up there, so steeply was the deck canted. It did us no good; there was nothing to be seen anywhere but fog.

Toole clung with one arm to the chain rail and puffed, "Can't see a thing down there, can you?"

I hung over the edge. "Can't even see the water line."

"Let's go down to the starboard side. She must be awash there."

She was. I stepped ankle-deep into sea water before I knew where I was. The sea was dead calm, and the fog was a solid thing; and something was holding the ship heeled over. I tell you, it was a nasty feeling. If only we knew what was under us! And then—we saw the ship being loaded.

May I never see another sight like that one. As if to tease and torture us, the fog swirled silently away from the ship's side, leaving a little dim island of visibility for us to peer into. We could see fifty or sixty feet of deck, and the chain rails fore and aft dipping into the sea at our feet; and we could see a round patch of still water with its edges wetting the curtain of fog. And on that patch of water were footprints. We both saw them at the same time and froze, speechless. Coming toward us over the water they were—dozens of them. The water was like a resilient, glossy sheet of paving, and the impression of dozens— hundreds—of feet ran across it to the ship. But there was nothing making the footprints. Just—footprints. Oh, my God!

There were big splay ones and big slow ones, and little swift ones and plodding ones. Once something long and invisible crept with many legs up to the ship, and once little pointed feet, high-arched, tripped soundlessly over the chains and *something* fell sprawling a yard from where we stood. There was no splash, but just the indentation in the water of a tiny, perfect body that rolled and squirmed back onto its feet and ran over to the deck and disappeared. I suddenly felt that I was in the midst of a milling crowd of—of people. Nothing touched me, and yet, all around me was the pressure of scores of beings who jostled each other and pushed and shoved, in their eagerness to get aboard. It was ghastly. There was no menace in it, nor anything to fear except that here was a thing that could not be understood.

The fog closed down suddenly, and for a long moment we stood there, feeling the pressure of that mob of "passengers"; and then I reached out and found the mate's arm and tugged him toward the midship house. We crawled up the canted ladder and stood by the glow from the lamp in the captain's room.

"It's a lot of goddam nonsense," I said weakly.

"Hm-m-m."

I didn't know whether or not Toole agreed with me.

The skipper's voice came loosely from the porthole. "Heh! I cert'n'y t'ank y'u for de Scotch, I du. Vat a deal, vat a deal!" And he burst out into a horrible sound that might have been laughter, in his cracked and grating voice. I stared in. He was nodding and grinning at the forward bulkhead, toasting it with a pony of fire water.

"He's seein' things," said the mate abruptly.

"Maybe all the rest of us are blind," I said; and the mate's dazed expression made me wonder, too, why I had said that. Without another word he went above to take over the bridge, while I went aft to quiet the crew.

We lay there for fourteen hours, and all the while that invisible invasion continued. There was nothing any of us could do. And crazy things began happening. Any one of them might have happened to any of us once in a while, but—well, judge for yourself, now.

When I came on watch that night there was nothing to do but stand by, since we were hove to, and I set Johnny to polishing brass. He got his polish and his rag and got to work. I mooned at the fog from the wheelhouse window, and in about ten minutes I heard Johnny cuss and throw rag and can over the side.

"What gives, Johnny?"

"Ain't no use doin' this job. Must be the fog." He pointed to the binnacle cover. "The tarnish smells the polish and fades off all around me rag. On'y where I rub it comes in stronger."

It was true. All the places he had rubbed were black-green, and around those spots the battered brass gleamed brilliantly! I told John to go have himself a cup of coffee and settled down on the stool to smoke.

No cigarettes in the right pocket of my dungarees. None in the left. I *knew* I'd put a pack there. "Damn!" I muttered. Now where the—what was I looking for? Cigarettes? But I had a pack of cigarettes in my hand! Was I getting old or something? I tried to shrug it off. I must have had them there all the time, only—well, things like that don't happen to me! I'm not absent-minded. I pulled out a smoke and stuck it in my chops, fumbling for a match. Now where— did some more cussing. No matches. What good is a fag to a guy without a— I gagged suddenly on too much smoke. Why was I looking for a match? My cigarette was lit!

When a sailor starts to get the jitters he usually begins to think about the girl he left behind him. It was just my luck to be tied up with one I didn't want to think about. I simply went into a daze while I finished that haunted cigarette. After a while Johnny came back carrying a cup of coffee for me.

Now I like my coffee black. Wet a spoon in it and dip it in the sugar barrel, and that's enough sugar for me. Johnny handed me the cup, and I took the saucer off the rim. The coffee was creamed—on a ship that means evaporated milk—and sweet as a soft caramel.

"Damn it, Johnny, you know how I like my coffee. What's the idea of this?"

"What?"

I showed him. When he saw the pale liquid he recoiled as if there had been a snake curled up on the saucer instead of a cup. "S'help me, third, I didn't put a drop of milk in that cup! Nor sugar, neither!"

I growled and threw cup and saucer over the side. I couldn't say anything to Johnny. I *knew* he was telling the truth. Oh, well, maybe there happened to be some milk and sugar in the cup he used and he didn't notice it. It was a weak sort of excuse, but I clung to it.

At six bells the second heaved himself up the ladder. "O.K.—you're relieved," he said.

"At eleven o'clock? What's the idea?"

"Aw—" His huge bulk pulsed as he panted, and he was sweating. "I couldn't sleep, that's all. Shove off."

"I'll be damned! First time I ever heard of you rolling out before you were called, Harry. What's the matter—this canting too much for you?" The ship still lay over at about 47°.

"Naw. I c'n sleep through twice that. It was— Oh, go below, third."

"O. K. Course 'n' speed the same—zero-zero. The wind is on the weather side, an' we're runnin' between the anchors. The bow is dead ahead and the smokestack is aft. The temperature—"

"Dry up, will ya?"

"The temperature is mighty hot around the second mate. What's eatin' you, Harry?"

"I'll tell you," he said suddenly very softly, so Johnny couldn't hear. "It was my bunk. It was full of spikes. I could feel 'em, but I couldn't see 'em. I've got the blue willies, third." He mopped his expansive face.

I slapped him on the back and went aft laughing. I was sorry I had laughed. When I turned in to my bunk it was full of cold, wet worms that crept and crawled and sent me mooning and shuddering to the deck, to roll up in the carpet for some shut-eye. No, I couldn't see them.

We left there—wherever "there" was—about fourteen hours after we struck. What it was that had stopped the ship we never did find out. We took soundings all around and got nothing but deep water. Whatever it was that the ship was lying on was directly underneath the turn of the bilge, so that no sounding lead could strike it. After the first surprise of it we almost got used to it—it and the fog, thick as banked snow, that covered everything. And all the while the "loading" went on. When it began, that invisible crowding centered around the section of the starboard well deck that was awash. But in a few hours it spread to every part of the ship. Everywhere you went you saw nothing and you actually felt nothing; and yet there was an increasing sense of being crowded—jostled.

It happened at breakfast, 7:20. The skipper was there, and the mate, though he should have been on the bridge. Harry rolled in, too, three hundred pounds of fretful wanness. I gathered that there were still spikes in his bunk. Being second mate, his watch was the twelve to four, and breakfast was generally something he did without.

The captain lolled back in his chair, leaning against the canted deck and grinning. It made me sore. I refused the bottle he shoved at me and ordered my eggs from the messman.

"Na, don't be dat vay," said the skipper. 'Everyt'ing is under control. Ve is all going to get a bonus, and nobody is going to get hurt."

"I don't savvy you, cap'n," I said brusquely. "Here we are high and dry in the middle of an African pea-souper, with everything aboard gone haywire, and you're tickled to death. If you know what's going on, you ought to tip us off."

The mate said, "He's got something there, captain. I want to put a boat over the side, at least, and have a look at what it is that's grounded us. I told you that last night, and you wouldn't let a boat leave the chocks. What's the idea—don't you want to know?"

The captain dipped a piece of sea bread into the remains of four eggs on his plate. "Look, boyss, didn't I pull y'u out of a lot of spots before dis? Did I ever let y'u down yet? Heh. Vell, I von't now."

The mate looked exasperated. "O.K., O.K., but this calls for a little more than seamanship, skipper."

"Not from y'u it don't," flared the captain. "I know vat goes on, but if I told y'u, y'u wouldn't believe it. Y'u'll make out all right."

I decided to take matters into my own hands. "Toole, he's got some silly idea that the ship is out of our hands. Told me the other night. He's seeing ghosts. He says we were surrounded by 'vimmin mit tails on.' "

The mate cocked an eyebrow at the Old Man. The captain lurched to his feet.

"Vell, it's true! An' I bat y'u y'ur trip's pay against mine dat I gat one for myself! Ve is taking on a cargo of—" He swallowed noisily and put his face so close to mine that our foreheads nearly touched. "Vare de hell y'u t'ink I got dis viskey?" he bellowed. "Somebody has chartered dis ship, and ve'll get paid. Vot y'u care who it is? Y'u never worried before!" He stamped out.

Harry laughed hollowly, his four pale chins bobbing. "I guess that tells you off, third."

"I'll be damned," I said hotly. "I trust the Old Man as much as anyone, but I'm not going to take much more of this."

"Take it easy, man," soothed Harry. He reached for the canned milk. "A lot of this is fog and imagination. Until the skipper does something endangering crew, ship or cargo we've got no kick."

"What do you call staying in his room when the ship rams something?"

"He seems to know it's all right. Let it go, mate. We're O.K., so far. When the fog clears, everything will be jake. You're letting your imagination run away with you." He stared at Toole and upended the milk can over his cup.

Ink came out.

I clutched the edge of the slanting table and looked away and back again. It was true enough—black ink out of a milk can I'd seen the messman open three minutes before. I didn't say anything because I couldn't. Neither Toole nor Harry noticed it. Harry put the can on the table and it slid down toward Toole.

"All right," said Toole, "we'll keep our traps shut until the skipper pulls something really phony. But I happen to know we have a cargo consigned to a Mediterranean port; and when and if we get off this sandbank, or whatever it is, I'm going to see to it that it's delivered. A charter is a charter." He picked up the can and poured.

Blood came out.

It drove me absolutely screwball. He wouldn't watch what he was doing! Harry was working on a pile of scrambled eggs, and the mate was looking at me, and my stomach was missing beats. I muttered something and went up to the bridge. Every time there was some rational explanation developing, something like that had to happen. Know why I couldn't pipe up about what I had seen? Because after the ink and the blood hit their coffee it was cream! You don't go telling people that you're bats!

It was ten minutes to eight, but as usual, Johnhy Weiss was early. He was a darn good quartermaster—one of the best I ever sailed with. A very steady guy, but I didn't go for the blind trust he expressed in the skipper. That was all right to a certain extent, but now—

"Anything you want done?" he asked me.

"No, Johnny, stand by. Johnny—what would you do if the officers decided the captain was nuts and put him in irons?"

"I'd borry one of the Old Man's guns an' shoot the irons off him," said my quartermaster laconically. "An' then I'd stand over him an' take his orders."

Johnny was a keynote in the crew. We were asking for real trouble if we tried anything. Ah, it was no use. All we could do was to wait for developments.

At eight bells on the button we floated again, and the lurch of it threw every man jack off his feet. With a splash and a muffled scraping, the *Dawnlight* settled deeply from under our feet, righted herself, rolled far over to the other side, and then gradually steadied. After I got up off my back I rang a "Stand-by" on the engine-room telegraph, whistled down the skipper's speaking tube, and motioned Johnny behind the wheel. He got up on the wheel mat as if we were leaving the dock in a seaport. Not a quiver! Old Johnny was one in a million.

I answered the engine room. "All steamed up and ready to go down here!" said the third engineer's voice. "And I think we'll have that generator running in another twenty minutes!"

"Good stuff!" I said, and whistled for the skipper. He must have felt that mighty lurch. I couldn't imagine why he wasn't on the bridge.

He answered sleepily: "Vell?"

"We're afloat" I spluttered.

"So?"

"What do you want to do—lay here? Or are we going some place?"

There was silence for a long time—so long that I called and asked him if he was still on the other end of the tube.

"I vas getting my orders," he said. "Yes, ve go. Full speed ahead."

"What course?"

"How should I know? I'm through now, third. You'll get y'ur orders."

"From Toole?"

"No!"

"Hey, if you ain't captain, who is?"

"I vouldn't know about dat. Full speed ahead!" The plug on his end of the tube clicked into place, and I turned toward Johnny, uncertain what to do.

"He said full ahead, didn't he?" asked Johnny quietly.

"Yeah, but—"

"Aye, aye, sir," he said with just a trace of sarcasm, and pulled the handle of the telegraph over from "Stand-by" to "Full ahead."

I put out my hand, and then shrugged and stuck it in my pocket. I'd tell

Toole about it when I came off watch. "As you go," I said, not looking at the compass.

"As she goes, sir," said Johnny, and began to steer as the shudder of the engines pounded through the ship.

The mate came up with Harry at noon, and we had a little confab. Toole was rubbing his hands and visibly expanding under the warmth of the bright sun, which had shone since three bells with a fierce brilliance, as if it wanted to make up for our three days of fog. "How's she go?" he asked me.

"Due west," I said meaningly.

"What? And we have a cargo for the Mediterranean?"

"I only work here," I said. "Skipper's orders."

Harry shrugged. "Then west it is, that's all I say," he grunted.

"Do you want to get paid this trip?" snapped Toole. He picked up the slip on which I had written the ship's position, which I'd worked out as soon as I could after the sun came out. "We're due south of the Madeiras and heading home," he went on. "How do you think those arms shippers are going to like our returning with their cargo? This is the payoff."

Harry tried to catch his arm, but he twisted away and strode into the wheelhouse. The twelve-to-four quartermaster hadn't relieved Johnny Weiss yet.

"Change course," barked the mate, his small, chunky body trembling. "East-nor'east!"

Johnny looked him over coolly and spat. "Cap'n changes course, mate."

"Then change course!" Toole roared. "The squarehead's nuts. From now on I'm running this ship!"

"I ain't been told of it," said Johnny quietly, and steadied on his westerly course.

"Well, by God, I'm the mate!" Toole said. "You've had no orders from that lunatic to disregard a command of a superior officer. Steer east!"

Weiss gazed out of the wheelhouse window, taking his time about thinking it over. The mate had made his point; to refuse further would be rank insubordination. Though Johnny was strong in his loyalty to the skipper, he was too much of a seaman to be pig-headed about this until he knew a little better where he stood.

"East it is, sir," he said, and his eyes were baleful. He hauled at the wheel, and a hint of a grin cracked his leathery face. "She—won't answer, sir!"

I saw red. "Go below!" I growled, and butted him from behind the wheel with my shoulder. He laughed aloud and went out.

I grasped the two top spokes, hunched my shoulders and gave a mighty heave. There was suddenly no resistance at all on the wheel, and my own violence threw me heels over crupper into the second mate, and we spun and tumbled, all his mass of lard on top of me. It was like lying under an anchor.

The wind was knocked out of him, and he couldn't move. I was smothering, and the mate was too surprised to do anything but stare. When Harry finally rolled off me it was a good two minutes before I could move.

"Damn that quartermaster," I gasped when we were on our feet again.

"Wasn't his fault," wheezed Harry. "He really tried to spin the wheel."

Knowing Johnny, I had to agree. He'd never pull anything like that. I scratched my head and turned to the mate. He was steering now, apparently without any trouble at all. "Don't tell me you can turn the ship?"

He grinned. "All it needed was a real helmsman," he ribbed me. And then the engines stopped, and the telegraph rang and spun over to "Stop," and the engine-room tube squealed.

"Now what?"

"I dunno," came the third's plaintive voice. "She just quit on us."

"O.K.; let us know when you've shot the trouble." The engineer rang off.

"Now what the hell?" said the mate.

I shrugged. "This is a jinxed trip," I said. I verified the "Stop" signal on the telegraph.

Harry said: "I don't know what's got into you guys. The skipper said somethin' about a new charter. He don't have to tell us who gave it to us."

"He don't have to keep us in the dark, either," said Toole. Then, glancing at the compass, he said, "Looka that! She's swingin' back to west!"

I looked over his shoulder. Slowly the ship was turning in the gentle swell, back to due west. And just as she came to 270° on the card—the engines began to pound.

"Ah!" said the mate, and verified the "Full ahead" gong that had just rung.

The third whistled up again and reported that he was picking fluff off his oilskins. "I'm going on the wagon," he said. "She quits by herself and starts by herself, an' I'm gonna bust out cryin' if it keeps up!"

And that's how we found out that the shp, with this strange cargo, insisted on having her head. For every time we tried to change course, the engines would stop, or a rudder cable would break, or the steering engine would quit. What could we do? We stood our watches and ran our ship as if nothing were the matter. If we hadn't we'd have gone as mad as we thought we already were.

Harry noticed a strange thing one afternoon. He told me about it when we came off watch.

"Y'know that box o' books in the chart room?" he asked me.

I did. It was an American Merchant Marine Library Association book chest, left aboard from the time the ship was honest. I'd been pretty well all through it. There were a few textbooks on French and Spanish, half a dozen detective novels, a pile of ten-year-old magazines, and a miscellaneous collection of pamphlets and unclassifiable.

"Well, about three o'clock I hear a noise in the chart room," said Harry, "an' I have a look. Well, sir, them books is heaving 'emselves up out of the chest and spilling on th' deck. Most of 'em was just tossed around, but a few was stackin' in a neat heap near the bulkhead. I on'y saw it for a second, and then it stopped, like I'd caught someone at the job, but I couldn't see no one there." He stopped and licked his lips and wheezed. "I looks at that pile o' books, an' they was all to do with North America an' the United States. A coupla history books, an atlas, a guidebook to New York City, a book on th' national parks— all sech. Well, I goes back into the wheelhouse, an' a few minutes later I peeks in again. All them books on America was open in different places in the chart room, an' the pages was turnin' like someone was readin' them, only—there just wasn't nobody there!"

What the *hell* was it that we had aboard, that wanted to know about the United States, that had replaced our captain with a string of coincidence, that had "chartered" the ship? I'd had enough. I firmly swore that if I ever got back to the States, police or no, I'd get off this scow and stay off her. A man can stand just so much.

About three days out the torpedo boat picked us up. She was a raider, small and gray and fast and wicked, and she belonged to a nation that likes to sink arms and runners. One of the nations, I mean. I had just come off watch, and was leaning on the taffrail when I saw her boiling along behind us, overtaking.

I ran forward, collaring an ordinary seaman. "Run up some colors," I said. "I don't give a damn what ones. Hurry!"

Pounding up the ladder. I hauled Toole out of the wheelhouse, pointed out the raider and dived for the radio shack, which was some good to us now that the generator was going again.

I sat down at the key and put on a headset. Sure enough, in a second or two I heard: "What ship is that? Where from? Where bound?" repeated in English, French, German and Spanish. I'd have called the skipper, but had given him up as a bad job. Toole came in.

"They want to know who we are," I said excitedly. "Who are we?"

"Wait'll I look at the flag the kid is running up," he said. He went to the door, and I heard him swear and whistle. "Give a look," he said.

Flying from the masthead was a brilliant green flag on which was a unicorn, rampant. I'd seen it—where was it? Years ago—oh, yes; that was it! In a book of English folk tales; that was supposed to be the standard of Oberon and Titania, King and Queen of . . . of the fairies, the Little Folk!

Dazed, I turned to the key and began pounding. I didn't even realize what I was sending. Some imp controlled my hand, and not until it was sent did I realize I had said, "*S.S. Princess of Birmingham,* Liverpool, bound for Calais with a load of airplane parts!"

"Thank you!" said the raider, and put a shell across our bow. Toole had gone back to the bridge, and I sat there sweating and wondering what the hell to do about this. Of all stupid things to say to an enemy raider!

The engine vibration suddenly became labored and the ship slowed perceptibly. Oh, of course, the old wagon would pick a time like this to become temperamental! I beat my skull with my fists and groaned. This was curtains.

The raider was abeam and angling toward us. "Heave to!" she kept buzzing through my phones. Through the porthole beside me I could already see the men moving about on her narrow decks. I turned to my key again and sent the commander of the raider some advice on a highly original way to amuse himself. In answer he brought his four swivel guns to bear on us.

The bridge tube whistled. Toole said, "What the hell did you say to him? He's fixin' to sink us!"

"I don't know," I wailed. "I don't know nothing!"

I ripped off the headset and put my elbows on the port ring across the room, staring out to sea with my back to the swiftly approaching raider. And there in the sunny waves was a conning tower, periscope and all!

Now get this. Here we were, lying helpless, going dead slow with crippled engines between a surface raider and a sub. We were meat for anyone working for any government. Most of us were Americans; if the raider took us it would mean an international incident at a time when no one could afford one. If the sub took us, it was the concentration camp for us. Either might, and probably would, sink us. We were outlaws.

I went up on the bridge. No sense doing anything now. If we got into boats, we'd likely be cut down by machine-gun bullets. Toole was frantically tugging at the handle of the engine-room telegraph.

"I'm trying to stop her!" he gasped. "She's going dead slow; there's something wrong with the engines. They're making such a racket back there that the first assistant can't hear the tube whistle. The telegraph is jammed! The helm won't answer! Oh, my God!"

"Where's your quartermaster?"

Toole jerked a thumb toward the bridge ladder. "I sent him aft to run down to the engine room, and he tripped and fell down to the boat deck! Knocked himself out!"

I ran to the port wing and looked out at the sub. True to her kind, she was attacking without asking questions. There was a jet of spume, and the swift wake of a torpedo cut toward us. At the rate we were going, it would strike us just between the after dry-cargo hold—where the "farm machinery" was stowed— and the fire room. It would get both the explosives and the boiler—good night nurse!

And then our "coincidental commander" took a hand. The crippled, laboring engines suddenly raced, shuddered and took hold. Grumbling in every plate, the *Dawnlight* sat down on her counter, raised her blunt nose eight feet, and scuttled forward at a speed that her builders would have denied. In fifty seconds she was doing fourteen knots. The torpedo swept close under our stern, and the raging wash of the tanker deflected it, so that it hurtled— straight toward the raider!

It struck just aft the stem piece, blowing away the gunboat's bow and turning her on her beam ends. She righted slowly lying far down by the head, and lay helpless. The sub, seeing her for the first time, came to the surface and men tumbled out of the hatches to man her four-incher. She began blasting away at the torpedo boat as fast as she could load, and the raider answered her, two shots to the sub's one. And there we left them, and for all I know they are blasting away yet, far too busy to pay attention to a crummy old tankship. And Toole and I—well, we cried on each other's shoulders for twenty minutes, and then we laughed ourselves sick.

The next four days were straight sailing, but for the pranks that were played on us. The skipper stuck to his cabin; we found out why later, and I can't really blame him. There was still no sign of the mob of beings that could be felt aboard, but for—again—the pranks that were played on us. We stood our watches and we ate our meals and we painted and chipped and scraped as usual. But for the—but I said that before.

Like the time the buff-colored paint the day gang was laying on the after bulkhead turned the steel transparent for forty-eight hours. Behind the bulkhead was the crew's washroom. The view from up forward was exquisite. As the four-to-eight fireman expressed it: "I wouldn't give a damn if the washroom was just fer washin'."

And lots of little things, like a spoonful of salt turning to thumbtacks in the Cajun's best gumbo soup, and live lobsters in the linen locker, and the toadstools in the bos'n's stores, and beautiful green grass, and acre of it, with four concentric fairy rings, growing on a flaked hawser in the forward cargo hold; and then there were the dice that, in the middle of a crap game, developed wickedly humorous caricatures of the six ship's officers—including me. That might not seem like much to you; but when you remember how clever they were, and when you could never meet one of your crew without his bursting into fits of laughter when he saw your face—well, it wasn't the best thing in the world for discipline.

About the captain— We got curious, Toole and I, about how he was getting on. He had locked himself in his room, and every once in a while would whistle for more food. He ate fish almost exclusively, in enormous quantities. We decided to do something about it. Some minor pretext to get a peek into his room. He wouldn't come to the door if we knocked; the portholes were the answer. Now, how could we get the curtain off from the outside without the irascible old man's coming out with a gun in each hand? We finally hit on something ideal. We'd get a broken spar with a snaggy end from somewhere, carry it past his porthole, and "accidentally" stick it in, tearing off the curtain and giving us a good look.

I'm sorry we did. We'd no business looking into the Old Man's private life that way. After all, we decided when we batted the wind about it afterward, the Old Man had a right, if he wanted to, to have a . . . a mermaid in his room! We saw her without being seen, and the skipper must have been in the inner room. She was very lovely, and I got a flash of scales and golden hair, and felt like a heel for looking.

Toole and I talked it over one afternoon as we neared the coast. The two of us had seen more of the whole screwy business than anyone else, and besides, Toole was an Irishman. No one will ever know if he was right or not, but his explanation is the only one that will fit all the facts. Pieced together from a two-hour conversation, this is about what he said, and now— I believe him:

"Third, this is a silly trip, hey? Ah, well. There are many things that you or I can't understand, and we're used to them, like the northern lights and the ways of a woman. I think that the skipper sold us out. No; no harm to us." He dragged on his cigar and stared out to sea as he talked. "Something, or somebody, made a deal with him the day after we sailed. Listen; hear that?"

Far out on the beam sounded the steady *smack-splash* of huge schools of porpoise. Oh, yes; they *might* have been porpoise.

"You told me what the skipper said to you about those critters. And they don't act like porpoises. I don't know if it was one of them or not; maybe it was something we couldn't see that talked. I think the skipper could. He's a squarehead, and they're seagoing people, and they know the sea from 'way back. He's been to sea half again as long as the oldest sailor aboard; you know that. I don't have to tell you that the sea is something that we'll never really understand. You can't know *all* about anything, even an atom; and the sea is so *damn* big.

"Well, he was made an offer; and it was probably a lifetime supply of whiskey and a week or so with that m-mermaid we—thought we saw in his room. What was the deal?

"That he should turn over his ship, and the crew to work it, to whatever party it was that wanted it for a trip from the African coast to America. There must have been provisions, if I know the skipper; he's a downy bird. He must have provided that the ship was to be protected against weather and bullets, mines and torps. He must have stipulated that no one aboard was to be harmed permanently, and—I'm sure of this—that ship and cargo were to be returned to him at the end of the trip. Everything else I've guessed at has turned out, hasn't it? Why not that? The only thing that really bothers me is the loss of time, because time is really big money in this racket. But you can bet that the squarehead wasn't beaten down. We'll find out—I'm certain of it.

"Now, about the passengers. Laugh at me and I'll dry up like a clam; but I believe I have the answer. The old country has inhabitants that men have dreamed and sung and written and told about a great deal, and seen more than seldom. I've spent a lot of time off watch reading about 'em, and my mother used to tell me—bless her! Anyway, there was ghosts and pixies, goblins and brownies, and dervishes and fairies and nymphs and peris and dryads and naiads and kelpies and sprites; gnomes and imps and elves and dwarves and nixies and ghouls and pigwidgeons, and the legion of the leprechauns, and many another. And some were good and some were not, and some helped and some hindered; but all were mischievous as hell. They weren't too bad, any more than are the snakes and spiders that eat mosquitoes, and many were downright beneficial.

"There's hell to pay in Europe now, third. You can't expect a self-respectin' pixie to hide in a shell hole and watch a baby torn to shreds. They sickened of it, and their boss man, whoever he is, got 'em together and made arrangements to ship 'em some place where there's a little peace and quiet once in a while, where they can work their harmless spells on a non-aggressive populace. They can't swim worth a damn, and you couldn't expect the sea folk to ferry 'em over; they're an unreliable lot anyway, to all accounts.

"I read a book once about Ol' Puck, and how the Little People were brought to the British Isles from the Continent. They couldn't swim even that, and they got a blind man to row and a deaf mute to stand lookout, and never a word was said of it until Puck himself told of it. This is the twentieth century, and it's a big ocean they've got to cross, and there are many more of them. Did ye notice, by the way," he broke off suddenly, "that though our tanks are empty an' we've used fuel and water and stores for near two weeks, that we're *low in the water?*" He laughed. "We've many and many of 'em aboard.

"We'll unload 'em, and we'll get our pay for the job. But this I'll tell you, and now you may laugh, for you're in the same boat. We're r'arin', tearin' lawbreakers aboard here, third, and we don't give a damn, or we wouldn't be here. But if there's any kind of a good place for us to go at the end of the voyage, then we'll go there for this week's work. It was always a good thing to help a war refugee."

I didn't laugh. I went away by myself and chewed and swallowed that, and I thought about it a bit, and now I believe what I believe, and maybe a little bit more. It's a big world, and these are crazy times.

Well, almost as we expected, we unloaded, but it only took us three hours instead of fourteen. Yes, we struck fog off the Carolinas, and the ship nosed up and heeled over in it, and we could feel the pressure getting less aboard. And when the *thing* under the ship sank and floated us again, and the sun came out—

Well, this is the part that is hard to explain. I won't try it. But look: It was the twenty-third day of September when we sailed from the drydock. And when we lay off the coast that way, just out of the fog, it was the twenty-fifth. And it would have taken just three days for us to reach there from the drydock. Somewhere we lost a week. Yeah.

And the bunkers were full of fuel. And the lockers were full of stores. And the fresh-water tanks were full of water, just as they had been. But—there's a difference. Any fuel we use is—or acts like—high-grade stuff. And our food tastes better, and the work is easier. Yeah, we're lawbreakers—outlaws. But we take our ship where we please, when we please, and never a warship do we see, and never a shell or mine touches us. Oh, yeah; they say she's haunted. No; there's another word for it. She is—*enchanted.* We're paid, and we're being paid. And we'll go anywhere and do anything, because we have the best skipper a man ever sailed under, and because, more than any other men on earth, we need not be afraid of death.

But I can't forget that there'll be hell an' all to pay ashore!

POKER FACE

I'm so very glad to see this one back in print. Written some time in
early 1940, this and the next four were written in an extraordinarily
prolific (for me) period in early 1940, during which my editor,
the late John Campbell, hoarded them and pieced them out; I saw
none of them in print until I returned to the States after managing a
hotel in Jamaica, then, when the U.S. got into the war, working as a
heavy equipment operator in Jamaica (for the Army) and in Puerto
Rico (for the Navy). From 1940 until late '46 I wrote only one story
(a novelette called *Killdozer*)—six solid years of "writers's block"—the
worst I have ever known.

But about *"Poker Face,"* 1940: I wonder what was in George Orwell's
mind just then, eight years before he wrote his terrifyingly prescient
1984?

We all had to get up early that morning, and we still hadn't sense enough to
get up from around the poker table. We'd called in that funny little guy from
the accounting department they called Face to make it a foursome with the
three of us. It had been nip and tuck from nine o'clock on—he played a nice
game of stud. But tonight there was no one lucky man, and when Harry
jokingly bet a nickel on a pair of fours and Delehanty took him up on it, the
game degenerated into penny-ante. After a while we forgot whose deal it was
and sat around just batting the breeze.

"Screwy game," said Delehanty. "What's the use of squattin' here all this time just to break even? Must be your influence, Face. Never happened before. We generally hand all our money over to Jack after four deals. Hey, Jack?"

I grinned. "The game still owes me plenty, bud," I said. "But I think you're right about Face. I don't know if you noticed it, but damn if that winning didn't go right around behind the deal—me, you, Face, Harry, me again. If I won two, everyone else would win two."

Face raised an eyebrow ridge because he hadn't any eyebrows. There wasn't anything particularly remarkable about his features, except that they were absolutely without hair. The others carried an a.m. stubble, but his face gleamed nakedly, half luminous. He'd been a last choice, but a pretty good one. He said little, watched everyone closely and casually, and seemed like a pretty nice guy. "Noticed that, did you?" he asked. His voice was a very full tenor.

"That's right," said Harry. "How about it, Face? What is this power you have over poker?"

"Oh, just one of those things you pick up," he said.

Delehanty laughed outright. "Listen at that," he said. "He's like the ol' mountain climber who saw a volcano erupting in the range he'd scaled the day before. 'By damn,' he says, 'why can't I be careful where I spit?'"

Everybody laughed but Face. "You think it just happened? Would you like to see it happen again?"

That stopped the hilarity. We looked at him queerly. Harry said, "What's the dope?"

"Play with chips," said Face. "No money, no hard feelings. If you like, I won't touch the cards. Just to make it easy, I'll put it this way. Deal our four hands of stud. Jack'll win the first with three threes. Delehanty next with three fours. Me next with three fives. Harry next with three sixes. Each three-spread will come out hearts, diamonds, clubs, in that order. You, Delehanty, start the deal. Go on—shuffle them all you like."

Delehanty was a little popeyed. "You wouldn't want to make a little bet on that, would you?" he breathed.

"I would not. I don't want to take your money that way. It would be like picking pockets."

"You're bats, Face," I said. "There's so little chance of a shuffled deck coming out that way that you might as well call it impossible."

"Try it," said Face quietly.

Delehanty counted the cards carefully, shuffled at least fifteen times with his very efficient gambler's rifle, and dealt around quickly. The cards flapped down in front of me—a jack face down, a six, and then—three threes; hearts, diamonds, clubs, in that order. Nobody said anything for a long time.

Finally, "Jack's got it," Harry breathed.

"Let me see that deck," snapped Harry. He swept it up, spread it out in his hands. "Seems O.K.," he said slowly, and turned to Face.

"Your deal," said Face woodenly.

Harry dealt quickly. I said, "Delehanty's s'posed to be next with three fours—right?" Yeah—right! Three fours lay in front of Delehanty. It was too much—cards shouldn't act that way. Wordlessly I reached for the cards, gathered them up, pitched them back over my shoulder. "Break out a new deck," I said. "Your deal, Face."

"Let Delehanty deal for me," said Face.

Delehanty dealt again, clumsily this time, for his hands trembled. That didn't matter—there were still three fives smiling up at Face when he was through.

"Your deal," whispered Harry to me, and turned half away from the table.

I took up the cards. I spent three solid minutes shuffling them. I had Harry cut them and then cut them again myself and then passed them to Delehanty for another cut. I dealt four hands, and Harry's was the winning hand, with three sixes—hearts, diamonds, clubs.

Delehanty's eyes were almost as big now as his ears. He said, "Heaven. All. Might. Tea," and rested his chin in his hands. I thought he was going to cry or something.

"Well?" said Face.

"Were we playing poker with this guy?" Harry asked no one in particular.

When, by a great deal of hard searching, I found my voice again, I asked Face, "Hey, do you do that just any time you feel like it, or does it come over you at odd moments?"

Face laughed. "Any time," he said. "Want to see a really pretty one? Shuffle and deal out thirteen cards to each of us, face down. Then look them over."

I gave him a long look and began to shuffle. Then I dealt. I think we were all a little afraid to pick up our cards. I know that when I looked at mine I felt as if someone had belted me in the teeth with a night stick. I had thirteen cards, and they were all spades. I looked around the table. Delehanty had diamonds. Face had hearts. Harry had clubs.

You could have heard a bedbug sneeze in the room until Harry began saying, "Ah, no. Ah, no. Ah, no," quietly, over and over, as if he were trying to tell himself something.

"Can they all do things like that where you come from?" I asked, and Face nodded brightly.

"Can everyone walk where you come from?" he returned. "Or see, or hear, or think? Sure."

"Just where do you come from?" asked Harry.

"I don't know," said Face. "I only know how I came and I couldn't explain it to you."

"Why not?"

"How could you explain an internal-combustion engine to an Australian bushman?"

"You might try," said Delehanty, piqued. "We's pretty smart bushmen, we is."

"Yeah," I chimed in. "I'm willing to allow you the brains to do those card tricks of yours; you ought to have enough savvy to put over an idea or two."

"Oh—the cards. That was easy enough. I felt the cards as you shuffled them."

"You felt with my fingers?"

"That's right. Want proof? Jack, your head is itching a little on the right side, near the top, and you're too lazy to scratch it just yet. Harry's got a nail pushing into the third toe of his right foot—not very bad, but it's there. Well, what do you say?"

He was right. I scratched. Harry shuffled his feet and said, "O.K., but what has that got to do with arranging the cards that way? Suppose you did feel them with our hands—then what?"

Face put his elbows on the table. "As for arranging the cards, that was done in the shuffle. You grasp half of the deck in each hand, bend them, let them flip out from under your thumbs. If you can control the pressure of each thumb carefully enough, you can make the right cards fall into the right places. You all shuffled at least four times; that made it that much easier for me."

Delehanty was popeyed again. "How did you know which cards were supposed to go in which places?"

"Memorized their order, of course," said Face. "I've seen that done in theaters even by men like you."

"So've I," said Harry. "But you still haven't told us how you arranged the deal. If you'd done the shuffling I could see it, but—"

"But I *did* do the shuffling," said Face. "I controlled that pressure of your thumbs."

"How about the cuts?" Delehanty put in, finding that at last we had him on the run. "When Jack dealt he handed the pack to Harry and me both to be cut."

"I not only controlled those cuts," said Face calmly, "but I made you do it."

"Go way," said Delehanty aggressively. "Don't give us that. How're you going to make a man do anything you like?"

"Skeptical animal, aren't you?" grinned Face; and Delehanty rose slowly, walked around the table, caught Harry by the shoulders and kissed him on both cheeks. Harry almost fell off his chair. Delehanty stood there rockily, his eyes positively bulging. Suddenly he expectorated with great violence. "What the dirty so and forth made me do that?" he wanted to know.

"Chummy, ain't you?" grinned Harry through his surprise.

Face said, "Satisfied, Delehanty?"

Delehanty whirled on him. "Why you little—" His fury switched off like a light going out. "Right again, Face." He went over and sat down. I never saw that Irishman back down like that before.

"You made him do that?" I asked.

Face regarded me gravely. "You doubt it?"

We locked glances for a moment, and then my feet gathered under me. I had a perverse desire to get on all fours and bark like a dog. It seemed the most natural thing in the world. I said quickly, "Not at all, Face, not at all!" My feet relaxed.

"You're the damnedest fellow I ever saw," said Harry. "What kind of a man are you, anyway?"

"Just a plain ordinary man with a job," said Face, and looked at Delehanty.

"So am I," said Harry, "but I can't make cards sit up and typewrite, or dumb Irishers snuggle up to their fellowmen."

"Don't let that bother you," said Face. "I told you before—there's nothing more remarkable in that than there is in walking, or seeing, or hearing. I was born with it, that's all."

"You said everyone was, where you come from," Harry reminded him. "Now spill it. Just where did you come from?"

"Geographically," said Face, "not very far from here. Chronologically, a hell of a way."

Harry looked over my way blankly. "Now what does all that mean?"

"As near as I can figure out," said Face, "it means just what I said. I come from right around here—fifty miles, maybe—but the place I came from is thirty-odd thousand years away."

"Years *away*?" I asked, by this time incapable of being surprised. "You mean 'ago,' don't you?"

"Away," repeated Face. "I came along duration, not through time itself."

"Sounds very nice," murmured Delehanty to a royal flush he had thumbed out for himself.

Face laughed. "Duration isn't time—it parallels it. Duration is a dimension. A dimension is essentially a measurement along a plane of existence. By that I mean that any given object has four dimensions, and these extend finitely, along four planes—length, width, height, duration. The last is no different from the others; nor is it any less tangible. You simply take it for granted.

"When you're ordering a piece of lumber, for instance, you name its measurements. You say you want a two by six, twelve feet long. You don't order its duration; you simply take for granted it will extend long enough in that dimension to suit your needs. You would build better if you measured it as carefully as you do the others, but your life span is too short for you to care that much."

"I think I savvy that," said Harry, who had been following carefully, "but what do you mean by saying that you came 'along' duration?"

"Again, just what I said. You can't move without moving along the plane of dimension. If you walk down the street, you move along its length. If you go up in an elevator, you move along its height. I came along duration."

"You mean you projected yourself into the fourth dimension?" asked Henry.

"No!" said Face violently, and snorted. "I told you—duration is a dimension, not another set of dimensions. Can you project yourself into length, or height, or into any one dimension? Of course not! The four are interdependent. That fourth-dimensional stuff you read is poppycock. There's no mystery about the fourth dimension. It isn't an impalpable word. It's a basis of measurement."

I said, "What's this business of your traveling along it?"

Face spread out his hands. "As I said before, duration is finite. Suppose you wanted to walk from Third Street to Fifth Street. First you'd locate a sidewalk that would take you in the direction you were going. You'd follow that until it ended. Then you'd locate one that would take you to your destination. Where the one stopped and the other started is Fourth Street. Now if you want to go twenty blocks instead of two, you simply repeat that process until you get where you're going.

"Traveling along duration is exactly the same thing. Just as you enter a street at a certain point in its length, so you encounter an object on the street at a certain point in its duration. Maybe it's near the beginning, maybe near the end. You follow it along that dimension—you don't project yourself into it. All objects have two terminations in duration—inception and destruction. You travel along an object's duration until it ceases to exist beside you because you have reached the end of it—or the beginning. Then you proceed to find another object so that you may continue in the same direction, exactly as you proceeded to find yourself another sidewalk in your little trek across town."

"I'll be damned," said Delehanty, "I can understand it!"

"Me, too," Harry said. "That much of it. But exactly how did you travel along duration? I can get the idea of walking beside a building's length, for instance, but I can't see myself walking along beside ... er ... how long it lasted, if you see what I mean. Or do *I* see what I mean?"

"Now you're getting to something that may be a little tough to explain," said Face. "You have few expressions in your language that could cover it. About the clearest way for me to put it is this: My ability to travel in that particular direction is the result of my ability to perceive it. If you could only perceive two dimensions, length and breadth, you would be completely in the dark about the source of an object which dropped on you from above. If you couldn't sense the distance from here to the door—if you didn't know the door existed, nor the distance to it, you wouldn't be able to make the trip. I can see along duration as readily as you can see up and down a road. I can move along it equally readily."

"Do you stay in one place while you travel duration?" I asked suddenly.

"I can. I don't have to, though. You can go forward and upward while you curve to the left, can't you? Mix 'em anyway you like."

Harry piped up. "You say you came thirty thousand years. How is that possible? You don't look as if you're much older than I am."

"I'm not," said Face, "in point of years existed. That is, I didn't live those years. I—passed them."

"How long did it take you?"

Face smiled. "Your question is ridiculous, Harry. 'How long' is a 'durational' term. It involves passage of time, which is a convenient falsehood. Time is static, objects mobile. I can't explain a true state of affairs from the basis of a false conception."

Harry shut up. I asked him something that had been bothering me. "Where did you come from, Face, and—why?"

He looked at me deeply, that eyebrow ridge rising a trifle. "I came—I was sent. I came because I was qualified for the job, I was sent because—well, someone had to be sent, to restore the balance of the city."

"What city?"

"I don't know. It had a name, I suppose, but it was forgotten. There was no need for a name. Do you name your toothbrush, or your bed sheets, or anything else that has been nearly a part of you all your life? No one ever left the city, no one ever arrived at it. There were other cities, but no one cared about them, where they were, who their people were and what they were like, and so on. There was no need to know. The city was independent and utterly self-sufficient. It was the ultimate government. It was not a democracy, for each individual was subjugated entirely to the city. But it was not a dictatorship as you know the term, for it had no dictators. It had no governing body, as a matter of fact. It didn't need one. It had no laws but those of habit and custom. It ran smoothly because all of its internal frictions had been worn smooth by the action of the centuries. It was an anarchistic society in the true sense of anarchism—society without need of government."

"That's an impossibility," said Harry, who had a reputation as a minor barroom sociologist.

"I came from that city," Face reminded him gently. "Why is it impossible? You must take certain things into account before you make such rash statements. Your human nature is against such an organization. Your people would be like lost sheep—possibly like lost wolverines—under such a set-up. But my people were not like that—not after centuries of breeding for the most desirable traits, living circumscribed ways of life, thinking stereotyped thoughts. Imagine it if you can.

"Now the city was divided into two halves, like the halves of a great brain. For every death there was a birth; for every loss there was a gain or an equal loss on the other side. The equation was kept balanced, the scales level. The city was permanent, inexorable, immortal and static."

"What did they do with their spare time?" asked Harry.

"They lay in their cubicles until they were needed."

"Were there no theaters, ball games—nothing like that?" asked Delehanty.

Face shook his head. "Amusement is for the relaxation of an imperfect mind," he said. "A mind that has been trained to do one thing and one thing only needs no stimulation or change of pace."

"Why was the city so big?" asked Harry. "Good gosh, a civilization like that doesn't *mean* anything. Why didn't it simply degenerate into the machines that ruled it? Why keep all those humans if they must live like machines?"

Face shrugged. "When the city was instituted, there was a population of that size to allow for. Then, it had a rigid human government, and there was crime and punishment and pain and happiness. They were disposed of in a few generations—they were not logical, you see, and the city was designed on the philosophy that what is not logical is also not necessary. By that time the city was too steeped in its own traditions; there was no one left to make such a radical change as to cut down on the population. The city could care for that many—likewise it could not exist as it was unless it did care for that many. Many human offices were disposed of as they became unnecessary and automatic. One of these was that of controller of population. The machines took care of that—they and the unbreakable customs."

"Hell!" said Delehanty explosively. "I wouldn't go for that. Why didn't the people push the whole thing over and get some fun out of life?"

"They didn't want it!" said Face, as if he were repeating a self-evident fact, and was surprised that he had to. "They had never had that sort of life; they never heard or read or saw anything of the sort. They had no more desire to do things like that than you have to play pattycake! They weren't constituted to enjoy it."

"You still haven't told us why you left the place," I reminded him.

"I was coming to that. In the city there was a necessity for the pursuance of certain knowledges, as a safety measure against the time when one or another of the machines might need rebuilding by a man who understood them.

"One of these men was an antiquarian named Hark Vegas, which is really not a name at all but a combination of sounds indicating a number. His field was history—the development of all about him, from its earliest recorded mythologies and beyond that to its most logical sources. In the interests of the city, he so applied himself to his work that he uncovered certain imponderables— historical trends which were neither logical nor in harmony with the records. They were of no importance, perhaps, but their existence interfered with the perfection of his understanding. The only way he could untangle these unimportant matters was to investigate them personally. And so—that is what he did.

"He waited until his successor was thoroughly trained, so that in any eventuality the city would not be left without an antiquarian for more than a very little while, and he studied carefully the records of the city's customs. These forbade any citizen's leaving the city, and carefully described the boundaries thereof. They were so very old, however, that they neglected to stipulate the boundaries along the duration dimension, since duration perception was a development of only the past four or five thousand years. As an antiquarian, Hark Vegas was familiar with the technique. He moved himself out along the duration of a metallic fragment and thus disappeared from the city.

"Now this unheard-of happening disturbed the timeless balance of the city, for Hark Vegas was nowhere to be found. Within seconds of his disappearance, news of it had reached the other half of the city, and the group of specialists there.

"The matter involved me immediately for several reasons. In the first place, my field was—damn it, there's no word for it in your language yet. It's a mental science and has to do with time perceptions. At any rate, I was the only one whose field enabled him to reason where Hark Vegas had gone. Secondly, Hark Vegas was my contemporary in the other half of the city. We would both be replaced within a week, but during that week there would be one too many in my half of the city, one too few in his—an intolerable, absolutely unprecedented state of affairs. There was only one thing to do, since I was qualified, and that was to find him and bring him back. My leaving would restore the balance; if I were successful in finding him, our return would not disturb it. It was the only thing to do, for the status quo had to be maintained at all costs. I acquired a piece of the metal he had used—an easy thing to do, since everything in the city was catalogued—and came away."

Face paused to light a cigarette. The man smoked, I had noticed, with more sheer enjoyment than anyone I had ever met.

"Well," said Harry impatiently, "did you find him?"

Face leaned back in a cloud of blue smoke and stared dreamily at the ceiling. "No," he said. "And I'll tell you why.

"I ran into a characteristic of dimensions that was so utterly simple that it had all but escaped me. Let me give you an example. How many sides has a cube?"

"Six," said Harry promptly.

Face nodded. "Exactly. Excluding the duration dimension, the cube is a three-dimensional body and has six sides. There are *two* sides as manifestations of each dimension. I think I overlooked that. You see, there are four dimensions, but eight—*directions!*"

He paused, while the three of us knotted our brows over the conception. "Right and left," he said. "Up and down. Forward and backward—and 'beginningwards' and 'endwards'—the two directions in the duration dimension!"

Delehanty raised his head slowly. "You mean you—didn't know which *way* to go?"

"Precisely. I entered the durational field and struck off blindly in the wrong direction! I went as far as I reasoned Hark Vegas had gone, and then stopped to look around. I found myself in such a bewildering, uproarious, chaotic world that I simply hadn't the mental equipment to cope with it. I had to retreat into a deserted place and develop it. I came into your world—here, about eight years ago. And when I had begun to get the ways of this world, I came out of hiding and began my search. It ended almost as soon as it had begun, for I stopped searching!

"Do you know what happened to me? Do you realize that never before had I seen color, or movement, or argument, or love, hate, noise, confusion, growth, death, laughter? Can you imagine my delighted first glimpses of a street fight, a traffic jam, a factory strike? I should have been horrified, perhaps—but never had I seen such beautiful marvels, such superb and profound and moving happenings. I threw myself into it. I became one of you. I became an accountant, throttling down what powers I alone of all this earth possess, striving for life as a man on an equal footing with the rest of men. You can't know my joy and my delight! I make a mistake in my entries, and the city—this city, does not care or suffer for it, but brawls on unheeding. My responsibilities are to myself alone, and I defy my cast-steel customs and laugh doing it. I'm living here, you see? Living! Go back? Hah!"

"Colors," I murmured. "Noise, and happy filth, and sorrows and screams. So they got you—*too!*"

Face's smile grew slowly and then flashed away. He stared at me like some alabaster-faced statue for nearly a full minute, and then the agile tendrils of his mind whipped out and encountered mine. We clutched each other thus, and the aura of our own forces around us struck two men dumb.

"Hark Vegas," he said woodenly.

I nodded.

He straightened, drew a deep breath, threw back his head and laughed. "This colossal joke," he said, wiping his eyes, "was thirty-eight thousand years in the making. Pleased to meet you—Jack."

We left then. Harry and Delehanty can't remember anything but a poker game.

MICROCOSMIC GOD

I have always disliked this story—not for its basic idea, which has been called unique, but for its writing. Just out of my 'teens, I had not yet learned that nobody is ever and altogether good, and nobody is all bad. Ignorant of that, one can produce 100% purified vintage dyed-in-the-wool cardboard characters. The story's basic idea, however, is indeed unique, and many years later, at the Artificial Intelligence offices in M.I.T., a truly great scientist introduced himself to me, to tell me (as many scientists have) that he had gotten into science in the first place because of reading science fiction as a youngster, and further, that he had gotten into microbiology because of this one story. And this is a guy who might win a Nobel Prize! So . . . what price literary judgments?

Here is a story about a man who had too much power, and a man who took too much, but don't worry; I'm not going political on you. The man who had the power was named James Kidder and the other was his banker.

Kidder was quite a guy. He was a scientist and he lived on a small island off the New England coast all by himself. He wasn't the dwarfed little gnome of a mad scientist you read about. His hobby wasn't personal profit, and he wasn't a megalomaniac with a Russian name and no scruples. He wasn't insidious, and he wasn't even particularly subversive. He kept his hair cut and his nails clean and lived and thought like a reasonable human being. He was slightly on the baby-faced side; he was inclined to be a hermit; he was short and plump and—brilliant. His specialty was biochemistry, and he was always called *Mr.* Kidder. Not "Dr." Not "Professor." Just Mr. Kidder.

He was an odd sort of apple and always had been. He had never graduated from any college or university because he found them too slow for him, and too rigid in their approach to education. He couldn't get used to the idea that perhaps his professors knew what they were talking about. That went for his texts, too. He was always asking questions, and didn't mind very much when they were embarrassing. He considered Gregor Mendel a bungling liar, Darwin an amusing philosopher, and Luther Burbank a sensationalist. He never opened his mouth without leaving his victim feeling breathless. If he was talking to someone who had knowledge, he went in there and got it, leaving his victim breathless. If he was talking to someone whose knowledge was already in his possession, he only asked repeatedly, "How do you know?" His most delectable pleasure was cutting a fanatical eugenicist into conversational ribbons. So people left him alone and never, never asked him to tea. He was polite, but not politic.

He had a little money of his own, and with it he leased the island and built himself a laboratory. Now I've mentioned that he was a biochemist. But being what he was, he couldn't keep his nose in his own field. It wasn't too remarkable when he made an intellectual excursion wide enough to perfect a method of crystalizing Vitamin B1 profitably by the ton—if anyone wanted it by the ton. He got a lot of money for it. He bought his island outright and put eight hundred men to work on an acre and a half of his ground, adding to his laboratory and building equipment. He got to messing around with sisal fiber, found out how to fuse it, and boomed the banana industry by producing a practically unbreakable cord from the stuff.

You remember the popularizing demonstration he put on at Niagara, don't you? That business of running a line of the new cord from bank to bank over the rapids and suspending a ten-ton truck from the middle of it by razor edges resting on the cord? That's why ships now moor themselves with what looks like heaving line, no thicker than a lead pencil, that can be coiled on reels like garden hose. Kidder made cigarette money out of that, too. He went out and bought himself a cyclotron with part of it.

After that money wasn't money any more. It was large numbers in little books. Kidder used little amounts of it to have food and equipment sent out to him, but after a while that stopped, too. His bank dispatched a messenger by sea-plane to find out if Kidder was still alive. The man returned two days later in a bemused state, having been amazed something awesome at the things he'd seen out there. Kidder was alive, all right, and he was turning out a surplus of good food in an astonishingly simplified synthetic form. The bank wrote immediately and wanted to know if Mr. Kidder, in his own interest, was willing to release the secret of his dirtless farming. Kidder replied that he would be glad to, and inclosed the formulas. In a P. S. he said that he hadn't sent the information ashore because he hadn't realized anyone would be interested. That from a man who was responsible for the greatest sociological change in the second half of the twentieth century—factory farming. It made him richer; I mean it made his bank richer. He didn't give a rap.

But Kidder didn't really get started until about eight months after the messenger's visit. For a biochemist who couldn't even be called "Doctor" he did pretty well. Here is a partial list of the things that he turned out:

A commercially feasible plan for making an aluminum alloy stronger than the best steel so that it could be used as a structural metal.

An exhibition gadget he called a light pump, which worked on the theory that light is a form of matter and therefore subject to physical and electromagnetic laws. Seal a room with a single light source, beam a cylindrical vibratory magnetic field to it from the pump, and the light will be led down it. Now pass the light through Kidder's "lens"—a ring which perpetuates an electric field along the lines of a high-speed iris-type camera shutter. Below this is the heart of the light pump—a ninety-eight-per-cent efficient light absorber, crystalline, which, in a sense, *loses* the light in its internal facets. The effect of darkening the room with this apparatus is slight but measurable. Pardon my layman's language, but that's the general idea.

Synthetic chlorophyll—by the barrel.

An airplane propeller efficient at eight times sonic speed.

A cheap goo you brush on over old paint, let harden, and then peel off like strips of cloth. The old paint comes with it. That one made friends fast.

A self-sustaining atomic disintegration of uranium's isotope 238, which is two hundred times as plentiful as the old stand-by, U-235.

That will do for the present. If I may repeat myself; for a biochemist who couldn't even be called "Doctor," he did pretty well.

Kidder was apparently unconscious of the fact that he held power enough on his little island to become master of the world. His mind simply didn't run to things like that. As long as he was left alone with his experiments, he was well content to leave the rest of the world to its own clumsy and primitive devices. He couldn't be reached except by radiophone of his own design, and its only counterpart was locked in a vault of his Boston bank. Only one man could operate it. The extraordinarily sensitive transmitter would respond only to Conant's own body vibrations. Kidder had instructed Conant that he was not to be disturbed except by messages of the greatest moment. His ideas and patents, what Conant could pry out of him, were released under pseudonyms known only to Conant—Kidder didn't care.

The result, of course, was an infiltration of the most astonishing advancements since the dawn of civilization. The nation profited—the world profited. But most of all, the bank profited. It began to get a little oversize. It began getting its fingers into other pies. It grew more fingers and had to bake more figurative pies. Before many years had passed, it was so big that, using Kidder's many weapons, it almost matched Kidder in power.

Almost.

Now stand by while I squelch those fellows in the lower left-hand corner who've been saying all this while that Kidder's slightly improbable; that no man could ever perfect himself in so many ways in so many sciences.

Well, you're right. Kidder was a genius—granted. But his genius was not creative. He was, too the core, a student. He applied what he knew, what he saw, and what he was taught. When first he began working in his new laboratory on his island he reasoned something like this:

"Everything I know is what I have been taught by the sayings and writings of people who have studied the sayings and writings of people who have—and so on. Once in a while someone stumbles on something new and he or someone cleverer uses the idea and disseminates it. But for each one that finds something really new, a couple of million gather and pass on information that is already current. I'd know more if I could get the jump on evolutionary trends. It takes too long to wait for the accidents that increase man's knowledge—my knowledge. If I had ambition enough now to figure out how to travel ahead in time, I could skim the surface of the future and just dip down when I saw something interesting. But time isn't that way. It can't be left behind or tossed ahead. What else is left?

"Well, there's the proposition of speeding intellectual evolution so that I can observe what it cooks up. That seems a bit inefficient. It would involve more labor to discipline human minds to that extent than it would to simply apply myself along those lines. But I can't apply myself that way. No one man can.

"I'm licked. I can't speed myself up, and I can't speed other men's minds up. Isn't there an alternative? There must be—somewhere, somehow, there's got to be an answer."

So it was on this, and not on eugenics, or light pumps, or botany, or atomic physics, that James Kidder applied himself. For a practical man he found the problem slightly on the metaphysical side; but he attacked it with typical thoroughness, using his own peculiar brand of logic. Day after day he wandered over the island, throwing shells impotently at sea gulls and swearing richly. Then came a time when he sat indoors and brooded. And only then did he get feverishly to work.

He worked in his own field, biochemistry, and concentrated mainly on two things—genetics and animal metabolism. He learned, and filed away in his insatiable mind, many things having nothing to do with the problem in hand, and very little of what he wanted. But he piled that little on what little he knew or guessed, and in time had quite a collection of known factors to work with. His approach was characteristically unorthodox. He did things on the order of multiplying apples by pears, and balancing equations by adding $\log \sqrt{-1}$ to one side and ^{00} to the other. He made mistakes, but only one of a kind, and later, only one of a species. He spent so many hours at his microscope that he had to quit work for two days to get rid of a hallucination that his heart was pumping his own blood through the mike. He did nothing by trial and error because he disapproved of the method as sloppy.

And he got results. He was lucky to begin with and even luckier when he formularized the law of probability and reduced it to such low terms that he knew almost to the item what experiments not to try. When the cloudy, viscous semifluid on the watch glass began to move itself he knew he was on the right track. When it began to seek food on its own he began to be excited. When it divided and, in a few hours, redivided, and each part grew and divided again, he was triumphant, for he had created life.

He nursed his brain children and sweated and strained over them, and he designed baths of various vibrations for them, and inoculated and dosed and sprayed them. Each move he made taught him the next. And out of his tanks and tubes and incubators came amoebalike creatures, and then ciliated animalcules, and more and more rapidly he produced animals with eye spots, nerve cysts, and then—victory of victories—a real blastopod, possessed of many cells instead of one. More slowly he developed a gastropod, but once he had it, it was not too difficult for him to give it organs, each with a specified function, each inheritable.

Then came cultured mollusklike things, and creatures with more and more perfected gills. The day that a nondescript thing wriggled up an inclined board out of a tank, threw flaps over its gills and feebly breathed air, Kidder quit work and went to the other end of the island and got disgustingly drunk. Hangover and all, he was soon back in the lab, forgetting to eat, forgetting to sleep, tearing into his problem.

He turned into a scientific byway and ran down his other great triumph—accelerated metabolism. He extracted and refined the stimulating factors in alcohol, cocoa, heroin, and Mother Nature's prize dope runner, *cannabis indica*. Like the scientist who, in analyzing the various clotting agents for blood treatments, found that oxalic acid and oxalic acid alone was the active factor, Kidder isolated the accelerators and decelerators, the stimulants and soporifics, in every substance that ever undermined a man's morality and/or caused a "noble experiment." In the process he found one thing he needed badly—a colorless elixir that made sleep the unnecessary and avoidable waster of time it should be. Then and there he went on a twenty-four-hour shift.

He artificially synthesized the substances he had isolated, and in doing so sloughed away a great many useless components. He pursued the subject along the lines of radiations and vibrations. He discovered something in the long reds which, when projected through a vessel full of air vibrating in the supersonics, and then polarized, speeded up the heartbeat of small animals twenty to one. They ate twenty times as much, grew twenty times as fast, and—died twenty times sooner than they should have.

Kidder built a huge hermetically sealed room. Above it was another room, the same length and breadth but not quite as high. This was his control chamber. The large room was divided into four sealed sections, each with its individual miniature cranes and derricks—handling machinery of all kinds. There were also trapdoors fitted with air locks leading from the upper to the lower room.

By this time the other laboratory had produced a warm-blooded, snake-skinned quadruped with an astonishingly rapid life cycle—a generation every eight days, a life span of about fifteen. Like the echidna, it was oviparous and mammalian. Its period of gestation was six hours; the eggs hatched in three; the young reached sexual maturity in another four days. Each female laid four eggs and lived just long enough to care for the young after they hatched. The male generally died, two or three hours after mating. The creatures were highly adaptable. They were small—not more than three inches long, two inches to the shoulder from the ground. Their forepaws had three digits and a triple-jointed, opposed thumb. They were attuned to life in an atmosphere with a large ammonia content. Kidder bred four of the creatures and put one group in each section of the sealed room.

Then he was ready. With his controlled atmospheres he varied temperatures, oxygen content, humidity. He killed them off like flies with excesses of, for instance, carbon dioxide, and the survivors bred their physical resistance into the next generation. Periodically he would switch the eggs from one sealed section to another to keep the strains varied. And rapidly, under these controlled conditions, the creatures began to evolve.

This, then, was the answer to his problem. He couldn't speed up mankind's intellectual advancement enough to have it teach him the things his incredible mind yearned for. He couldn't speed himself up. So he created a new race—a race which would develop and evolve so fast that it would surpass the civilization of man; and from them he would learn.

They were completely in Kidder's power. Earth's normal atmosphere would poison them, as he took care to demonstrate to every fourth generation. They would make no attempt to escape from him. They would live their lives and progress and make their little trial-and-error experiments hundreds of times faster than man did. They had the edge on man, for they had Kidder to guide them. It took man six thousand years really to discover science, three hundred to put it to work. It took Kidder's creatures two hundred days to equal man's mental attainments. And from then on—Kidder's spasmodic output made the late, great Tom Edison look like a home handicrafter.

He called them Neoterics, and he teased them into working for him. Kidder was inventive in an ideological way; that is, he could dream up impossible propositions providing he didn't have to work them out. For example, he wanted the Neoterics to figure out for themselves how to build shelters out of porous material. He created the need for such shelters by subjecting one of the sections to a high-pressure rainstorm which flattened the inhabitants. The Neoterics promptly devised waterproof shelters out of the thin waterproof material he piled in one corner. Kidder immediately blew down the flimsy structures with a blast of cold air. They built them up again so that they resisted both wind and rain. Kidder lowered the temperature so abruptly that they could not adjust their bodies to it. They heated their shelters with tiny braziers. Kidder promptly turned up the heat until they began to roast to death. After a few deaths, one of their bright boys figured out how to build a strong insulant house by using three-ply rubberoid, with the middle layer perforated thousands of times to create tiny air pockets.

Using such tactics, Kidder forced them to develop a highly advanced little culture. He caused a drought in one section and a liquid surplus in another, and then opened the partition between them. Quite a spectacular war was fought, and Kidder's notebooks filled with information about military tactics and weapons. Then there was the vaccine they developed against the common cold—the reason why that affliction has been absolutely stamped out in the world today, for it was one of the things that Conant, the bank president, got hold of. He spoke to Kidder over the radiophone one winter afternoon with a voice so hoarse from laryngitis that Kidder sent him a vial of vaccine and told him briskly not to ever call him again in such a disgustingly inaudible state. Conant had it analyzed and again Kidder's accounts and the bank's swelled.

At first, Kidder merely supplied the materials he thought they might need, but when they developed an intelligence equal to the task of fabricating their own from the elements at hand, he gave each section a stock of raw materials. The process for really strong aluminum was developed when he built in a huge plunger in one of the sections, which reached from wall to wall and was designed to descend at the rate of four inches a day until it crushed whatever was at the bottom. The Neoterics, in self-defense, used what strong material they had in hand to stop the inexorable death that threatened them. But Kidder had seen to it that they had nothing but aluminum oxide and a scattering of other elements, plus plenty of electric power. At first they ran up dozens of aluminum pillars; when these were crushed and twisted they tried shaping them so that the soft metal would take more weight. When that failed they quickly built stronger ones; and when the plunger was halted, Kidder removed one of the pillars and analyzed it. It was hardened aluminum, stronger and tougher than molybd steel.

Experience taught Kidder that he had to make certain changes to increase his power over his Neoterics before they got too ingenious. There were things that could be done with atomic power that he was curious about; but he was not willing to trust his little superscientists with a thing like that unless they could be trusted to use it strictly according to Hoyle. So he instituted a rule of fear. The most trivial departure from what he chose to consider the right way of doing things resulted in instant death of half a tribe. If he was trying to develop a Diesel-type power plant, for instance, that would operate without a flywheel, and a bright young Neoteric used any of the materials for architectural purposes, half the tribe immediately died. Of course, they had developed a written language; it was Kidder's own. The teletype in a glass-enclosed area in a corner of each section was a shrine. Any directions that were given on it were obeyed, or else. . . . After this innovation, Kidder's work was much simpler. There was no need for any indirection. Anything he wanted done was done. No matter how impossible his commands, three or four generations of Neoterics could find a way to carry them out.

This quotation is from a paper that one of Kidder's high-speed telescopic cameras discovered being circulated among the younger Neoterics. It is translated from the highly simplified script of the Neoterics.

"These edicts shall be followed by each Neoteric upon pain of death, which punishment will be inflicted by the tribe upon the individual to protect the tribe against him.

"Priority of interest and tribal and individual effort is to be given the commands that appear on the word machine.

"Any misdirection of material or power, or use thereof for any other purpose than the carrying out of the machine's commands, unless no command appears, shall be punishable by death.

"Any information regarding the problem at hand, or ideas or experiments which might conceivably bear upon it, are to become the property of the tribe.

"Any individual failing to cooperate in the tribal effort, or who can be termed guilty of not expending his full efforts in the work; or the suspicion thereof shall be subject to the death penalty."

Such are the results of complete domination. This paper impressed Kidder as much as it did because it was completely spontaneous. It was the Neoterics' own creed, developed by them for their own greatest good.

And so at last Kidder had his fulfillment. Crouched in the upper room, going from telescope to telescope, running off slowed-down films from his high-speed cameras, he found himself possessed of a tractable, dynamic source of information. Housed in the great square building with its four half-acre sections was a new world, to which he was god.

Conant's mind was similar to Kidder's in that its approach to any problem was along the shortest distance between any two points, regardless of whether that approach was along the line of most or least resistance. His rise to the bank presidency was a history of ruthless moves whose only justification was that they got him what he wanted. Like an over-efficient general, he would never vanquish an enemy through sheer force of numbers alone. He would also skillfully flank his enemy, not on one side, but on both. Innocent bystanders were creatures deserving no consideration.

The time he took over a certain thousand-acre property, for instance, from a man named Grady, he was not satisfied with only the title to the land. Grady was an airport owner—had been all his life, and his father before him. Conant exerted every kind of pressure on the man and found him unshakable. Finally judicious persuasion led the city officials to dig a sewer right across the middle of the field, quite efficiently wrecking Grady's business. Knowing that this would supply Grady, who was a wealthy man, with motive for revenge, Conant took over Grady's bank at half again its value and caused it to fold up. Grady lost every cent he had and ended his life in an asylum. Conant was very proud of his tactics.

Like many another who has had Mammon by the tail, Conant did not know when to let go. His vast organization yielded him more money and power than any other concern in history, and yet he was not satisfied. Conant and money were like Kidder and knowledge. Conant's pyramided enterprises were to him what the Neoterics were to Kidder. Each had made his private world; each used it for his instruction and profit. Kidder, though, disturbed nobody but his Neoterics. Even so, Conant was not wholly villainous. He was a shrewd man, and had discovered early the value of pleasing people. No man can rob success-fully over a period of years without pleasing the people he robs. The technique for doing this is highly involved, but master it and you can start your own mint.

Conant's one great fear was that Kidder would some day take an interest in world events and begin to become opinionated. Good heavens—the potential power he had! A little matter like swinging an election could be managed by a man like Kidder as easily as turning over in bed. The only thing he could do was to call him periodically and see if there was anything that Kidder needed to keep himself busy. Kidder appreciated this. Conant, once in a while, would suggest something to Kidder that intrigued him, something that would keep him deep in his hermitage for a few weeks. The light pump was one of the results of Conant's imagination. Conant bet him it couldn't be done. Kidder did it.

One afternoon Kidder answered the squeal of the radiophone's signal. Swearing mildly, he shut off the film he was watching and crossed the compound to the old laboratory. He went to the radiophone, threw a switch. The squealing stopped.

"Well?"

"Hello," said Conant. "Busy?"

"Not very," said Kidder. He was delighted with the pictures his camera had caught, showing the skillful work of a gang of Neoterics synthesizing rubber out of pure sulphur. He would rather have liked to tell Conant about it, but somehow he had never got around to telling Conant about the Neoterics, and he didn't see why he should start now.

Conant said, "Er ... Kidder, I was down at the club the other day and a bunch of us were filing up an evening with loose talk. Something came up which might interest you."

"What?"

"Couple of the utilities boys there. You know the power setup in this country, don't you? Thirty per cent atomic, the rest hydroelectric, Diesel and steam?"

"I hadn't known," said Kidder, who was as innocent as a babe of current events.

"Well, we were arguing about what chance a new power source would have. One of the men there said it would be smarter to produce a new power and then talk about it. Another one waived that; said he couldn't name that new power, but he could describe it. Said it would have to have everything that present power sources have, plus one or two more things. It could be cheaper, for instance. It could be more efficient. It might supersede the others by being easier to carry from the power plant to the consumer. See what I mean? Any one of these factors might prove a new source of power competitive to the others. What I'd like to see is a new power with *all* of these factors. What do you think of it?"

"Not impossible."

"Think not?"

"I'll try it."

"Keep me posted." Conant's transmitter clicked off. The switch was a little piece of false front that Kidder had built into the set, which was something that Conant didn't know. The set switched itself off when Conant moved from it. After the switch's sharp crack, Kidder heard the banker mutter, "If he does it, I'm all set. If he doesn't, at least the crazy fool will keep himself busy on the isl—"

Kidder eyed the radiophone for an instant with raised eyebrows, and then shrugged them down again with his shoulders. It was quite evident that Conant had something up his sleeve, but Kidder wasn't worried. Who on earth would want to disturb him? He wasn't bothering anybody. He went back to the Neoterics' building, full of the new power idea.

Eleven days later Kidder called Conant and gave specific instructions on how to equip his receiver with a facsimile set which would enable Kidder to send written matter over the air. As soon as this was done and Kidder informed, the biochemist for once in his life spoke at some length.

"Conant—you implied that a new power source that would be cheaper, more efficient and more easily transmitted than any now in use did not exist. You might be interested in the little generator I have just set up.

"It has power, Conant—unbelievable power. Broadcast. A beautiful little tight beam. Here—catch this on the facsimile recorder." Kidder slipped a sheet of paper under the clips of his transmitter and it appeared on Conant's set. "Here's the wiring diagram for a power receiver. Now listen. The beam is so tight, so highly directional, that not three-thousandths of one per cent of the power would be lost in a two-thousand-mile transmission. The power system is closed. That is, any drain on the beam returns a signal along it to the transmitter, which automatically steps up to increase the power output. It has a limit, but it's way up. And something else. This little gadget of mine can send out eight different beams with a total horsepower output of around eight thousand per minute per beam. From each beam you can draw enough power to turn the page of a book or fly a superstratosphere plane. Hold on—I haven't finished yet. Each beam, as I told you before, returns a signal from receiver to transmitter. This not only controls the power output of the beam, but directs it. Once contact is made, the beam will never let go. It will follow the receiver anywhere. You can power land, air or water vehicles with it, as well as any stationary plant. Like it?"

Conant, who was a banker and not a scientist, wiped his shining pate with the back of his hand and said, "I've never known you to steer me wrong yet, Kidder. How about the cost of this thing?"

"High," said Kidder promptly. "As high as an atomic plant. But there are no high-tension lines, no wires, no pipelines, no nothing. The receivers are little more complicated than a radio set. Transmitter is—well, that's quite a job."

"Didn't take you long," said Conant.

"No," said Kidder, "it didn't, did it?" It was the lifework of nearly twelve hundred highly cultured people, but Kidder wasn't going into that. "Of course, the one I have here's just a model."

Conant's voice was strained. "A—model? And it delivers—"

"Over sixty-thousand horsepower," said Kidder gleefully.

"Good heavens! In a full-sized machine—why, one transmitter would be enough to—" The possibilities of the thing choked Conant for a moment. "How is it fueled?"

"It isn't," said Kidder. "I won't begin to explain it. I've tapped a source of power of unimaginable force. It's—well, big. So big that it can't be misused."

"What?" snapped Conant. "What do you mean by that?"

Kidder cocked an eyebrow. Conant *had* something up his sleeve, then. At this second indication of it, Kidder, the least suspicious of men, began to put himself on guard. "I mean just what I say," he said evenly. "Don't try too hard to understand—I barely savvy it myself. But the source of this power is a monstrous resultant caused by the unbalance of two previously equalized forces. Those equalized forces are cosmic in quantity. Actually, the forces are those which make suns, crush atoms the way they crushed those that compose the companion of Sirius. It's not anything you can fool with."

"I don't—" said Conant, and his voice ended puzzledly.

"I'll give you a parallel of it," said Kidder. "Suppose you take two rods, one in each hand. Place their tips together and push. As long as your pressure is directly along their long axes, the pressure is equalized; right and left hands cancel each other. Now I come along; I put out one finger and touch the rods ever so lightly where they come together. They snap out of line violently; you break a couple of knuckles. The resultant force is at right angles to the original forces you exerted. My power transmitter is on the same principle. It takes an infinitesimal amount of energy to throw those forces out of line. Easy enough, when you know how to do it. The important question is whether or not you can control the resultant when you get it. I can."

"I—see." Conant indulged in a four-second gloat. "Heaven help the utility companies. I don't intend to. Kidder—I want a full-size power transmitter."

Kidder clucked into the radiophone. "Ambitious, aren't you? I haven't a staff out here, Conant—you know that. And I can't be expected to build four or five thousand tons of apparatus myself."

"I'll have five hundred engineers and laborers out there in forty-eight hours."

"You will not. Why bother me with it? I'm quite happy here, Conant, and one of the reasons is that I've no one to get in my hair."

"Oh, now, Kidder—don't be like that—I'll pay you—"

"You haven't got that much money," said Kidder briskly. He flipped the switch on his set. *His* switch worked.

Conant was furious. He shouted into the phone several times, then began to lean on the signal button. On his island, Kidder let the thing squeal and went back to his projection room. He was sorry he had sent the diagram of the receiver to Conant. It would have been interesting to power a plane or a car with the model transmitter he had taken from the Neoterics. But if Conant was going to be that way about it—well, anyway, the receiver would be no good without the transmitter. Any radio engineer would understand the diagram, but not the beam which activated it. And Conant wouldn't get his beam.

Pity he didn't know Conant well enough.

Kidder's days were endless sorties into learning. He never slept, nor did his Neoterics. He ate regularly every five hours, exercised for half an hour in every twelve. He did not keep track of time, for it meant nothing to him. Had he wanted to know the date or the year, even, he knew he could get it from Conant. He didn't care, that's all. The time that was not spent in observation was used in developing new problems for the Neoterics. His thoughts just now ran to defense. The idea was born in his conversation with Conant; now the idea was primary, its motivation something of no importance. The Neoterics were working on a vibration field of quasi-electrical nature. Kidder could see little practical value in such a thing—an invisible wall which would kill any living thing which touched it. But still—the idea was intriguing.

He stretched and moved away from the telescope in the upper room through which he had been watching his creations at work. He was profoundly happy here in the large control room. Leaving it to go to the old laboratory for a bite to eat was a thing he hated to do. He felt like bidding it good-bye each time he walked across the compound, and saying a glad hello when he returned. A little amused at himself, he went out.

There was a black blob—a distant power boat—a few miles off the island, toward the mainland. Kidder stopped and stared distastefully at it. A white petal of spray was affixed to each side of the black body—it was coming toward him. He snorted, thinking of the time a yachtload of silly fools had landed out of curiosity one afternoon, spewed themselves over his beloved island, peppered him with lame-brained questions, and thrown his nervous equilibrium out for days. Lord, how he hated *people!*

The thought of unpleasantness bred two more thoughts that played half-consciously with his mind as he crossed the compound and entered the old laboratory. One was that perhaps it might be wise to surround his buildings with a field of force of some kind and post warnings for trespassers. The other thought was of Conant and the vague uneasiness the man had been sending to him through the radiophone these last weeks. His suggestion, two days ago, that a power plant be built on the island—horrible idea!

Conant rose from a laboratory bench as Kidder walked in.

They looked at each other wordlessly for a long moment. Kidder hadn't seen the bank president in years. The man's presence, he found, made his scalp crawl.

"Hello," said Conant genially. "You're looking fit."

Kidder grunted. Conant eased his unwieldy body back onto the bench and said, "Just to save you the energy of asking questions, Mr. Kidder, I arrived two hours ago on a small boat. Rotten way to travel. I wanted to be a surprise to you; my two men rowed me the last couple of miles. You're not very well equipped here for defense, are you? Why, anyone could slip up on you the way I did."

"Who'd want to?" growled Kidder. The man's voice edged annoyingly into his brain. He spoke too loudly for such a small room; at least, Kidder's hermit's ears feel that way. Kidder shrugged and went about preparing a light meal for himself.

"Well," drawled the banker. "I might want to." He drew out a Dow-metal cigar case. "Mind if I smoke?"

"I do," said Kidder sharply.

Conant laughed easily and put the cigars away. "I might," he said, "want to urge you to let me build that power station on this island."

"Radiophone work?"

"Oh, yes. But now that I'm here you can't switch me off. Now—how about it?"

"I haven't changed my mind."

"Oh, but you should, Kidder, you should. Think of it—think of the good it would do for the masses of people that are now paying exorbitant power bills!"

"I hate the masses! Why do you have to build here?"

"Oh, that. It's an ideal location. You own the island; work could begin here without causing any comment whatsoever. The plant would spring full-fledged on the power markets of the country, having been built in secret. The island can be made impregnable."

"I don't want to be bothered."

"We wouldn't bother you. We'd build on the north end of the island—a mile and a quarter from you and your work. Ah—by the way—where's the model of the power transmitter?"

Kidder, with his mouth full of synthesized food, waved a hand at a small table on which stood the model, a four-foot, amazingly intricate device of plastic and steel and tiny coils.

Conant rose and went over to look at it. "Actually works, eh?" He sighed deeply and said, "Kidder, I really hate to do this, but I want to build that plant rather badly. Carson! Robbins!"

Two bull-necked individuals stepped out from their hiding places in the corners of the room. One idly dangled a revolver by its trigger guard. Kidder looked blankly from one to the other of them.

"These gentlemen will follow my orders implicitly, Kidder. In half an hour a party will land here—engineers, contractors. They will start surveying the north end of the island for the construction of the power plant. These boys here feel about the same way I do as far as you are concerned. Do we proceed with your cooperation or without it? It's immaterial to me whether or not you are left alive to continue your work. My engineers can duplicate your model."

Kidder said nothing. He had stopped chewing when he saw the gunmen, and only now remembered to swallow. He sat crouched over his plate without moving or speaking.

Conant broke the silence by walking to the door. "Robbins—can you carry that model there?" The big man put his gun away, lifted the model gently, and nodded. "Take it down to the beach and meet the other boat. Tell Mr. Johansen, the engineer, that this is the model he is to work from." Robbins went out. Conant turned to Kidder. "There's no need for us to anger ourselves," he said oilily. "I think you are stubborn, but I don't hold it against you. I know how you feel. You'll be left alone; you have my promise. But I mean to go ahead on this job, and a small thing like your life can't stand in my way."

Kidder said, "Get out of here." There were two swollen veins throbbing at his temples. His voice was low, and it shook.

"Very well. Good day, Mr. Kidder. Oh—by the way—you're a clever devil." No one had ever referred to the scholastic Mr. Kidder that way before. "I realize the possibility of your blasting us off the island. I wouldn't do it if I were you. I'm willing to give you what you want—privacy. I want the same thing in return. If anything happens to me while I'm here, the island will be bombed by someone who is working for me. I'll admit they might fail. If they do, the United States government will take a hand. You wouldn't want that, would you? That's rather a big thing for one man to fight. The same thing goes if the plant is sabotaged in any way after I go back to the mainland. You might be killed. You will most certainly be bothered interminably. Thanks for your . . . er . . . cooperation." The banker smirked and walked out, followed by his taciturn gorilla.

Kidder sat there for a long time without moving. Then he shook his head, rested it in his palms. He was badly frightened; not so much because his life was in danger, but because his privacy and his work—his world—were threatened. He was hurt and bewildered. He wasn't a businessman. He couldn't handle men. All his life he had run away from human beings and what they represented to him. He was like a frightened child when men closed in on him.

Cooling a little, he wondered vaguely what would happen when the power plant opened. Certainly the government would be interested. Unless—unless by then Conant was the government. That plant was an unimaginable source of power, and not only the kind of power that turned wheels. He rose and went back to the world that was home to him, a world where his motives were understood, and where there were those who could help him. Back at the Neoterics' building, he escaped yet again from the world of men into his work.

Kidder called Conant the following week, much to the banker's surprise. His two days on the island had got the work well under way, and he had left with the arrival of a shipload of laborers and material. He kept in close touch by radio with Johansen, the engineer in charge. It had been a blind job for Johansen and all the rest of the crew on the island. Only the bank's infinite resources could have hired such a man, or the picked gang with him.

Johansen's first reaction when he saw the model had been ecstatic. He wanted to tell his friends about this marvel; but the only radio set available was beamed to Conant's private office in the bank, and Conant's armed guards, one to every two workers, had strict orders to destroy any other radio transmitter on sight. About that time he realized that he was a prisoner on the island. His instant anger subsided when he reflected that being a prisoner at fifty thousand dollars a week wasn't too bad. Two of the laborers and an engineer thought differently, and got disgruntled a couple of days after they arrived. They disappeared one night—the same night that five shots were fired down on the beach. No questions were asked, and there was no more trouble.

Conant covered his surprise at Kidder's call and was as offensively jovial as ever. "Well, now! Anything I can do for you?"

"Yes," said Kidder. His voice was low, completely without expression. "I want you to issue a warning to your men not to pass the white line I have drawn five hundred yards north of my buildings, right across the island."

"Warning? Why, my dear fellow, they have orders that you are not to be disturbed on any account."

"You've ordered them. All right. Now warn them. I have an electric field surrounding my laboratories that will kill anything living which penetrates it. I don't want to have murder on my conscience. There will be no deaths unless there are trespassers. You'll inform your workers?"

"Oh, now Kidder," the banker expostulated. "That was totally unnecessary. You won't be bothered. Why—" But he found he was talking into a dead mike. He knew better than to call back. He called Johansen instead and told him about it. Johansen didn't like the sound of it, but he repeated the message and signed off. Conant liked that man. He was, for a moment, a little sorry that Johansen would never reach the mainland alive.

But that Kidder—he was beginning to be a problem. As long as his weapons were strictly defensive he was no real menace. But he would have to be taken care of when the plant was operating. Conant couldn't afford to have genius around him unless it was unquestionably on his side. The power transmitter and Conant's highly ambitious plans would be safe as long as Kidder was left to himself. Kidder knew that he could, for the time being, expect more sympathetic treatment from Conant than he could from a horde of government investigators.

Kidder only left his own enclosure once after the work began on the north end of the island, and it took all of his unskilled diplomacy to do it. Knowing the source of the plant's power, knowing what could happen if it were misused, he asked Conant's permission to inspect the great transmitter when it was nearly finished. Insuring his own life by refusing to report back to Conant until he was safe within his own laboratory again, he turned off his shield and walked up to the north end.

He saw an awe-inspiring sight. The four-foot model was duplicated nearly a hundred times as large. Inside a massive three-hundred-foot tower a space was packed nearly solid with the same bewildering maze of coils and bars that the Neoterics had built so delicately into their machine. At the top was a globe of polished golden alloy, the transmitting antenna. From it would stream thousands of tight beams of force, which could be tapped to any degree by corresponding thousands of receivers placed anywhere at any distance. Kidder learned that the receivers had already been built, but his informant, Johansen, knew little about that end of it and was saying less. Kidder checked over every detail of the structure, and when he was through he shook Johansen's hand admiringly.

"I didn't want this thing here," he said shyly, "and I don't. But I will say that it's a pleasure to see this kind of work."

"It's a pleasure to meet the man that invented it."

Kidder beamed. "I didn't invent it," he said. "Maybe some day I'll show you who did. I—well, good-by." He turned before he had a chance to say too much and marched off down the path.

"Shall I?" said a voice at Johansen's side. One of Conant's guards had his gun out.

Johansen knocked the man's arm down. "No." He scratched his head. "So that's the mysterious menace from the other end of the island. Eh! Why, he's a hell of a nice little feller!"

Built on the ruins of Denver, which was destroyed in the great Battle of the Rockies during the Western War, stands the most beautiful city in the world— our nation's capital. New Washington. In a circular room deep in the heart of the White House, the president, three army men and a civilian sat. Under the president's desk a dictaphone unostentatiously recorded every word that was said. Two thousand and more miles away, Conant hung over a radio receiver, tuned to receive the signals of the tiny transmitter in the civilian's side pocket.

One of the officers spoke.

"Mr. President, the 'impossible claims' made for this gentleman's product are absolutely true. He has proved beyond doubt each item on his prospectus."

The president glanced at the civilian, back at the officer. "I won't wait for your report," he said. "Tell me—what happened?"

Another of the army men mopped his face with a khaki bandanna. "I can't ask you to believe us, Mr. President, but it's true all the same. Mr. Wright here has in his suitcase three or four dozen small . . . er . . . bombs—"

"They're not bombs," said Wright casually.

"All right. They're not bombs. Mr. Wright smashed two of them on an anvil with a sledge hammer. There was no result. He put two more in an electric furnace. They burned away like so much tin and cardboard. We dropped one down the barrel of a field piece and fired it. Still nothing." He paused and looked at the third officer, who picked up the account:

"We really got started then. We flew to the proving grounds, dropped one of the objects and flew to thirty thousand feet. From there, with a small hand detonator no bigger than your fist, Mr. Wright set the thing off. I've never seen anything like it. Forty acres of land came straight up at us, breaking up as it came. The concussion was terrific—you must have felt it here, four hundred miles away."

The president nodded. "I did. Seismographs on the other side of the Earth picked it up."

"The crater it left was a quarter of a mile deep at the center. Why, one plane load of those things could demolish any city! There isn't even any necessity for accuracy!"

"You haven't heard anything yet," another officer broke in. "Mr. Wright's automobile is powered by a small plant similar to the others. He demonstrated it to us. We could find no fuel tank of any kind, or any other driving mechanism. But with a power plant no bigger than six cubic inches, that car, carrying enough weight to give it traction, outpulled an army tank!"

"And the other test!" said the third excitedly. "He put one of the objects into a replica of a treasury vault. The walls were twelve feet thick, super-reinforced concrete. He controlled it from over a hundred yards away. He . . . he burst that vault! It wasn't an explosion—it was as if some incredibly powerful expansive force inside filled it and flattened the walls from inside. They cracked and split and powdered, and the steel girders and rods came twisting and shearing out like . . . like—*whew!* After that he insisted on seeing you. We knew it wasn't usual, but he said he has more to say and would say it only in your presence."

The president said gravely, "What is it, Mr. Wright?"

Wright rose, picked up his suitcase, opened it and took out a small cube, about eight inches on a side, made of some light-absorbent red material. Four men edged nervously away from it.

"These gentlemen," he began, "have seen only part of the things this device can do. I'm going to demonstrate to you the delicacy of control that is possible with it." He made an adjustment with a tiny knob on the side of the cube, set it on the edge of the president's desk.

"You have asked me more than once if this is my invention or if I am representing someone. The latter is true. It might also interest you to know that the man who controls this cube is right now several thousand miles from here. He and he alone, can prevent it from detonating now that I—" He pulled his detonator out of the suitcase and pressed a button—"have done this. It will explode the way the one we dropped from the plane did, completely destroying this city and everything in it, in just four hours. It will also explode—" He stepped back and threw a tiny switch on his detonator—"if any moving object comes within three feet of it or if anyone leaves this room but me—it can be compensated for that. If, after I leave, I am molested, it will detonate as soon as a hand is laid on me. No bullets can kill me fast enough to prevent me from setting it off."

The three army men were silent. One of them swiped nervously at the beads of cold sweat on his forehead. The others did not move. The president said evenly:

"What's your proposition?"

"A very reasonable one. My employer does not work in the open, for obvious reasons. All he wants is your agreement to carry out his orders; to appoint the cabinet members he chooses, to throw your influence in any way he dictates. The public—Congress—anyone else—need never know anything about it. I might add that if you agree to this proposal, this 'bomb,' as you call it, will not go off. But you can be sure that thousands of them are planted all over the country. You will never know when you are near one. If you disobey, it means instant annihilation for you and everyone else within three or four square miles.

"In three hours and fifty minutes—that will be at precisely seven o'clock—there is a commercial radio program on Station RPRS. You will cause the announcer, after his station identification, to say 'Agreed.' It will pass unnoticed by all but my employer. There is no use in having me followed; my work is done. I shall never see nor contact my employer again. That is all. Good afternoon, gentlemen!"

Wright closed his suitcase with a businesslike snap, bowed, and left the room. Four men sat staring at the little red cube.

"Do you think he can do all he says?" asked the president.

The three nodded mutely. The president reached for his phone.

There was an eavesdropper to all of the foregoing. Conant, squatting behind his great desk in the vault, where he had his sanctum sanctorum, knew nothing of it. But beside him was the compact bulk of Kidder's radiophone. His presence switched it on, and Kidder, on his island, blessed the day he had thought of that device. He had been meaning to call Conant all morning, but was very hesitant. His meeting with the young engineer Johansen had impressed him strongly. The man was such a thorough scientist, possessed of such complete delight in the work he did, that for the first time in his life Kidder found himself actually wanting to see someone again. But he feared for Johansen's life if he brought him to the laboratory, for Johansen's work was done on the island, and Conant would most certainly have the engineer killed if he heard of his visit, fearing that Kidder would influence him to sabotage the great transmitter. And if Kidder went to the power plant he would probably be shot on sight.

All one day Kidder wrangled with himself, and finally determined to call Conant. Fortunately he gave no signal, but turned up the volume on the receiver when the little red light told him that Conant's transmitter was functioning. Curious, he heard everything that occurred in the president's chamber three thousand miles away. Horrified, he realized what Conant's engineers had done. Built into tiny containers were tens of thousands of power receivers. They had no power of their own, but, by remote control, could draw on any or all of the billions of horsepower the huge plant on the island was broadcasting.

Kidder stood in front of his receiver, speechless. There was nothing he could do. If he devised some means of destroying the power plant, the government would certainly step in and take over the island, and then—what would happen to him and his precious Neoterics?

Another sound grated out of the receiver—a commercial radio program. A few bars of music, a man's voice advertising stratoline fares on the installment plan, a short silence, then:

"Station RPRS, voice of the nation's Capital, District of South Colorado."

The three-second pause was interminable.

"The time is exactly ... er ... *agreed.* The time is exactly seven P.M., Mountain Standard Time."

Then came a half-insane chuckle. Kidder had difficulty believing it was Conant. A phone clicked. The banker's voice:

"Bill? All set. Get out there with your squadron and bomb up the island. Keep away from the plant, but cut the rest of it to ribbons. Do it quick and get out of there."

Almost hysterical with fear, Kidder rushed about the room and then shot out the door and across the compound. There were five hundred innocent workmen in barracks a quarter mile from the plant. Conant didn't need them now, and he didn't need Kidder. The only safety for anyone was in the plant itself, and Kidder wouldn't leave his Neoterics to be bombed. He flung himself up the stairs and to the nearest teletype. He banged out, "Get me a defense. I want an impenetrable shield. Urgent!"

The words ripped out from under his fingers in the functional script of the Neoterics. Kidder didn't think of what he wrote, didn't really visualize the thing he ordered. But he had done what he could. He'd have to leave them now, get to the barracks; warn those men. He ran up the path toward the plant, flung himself over the white line that marked death to those who crossed it.

A squadron of nine clip-winged, mosquito-nosed planes rose out of a cove on the mainland. There was no sound from the engines, for there were no engines. Each plane was powered with a tiny receiver and drew its unmarked, light-absorbent wings through the air with power from the island. In a matter of minutes they raised the island. The squadron leader spoke briskly into a microphone.

"Take the barracks first. Clean 'em up. Then work south."

Johansen was alone on a small hill near the center of the island. He carried a camera, and though he knew pretty well that his chances of ever getting ashore again were practically nonexistent, he liked angle shots of his tower, and took innumerable pictures. The first he knew of the planes was when he heard their whining dive over the barracks. He stood transfixed, saw a shower of bombs hurtle down and turn the barracks into a smashed ruin of broken wood, metal and bodies. The picture of Kidder's earnest face flashed into his mind. Poor little guy—if they ever bombed his end of the island he would—But his tower! Were they going to bomb the plant?

He watched, utterly appalled, as the planes flew out to sea, cut back and dove again. They seemed to be working south. At the third dive he was sure of it. Not knowing what he could do, he nevertheless turned and ran toward Kidder's place. He rounded a turn in the trail and collided violently with the little biochemist. Kidder's face was scarlet with exertion, and he was the most terrified-looking object Johansen had ever seen.

Kidder waved a hand northward. "Conant!" he screamed over the uproar. "It's Conant! He's going to kill us all!"

"The plant?" said Johansen, turning pale.

"It's safe. He won't touch *that!* But . . . my place . . . what about all those men?"

"Too late!" shouted Johansen.

"Maybe I can— Come on!" called Kidder, and was off down the trail, heading south.

Johansen pounded after him. Kidder's little short legs became a blur as the squadron swooped overhead, laying its eggs in the spot where they had met.

As they burst out of the woods, Johansen put on a spurt, caught up with the scientist and knocked him sprawling not six feet from the whiteline.

"Wh . . . wh—"

"Don't go any farther, you fool! Your own damned force field—it'll kill you!"

"Force field? But—I came through it on the way up—Here. Wait. If I can—" Kidder began hunting furiously about in the grass. In a few seconds he ran up to the line, clutching a large grasshopper in his hand. He tossed it over. It lay still.

"See?" said Johansen. "It—"

"Look! It jumped! Come on! I don't know what went wrong, unless the Neoterics shut it off. They generated that field—I didn't."

"Neo—huh?"

"Never mind," snapped the biochemist, and ran.

They pounded gasping up the steps and into the Neoterics' control room. Kidder clapped his eyes to a telescope and shrieked in glee. "They've done it! They've done it!"

"Who's—"

"My little people! The Neoterics! They've made the impenetrable shield! Don't you see—it cut through the lines of force that start up that field out there. Their generator is still throwing it up, but the vibrations can't get out! They're safe! They're safe!" And the overwrought hermit began to cry. Johansen looked at him pityingly and shook his head.

"Sure—your little men are all right. But we aren't," he added as the floor shook to the detonation of a bomb.

Johansen closed his eyes, got a grip on himself and let his curiosity overcome his fear. He stepped to the binocular telescope, gazed down it. There was nothing there but a curved sheet of gray material. He had never seen a gray quite like that. It was absolutely neutral. It didn't seem soft and it didn't seem hard, and to look at it made his brain reel. He looked up.

Kidder was pounding the keys of a teletype, watching the blank yellow tape anxiously.

"I'm not getting through to them," he whimpered. "I don't know what's the mat—Oh, of *course!*"

"What?"

"The shield is absolutely impenetrable! The teletype impulses can't get through or I could get them to extend the screen over the building—over the whole island! There's *nothing* those people can't do!"

"He's crazy," Johansen muttered. "Poor little—"

The teletype began clicking sharply. Kidder dove at it, practically embraced it. He read off the tape as it came out. Johansen saw the characters, but they meant nothing to him.

"Almighty," Kidder read falteringly, "pray have mercy on us and be forebearing until we have said our say. Without orders we have lowered the screen you ordered us to raise. We are lost, O great one. Our screen is truly impenetrable, and so cut off your words on the word machine. We have never, in the memory of any Neoteric, been without your word before. Forgive us our action. We will eagerly await your answer."

Kidder's fingers danced over the keys. "You can look now," he gasped. "Go on—the telescope!"

Johansen, trying to ignore the whine of sure death from above, looked.

He saw what looked like land—fantastic fields under cultivation, a settlement of some sort, factories, and—beings. Everything moved with incredible rapidity. He couldn't see one of the inhabitants except as darting pinky-white streaks. Fascinated, he stared for a long minute. A sound behind him made him whirl. It was Kidder, rubbing his hands together briskly. There was a broad smile on his face.

"They did it," he said happily. "You see?"

Johansen didn't see until he began to realize that there was a dead silence outside. He ran to a window. It was night outside—the—blackest night—when it should have been dusk. "What happened?"

"The Neoterics," said Kidder, and laughed like a child. "My friends downstairs there. They threw up the impenetrable shield over the whole island. We can't be touched now!"

And at Johansen's amazed questions, he launched into a description of the race of beings below them.

Outside the shell, things happened. Nine airplanes suddenly went dead-stick. Nine pilots glided downward, powerless, and some fell into the sea, and some struck the miraculous gray shell that loomed in place of an island; slid off and sank.

And ashore, a man named Wright sat in a car half dead with fear, while government men surrounded him, approached cautiously, daring instant death from a now-dead source.

In a room deep in the White House, a high-ranking army officer shrieked, "I can't stand it any more! I can't!" and leaped up, snatched a red cube off the president's desk, ground it to ineffectual litter under his shining boots.

And in a few days they took a broken old man away from the bank and put him in an asylum, where he died within a week.

The shield, you see, was truly impenetrable. The power plant was untouched and sent out its beams; but the beams could not get out, and anything powered from the plant went dead. The story never became public, although for some years there was heightened naval activity off the New England coast. The navy, so the story went, had a new target range out there—a great hemiovoid of gray material. They bombed it and shelled it and rayed it and blasted all around it, but never even dented its smooth surface.

Kidder and Johansen let it stay there. They were happy enough with their researches and their Neoterics. They did not hear or feel the shelling, for the shield was truly impenetrable. They synthesized their food and their light and air from the materials at hand, and they simply didn't care. They were the only survivors of the bombing, with the exception of three poor maimed devils who died soon afterward.

All this happened many years ago, and Kidder and Johansen may be alive today, and they may be dead. But that doesn't matter too much. The important thing is that the great gray shell will bear watching. Men die, but races live. Some day the Neoterics, after innumerable generations of inconceivable advancement, will take down their shield and come forth. When I think of that I feel frightened.

TWO PERCENT INSPIRATION

More early don't-give-a-damn fun; actually a lampoon on some of the more dreadful contemporary (1940) examples of science fiction. So come on and meet Satan Strong, Scourge of the Spaceways, Supporter of the Serialized Short Story, and Specialist in Science On The Spot.

Dr. Bjornsen ws a thorough man. He thought that way and acted that way and expected others to exceed him in thoroughness. Since this was an impossibility, he expressed an almost vicious disappointment in incompetents, and took delight in pointing out the erring one's shortcomings. He was in an ideal position for this sort of thing, being principal of the Nudnick Institute.

Endowed by Professor Thaddeus MacIlhainy Nudnick, the institute was conducted for the purpose of supplying brilliant young assistants to Professor Nudnick. It enrolled two thousand students every year, and the top three of the graduating class were given subsistence and a considerable salary for the privilege of entering Nudnick's eight-year secondary course, where they underwent some real study before they began as assistants in the Nudnick laboratories.

Bjornsen never congratulated an honor student, for they had behaved as expected. He found many an opportunity of delivering a kick or two in the slats of those who had fallen by the wayside; and of these opportunities, the ones that pleased him the most were the ones involving expulsion. He considered himself an expert disciplinarian, and he was more than proud of his forte for invective.

It was with pleasurable anticipation that he summoned one Hughie McCauley to his office one afternoon. Hughie was a second-year student, and made ideal bait for Bjornsen's particular line of attack. The kid was intelligent to a degree, and fairly well read, so that he could understand Bjornsen's more subtle insults. He was highly sensitive, so that he could be hurt by what Bjornsen said, and he showed it. He lacked sense, so that he continually retorted to Bjornsen's comments, giving the principal blurted statements to pick meticulously apart while the victim writhed. Hughie was such perfect material for persecution that Bjornsen rather hated to expel him; but he comforted himself by recalling the fact that there were hundreds of others who could be made to squirm. He'd take his time with Hughie, however; stretch it out, savor the boy's suffering before he kicked him out of the school.

"Send him in," Bjornsen told the built-in communicator on his luxurious desk. He leaned back in his chair, put the tips of his fingers together, lowered his head so that only the whites of his eyes were visible as he stared through his shaggy brows at the door, and waited.

Hughie came in, his hair plastered unwillingly down, his fear and resentment sticking out all over him. The kid's knees knocked together so that he stumbled against the doorpost. There was a gloss of cold sweat on his forehead. From previous experience, he had no difficulty in taking up the front-and-center position before the principal's desk.

"Y-yes sir!"

Bjornsen made a kissing noise with his wrinkled lips before he spoke, threw back his head and glared. "You might," he said quietly, "have washed your ears before you came in here." He knew that there is no more painfully undignified attack for an adolescent, particularly if it is not true. Hughie flushed and stuck out his lower lip.

Bjornsen said, "You are an insult to this institution. You were in a position, certainly, to know yourself before you applied for admission; therefore, the very act of applying was dishonest and insincere. You must have known that you were unfit even to enter these buildings, to say nothing of daring to perpetuate the mistake of the board of examiners in staying here. I am thoroughly disgusted with you." Bjornsen smiled his disgust, and it was a smile that perfectly matched his words. He bent to flip the switch on the communicator, cutting off its mellow buzz. "Yes?"

"Dr. Bjornsen! Professor Nudnick is—"

The annunciator's hollow voice was drowned out in the crashing of a hard, old foot against the door. Nudnick kicked it open because he knew it could not be slammed, and he liked startling Bjornsen. "What sort of nonsense is this?" he demanded, in a voice that sounded like flatulence through ten feet of lead pipe. "Since when has that vinegar-visaged female out there been instructed to announce me? Damn it, you'll see me whether you're busy or not!"

Bjornsen had bounced out of his chair to indulge in every sort of sycophantism short of curtsying. "Professor Nudnick! I am delighted to see you!" This was perfect. The only thing that could possibly increase Hughie McCauley's agony was to have an audience to his dismissal; and what better audience could he have than the great endower of the school himself? Bjornsen rubbed his hands, which yielded an unpleasant dry sound, and began.

"Professor Nudnick," he said, catching Hughie's trembling shoulder and using it to thrust the attached boy between him and Nudnick, "you could not have picked a better time to arrive. This shivering example of negation is typical of the trash that has been getting by the examiners recently. Now I may prove to you that my recent letter on the subject was justified."

Nudnick looked calmly at Hughie. "I don't read your letters," he said. "They bore me. What's he done?"

Bjornsen, a little taken aback, put this new resentment into his words. "Done? What he hasn't done is more important. He has neglected to tidy up his thinking habits. He indulges in reading imaginative fiction during his hours of relaxation instead of reading books pertaining in some way to his studies. He whistles in corridors. He asks impertinent questions of his instructors. He was actually discovered writing a letter to a . . . a *girl!*"

"*Tsk, tsk,*" chuckled the professor. "This during classes?"

"Certainly not! Even he would not go that far, though I expect it hourly."

"Hm-m-m. Is he intelligent?"

"Not very."

"What kind of questions does he ask?"

"Oh—stupid ones. About the nature of a space-warp, whatever that may be, and about whether or not time travel is possible. A dreamer—that's what he is, and a scientific institution is no place for dreamers."

"What are you going to do with him?"

"Expel him, of course."

Nudnick reached over and pulled the boy out of Bjornsen's claw. "Then why not post him as expelled and spare him this agony? It so happens, Bjornsen, that this is just the kind of boy I came here to get. I'm going to take him with me on a trip to the Asteroid Belt. Salary at two thousand a month, if he's willing. Are you, what's-your-name?"

Hughie nodded swimmingly.

"Eh." Beckoning the boy, Nudnick started for the door. "My advice to you, Bjornsen," grated the scientist, "is as follows. Keep your nose out of the students' lives on their off hours. If you must continue in these little habits of yours, take it out in pulling the wings off flies. And get married. Take this advice or hand in your resignation effective this date next month."

Hughie paused at the door, looking back. Nudnick gave him a quick look, shoved him toward Bjornsen. "Go ahead, kid. I'd like it, too."

Hughie grinned, walked up to Bjornsen, and with a quick one-two knocked the principal colder than a cake of ice.

They were eight days out now, and these were the eight:

The day when the unpredictable Professor Nudnick had whisked Hughie up to his mountain laboratory, and had put him to work loading the last of an astonishingly inclusive list of stores into the good ship *Stoutfella.* Hughie began to regard the professor as a little less than the god he had imagined, and a little more as a human being. The old man was perpetually cheerful, pointing out Hughie's stupidities and his little triumphs without differentiating between them. He treated Hughie with a happy tolerance, and seemed to be more delighted with the lad's ignorance than by his comparatively meager knowledge. When Hughie had haltingly asked if he might take a suitcase full of fiction with him, Nudnick had chuckled dryly and sent him off to the nearest town with a pocketful of money. Hughie arrived back at the laboratory laden and blissful. They took off.

And the day when they heard the last broadcast news report before they whisked through the Heaviside layer, among other items was one to the effect that Dr. Emil Bjornsen, principal of the Nudnick Institute, had resigned to accept a government job. Hughie had laughed gleefully at this, but Nudnick shook his shaggy old head. "Not funny, Hughie," he said. "Bjornsen's a shrewd man. I've an idea why he did that, and it has nothing to do with my . . . our . . . ultimatum."

Struck by the scientist's sober tone, Hughie calmed down to ask, "What did he do it for?"

Nudnick clapped a perforated course card into the automatic pilot, reeled its lower edge into the integrator, and checked his controls before switching them over to the "Iron Mike."

"It has to do with this trip," he said, waving the kid into the opposite seat, "and it's about time you knew what this is all about. What we're after is a mineral deposit of incalculable value. How it is, I don't know, but somewhere in that mess of nonsense out there"—he indicated the Asteroid Belt—"is a freak. It's a lump like the rest of the asteroids, but it differs from the rest of them. It must've been a wanderer, drifting heaven alone knows how far in space until it got caught in the Belt. It's almost pure, through and through—an oxide of prosydium. That mean anything to you?"

Hughie pushed a couple of freckles together over his nose. "Yeah. Rare Earth element. Used for . . . lessee . . . something to do with Nudnick Metal, isn't it?"

"That's right: Do you know what Nudnick Metal is?"

"No. Far as I know it's a trade secret, known only to the workers in the Isopolis Laboratories." The Isopolis Laboratories were half heaven and half prison. By government grant, the great Nudnick plant there turned out the expensive metal. It was manned by workers who would never again set foot outside the walls—men who did not have to, for everything they could possibly want was supplied them. There was no secret about the way they lived, nor about anything in the fifty-square-mile enclosure except the process itself. "Nudnick's Metal is a synthetic element, thousands of times denser than anything else known. That's about all I remember," Hughie finished lamely.

Nudnick chuckled. "I'll let you in on it. The metal is the ideal substance for coating spaceships, because it's as near being impenetrable as anything in the Universe. This ship, for instance, is coated with a layer of the stuff less than one one-hundred-fifty-thousandths of an inch thick, and yet is protected against practically anything. We could run full tilt into an object the size of Earth, and though the impact would drill a molten hole thirty miles deep and most likely kill us a little bit, the hull wouldn't even be scratched. Heh. Want to know what Nudnick Metal is? I'll tell you. Copper. Just plain, ordinary, everyday Cu!"

Hughie said, "Copper? But what makes it—How is it—"

"Easy enough. You know, Hughie, it's the simple things that are really effective. Try to remember that. Nudnick Metal is *collapsed* copper; collapsed in the way that the elements of the companions of Sirius and Procyon are collapsed. You know the analogy—pile wine-glasses into a barrel, and there'll be a definite, small number of glasses that can be packed in. But crush them to fine powder, and then start packing. The barrel will hold thousands upon thousands more. The molecules of Nudnick Metal are crushed that way. You could build four hundred ships this size, from stem to stern of solid copper, and you'd use less copper than that which was used to coat this hull.

"The process is only guessed at because copper is synthesized from the uranium we ship into Isopolis ostensibly for power. As you just said, it is known that we import prosydium. That's the only clue anyone but I and the Isopolites have as to the nature of the process. But prosydium isn't an ingredient. It's more like a catalyst. Of all the elements, only prosydium can, by its atomic disintegration, absorb the unbelievable heat liberated by the collapse of the copper molecules. I won't go into the details of it, but the energy thus absorbed and transmuted can be turned back to hasten the collapsing process. The tough thing about prosydium is that it's as rare as a hairy egg, and so far no one's been able to synthesize it in usable quantities. All of which makes Nudnick Metal a trifle on the expensive side. This lump of prosydium in the Belt will cut the manufacturing cost way down, and the man or concern or planet that gets hold of it can write his—its—own ticket. See?"

"I will," said Hughie slowly, "if you'll say all that over again a few thousand times a day for the next couple of years." The boy was enormously flattered by the scientist's confiding in him. Though he himself was not qualified to use it, he knew that the information he had just received was worth countless millions in the right quarters. It frightened him a little. He wanted to keep the old man talking, and so reached for a question. "Why do we have to sneak out in a little ship like this? Why not take a flotilla of destroyers from Earth and take possession?"

"Can't do things that way, son. The Joint Patrol puts the kibosh on that. You can blame the jolly old idealism of the Interplanetary Peace Congress for that, and the Equal Armament Amendment. You see, Mars and Earth are forced by mutual agreement to maintain absolutely equal armament, to share all new developments and to police space with a Joint Patrol. A flotilla of Earth ships taking off without the knowledge or consent of the Patrol constitutes an act of war. War is a nasty business for a lot of people who weren't in on starting it. We can't do it that way. But if I turn over the location of my find to the Patrol, it becomes the property of the Joint Patrol, neatly tied up in red tape, and it doesn't do anybody any good—particularly the Nudnick Laboratories. However—here's where we come in.

"If an independent expedition lands on, or takes in tow, any body in space that is not the satellite of a planet, said body becomes the sole property of that expedition. Therefore, I've got to keep this expedition as secret from Earth as from Mars, so that Earth—and Nudnick—can get the ultimate benefit. In two months my little treasure will be in opposition with Earth. If I have taken it in tow by then, I can announce my discovery by ultraradio. The signal reaches Earth before it reaches Mars; by the time the little red men can send out a pirate to erase me, I am surrounded by a Patrol Fleet, and quite safe. But if Mars gets wind of what I am up to, son, we are going to be intercepted, followed, and rubbed out for the glory and profit of the red planet. Get it?"

"I get it. But what's all this got to do with Bjornsen?"

The old scientist scratched his nose. "I don't know. Bjornsen's a most peculiar egg, Hughie. He worked most of his life to get to be principal of the institute, and it seems to me he didn't do it just for the salary and prestige attached. More than once that egocentric martinet tried to pump me for information about what I was doing, about the Nudnick Metal process, about a hundred things of the sort. I'm sure he hasn't got any real information, but he might possibly have a hunch. A good hunch is plenty to put a Martian ship on our tail and a lot of money in Bjornsen's pocket. We'll see."

And then there was the day when Hughie had made bold enough to ask Nudnick why he had picked him for the trip, when he had his choice of thousands upon thousands of other assistants. Nudnick unwrapped his white teeth in one of his indescribable grins.

"Lots of reasons, son, among which are the fact that I delight in displeasing the contents of Bjornsen's stuffed shirt, and the fact that I dislike being bored, and since I must make this trip myself, I might as well be amused while I am cooped up. Also, I have found that baby geniuses are inclined to be a little cocky about what they know, and the fact that they knew it at such a tender age. A trained assistant, on the other hand, is almost certain to be a specialist of sorts, and specialists have inflexible and dogmatic minds. Bjornsen said that one of your cardinal crimes was that you relaxed in fantasy. I, with all of my scientific savvy, can find it in me to admire a mind which can conceive of the possibility of a space-warp, or time-travel. Don't look at me that way—I'm not kidding you. I can't possibly imagine such a thing—my mind is far too cluttered up with facts. I don't know whether or not a Martian ship will pick up our trail on this trip. If one does, it will take fantastic thinking to duck him. I'm incapable of thinking that way, so it's up to you."

Hughie, hearing the old man's voice, watching his eyes as he spoke, recognized the sincerity there, and began to realize that he carried an unimaginable responsibility on his shoulders.

On the fourth and fifth days out, there was little to do and Hughie amused both of them by reading aloud, at Nudnick's insistence, from some of his store of books and magazines. At first Hughie was diffident; he could not believe that Nudnick, who had so outdone any fictional scientist, could be genuinely interested; but Nudnick put it as an order, and Hughie began to read, with many a glance at the old man to see if he could find the first glimmerings of derision. He found difficulty in controlling his voice and his saliva until Nudnick slowed him down. Soon he was lost in the yarn. It was a good one.

It concerned one Satan Strong, Scientist, Scourge of the Spaceways and Supporter of the Serialized Short Story. Satan was a bad egg whose criminality was surpassed only by his forte for Science on the Spot. Pursued particularly by the Earth sections of the Space Patrol, Satan Strong was always succeeding in the most dastardly deeds, which always turned out to be preliminaries to greater evils which were always thwarted by the quick thinking of Captain Jaundess of the Patrol, following which, by "turning to the micro-ultraphiltmeter he rapidly tore out a dozen connections, spot-welded twenty-seven busbars, and converted the machine into an improved von Krockmeier hyperspace lever, which bent space like the blade of a rapier and hurtled him in a flash from hilt to point" and effected his escape until the next issue. Nudnick was entranced.

"It's pseudoscience," he chuckled. "I might even say that it's pseudological pseudoscience. But, it's lovely!" He regarded his withered frame quizzically. "Pity I don't have muscles and a widow's peak," he said. "I've got the science but I rather fear I lack glamour. Have you the next issue?"

Hughie had.

Then, on the sixth day, Hughie's reading was interrupted by a shrill whine from the forward instrument panel. A light flashed under a screen; Nudnick walked over to it and flipped a switch. The screen glowed, showing the blackness of space and its crystal points of light. He turned a knob; the points of light swung slowly across the screen until the tiny black ring at the juncture of the crosshairs encircled a slightly luminous spot.

"What is it?" Hughie asked, regretfully laying down his book.

"Company," said Nudnick tersely. "No telling who it is at this distance, unless they want to tell us about themselves by ultraradio. They're on our course, and overtaking."

Hughie stared into the screen. "You had this stern detector running all the time, didn't you? Gee—You don't think it's a pirate, do you?" There was something hopeful in Hughie's tone. Nudnick laughed.

"You want to see science in action, don't you? Heh. I'm afraid I'm going to be a disappointment to you, youngster. We can't travel any faster than we are going now, and that ship quite obviously can."

Hughie flushed. "Well, professor, if you think it's all right—"

Nudnick shook his head. "I don't think it's all right," he said. "Now that we have established that fact, let's get back to your story. To think that Captain Juandess would be careless enough to let his betrothed get into the clutches of that evil fellow! What will he do to her?"

"But, Professor Nudnick—"

Nudnick took Hughie's arm and steered him across the control room to his chair. "My dear, overanxious young crew, the ship that is pursuing us presents no problem until it overtakes us. That will be in forty-eight hours. In the meantime, Captain Jaundess' girl friend is in far greater danger than we are. Pray proceed."

Most unwillingly, Hughie read on.

Forty-eight hours later, the brisk crackle of an ultraradio ordered them to stand by to be boarded in the name of the Joint Patrol. The destroyer pulled alongside, and a lifeboat carried a slim, strong cable around the *Stoutfella* and, through the mooring eyes, back to the Patrol ship. The cable was used because magnetic grapples are useless on a Nudnick Metal hull. A winch drew the craft together, and a "wind tunnel" boarding stage groped against the outside of the *Stoutfella*'s air lock.

"What are you going to do?" asked Hughie desperately.

"We are going to say as little as possible," said Nudnick meaningly, "and we are going to let them in, of course." He actuated the air-lock controls; the boarding stage was hermetically sealed to their hull as the outer and inner doors slid back.

A purple-uniformed Martian yeoman stepped down into the room, followed by his equally ranking shipmate from Earth. The Martian swore and shut his nostril flaps on the sides of his stringy neck with an unpleasant click. "This air is saturated," he squeaked. "You might have had the courtesy to dehydrate it."

"What?" grinned the Earth Patrolman. "And deprive me of the only breath of decent air I've had in nineteen days?" He drew a grateful breath, letting the moisture sink into his half-parched lungs.

The air in Patrol ships was always, since there was no happy medium, too dry for Earthlings and too humid for Martians; for the Martians, living for countless generations on a water-starved planet had developed a water-hoarding metabolism which had never evolved a use for a water surplus.

"Who is in command?" piped the Martian. Nudnick gestured; the Martian immediately turned his back on Hughie. "We have orders from headquarters that this ship is to be searched and disarmed according to Section 398 of the Earth-Mars Code."

"Suspicion of piracy," supplemented the Earthman.

"Piracy?" shouted Hughie, his resentment at last breaking through. "Piracy? Who do you think you are? What do you mean by—"

Three tiny eyes in the back of the Martian's head flipped open. "Has this unpleasantly noisy infant a function?" he demanded, fingering the blaster at his hip.

"He's my crew. Be quiet, Hughie."

"Yeah—take it easy, kiddo," said the Earthman, not unkindly. "Orders are orders in this outfit. You got no fight with us. We just work here."

"Let them alone, Hughie," chimed in Nudnick. "We've little enough armament and they're welcome to it. They have every right." While the Martian stalked out, the scientist turned to the other Patrolman. "This is a Patrol Council order?"

"Of course."

"Who signed it?"

"Councilman Emil Bjornsen."

"Bjornsen? The new member? How has he the right?"

"Council regulations. 'If any matter should be put to a vote, the resulting decision shall be executed in the name of the president of the council, except in such cases where the decision is carried by one vote, when the order shall be executed in the name of the councilman whose vote carried the measure.' Bjornsen, as the most recently appointed councilman, has the last vote. In this case the action was deadlocked and his vote carried it."

"I see. Thank you. I suppose you can't tell me who proposed this order?"

"Sorry."

The Patrolman moved swiftly about the room, covering every inch of space. In spite of his resentment, Hughie had to admire the man's efficiency. The kid stood sullenly against the bulkhead; when the man came to him, he ran his hands quickly over the boy, and with the skill of a practiced "dip," extracted a low-powered pellet-gun from Hughie's side pocket. "You won't want this," he said. "It won't kill anything but cockroaches, and they're too easily fumigated."

Glancing around swiftly to see if the Martian had returned from the storerooms yet, he clapped his hand over Hughie's mouth and whispered something. When the Martian came back, the Patrolman was finishing up on the other side of the room, and Hughie was staring at him with an affectionately resentfull wonderment.

"Hardly a thing," complained the Martian shrilly, displaying a sparse armload of side arms and one neuro ray bow chaser. "Never heard of a Martian councilman sending a destroyer after a couple of nitwits on a pleasure cruise."

They saluted and left. In two minutes the ships drifted apart; in five, the destroyer was nothing but a memory and a dwindling spot on the stern visiscreen. Nudnick smiled at Hughie.

"*Tsk!* You certainly flew off the handle, Hughie. When that fellow took away your peashooter, I thought you were going to bite him."

"Nah," said Hughie embarrassed. "He was O.K. I guess I didn't want the gun much anyhow."

There was a silence, while Nudnick inspected the inner air-lock gate and then the air-pressure indicator. Finally Nudnick asked:

"Well, aren't you going to tell me?"

"What?"

"What it was that the Patrolman whispered in your ear. Or are you going to save it for a climax in the best science-fiction tradition?"

Hughie was saving it for just that. "You don't miss much do you?" he said. "It wasn't nothing much. He said, 'There's a lousy little Martian private ship on your tail. Probably will stay on our spot on your visiscreen for a few days and be on top of you before you know it. Better watch him.' "

"Hm-m-m." Nudnick stared at the screen. "Anything else?" He spoke as if he knew damn well there was something else. Hughie blushed, robbed of the choicest part of his secret.

"Only just that Bjornsen's aboard."

"That still isn't all." Nudnick approached the boy, absolutely dead pan.

"Honest," stammered Hughie, wide-eyed.

Nudnick shook his head, put his hand in his pocket, gave something to Hughie. "There's just this," he said. "He slipped it into my pocket on the way out, just as easily as he slipped it out of yours."

Hughie stared at the gun in his hand with a delight approaching tears.

"A very efficient young man," said Nudnick. "You will notice that he unloaded it."

Three weeks later Professor Nudnick took it upon himself to disconnect the stern visiscreen because Hughie could not pry himself loose from it. The Patrolman had been right; the destroyer had dwindled there until it reached a .008 intensity and then had stayed right there for several days, after which it had grown again until the boy could make out the ship itself. It was no longer the destroyer, it was a plump-lined wicked little Martian sportster. He knew without asking that the little ship was fast and maneuverable beyond all comparison with the *Stoutfella*. It annoyed him almost as much as Nudnick's calm acceptance of the fact that they were being followed, and that there was every possibility of their never returning to Earth, to say nothing of locating and claiming the prosydium asteroid. He took the trouble to say as much. Nudnick merely raised his eyebrows to uncover his logic and said:

"Don't go off half-cocked, younker. Granted, the Martian is following us. I was apparently right about Bjornsen's hunch; he knows that I have been looking all over the System for prosydium and that it is rather unusual for me to go sailing off personally into space. Ergo, I must have found some. But he doesn't want me, or you. All he wants is the prosydium. He can get it only by following this ship. Until we tie on to something, we're as safe as a babe in a bassinet. So why worry?"

"Why worry?" The kid's brains almost crackled audibly in their attempt to transmit his worry to the scientist. "Here's something! Has it occurred to you that all the Martian has to do is to determine our course, continue it ahead on a chart, and then know our destination?"

"It has occurred to me," said Nudnick gently. "Our course will intercept Mercury in twenty days."

"Mercury!" Hughie cried. "You told me the prosydium was on an asteroid!"

"It is an asteroid." Nudnick was being assiduously patient. "You know it, and I know it. But our course is for Mercury. That's all *they* know. If we lose them, we will change course for the Belt. If we don't lose them, we will go to Mercury. If they're persistent, we'll go back to Earth and try again some time, though I will admit that there's only a billion to one chance of our slipping away without being followed again."

"I'm sorry," said Hughie after a while. "I have no business in trying to tell you off, Professor Nudnick. Only I hate like hell to see that Bjornsen guy keep you away from what you want to get. That heel. That lousy wart on the nose of progress!"

"End quotes," said Nudnick dryly. "Captain Jaundess."

"O.K., O.K.," said Hughie, grinning in spite of himself. "But I can't seem to get over that guy Bjornsen. He got in my hair for nearly two years at school, and now that he's kicked me out he seems to want to get under my scalp as well. I dunno—I never saw a guy like that before. I can't figger him—the way he thinks. That rotten business of ganging up on kids. He's inhuman!"

"You may be right," said Nudnick slowly. "You may just possibly be right." After a long pause, he said, "I picked the right assistant, Hughie. You're doing fine."

Hughie was so tickled by that remark that he didn't think to ask what provoked it.

Two days before they were due on Mercury, the professor heaved a sigh, glanced at Hughie, and connected up the stern visiscreen. "There you are," he said quietly. Hughie looked up from his magazine, dropped it with a gasp of horror. The Martian ship was not two hundred yards behind them, looming up, filling the screen. He sprang to his feet.

"Professor Nudnick! *Do* something!"

Nudnick shook his head, spread his hands. "Any ideas?"

"There must be something. Can't you blast them, professor?"

"With what? The Patrol took even our little neuro ray."

Hughie waved the defeatist philosophy aside impatiently. "There ought to be something you could do. Heck—you're supposed to be ten times the scientist that Harry Petrou is—"

"I beg your pardon?"

"Harry Petrou ... Petrou!" Hughie swept up the magazine, thrust the too-bright cover in the scientist's face. "The writer! The author of—"

"Satan Strong!" The dried-up old man let out an astonishingly hearty peal of laughter.

"Well," said Hughie defensively, "anyway—" Furiously he began to shout half hysterical phrases. He was scared, and he had a bad case of hero worship, and he was also very young. He said, "You go ahead and laugh. But Harry Petrou has some pretty damn good ideas. Maybe they're not scientific. Not what you'd call scientific. Why doesn't anybody ever do anything scientific without studying for fifty years in a dusty old laboratory? Why does one of the greatest scientists in history," he half sobbed, "sit back and b-be bullied by a l-louse like Bjornsen?"

"Hughie—take it easy, there." Nudnick put out his hand, then turned away from those young, accusing eyes. "Things aren't done that way, Hughie. Science isn't like that—made to order for melodramatic adventures. I know—you'd like me to burrow into the air conditioner, throw a few connections around, and come out with a space-warp."

Hughie turned on the lower forward screen. It showed, blindingly, the flaming crescent of the inner planet. They were descending swiftly toward the night-edge of the twilight strip, the automatic pilot taking care of every detail of deceleration and gravity control.

"You're quitting," said Hughie, his lip quivering. "You're running away!" And he turned his back to Nudnick, to stare at the evil menacing bulk of the Martian ship.

Nudnick sighed, went and sat at the controls, and took over the ship from the pilot.

After two silent hours, Hughie observed that Nudnick was preparing to land. He said, in a dead voice:

"If you land, they'll catch us."

"That's right." Nudnick's voice was brisk.

"And if they catch us, they'll torture us."

"Yep." Nudnick glanced over his shoulder. "Will you obey my orders implicitly?"

"Sure," said Hughie hopelessly. His eyes were fixed in fearful fascination on the Martian ship.

"Start now, then. Get rid of all the metal on your clothes. Belt buckle, buttons—everything. You have fiber soled boots?"

"Mm-m-m."

"Put them on. Snap into it!"

An hour later the *Stoutfella* grated on a sandy clearing not far from a red and rocky bluff. The choking atmosphere of Mercury swirled about the portholes. Nudnick climbed out of the pilot seat and tore a pair of fiber boots out of a locker. He had already ripped his buttons off, tossed his wrist radio and identification ring on the chart table. "Come on!" he snapped.

"You . . . we're not going out there?"

"You're damn right we are."

Hughie looked at him. If this old man was willing—He shrugged, picked up a magazine. It seemed as if he—stroked it. Then he tossed it aside and strode with Nudnick into the air lock.

As the inner gate shut them out of the little world that the ship afforded, Nudnick clapped him on the back. "Chin up, kiddo," he said warmly. "Now listen—do exactly as I tell you. When we get outside, move as fast as you can toward that bluff. The Martians won't shoot as long as they think we have any information. Na—no questions—there isn't time! Listen. It's hot out there. As hot as the oven my dear old mother used to bake ten-egg cakes in. The air is not so good, but we can breathe it—for a while. Long enough, I guess. Ready?"

The outer gate slid back and they plunged out.

It was hot. In seconds acrid dust was packing on Hughie's skin, washing away in veritable gushes of sweat, packing the pores again. He saw the reason for taking off metal clothing. He had left his identification ring on; it began to sear his hand. He tore it off, and blistered flesh with it.

The air lacerated his throat, stung his eyes. Somehow he knew the location of three things—the red bluff, the hovering Martian ship, and the professor. He pounded on. Once he tripped, went down on one knee. His breeches burst into flame. Nudnick saw and helped him slap it out. Inside the charred edges of cloth he caught a glimpse of his own kneecap, a tiny spot of bone amid a circle of cooked flesh, where his knee had ground into the burning sand.

Nudnick tugged at his elbow. "How far do you think we are?" he wheezed.

Hughie suddenly realized that Nudnick's old eyes couldn't see very far in this kind of heat; he had to be eyes for two people now. "Ship—hundred and fifty—yards—"

"Not—far enough! Go—on!"

They struggled on, helping each other, hindering each other. The ground rose sharply; Nudnick stopped. "Beginning of . . . bluff . . . far . . . enough—" He began coughing.

Hughie held him up until he had finished. He began to understand. He had heard vague stories about Martian torture. Nudnick would rather die this way, then. They could have starved slowly in the ship. Maybe this was better—

Nudnick's shrill, dust-choked whisper reached him. "Martians?"

Hughie put one hand over his eyes and peered through the fingers. The Martian ship had settled down beside the *Stoutfella*. The port swung open, three figures, two tall and lanky, one short and shriveled. "Three . . . coming . . . two Martians . . . Bjornsen." Talking was torture. Breathing was pulling fire into the lungs. He heard a noise and looked down. Nudnick was clutching him and making the noise. Slowly he realized that the old man was laughing.

They lurched toward the three figures, clinging to each other. The two Martians grasped them, and just in time, or they would have fallen and died.

"Of all the crazy damn things to do!" shrilled Bjornsen. In spite of the blazing breeze, the insufferable heat, the old gestures returned to him, and he rubbed his hands together in that familiar, despised gesture.

Nudnick forced his eyes open and stared at the councilman worriedly, and then turned to each of the Martians. They were wilting a little bit in the heat, but their grip was still strong. Bjornsen spoke a few squeaky words in the Martian tongue, and the five of them began to struggle toward the ships.

Suddenly the Martian who had Hughie's arm began to cry out in a piercing, undulating whine. It was quite the most ghastly sound the boy had ever heard; he shuddered in spite of the heat and thrust at the creature. To his utter amazement the Martian slumped to the ground, arched his back as it began to scorch, screamed deafeningly and then lay still. Nudnick laughed cacklingly again and shoved at his Martian, tripping him at the same time. The second Martian stumbled, regained his balance, and then began screaming. In a matter of seconds he fell. He took longer, but died also—

Bjornsen stood in front of them, watching the Martians, and then, shouting agonized curses, began a stumbling run toward his ship.

"Damn it, he's going to make it!" cried Nudnick; and stooping, he caught up a hot stone and hurled it.

Straight as an explosive pellet it flew, and caught Bjornsen between his narrow shoulders. Bjornsen threw up his hands, trying wildly to keep his feet. Gibbering crazily, Nudnick threw another stone. It missed by twenty feet. Hughie caught the old man as he fell exhausted. When next he looked at

Bjornsen, the councilman was down on his knees, his hand clutching at the sill of the Martian's air lock. He sagged, writhed, and died there.

Hughie stood for five seconds, tottering; then he shook his head, bent and let the scientist's limp body fall across his shoulder. It took him an eternity to straighten up, and then eternities to locate his nearby ship and begin that long, long, fifty-foot journey. Hughie knew later that if it had been five—three—feet more, he could not possibly have made it. But somehow he did—somehow he tumbled the old man into the lock, pitched forward on top of him. He scrabbled weakly around, found the lock control, pressed it.

Hughie screamed when he came out of it. Then he opened his eyes and saw that he wasn't in that fiery desert. He closed them again and realized that his knee hurt terribly. Then Nudnick was beside him, bathing his face, talking.

"Good stuff, kid. Fix you up in no time. Heh! Long chance just for a few tons of prosydium, eh? Well, we'll get it now. No one else around. No one else around."

"Bjornsen?"

"Dead. Remember? Like the Martians."

"Martians." The words brought horror into the heat-reddened young face. He raised his head and Nudnick slipped another pillow under it. "What happened to those Martians?"

Nudnick grinned. "They died of ignorance, son, and let that be a lesson to you." Hughie just stared. "You see, for generations now, Martians have lived on Earth and Earthmen on Mars. It made 'em forget something—that one little fact I was talking about before we landed. Water-hoarders, Hughie. *Martians can't sweat!* You see? A human can live beside a steak that's cooking, because he sweats. The evaporation cools him down. A Martian can't stand that kind of heat—he cooks like a steak!"

"But . . . Bjornsen wasn't—"

"Ah. You're wrong there. Bjornsen *was!* A freak, Hughie. Look at Martians. Unemotional—logical— well, isn't that Bjornsen? Y'know, when I walked in on him when he was ganging up on you at the Institute, I heard him rub his hands together. I'd heard it somewhere before, but I didn't know just where. But the other day when you said he was inhuman, it clicked. Bjornsen didn't have no mamma and no poppa, kiddo. He came out of a Martian biochemical laboratory, or I miss my guess. Clever fellers, those Martians. Trained him from birth for that job. A key man in the middle of my little old institute, There may be more like him. I'll see to that. Heh! I won't be the first boss that's told his employees, 'Work up a sweat or get canned!' "

Hughie at last managed to grin a little. Nudnick kept on talking happily. "The knee'll be all right in a couple weeks. By that time we'll hook on to the prosydium. You're fixed for life, fella. Ah—hey, I've got a confession to make to you."

Hughie turned weak, amused eyes on him. The old man wagged his head. "Yep. About that prosydium. Didn't you wonder how I knew about it? I'll tell you. I was coming from Mars last year on a Martian liner. Very elegant. Humidifiers in every room. Radio. Recorded music. Lots of apparatus built into the staterooms. Would've delighted the heart of Satan Strong. Anyway, I got messing around I . . . er—" He paused guiltily, then went on. "I sort of tore out some connections and spot-welded some busbars. Built me a dandy little detectograph. Located that prosydium as we passed the edge of the Belt. Sheer luck. Spotted it, by golly, right from a stateroom in a Martian ship!"

Hughie laughed admiringly. "You old son of a gun," he said disrespectfully. "And you sneered at Satan Strong!"

"Me?" The old man shook his head and stood up. "Why should I sneer at Satan Strong? I *like* Satan Strong. I ought to. I *write* those stories!"

BRAT

Not fun. A horrid little fantasy, derived from true-life observations by a man who loved children, but not children like this one. Those ones.

"It's strictly a short-order proposition," said Michaele, tossing her searchlight hair back on her shoulders. "We've got to have a baby eight days from now or we're out a sweet pile of cash."

"We'll get one somewhere. Couldn't we adopt one or something?" I said, plucking a stalk of grass from the bank of the brook and jamming it between my front teeth.

"Takes weeks. We could kidnap one, maybe."

"They got laws. Laws are for the protection of people."

"Why does it always have to be other people?" Mike was beginning to froth up. "Shorty, get your bulk up off the ground and think of something."

"Think better this way," I said. "We could borrow one."

"Look," said Mike. "When I get my hands on a kid, that child and I have to go through a short but rigorous period of training. It's likely to be rough. If I had a baby and someone wanted to borrow it for any such purpose, I'd be damned if I'd let it go."

"Oh, you wouldn't be too tough," I said. "You've got maternal instincts and stuff."

"Shortly, you don't seem to realize that babies are very delicate creatures and require the most skilled and careful handling. I don't know *anything* about them. I am an only child, and I went right from high school into business college and from there into an office. The only experience I ever had with a baby was once when I minded one for an afternoon. It cried all the time I was there."

"Should've changed its diapers."

"I did."

"Must've stuck it with a pin then."

"I did not! You seem to know an awful lot about children," she said hotly.

"Sure I do. I was one myself once."

"Heel!" She leaped on me and rolled me into the brook, I came up spluttering and swearing. She took me by the neck, pulled me half up on the bank and began thudding my head on the soft bank.

"Let go my apple," I gasped. "This is no choking matter."

"Now will you cooperate? Shorty, quit your kidding. This is serious. Your Aunt Amanda has left us thirty grand, providing we can prove to her sister Jonquil that we are the right kind of people. 'Those who can take care of a baby can take care of money,' she used to say. We've got to be under Jonquil's eye for thirty days and take care of a baby. No nursemaids, no laundresses, no nothing."

"Let's wait till we have one of our own."

"Don't be stupid! You know as well as I do that that money will set you up in a business of your own as well as paying off the mortgage on the shack. *And* decorating it. *And* getting us a new car."

"And a fur coat. *And* a star sapphire. Maybe I'll even get a new pair of socks."

"Shorty!" A full lip quivered, green eyes swam.

"Oh, darling, I didn't mean— Come here and be kissed."

She did. Then she went right on where she had left off. She's like that. She can puddle up at the drop of a cynicism, and when I apologize she sniffs once and the tears all go back into her eyes without being used. She holds them for when they'll be needed instead of wasting them. "But you know perfectly well that unless we get our hands on money—lots of it—and darn soon, we'll lose that barn and the garage that we built just to *put* a new car in. Wouldn't that be silly?"

"No. No garage, no need for a car. Save lots of money!"

"Shorty—please."

"All right, all right. The fact that everything you say is correct doesn't help to get us a baby for thirty days. Damn money anyway! Money isn't everything!"

"Of course it isn't, darling," said Michaele sagely, "but it's what you buy everything with."

A sudden splash from the brook startled us. Mike screamed. "Shortly—grab him!"

I plunged into the water and hauled out a very tiny, very dirty—baby. It was dressed in a tattered romper, and it had an elfin face, big blue eyes and a golden topknot. It looked me over and sprayed me—*b-b-b-b-b-br-r-r*—with a combination of a mouthful of water and a Bronx cheer.

"Oh, the poor darling little angel!" said Mike. "Give him to me, Shorty! You're handling him like a bag of sugar!"

I stepped gingerly out of the brook and handed him over. Michaele cradled the filthy mite in her arms, completely oblivious to the child's effect on her white linen blouse. The same white linen blouse, I reflected bitterly, that I had been kicked out of the house for, when I pitched some cigar ashes on it. It made me feel funny, watching Mike handle that kid. I'd never pictured her that way.

The baby regarded Mike gravely as she discoursed to it about a poor drowned woofum-wuffums, and did the bad man treat it badly, then. The baby belched eloquently.

"He belches in English!" I remarked.

"Did it have the windy ripples?" cooed Mike. "Give us a kiss, honey lamb."

The baby immediately flung its little arms around her neck and planted a whopper on her mouth.

"Wow!" said Mike when she got her breath. "Shorty, could you take lessons!"

"Lessons my eye," I said jealously. "Mike, that's no baby, that's some old guy in his second childhood."

"The idea." She crooned to the baby for a moment, and then said suddenly. "Shorty—what were we talking about before heaven opened up and dropped this little bundle of—" Here the baby tried to squirm out of her arms and she paused to get a better grip.

"Bundle of what?" I asked, deadpan.

"Bundle of joy."

"Oh! Bundle of joy. What were we talking about? Ba— Hey! Babies!"

"That's right. And a will. And thirty grand."

I looked at the child with new eyes. "Who do you think belongs to the younker?"

"Someone who apparently won't miss him if we take him away for thirty days" she said. "No matter what bungling treatment I give him, it's bound to be better than what he's used to. Letting a mere babe crawl around in the woods! Why, it's awful!"

"The mere babe doesn't seem to mind" I said. "Tell you what we'll do— we'll take care of him for a few days and see if anyone claims him. We'll listen to the radio and watch the papers and the ol' grapevine. If anybody does claim him, maybe we can make a deal for a loan. At any rate we'll get to work on him right away."

At this juncture the baby eeled out of Mike's arms and took off across the grass. "Sweet Sue! Look at him go!" she said, scrambling to her feet. "Get him, Shorty!"

The infant, with twinkling heels, was crawling—running, on hands and knees—down toward the brook. I headed him off just as he reached the water, and snagged him up by the slack of his pants. As he came up off the ground he scooped up a handful of mud and pitched it into my eyes. I yelped and dropped him. When I could see a little daylight again I beheld Michaele taking a running brodie into a blackberry bush. I hurried over there, my eyelids making a nasty grating sound. Michaele was lying prone behind the baby, who was also lying prone, his little heels caught tightly in Mike's hands. He was nonchalantly picking blackberries.

Mike got her knees and then her feet under her, and picked up the baby, who munched contentedly. "I'm disgusted with you," she said, her eyes blazing. "Flinging an innocent child around like that! Why, it's a wonder you didn't break every bone in his poor little body!"

"But I—He threw mud in my—"

"Pick on someone your size, you big bully! I never knew till now that you were a sadist with an inferiority complex."

"And I never knew till now that it's true what they say about the guy in the three-cornered pants—the king can do no wrong! What's happened to your sense of justice, woman? That little brat there—"

"Shorty! Talking that way about a poor little baby! He's beautiful! He didn't mean anything by what he did. He's too young to know any better."

In the biggest, deepest bass voice I have ever heard, the baby said, "Lady, I do know what I'm doin'. I'm old enough!"

We both sat down.

"Did you say that?" Mike wanted to know.

I shook my head dazedly.

"Coupla dopes," said the baby.

"Who— What are you?" asked Mike breathlessly.

"What do I look like?" said the baby, showing his teeth. He had very sharp, very white teeth—two on the top gum and four on the lower.

"A little bundle of—"

"Shorty!" Mike held up a slim finger.

"Never mind him," growled the child. "I know lots of four-letter words. Go ahead, bud."

"You go ahead. What are you—a midget?"

I no sooner got the second syllable of that word out when the baby scuttled over to me and rocked my head back with a surprising right to the jaw. "That's the last time I'm going to be called that by anybody!" He roared deafeningly.

"No! I'm not a . . . a . . . what you said. I'm a pro tem changeling, and that's all."

"What on earth is that?" asked Mike.

"Just what I said!" snapped the baby, "a pro tem changeling. When people treat their babies too well—or not well enough—I show up in their bassinets and give their folks what for. Only I'm always the spitting image of their kid. When they wise up in the treatment, they get their kids back—not before."

"Who pulls the switch? I mean, who do you work for?"

The baby pointed to the grass at our feet. I had to look twice before I realized what he was pointing at. The blades were dark and glossy and luxuriant in a perfect ring about four feet in diameter.

Michaele gasped and put her knuckles to her lips. "The Little People!" she breathed.

I was going to say, "Don't be silly, Mike!" but her taut face and the baby's bland, nodding head stopped me.

"Will you work for us?" she asked breathlessly. "We need a baby for thirty days to meet the conditions of a will."

"I heard you talking about it," said the baby. "No."

"No?"

"No."

A pause. "Look, kid," I said, "what do you like? Money? Food? Candy? Circuses?"

"I like steaks," said the child gruffly. "Rare, fresh, thick. Onions. Cooked so pink they say, 'Moo!' when you bite 'em. Why?"

"Good," I said. "If you work for us, you'll get all the steaks you can eat."

"No."

"What would you want to work for us?"

"Nothin'. I don't wanna work for you."

"What are we going to do?" I whispered to Mike. "This would be perfect!"

"Leave it to me. Look—baby—what's your name, anyway?"

"Percival. But don't call me Percival! Butch."

"Well, look, Butch; we're in an awful jam. If we don't get hold of a sockful of money darn soon, we'll lose that pretty little house over there."

"What's the matter with *him?* Can't he keep up the payments? What is he—a bum?"

"Hey, you—"

"Shut up, Shorty. He's just beginning, Butch. He's a graduate caterer. But he has to get a place of his own before he can make any real money."

"What happens if you lose th' house?"

"A furnished room. The two of us."

"What's the matter with that?"

I tensed. This was a question I had asked her myself.

"Not for me. I just couldn't live that way." Mike would wheedle, but she wouldn't lie.

Butch furrowed his nonexistent eyebrows. "Couldn't? Y' know, I like that. High standards." His voice deepened; the question lashed her. "Would you live with him in a furnished room if there were no other way?"

"Well, of course."

"I'll help you," said Butch instantly.

"Why?" I asked. "What do you expect to get out of it?"

"Nothing—some fun, maybe. I'll help you because you need help. That's the only reason I ever do anything for anybody. That's the only thing you should have told me in the first place—that you were in a jam. You and your bribes!" he snapped at me, and turned to Mike. "I ain't gonna like that guy," he said.

I said, "I already don't like you."

As we started back to the house Butch said, "But I'm gonna get my steaks?"

Aunt Jonquil's house stood alone in a large lot with its skirts drawn primly up and an admonishing expression on its face. It looked as if it had squeezed its way between two other houses to hide itself, and some scoundrel had taken the other houses away.

And Aunt Jonquil, like her house, was five times as high as she was wide, extremely practical, unbeautifully ornate, and stood alone. She regarded marriage as an unfortunate necessity. She herself never married because an unkind nature had ruled that she must marry a man, and she thought that men were uncouth. She disapproved of smoking, drinking, swearing, gambling, and loud laughter. Smiles she enjoyed only if she could fully understand what was being smiled at; she mistrusted innuendo. A polite laugh was a thing she permitted herself perhaps twice a week, providing it was atoned for by ten minutes of frozen-faced gravity. Added to which, she was a fine person. Swell.

On the way to the city, I sat through this unnerving conversation.

Butch said, "Fathead! Drive more carefully!"

"He's doing all right," said Mike. "Really. It surprises me. He's usually an Indian." She was looking very lovely in a peagreen linen jacket and a very simple white skirt and a buff straw hat that looked like a halo.

Butch was wearing a lace-edged bonnet and an evil gleam in his eye to offset the angelic combination of a pale-blue sweater with white rabbits applied on the sides, and fuzzy Angora booties on which he had insisted because I was wearing a navy-blue and he knew it would come off all over me. He was, I think, a little uncomfortable due to my rather unskilled handling of his diapering. And the reason for my doing that job was to cause us more trouble than a little bit. Butch's ideas of privacy and the proprieties were advanced. He would no more think of letting Mike bathe or change him than I would think of letting Garbo change me. Thinking about this, I said:

"Butch, that prudishness of yours is going to be tough to keep up at Aunt Jonquil's."

"You'll keep it up, son," said the infant, "or I'll quit working. I ain't going to have no women messin' around me that way. What d'ye think I am—an exhibitionist?"

"I think you're a liar," I said. " And I'll tell you why. You said you made a life's work of substituting for children. How could you with ideas like that? Who you trying to horse up?"

"Oh," said Butch, "that. Well, I might's well confess to you that I ain't done that kind of work in years. I got sick of it. I was gettin' along in life and . . . well, you can imagine. Well, about thutty years ago I was out on a job an' the woman was changin' my drawers when a half-dozen babes arrived from her sewin' circle. She left off workin' right where she was and sang out for them all to come in and see how pretty I looked the way I was. I jumped out o' th' bassinet, grabbed a diaper off th' bed an' held it in front of me while I called a whole bunch of 'em what they were and told them to get out of there. I got fired for it. I thought they'd put me to work hauntin' houses or cleanin' dishes for sick people or somethin', but no—they cracked down on me. Told me I'd have to stay this way until I was repentant."

"Are you?" giggled Mike.

Butch snorted. "Not so you'd notice it," he growled. "Repentant because I believe in common decency? Heh?"

"We waited a long time after we rang the bell before Jonquil opened the door. That was to give her time to peep out at us from the tumorous bay window and compose her features to meet the niece by marriage her unfastidious nephew had acquired.

"Jonquil!" I said heartily, dashing forward and delivering the required peck on her cheek. Jonquil expected her relatives to use her leathery cheek precisely as she herself used a napkin. Pat. Dry surface on dry surface. Moisture is vulgar.

"And this is Michaele," I said, stepping aside.

Mike said, "How do you do?" demurely, and smiled.

Aunt Jonquil stepped back a pace and held her head as if she were sighting at Mike through her nostrils. "Oh, yes," she said without moving her lips. The smile disappeared from Mike's face and came back with an effort of will that hurt. "Come in," said Jonquil at last, and with some reluctance.

We trailed through a foyer and entered the parlor. It wasn't a living room, it was an honest-to-goodness front parlor with antimacassars and sea shells. The tone of the room was sepia—light from the background of the heavily flowered wallpaper, dark for the furniture. The chairs and a hard-looking divan were covered with a material that looked as if it had been bleeding badly some months ago. When Butch's eye caught the glassed-in monstrosity of hay and dead flowers over the mantelpiece, he retched audibly.

"What a lovely place you have here," said Mike.

"Glad you like it," acknowledged Jonquil woodenly. "Let's have a look at the child." She walked over and peered at Butch. He scowled at her. "Good heavens!" she said.

"Isn't he lovely?" said Mike.

"Of course," said Jonquil without enthusiasm, and added, after searching her store of ready-made expressions, "the little wudgums!" She kitchy-cooed his chin with her sharp forefinger. He immediately began to wail, with the hoarse, high-pitched howl of a genuine baby.

"The poor darling's tired after his trip," said Mike.

Jonquil, frightened by Butch's vocal explosion, took the hint and led the way upstairs.

"Is the whole damn house like this?" whispered Butch hoarsely.

"No. I don't know. Shut up," said Mike. My sharp-eared aunt swiveled on the steps. "And go to sleepy-bye," she crooned aloud. She bent her head over his and hissed, "And keep on crying, you little wretch!"

Butch snorted and then complied.

We walked into a bedroom, austerely furnished, the kind of room they used in the last century for sleeping purposes only, and therefore designed so that it was quite unattractive to anyone with anything but sleep on his mind. It was all gray and white; the only spot of color in the room was the bedstead, which was a highly polished pipe organ. Mike laid the baby down on the bed and stripped off his booties, his shirt and his sweater. Butch put his fist in his mouth and waited tensely.

"Oh—I almost forgot. I have the very same bassinet you used, up in the attic," said Jonquil. "I should have had it ready. Your telegram was rather abrupt, Horace. You should have let me know sooner that you'd come today." She angled out of the room.

"Horace! I'll be— Is your name Hoarce?" asked Butch in delight.

"Yes," I said gruffly. "But it's Shorty to you, see, little man?"

"And I was worried about you callin' me Percival!"

I helped set up the bassinet and we tucked Butch in for his nap. I managed to be fooling around with his bedclothes when Mike bent over dutifully to give him a kiss. I grabbed Butch's chin and held it down so the kiss landed on his forehead. He was mightily wroth, and bit my finger till it bled. I stuck it in my pocket and told him, "I'll see you later, bummy-wummy!" He made a noise, and Jonquil fled, blushing.

We convened in the kitchen, which was far and away the pleasantest room in the house. "Where on earth did you get that child?" Jonquil asked, peering into a nice-smelling saucepan on the old-fashioned range.

"Neighbor's child," I said. "They were very poor and were glad to have him off their hands for a few weeks."

"He's a foundling," Mike ingeniously supplemented. "Left on their doorstep. He's never been adopted or anything."

"What's his name?"

"We call him Butch."

"How completely vulgar!" said Jonquil. "I will have no child named Butch in my house. We shall have to give him something more refined."

I had a brain wave. "How about Percival?" I said.

"Percival. Percy," murmured Jonquil, testing it out. "That is much better. That will do. I knew somebody called Percival once."

"Oh—you better not call him Percival," said Mike, giving me her no-good-can-come-of-this look.

"Why not?" I said blandly. "Lovely name."

"Yeah," said Mike. "Lovely."

"What time does Percival get his dinner?" asked Jonquil.

"Six o'clock."

"Good," said Jonquil. "I'll feed him!"

"Oh no, Aunt J—I mean, Miss Timmins. That's our job."

I think Jonquil actually smiled. "I think I'd like to do it," she said. "You're not making an inescapable duty out of this, are you?"

"I don't know what you mean," said Mike, a little coldly. "We *like* that child."

Jonquil peered intently at her. "I believe you do," she said in a surprised tone, and started out of the room. At the door she called back, "You needn't call me Miss Timmins," and she was gone.

"Well!" said Mike.

"Looks like you won the war, babe."

"Only the first battle, honey, and don't think I don't know it. What a peculiar old duck she is!" She busied herself at the stove, warming up some strained carrots she had taken out of a jar, sterilizing a bottle and filling it with pineapple juice. We had read a lot of baby manuals in the last few days!

Suddenly, "Where's your aunt?" Mike asked.

"I dunno. I guess she's—Good grief!"

There was a dry-boned shriek from upstairs and then the sound of hard heels pounding along the upper hallway toward the front stairs. We went up the back stairs two at a time, and saw the flash of Jonquil's dimity skirts as she disappeared downstairs. We slung into the bedroom. Butch was lying in his bassinet doubled up in some kind of spasm.

"Now what?" I groaned.

"He's choking," said Mike. "What are we going to do, Shorty?"

I didn't know. Mike ran and turned him over. His face was all twisted up and he was pouring sweat and gasping. "Butch! Butch —What's the matter?"

And just then he got his wind back. *"Ho ho ho!"* he roared in his bullfrog voice, and lost it again.

"He's laughing!" Mike whispered.

"That the funniest way I ever saw anyone commit sideways," I said glumly. I reached out and smacked him across the puss. "Butch! Snap out of it!"

"Ooh!" said Butch. "You lousy heel. I'll get you for that."

"Sorry, Butch. But I thought you were strangling."

"Guess I was at that," he said, and started to laugh again. "Shorty, I couldn't help it. See, that ol' vinegar visage come in here and started staring at me. I stared right back. She bends over the bassinet. I grin. She grins. I open my mouth. She opens her mouth. I reach in and pull out her bridgework and pitch it out the windy. Her face sags down in the middle like a city street in Scranton. She does the steam-siren act and hauls out o' here. But Shorty—Mike"—and he went off into another helpless spasm—"you shoulda seen her *face!"*

We all subsided when Jonquil came in again. "Just tending to my petunias," she said primly. "Why—you have dinner on the table. Thank you, child."

"Round two," I said noncommittally.

Around two in the morning I was awakened by a soft thudding in the hallway. I came up on one elbow. Mike was fast asleep. But the bassinet was empty. I breathed an oath and tiptoed out into the hall. Halfway down was Butch, crawling rapidly. In two strides I had him by the scruff of the neck.

"Awk!"

"Shut up! Where do you think you're going?"

He thumbed at a door down the hall."

"No, Butch. Get on back to bed. You can't go there."

He looked at me pleadingly. "I can't? Not for *nothin'?"*

"Not for nothin'."

"Aw—Shorty. Gimme a break."

"Break my eyebrow. You belong in that bassinet."

"Just this once, huh, Shorty?"

I looked worriedly at Jonquil's bedroom door. "All right, dammit. But make it snappy."

Butch went on strike the third day. He didn't like those strained vegetables and soups to begin with, and then one morning he heard the butcher boy downstairs, singing out, "Here's yer steaks, Miss Timmins!" That was enough for little Percival.

"There's got to be a new deal around here, chum," he said the next time he got me in the room alone. "I'm gettin' robbed."

"Robbed? Who's taking what?"

"Youse. You promise me steaks, right? Listen, Shorty, I'm through with that pap you been feedin' me. I'm starvin' to death on it."

"What would you suggest?" I asked calmly. "Shall I have one done to your taste and delivered to your room, sir?"

"You know what, Shorty? You're kiddin'." He jabbed a tiny forefinger into the front of my shirt for emphasis. "You're kiddin', but I ain't. An' what you just said is a pretty good idea. I want a steak once a day—here in this room. I mean it, son."

I opened my mouth to argue and then looked deep into those baby eyes. I saw an age-old stubborness, an insurmountable firmness of character there. I shrugged and went out.

In the kitchen I found Mike and Jonquil deeply engaged in some apparently engrossing conversation about rayon taffeta. I broke it up by saying, "I just had an idea. Tonight I'm going to eat my supper upstairs with Bu . . . Percival. I want you to get to know each other better, and I would commune with another male for a spell. I'm outnumbered down here."

Jonquil actually did smile this time. Smiles seemed to be coming to her a little more easily these days. "I think that's a lovely idea," she said. "We're having steak tonight, Horace. How do you like yours?"

"Broiled," said Mike, "and well d—"

"Rare!" I said, sending a glance at Mike. She shut up, wonderingly.

And that night I sat up in the bedroom, watching that miserable infant eat my dinner. He did it with gusto, with much smacking of the lips and grunting in ecstasy.

"What do you expect me to do with this?" I asked, holding up a cupful of lukewarm and sticky strained peas.

"I don't know," said Butch with his mouth full. "That's your problem."

I went to the window and looked out. Directly below was a spotless concrete walk which would certainly get spattered if I pitched the unappetizing stuff out there. "Butch—won't you get rid of the stuff for me?"

He sighed, his chin all greasy from my steak. "Thanks, no," he said luxuriously. "Couldn't eat another bite."

I tasted the peas tentatively, held my nose and gulped them down. As I swallowed the last of them I found time to direct a great many highly unpleasant thoughts at Butch. "No remarks, *Percy*," I growled.

He just grinned. I picked up his plates and the cup and started out. "Haven't you forgotten something?" he asked sleepily.

"What?" He nodded toward the dresser and the bottle which stood on it. Boiled milk with water and corn syrup added. "Damned if I will!" I snapped.

He grinned, opened his mouth and started to wail.

"Shut up!" I hissed. "You'll have them women up here claiming I'm twisting your tail or something."

"That's the idea," said Butch. "Now drink your milk like a good little boy and you can go out and play."

I muttered something impotently, ripped the nipple off the bottle and gulped the contents.

"That's for telling the old lady to call me Percy," said Butch. "I want another steak tomorrow. 'Bye now."

And that's how it came about that I, a full-grown man in good health, lived for close to two weeks on baby food. I think that the deep respect I have for babies dates from this time, and is founded on my realization of how good-natured they are on the diet they get. It sure didn't work that way with me. What really griped me was having to watch him eat my meals. Brother, I was earning that thirty grand the hard way.

About the beginning of the third week Butch's voice began to change. Mike noticed it first and came and told me.

"I think something's the matter with him," she said. "He doesn't seem as strong as he was, and his voice is getting high-pitched."

"Don't borrow trouble, beautiful," I said, putting my arm around her. "Lord knows he isn't losing any weight on the diet he's getting. And he has plenty of lung power."

"That's another thing," she said in a puzzled tone. "This morning he was crying and I went in to see what he wanted. I spoke to him and shook him but he went on crying for almost five minutes before he suddenly sat up and said 'What? What? Eh—it's you, Mike.' I asked him what he wanted; he said nothing and told me to scram."

"He was kidding you."

She twisted out of my arms and looked up at me, her golden brows just touching over the snowy crevasse of her frown. "Shorty—he was crying—*real tears.*"

That was the same day that Jonquil went in to town and bought herself a half dozen bright dresses. And I strongly suspect she had something done to her hair. She looked fifteen years younger when she came in and said, "Horace—it seems to me you used to smoke."

"Well . . . yes—"

"Silly boy! You've stopped smoking just because you think I wouldn't approve! I like to have a man smoking around the house. Makes it more homey. Here."

She pressed something into my hand and fled, red-faced and bright-eyed. I looked at what she had given me. Two packs of cigarettes. They weren't my brand, but I don't think I have ever been so deeply touched.

*   *   *

I went and had a talk with Butch. He was sleeping lightly when I entered the room. I stood there looking down at him. He was awful tiny, I thought. I wonder what it is these women gush so much about.

Butch's eyes were so big under his lids that they seemed as if they just couldn't stay closed. The lashes lay on his cheek with the most gentle of delicate touches. He breathed evenly, with occasionally a tiny catch. It made nice listening, somehow. I caught a movement out of the corner of my eye—his hand, clenching and unclenching. It was very rosy, and far too small to be so perfect. I looked at my own hand and at his, and I just couldn't believe it . . .

He woke suddenly, opening his eyes and kicking. He looked first at the window, and then at the wall opposite. He whimpered, swallowed, gave a little cry. Then he turned his head and saw me. For a long moment he watched me, his deep eyes absolutely unclouded; suddenly he sat up and shook his head. "Hello," he said sleepily.

I had the strange sensation of watching a person wake up twice. I said, "Mike's worried about you," I told him why.

"Really?" he said. "I—don't feel much different. Heh! Imagine this happening to me!"

"Imagine what happening?"

"I've heard of it before, but I never . . . Shorty, you won't laugh at me, will you?"

I thought of all that baby food, and all those steaks. "Don't worry. You ain't funny."

"Well, you know what I told you about me being a changeling. Changelings is funny animals. Nobody likes 'em. They raise all kinds of hell. Fathers resent 'em because they cry all night. Mothers get panicky if they don't know it's a changeling, and downright resentful if they do. A changeling has a lot of fun bein' a brat, but he don't get much emotional sugar, if you know what I mean. Well, in my case . . . dammit, I can't get used to it! Me, of all people . . . well, someone around here . . . uh . . . loves me."

"Not me," I said quickly, backing away.

"I know, not you." He gave me a sudden, birdlike glance and said softly, "You're a pretty good egg, Shorty."

"Huh? Aw—"

"Anyway, they say that if any woman loves a changeling, he loses his years and his memories, and turns into a real human kid. But he's got to be loved for himself, not for some kid he replaces." He shifted uneasily. "I don't . . . I can't get used to it happening to me, but . . . oh oh!" A pained expression came across his face and he looked at me helplessly. I took in the situation at a glance.

A few minutes later I corralled Mike. "Got something for you," I said, and handed her something made of layette cloth.

"What's . . . Shorty! Not—"

I nodded. "Butch's getting infantile," I said.

While she was doing the laundry a while later I told her what Butch had said. She was very quiet while I told her, and afterward.

"Mike—if there is anything in all this fantastic business, it wouldn't be you, would it, that's making this change in him?"

She thought it over for a long time and then said, "I think he's terribly cute, Shorty."

I swung her around. She had soapsuds on her temple, where her fingers had trailed when she tossed her bright hair back with her wrist.

"Who's the number one man around here?" I whispered. She laughed and said I was silly and stood on tiptoe to kiss me. She's a little bit of a thing.

The whole thing left me feeling awful funny.

Our thirty days were up, and we packed. Jonquil helped us, and I've never seen her so full of life. Half the time she laughed, and once in a while she actually broke down and giggled. And at lunch she said to us, "Horace—I'm afraid to let you take little Percy back with you. You said that those people who had him were sort of ne'er-do-wells, and they wouldn't miss him much. I wish you'd leave him with me for a week or so while you find out just what their home life is like, and whether they really want him back. If not, I . . . well, I'll see that he gets a good place to live in."

Mike and I looked at each other, and then Mike looked up at the ceiling, toward the bedroom. I got up suddenly. "I'll ask him," I said, and walked upstairs.

Butch was sitting up in the bassinet trying to catch a sunbeam. "Hey!" I said. "Jonquil wants you to stick around. What do you say?"

He looked at me, and his eyes were all baby, nothing else.

"Well?"

He made some tremendous mental effort, pursed his lips, took a deep breath, held it for an unconscionable time, and then one word burst out. "Percy!"

"I get it," I said. "So long, fella."

He didn't say anything; just went back to his sunbeam.

"It's O.K. with him," I said when I got back to the table.

"You never struck me as the kind of man who would play games with children," laughed Jonquil. "You'll do . . . you'll do. Michaele, dear—I want you to write to me. I'm so glad you came."

So we got our thirty grand. We wrote as soon as we reached the shack—*our* shack, now—that no, the people wouldn't want Percy back, and that his last name was—Fay. We got a telegram in return thanking us and telling us that Jonquil was adopting the baby.

"You goin' to miss ol' Butch?" I asked Mike.

"No," she said. "Not too much. I'm sort of saving up."

"Oh," I said.

MEDUSA

This is fun too, but of a whole different order of magnitude. Some fun is, by its nature, trivial. This kind, however, is at base deeply thoughtful, though it masquerades as a comedy. It is, in short— metaphor.

I wasn't sore at them. I didn't know what they'd done to me, exactly—I knew that some of it wasn't so nice, and that I'd probably never be the same again. But I was a volunteer, wasn't I? I'd asked for it. I'd signed a paper authorizing the department of commerce of the league to use me as they saw fit. When they pulled me out of the fleet for routine examinations, and when they started examinations that were definitely not routine, I didn't kick. When they asked for volunteers for a project they didn't bother to mention by name, I accepted it sight unseen. And now—

"How do you feel, Rip?" old Doc Renn wanted to know. He spoke to me easylike, with his chin on the backs of his hands and his elbows on the table. The greatest name in psychoscience, and he talks to me as if he were my old man. Right up there in front of the whole psycho board, too.

"Fine, sir," I said. I looked around. I know all the doctors and one or two of the visitors. All the medicos had done one job or another on me in the last three years. Boy, did they put me through the mill. I understood only a fraction of it all—the first color tests, for instance, and the electro-coordination routines. But that torture machine of Grenfell's, and that copper helmet that Winton made me wear for two months—talk about your nightmares! What they were doing to or for me was something I could only guess at. Maybe they were testing me for something. Maybe I was just a guinea pig. Maybe I was in training for something. It was no use asking, either. I volunteered, didn't I?

"Well, Rip," Doc Renn was saying, "it's all over now—the preliminaries, I mean. We're going ahead with the big job."

"Preliminaries?" I goggled. "You mean to tell me that what I've been through for the last three years was all preliminaries?"

Renn nodded, watching me carefully. "You're going on a little trip. It may not be fun, but it'll be interesting."

"Trip? Where to?" This was good news; the repeated drills on spaceship techniques, the refresher courses on astrogation, had given me a good-sized itch to get out into the black again.

"Sealed orders," said Renn, rather sharply. "You'll find out. The important thing for you to remember is that you have a very important role to play." He paused; I could see him grimly ironing the snappiness out of his tone. Why in Canaan did he have to be so careful with *me*? "You will be put aboard a Forfield Super—the latest and best equipped that the league can furnish. Your job is to tend the control machinery, and to act as assistant astrogator no matter what happens. Without doubt you will find your position difficult at times. You are to obey your orders as given, without question, and without the use of force where possible."

This sounded screwy to me. "That's all written up, just about word for word, in the 'Naval Manual,' " I reminded him gently, "under 'Duties of Crew.' I've had to do all you said every time I took a ship out. Is there anything special about this one, that it calls for all this underlining?"

He was annoyed, and the board shuffled twenty-two pairs of feet. But his tone was still friendly, half-persuasive when he spoke. "There is definitely something special about this ship, and—its crew. Rip, you've come through everything we could hand you, with flying colors. Frankly, you were subjected to psychic forces that were enough to drive a normal man quite mad. The rest of the crew—it is only fair to tell you—are insane. The nature of this expedition necessitates our manning the ship that way. Your place on the ship is a key position. Your responsibility is a great one."

"Now—hold on, sir," I said. "I'm not questioning your orders, sir, and I consider myself under your disposition. May I ask a few questions?"

He nodded.

"You say the crew is insane. Isn't that a broad way of putting it—" I couldn't help needling him; he was trying so hard to keep calm—"for a psychologist?"

He actually grinned. "It is. To be more specific, they're schizoids—dual personalities. Their primary egos are paranoiac. They're perfectly rational except on the subject of their particular phobia—or mania, as the case may be. The recessive personality is a manic depressive."

Now, as I remembered it, most paranoiacs have delusions of grandeur coupled with a persecution mania. And a manic depressive is the "Yes master" type. They just didn't mix. I took the liberty of saying as much to one of Earth's foremost psychoscientists.

"Of course they don't mix," snapped Renn. "I didn't say they did. There's no interflowing of egos in these cases. They are schizoids. The cleavage is perfect."

I have a mole under my arm that I scratch when I'm thinking hard. I scratched it. "I didn't know anything like that existed," I said. Renn seemed bent on keeping this informal, and I was playing it to the limit. I sensed that this was the last chance I'd have to get any information about the expedition.

"There never were any cases like that until recently," said Renn patiently. "Those men came out of our laboratories."

"Oh. Sort of made-to-order insanity?" He nodded.

"What on earth for, sir?"

"Sealed orders," he said immediately. His manner became abrupt again. "You take off tomorrow. You'll be put aboard tonight. Your commanding officer is Captain William Parks." I grinned delightedly at this. Parks—the horny old fireater! They used to say of him that he could create sunspots by spitting straight up. But he was a real spaceman—through and through. "And don't forget, Rip," Renn finished. "There is only one sane man aboard that ship. That is all."

I saluted and left.

A Forfield Super is as sweet a ship as anything ever launched. There's none of your great noisy bulk pushed through the ether by a cityful of men, nor is it your completely automatic "Eyehope"—so called because after you slipped your master control tape into the automatic pilot you always said, "you're on your way, you little hunk of tinfoil—I hope!"

With an eight-man crew, a Forfield can outrun and outride anything else in space. No rockets—no celestial helices—no other such clumsy nonsense drives it. It doesn't go places by going—it gets there by standing still. By which I mean that the ship achieves what laymen call "Universal stasis."

The Galaxy is traveling in an orbit about the mythical Dead Center at an almost incredible velocity. A Forfield, with momentum nullified, just stops dead while the Galaxy streams by. When the objective approaches, momentum is resumed, and the ship appears in normal space with only a couple of thousand miles to go. That is possible because the lack of motion builds up a potential in motion; motion, being a relative thing, produces a set of relative values.

Instead of using the terms "action" and "reaction" in speaking of the Forfield drive, we speak of "stasis" and "re-stasis." I'd explain further but I left my spherical slide rule home. Let me add only that a Forfield can achieve stasis in regard to planetary, solar, galactic or universal orbits. Mix 'em in the right proportions, and you get resultants that will take you anywhere, fast.

I was so busy from the instant I hit the deck that I didn't have time to think of all the angles of this more-than-peculiar trip. I had to check and double-check every control and instrument from the milliammeter to the huge compound integrators, and with a twenty-four-hour deadline that was no small task. I also had to take a little instruction from a league master mechanic who had installed a couple of gadgets which had been designed and tested at the last minute expressly for this trip. I paid little attention to what went on round me; I didn't even know the skipper was aboard until I rose from my knees before the integrators, swiveled around on my way to the control board, and all but knocked the old war horse off his feet.

"Rip! I'll be damned!" he howled. "Don't tell me—you're not signed on here?"

"Yup," I said. "Let go my hand, skipper—I got to be able to hold a pair of needle noses for another hour or so. Yeah, I heard you were going to captain this barrel. How do you like it?"

"Smooth," he said, looking around, then bringing his grin back to me. He only grinned twice a year because it hurt his face; but when he did, he did it all over. "What do you know about the trip?"

"Nothing except that we have sealed orders."

"Well, I'll bet there's some kind of a honkatonk at the end of the road," said Parks. "You and I've been on . . . how many is it? Six? Eight . . . anyway, we've been on plenty of ships together, and we managed to throw a whingding ashore every trip. I hope we can get out Aldeberan way. I hear Susie's place is under new management again. Heh! Remember the time we—"

I laughed. "Let's save it, skipper. I've got to finish this check-up, and fast. But, man, it's good to see you again." We stood looking at each other, and then something popped into my head and I felt my smile washing off. What was it that Dr. Renn had said—"Remember there's only one sane man aboard!" Oh, no—they hadn't put Captain Parks through that! Why—

I said, "How do you—feel, cap'n?"

"Swell," he said. He frowned. "Why? You feel all right?"

Not right then, I didn't. Captain Parks batty? That was just a little bit lousy. If Renn was right—and he was always right—then his board had given Parks the works, as well as the rest of the crew. All but me, that is. I knew I wasn't crazy. I didn't feel crazy. "I feel fine," I said.

"Well, go ahead then," said Parks, and turned his back.

I went over to the control board, disconnected the power leads from the radioscope, and checked the dials. For maybe five minutes I felt the old boy's eyes drilling into the nape of my neck, but I was too upset to say anything more. It got very quiet in there. Small noises drifted into the control room from other parts of the ship. Finally I heard his shoulder brush the doorpost as he walked out.

How much did the captain know about this trip? Did he know that he had a bunch of graduates from the laughing academy to man his ship? I tried to picture Renn informing Parks that he was a paranoiac and a manic depressive, and I failed miserably. Parks would probably take a swing at the doctor. Aw, it just didn't make sense. It occurred to me that "making sense" was a criterion that we put too much faith in. What do you do when you run across something that isn't even supposed to make sense?

I slapped the casing back on the radioscope, connected the leads, and called it quits. The speaker over the forward post rasped out, "All hands report to control chamber!" I started, stuck my tools into their clips under the chart table and headed for the door. Then I remembered I was already in the control room, and subsided against the bulkhead.

They straggled in. All hands were in the pink, well fed and eager. I nodded to three of them, shook hands with another. The skipper came in without looking at me—I rather thought he avoided my eyes. He went straight forward, faced about and put his hands low enough on the canted control board so he could sit on them. Seabiscuit, the quartermaster, and an old shipmate of mine, came and stood beside me. There was an embarrassed murmur of voices while we all awaited the last two stragglers.

Seabiscuit whispered to me, "I once said I'd sail clear to Hell if Bill Parks was cap'n of the ship."

I said, out of the side of my face, "So?"

"So it looks like I'm goin' to," said the Biscuit.

The captain called the roll. That crew was microscopically hand picked. I had heard every single one of the names he called in connection with some famous escapade or other. Harry Voight was our chemist. He is the man who kept two hundred passengers alive for a month with little more than a week's supply of air and water to work with, after the liner crossed bows with a meteorite on the Pleione run. Bort Brecht was the engineer, a man who could do three men's work with his artificial hand alone. He lost it in the *Pretoria* disaster. The gunner was Hoch McCoy, the guy who "invented" the bow and arrow and saved his life when he was marooned on an asteroid in the middle of a pack of poison-toothed "Jackrabbits." The mechanics were Phil and Jo Hartley, twins, whose resemblance enabled them to change places time and again during the Insurrection, thus running bales of vital information to the league high command.

"Report," he said to me.

"All's well in the control chamber, sir," I said formally.

"Brecht?"

"All's well back aft, sir."

"Quartermaster?"

"Stores all aboard and stashed away, sir," said the Biscuit.

Parks turned to the control board and threw a lever. The air locks slid shut, the thirty-second departure signal began to sound from the oscillator on the hull and from signals here and in the engineer's chamber. Parks raised his voice to be heard over their clamor.

"I don't know where we're goin'," he said, with an odd smile, "but—" the signals stopped, and that was deafening—"we're on our way!"

The master control he had thrown had accomplished all the details of taking off—artificial gravity, "solar" and "planetary" stases, air pumps, humidifiers—everything. Except for the fact that there was suddenly no light streaming in through the portholes any more, there was no slightest change in sensation. Parks reached out and tore the seals off the tape slot on the integrators and from the door of the orders file. He opened the cubbyhole and drew out a thick envelope. There was something in my throat I couldn't swallow.

He tore it open and pulled out eight envelopes and a few folded sheets of paper. He glanced at the envelopes and, with raised eyebrows, handed them to me. I took them. There was one addressed to each member of the crew. At a nod from the skipper I distributed them. Parks unfolded his orders and looked at them.

"Orders," he read. "By authority of the Solar League, pertaining to destination and operations of Xantippean Expedition No. 1."

Startled glances were batted back and forth. Xantippe! No one had ever been to Xantippe! The weird, cometary planet of Betelgeuse was, and had always been, taboo—and for good reason.

Parks's voice was tight. "Orders to be read to crew by the captain immediately upon taking off." The skipper went to the pilot chair, swiveled it, and sat down. The crew edged closer.

"The league congratulates itself on its choice of a crew for this most important mission. Out of twenty-seven hundred volunteers, these eight men survived the series of tests and conditioning exercises provided by the league.

"General orders are to proceed to Xantippe. Captain and crew have been adequately protected against the field. Object of the expedition is to find the cause of the Xantippe Field and to remove it.

"Specific orders for each member of the crew are enclosed under separate sealed covers. The crew is ordered to read these instructions, to memorize them, and to destroy the orders and envelopes. The league desires that these orders be read in strictest secrecy by each member of the crew, and that the individual contents of the envelopes be held as confidential until contrary orders are issued by the league." Parks drew a deep breath and looked around at his crew.

They were a steady lot. There was evidence of excitement, of surprise, and in at least one case, of shock. But there was no fear. Predominantly, there was a kind of exultance in the spaceburned, hard-bitten faces. They bore a common glory, a common hatred. "That isn't sensible," I told myself. "It isn't natural, or normal, or sane, for eight men to face madness, years of it, with that joyous light in their eyes. But then—they're mad already, aren't they? *Aren't they?*"

It was catching, too. I began to hate Xantippe. Which was, I suppose, silly. Xantippe was a planet, of a sort. Xantippe never killed anybody. It drove men mad, that was all. More than mad—it fused their synapses, reduced them to quivering, mindless hulks, drooling, their useless minds turned super-cargo in a useless body. Xantippe had snared ship upon ship in the old days; ships bound for the other planets of the great star. The mad planet used to blanket them in its mantle of vibrations, and they were never heard from again. It was years before the league discovered where the ships had gone, and then they sent patrols to investigate. They lost eighteen ships and thirty thousand men that way.

And then came the Forfield drive. In the kind of static hyperspace which these ships inhabited, surely they would pass the field unharmed. There were colonists out there on the other planets, depending on supplies from Sol. There were rich sources of radon, uranium, tantalum, copper. Surely a Forfield ship could—

But they couldn't. They were the first ships to penetrate the field, to come out on the other side. The ships were intact, but their crews could use their brains for absolutely nothing. Sure, I hated Xantippe. Crazy planet with its cometary orbit and its unpredictable complex ecliptic. Xantippe had an enormous plot afoot. It was stalking us—even now it was ready to pounce on us, take us all and drain our minds—

I shook myself and snapped out of it. I was dreaming myself into a case of the purple willies. If I couldn't keep my head on my shoulders aboard this spacegoing padded cell, then who would? Who else could?

The crew filed out, muttering. Parks sat on the pilot's chair, watching them, his bright gaze flitting from face to face. When they had gone he began to watch me. Not look at me. Watch me. It made me sore.

"Well?" he said after a time.

"Well *what?*" I barked, insubordinately.

"Aren't you going to read your bedtime story? I am."

"Bed—oh." I slit the envelope, unfolded my orders. The captain did likewise at the extreme opposite side of the chamber. I read:

"Orders by authority of the Solar League pertaining to course of action to be taken by Harl Ripley, astromechanic on Xantippean Expedition No. 1.

"Said Harl Ripley shall follow the rules and regulations as set forth in the naval regulations, up until such time as the ship engages the Xantippean Field.

He is then to follow the orders of the master, except in case of the master's removal from active duty from some unexpected cause. Should such an emergency arise, the command does not necessarily revert to said Harl Ripley, but to the crew member who with the greatest practicability outlines a plan for the following objective: The expedition is to land on Xantippe; if uninhabited, the planet is to be searched until the source of the field is found and destroyed. If inhabited, the procedure of the pro-tem commander must be dictated by events. He is to bear in mind, however, that the primary and only purpose of the expedition is to destroy the Xantippean Field."

That ended the orders; but scrawled across the foot of the page was an almost illegible addendum: "Remember your last board meeting, Rip. And good luck!" The penciled initials were C. Renn, M. Ps. S. That would be Doc Renn.

I was so puzzled that my ears began to buzz. The government had apparently spent a huge pile of money in training us and outfitting the expedition. And yet our orders were as hazy as they could possibly be. And what was the idea of giving separate orders to each crew member? And such orders! "The procedure of the pro-tem commander must be dictated by events." That's what you'd call putting us on our own! It wasn't like the crisp, detailed commands any navy man is used to. It was crazy.

Well, of course it was crazy, come to think of it. What else could you expect with this crew? I began to wish sincerely that the board had driven me nuts along with the rest of them.

I was at the chart table, coding up the hundred-hour log entry preparatory to slipping it into the printer, when I sensed someone behind me. The skipper, of course. He stayed there a long time, and I knew he was watching me.

I sat there until I couldn't stand it any longer. "Come on in," I said without moving. Nothing happened. I listened carefully until I could hear his careful breathing. It was short, swift. He was trying to breathe in a whisper. I began to be really edgy. I had a nasty suspicion that if I whirled I would be just in time to catch a bolt from a by-by gun.

Clenching my jaw till my teeth hurt, I rose slowly, and without looking around, went to the power-output telltales and looked at them. I didn't know what was the matter with me. I'd never been this way before—always expecting attack from somewhere. I used to be a pretty nice guy. As a matter of fact, I used to be the nicest guy I knew. I didn't feel that way any more.

Moving to the telltales took me another six or eight feet from the man at the door. Safer for both of us. And this way I had to turn around to get back to the table. I did. It wasn't the skipper. It was the chemist, Harry Voight. We were old shipmates, and I knew him well.

"Hello, Harry. Why the dark-companion act?"

He was tense. He was wearing a little mustache of perspiration on his upper lip. His peculiar eyes—the irises were as black as the pupils—were set so far back in his head that I couldn't see them, for the alleyway light was directly over his head. His bald, bulging forehead threw two deep purple shadows, and out of them he watched me.

"Hi, Rip. Busy?"

"Not too busy. Put it in a chair."

He came in and sat down. He turned as he passed me, backed into the pilot's seat. I perched on the chart table. It looked casual, and it kept my weight on one foot. If I had to move in any direction, including up, I was ready to.

After a time he said, "What do you think of this, Rip?" His gesture took in the ship, Xantippe, the league, the board.

"I only work here," I quoted. That was the motto of the navy. Our insignia is the league symbol superimposed on a flaming sun, under which is an ultraradio screen showing the words, "I only work here." The famous phrase expresses the utmost in unquestioning, devoted duty.

Harry smiled a very sickly smile. If ever I saw a man with something eating him, it was Harry Voight. "S'matter," I asked quietly. "Did somebody do you something?"

He looked furtively about him, edged closer. "Rip, I want to tell you something. Will you close the door?"

I started to refuse, and then reflected that regulations could stand a little relaxing in a coffin like this one. I went and pressed the panel, and it slid closed. "Make it snappy," I said. "If the skipper comes up here and finds that door closed he'll slap some wrists around here."

As soon as the door closed, Harry visibly slumped. "This is the first time in two days I've felt—comfortable," he said. He looked at me with sudden suspicion. "Rip—when we roomed together in Venus City, what color was that jacket I used to keep my 'Naval Manual' in?"

I frowned. I'd only seen the thing a couple of times—"Blue," I said.

"That's right." He wiped his forehead. "You're O.K." He made a couple of false starts and then said, "Rip, will you keep everything I say strictly to yourself? Nobody can be trusted here—nobody!" I nodded. "Well," he went on in a strained voice, "I know that this is a screwy trip. I know that the crew is—has been made—sort of—well, not normal—"

He said, with conviction, "The league has its own reason for sending us, and I don't question them. But something has gone wrong. You think Xantippe is going to get us? Ha! Xantippe is getting us now!" He sat back triumphantly.

"You don't say!"

"But I do! I know she's countless thousands of light years away. But I don't have to tell you of the power of Xantippe. For a gigantic power like that, a little project like what they're doing to us is nothing. Any force that can throw out a field three quarters of a billion miles in diameter can play hell with us at a far greater distance."

"Could be," I said. "Just what are they doing?"

"They're studying us," he hissed. "They're watching each of us, our every action, our every mental reflex. And one by one they are—taking us away! They've got the Hartley twins, and Bort Brecht, and soon they'll have me. I don't know about the others, but their turns will come. They are taking away our personalities, and substituting their own. I tell you, those three men—and soon now, I with them—those men are not humans, but Xantippeans!"

"Now wait," I said patiently. "Aren't you going on guesswork? Nobody knows if Xantippe's inhabited. And I doubt that this substitution you speak of can be done."

"You don't think so? For pity's sake, Rip—for your own good, try to believe me! The Xantippean Field is a thought force, isn't it? And listen—I know it if you don't—this crew was picked for its hatred of Xantippe. Don't you see why? The board expects that hatred to act as a mental 'fender'—to partly ward off the field. They think there might be enough left of our minds when we're inside the field to accomplish our objective. They're wrong, Rip—*wrong!* The very existence of our communal hatred is the thing that has given us away. They have been ready for us for days now—and they are already doing their work aboard."

He subsided, and I prodded him with gentle questions.

"How do you know the Xantippeans have taken away those three men?"

"Because I happened to overhear the Hartley twins talking in the messroom two days ago. They were talking about their orders. I know I should not have listened, but I was already suspicious."

"They were talking about their orders? I understood that the orders were confidential."

"They were. But you can't expect the Hartleys to pay much attention to that. Anyway, Jo confided that a footnote on his orders had intimated that there was only one sane man aboard. Phil laughed that off. He said he knew he was sane, and he knew that Jo was sane. Now, I reason this way. Only a crazy man would question the league; a crazy man or an enemy. Now the Hartleys may be unbalanced, but they are still rational. They are still navy men. Therefore, they must be enemies, because navy men never question the league."

I listened to that vague logic spoken in that intense, convincing voice, and I didn't know what to think. "What about Bort Brecht—and yourself?"

"Bort! Ahh!" His lips curled. "I can sense an alien ego when I speak to him. It's overwhelming. I hate Xantippe," he said wildly, "but I hate Bort Brecht more! The only thing I could possibly hate more than Xantippe would be a Xantippean. That proves my point!" He spread his hands. "As for me—Rip, I'm going mad. I feel it. I see things—and when I do, I will be another of them. And then we will all be lost. For there is only one sane man aboard this ship, and that is me, and when I'm turned into an Xantippean, we will be doomed, and I want you to kill me!" He was half hysterical. I let him simmer down.

"And do I look crazy?" I asked. "If you are the only sane man—"

"Not crazy," he said quickly. "A schizoid—but you're perfectly rational. You must be, or you wouldn't have remembered what color my book jacket was."

I got up, reached out a hand to help him to his feet. He drew back. "Don't touch me!" he screamed, and when I recoiled, he tried to smile. "I'm sorry, Rip, but I can't be sure about anything. You may be a Xantippean by now, and touching me might . . . I'll be going now . . . I—" He went out, his black, burning eyes half closed.

I stood at the door watching him weave down the alleyway. I could guess what was the matter. Paranoia—but bad! There was the characteristic persecution mania, the intensity of expression, the peculiar single-track logic—even delusions of grandeur. Heh! He thought *he* was the one mentally balanced man aboard!

I walked back to the chart table, thinking hard. Harry always had been pretty tight-lipped. He probably wouldn't spread any panic aboard. But I'd better tip the captain off. I was wondering why the Hartley twins and Harry Voight had all been told that all hands but me were batty, when the skipper walked in.

"Rip," he said without preamble. "Did you ever have a fight with Hoch McCoy?"

"Good gosh, no!" I said. "I never saw him in my life until the day we sailed. I've heard of him, of course. Why?"

Parks looked at me oddly. "He just left my quarters. He had the most long-winded and detailed song and dance about how you were well known as an intersolar master saboteur. Gave names and dates. The names I know well. But the dates—well, I can alibi you for half of 'em. I didn't tell him that. But—Lord! He almost had me convinced!"

"Another one!" I breathed. And then I told him about Harry Voight.

"I don't imagine Doc Renn thought they would begin to break so soon," said Parks when I had finished. "These boys were under laboratory conditions for three solid years, you know."

"I didn't know," I said. "I don't know a damn thing that's going on around here and I'd better learn something before I go off my kilter, too."

"Why, Ripley," he said mockingly. "You're overwrought!" Well, I was. Parks said, "I don't know much more than you do, but that goofy story of Harry Voight's has a couple of pretty shrewd guesses in it. For instance, I think he was right in assuming that the board had done something to the minds of . . . ah . . . some of the crew as armor against the field. Few men have approached it consciously—those who have were usually scared half to death. It's well known that fear forms the easiest possible entrance for the thing feared—ask any good hypnotist. Hate is something different again. Hate is a psychological block against fear and the thing to be feared. And the kind of hate that these guys have for Xantippe and the field is something extra special. They're mad, but they're not afraid—and that's no accident. When we do hit the field, it's bound to have less effect on us than it had on the crews of poor devils who tried to attack it."

"That sounds reasonable. Er . . . skipper, about this 'one sane man' business. What do you think of that?"

"More armor," said Parks. "But armor against the man himself. Harry, for instance, was made a paranoiac, which is a very sensible kind of nut; but at the same time he was convinced that he alone was sane. If he thought his mind had been actually tampered with instead of just—tested, he'd get all upset about it and, like as not, undo half the Psy Board's work."

Some of that struck some frightening chords in my memory. "Cap'n—do you believe that there is one sane, normal man aboard?"

"I do. One." He smiled slowly. "I know what you're thinking. You'd give anything to compare your orders with mine, wouldn't you?"

"I would. But I won't do it. Confidential. I couldn't let myself do it even if you agreed, because—" I paused.

"Well?"

"Because you're an officer and I'm a gentleman."

In my bunk at last, I gave over wishing that we'd get to the field and have it over with, and tried to do some constructive thinking. I tried to remember exactly what Doc Renn had said, and when I did, I was sorry I'd made the effort. "You are sane," and "You have been subjected to psychic forces that are sufficient to drive a normal man quite mad" might easily be totally different things. I'd been cocky enough to assume that they meant the same thing. Well, face it. Was I crazy? I didn't feel crazy. Neither did Harry Voight. He thought he was going crazy, but he was sure he hadn't got there yet. And what was "crazy," anyway? It was normal, on this ship, to hate Xantippe so much that you felt sick and sweated cold when you thought of it. Paranoia—persecution. Did I feel persecuted? Only by the thought of our duty toward Xantippe, and the persecution was Xantippe, not the duty. Did I have delusions of grandeur? Of course not; and yet—hadn't I blandly assumed that Voight had such delusions because he thought *he* was the one sane man aboard?

What was the idea of that, anyway? Why had the board put one sane man aboard—if it had? Perhaps to be sure that one man reacted differently to the others at the field, so that he could command. Perhaps merely to make each man feel that he was sane, even though he wasn't. My poor, tired brain gave it up and I slept.

*   *   *

We had two casualties before we reached the field. Harry Voight cut his throat in the washroom, and my gentle old buddy, Seabiscuit, crushed in the back of Hoch McCoy's head. "He was an Insurrectionist spy," he insisted mildly, time and again, while we were locking him up.

After that we kept away from each other. I don't think I spoke ten words to anyone outside of official business, from that day until we snapped into galactic stasis near Betelgeuse. I was sorry about Hoch, because he was a fine lad. But my sorrow was tempered by the memory of his visit to the captain. There had been a pretty fine chance of his doing that to me!

In normal space once more, we maneuvered our agile little craft into an orbit about the huge sun and threw out our detectors. These wouldn't tell us much when the time came, for their range wasn't much more than the radius of the field.

The mad planet swam up onto the plates and I stared at it as I buzzed for the skipper. Xantippe was a strangely dull planet, even this close to her star. She shone dead silver, like a moonlit corpses's flesh. She was wrinkled and patched, and—perhaps it was an etheric disturbance—she seemed to pulsate slowly from pole to pole. She wasn't quite round; more nearly an ovoid, with the smaller end toward Betelgeuse! She was between two and three times the size of Luna. Gazing at her, I thought of the thousands of men of my own service who had fallen prey to her, and of the fine ships of war that had plunged into the field and disappeared. Had they crashed? Had they been tucked into some weird warp of space? Were they captives of some strange and horrible race?

Xantippe had defied every type of attack so far. She swallowed up atomic mines and torpedoes with no appreciable effect. She was apparently impervious to any rayed vibration known to man; but she was matter, and should be easy meat for an infragun—if you could get an infragun close enough. The gun's twin streams of highly charged particles, positrons on one side, mesatrons on the other, would destroy anything that happened to be where they converged. But an infragun has an effective range of less than five hundred miles. Heretofore, any ship which carried the weapon that close to Xantippe carried also a dead or mindless crew.

Captain Parks called the crew into the control room as soon as he arrived. No one spoke much; they didn't need any more information after they had glanced at the view-plate which formed the forward wall of the chamber. Bort Brecht, the swarthy engineer, wanted to know how soon we'd engage the field.

"In about two hours," said the captain glibly. I got a two-handed grip on myself to keep from yapping. He was a cold-blooded liar—we'd hit it in half an hour or less, the way I figured it. I guessed that he had his own reasons. Perhaps he thought it would be easier on the crew that way.

Parks leaned casually against the integrators and faced the crew. "Well, gentlemen," he said as if he were banqueting on Earth, "we'll soon find out what this is all about. I have instructions from the league to place certain information at your disposal.

"All hands are cautioned to obey the obvious commander once we're inside the field. That commander may or may not be myself. That has been arranged for. Each man must keep in mind the objective—the destruction of the Xantippean Field. One of us will lead the others toward that objective. Should no one seem to be in command a pro-tem captain is to be elected."

Brecht spoke up. "Cap'n, how do we know that this 'commander' that has been arranged for isn't Harry Voight or Hoch McCoy?"

"We don't know," said Parks gravely. "But we will. We will."

Twenty-three minutes after Xantippe showed up on the plates, we engaged her field.

All hands were still in the control room when we plunged in. I remember the sudden weakness of my limbs, and the way all five of the others slipped and slid down to the deck. I remember the Biscuit's quaver, "I tell you it's all a dirty Insurrectionist plot." And then I was down on the deck, too.

Something was hurting me, but I knew exactly where I was. I was under Dr. Grenfell's torture machine; it was tearing into my mind, chilling my brain. I could feel my brains, every last convolution of them. They were getting colder and colder, and bigger and bigger, and pretty soon now they would burst my skull and the laboratory and the buildings and chill the earth. Inside my chest I was hot, and of course I knew why. I was Betelgeuse, mightiest of suns, and with my own warmth I warmed half a galaxy. Soon I would destroy it, too, and that would be nice.

All the darkness in Great Space came to me.

Leave me alone. I don't care what you want done. I just want to lie here and— But nobody wanted me to do anything. What's all the hollering about, then? Oh. *I* wanted something done. There's something that has to be done, so get up, get up, get—

"He *is* dead. Death is but a sleep and a forgetting, and he's asleep, and he's forgotten everything, so he must be dead!" It was Phil Hartley. He was down on his hunkers beside me, shrieking at the top of his voice, mouthing and pointing like an ape completely caught up in the violence of his argument. Which was odd, because he wasn't arguing with anybody. The skipper was sitting silently in the pilot's chair, tears streaming down his cheeks. Jo Hartley was dead or passed out on the deck. The Biscuit and Bort Brecht were sitting on the deck holding hands like children, staring entranced into the viewplate. It showed a quadrant of Xantippe, filling the screen. The planet's surface did indeed pulsate, and it was a beautiful sight. I wanted to watch it drawing closer and closer, but there was something that had to be done first.

I sat up achingly. "Get me some water," I muttered to Phil Hartley. He looked at me, shrieked, and went and hid under the chart table.

The vision of Xantippe caught and held me again, but I shook it off. It was the most desirable thing I'd ever seen, and it promised me all I could ever want, but there was something I had to do first. Maybe someone could tell me. I shook the skipper's shoulder.

"Go away," he said. I shook him again. He made no response. Fury snapped into my brain. I cuffed him with my open hand, front and back, front and back. He leaped to his feet, screamed, "Leave me alone!" and slumped back into the chair. At the sound Bort Brecht lurched to his feet and came over to us. When he let go Seabiscuit's hand, the Biscuit began to cry quietly.

"I'm giving the orders around here," Bort said.

I was delighted. There had been something, a long time ago, about somebody giving orders. "I have to do something," I said. "Do you know what it is?"

"Come with me." He led the way, swaggering, to the screen. "Look," he commanded, and then sat down beside Seabiscuit and lost himself in contemplation. Seabiscuit kept on crying.

"That's not it," I said doubtfully. "I think you gave me the wrong orders."

"Wrong?" he bellowed. "Wrong? I am never wrong!" He got up, and before I knew what was coming, he hauled off and cracked three knuckles with my jawbone. I hit the deck with a crash and slid up against Jo Hartley. Jo didn't move. He was alive, but he just didn't seem to give a damn. I lay there for a long time before I could get up again. I wanted to kill Bort Brecht, but there was something I had to do first.

I went back to the captain and butted him out of the chair. He snarled at me and went and crouched by the bulkhead, tears still streaming down his cheeks. I slumped into the seat, my fingers wandering idly about the controls without touching them, my eyes desperately trying to avoid the glory of Xantippe.

It seemed to me that I was very near to the thing I was to do. My right hand touched the infragun activator switch, came away, went back to it, came away. I boldly threw another switch; a network of crosshairs and a bright central circle appeared on the screen. This was it, I thought. Bort Brecht yelped like a kicked dog when the crosshairs appeared, but did not move. I activated the gun, and grasped the range lever in one hand and the elevation control in the other. A black-centered ball of flame hovered near the surface of the planet.

This was it! I laughed exultantly and pushed the range lever forward. The ball plunged into the dull-silver mystery, leaving a great blank crater. I pulled and pushed at the elevation control, knowing that my lovely little ball was burning and tearing its inexorable way about in the planet's vitals. I drew it out to the surface, lashed it up and down and right and left, cut and slashed and tore.

Bort Brecht was crouched like an anthropoid, knees bent, knuckles on the deck, fury knotting his features, eyes fixed on the scene of destruction. Behind me Phil Hartley was teetering on tiptoe, little cries of pain struggling out of his lips every time the fireball appeared. Bort spun and was beside me in one great leap. "What's happening? Who's doing that?"

"He is," I said immediately, pointing at Jo Hartley. I knew that this was going to be tough on Jo, but I was doing the thing I had to do, and I knew Bort would try to stop me. Bort leaped on the prone figure, using teeth and nails and fists and feet; and Phil Hartley hesitated only a minute, torn between the vision of Xantippe and something that called to him from what seemed a long, long while ago. Then Jo cried out in agony, and Phil, a human prototype of my fireball, struck Bort amidships. Back and forth, fore and aft, the bloody battle raged, while Seabiscuit whimpered and the skipper, still sunk in his introspective trance, wept silently. And I cut and stabbed and ripped at Xantippe.

I took care now, and cut a long slash almost from pole to pole; and the edges opened away from the wound as if the planet had been wrapped in a paper sheath. Underneath it was an olive-drab color, shot with scarlet. I cut at this incision again and again, sinking my fireball in deeper at each slash. The weakened ovoid tended to press the edges together, but the irresistible ball sheared them away as it passed; and when it had cut nearly all the way through, the whole structure fell in on itself horribly. I had a sudden feeling of lightness, and then unbearable agony. I remember stretching back and back over the chair in the throes of some tremendous attack from inside my body, and then I struck the deck with my head and shoulders, and I was all by myself again in the beautiful black.

There was a succession of lights that hurt, and soothing smells, and the sound of arcs and the sound of falling water. Some of them were weeks apart, some seconds. Sometimes I was conscious and could see people tiptoeing about. Once I thought I heard music.

But at last I awoke quietly, very weak, to a hand on my shoulder. I looked up. It was Dr. Renn. He looked older.

"How do you feel, Rip?"

"Hungry."

He laughed. "That's splendid. Know where you are?"

I shook my head, marveling that it didn't hurt me.

"Earth," he said. "Psy hospital. You've been through the mill, son."

"What happened?"

"Plenty. We got the whole story from the picrecording tapes inside and outside of your ship. You cut Xantippe all to pieces. You incidentally got Bort Brecht started on the Hartley family, which later literally cut *him* to pieces. It cost three lives, but Xantippe is through."

"Then—I destroyed the projector, or whatever it was—"

"You destroyed Xantippe. You—killed Xantippe. The planet was a . . . a thing that I hardly dare think about. You ever see a hydromedusa here on Earth?"

"You mean one of those jellyfish that floats on the surface of the sea and dangles paralyzing tentacles down to catch fish?"

"That's it. Like a Portuguese man-of-war. Well, that was Xantippe, with that strange mind field about her for her tentacles. A space dweller; she swept up anything that came her way, killed what was killable, digested what was digestible to her. Examination of the pictures, incidentally, shows that she was all set to hurl out a great cloud of spores. One more revolution about Betelgeuse and she'd have done it."

"How come I went under like that?" I was beginning to remember.

"You weren't as well protected as the others. You see, when we trained that crew we carefully split the personalities; paranoiac hatred to carry them through the field and an instant reversion to manic depressive under the influence of the field. But yours was the only personality we couldn't split. So you were the leader—you were delegated to do the job. All we could do to you was to implant a desire to destroy Xantippe. You did the rest. But when the psychic weight of the field was lifted from you, your mind collapsed. We had a sweet job rebuilding it, too, let me tell you!"

"Why all that business about the 'one sane man?' "

Renn grinned. "That was to keep the rest of the crew fairly sure of themselves, and to keep you from the temptation of taking over before you reached the field, knowing that the rest, including the captain, were not responsible for their actions."

"What about the others, after the field disappeared?"

"They reverted to something like normal. Not quite, though. The quartermaster tied up the rest of the crew just before they reached Earth and handed them over to us as Insurrectionist spies!

"But as for you, there's a command waiting for you if you want it."

"I want it," I said. He clapped me on the shoulder and left. Then they brought me a man-sized dinner.

THE MARTIAN AND THE MORON

This is one of the first writings after that long period of silence. Oddly enough it comes out as comedy—sheer joyous comedy for itself, with no effort to be metaphor or anything else but itself. The events concerning the cessation of all broadcasts during the near approach of Mars in the 'twenties, did indeed happen; and back in those days of newspaper articles about guys who built crystal sets into peanuts, of 100-foot braided copper antennas enabling you to pick up Chicago all the way from Philadelphia, late at night, of cats-whiskers and variocouplers (anybody out there know what a variocouple is? I mean, was?) back in those days, there was surely more than one radio buff with flanged-up equipment like that "dad" built in his basement. As for that girl—I think I met that girl one time at a party. *Nov shmoz ka pop!*

In 1924, when I was just a pup, my father was a thing currently known as a "radio bug." These creatures were wonderful. They were one part fanatic, one part genius, a dash of childlike wonderment, and two buckets full of trial-and-error. Those were the days when you could get your picture in the paper for building a crystal set in something smaller and more foolish than the character who had his picture in the paper the day before. My father had his picture in there for building a "set" on a pencil eraser with a hunk of galena in the top and about four thousand turns of No. 35 enamelled wire wrapped around it. When they came around to take his picture he dragged out another one built into a peanut. Yes, a real peanut which brought in WGBS, New York. (You see,

I really do remember.) They wanted to photograph that too, but Dad thought it would be a little immodest for him to be in the paper twice. So they took Mother's picture with it. The following week they ran both pictures, and Dad got two letters from other radio bugs saying his eraser radio wouldn't work and Mother got two hundred and twenty letters, forwarded from the paper, twenty-six of which contained proposals of marriage. (Of course Mother was a YL and not an OW then.)

Oddly enough, Dad never did become a radio ham. He seemed satisfied to be the first in the neighborhood to own a set, then to build a set—(after the spiderweb coil phase he built and operated a one-tube regenerative set which featured a UX-11 detector and a thing called a vario-coupler which looked like a greasy fist within a lacquered hand, and reached his triumph when he hooked it into a forty-'leven-pound "B-eliminator" and ran it right out of the socket like a four-hundred-dollar "electric" radio) and first in the state to be on the receiving end of a court-order restraining him from using his equipment (every time he touched the tuning dials—three—the neighboring radios with which Joneses were keeping up with each other, began howling unmercifully). So for a time he left his clutter of forms and wire and solder-spattered "bathtub" condensers shoved to the back of his cellar workbench, and went back to stuffing field mice and bats, which had been his original hobby. I think Mother was glad, though she hated the smells he made down there. That was after the night she went to bed early with the cramps, and he DX'd WLS in Chicago at 4:30 one morning with a crystal set, and wanted to dance. (He learned later that he had crossed aerials with Mr. Bohackus next door, and had swiped Mr. Bohackus' fourteen-tube Atwater-Kent signal right out of Mr. Bohackus' gooseneck-megaphone speaker. Mr. Bohackus was just as unhappy as Mother to hear about this on the following morning. They had both been up all night.)

Dad never was one to have his leg pulled. He got very sensitive about the whole thing, and learned his lesson so well that when the last great radio fever took him, he went to another extreme. Instead of talking his progress all over the house and lot, he walled himself up. During the late war I ran up against security regulations—and who didn't—but they never bothered me. I had my training early.

He got that glint in his eyes after grunting loudly over the evening paper one night. I remember Mother's asking him about it twice, and I remember her sigh—her famous "here we go again" sigh—when he didn't answer. He leapt up, folded the paper, got out his keys, opened the safe, put the paper in it, locked the safe, put his keys away, looked knowingly at us, strode out of the room, went down into the cellar, came up from the cellar, took out his keys, opened the safe, took out the paper, closed the safe, looked knowingly at us again, said, "Henry, your father's going to be famous," and went down into the cellar.

Mother said, "I knew it. I *knew* it! I should have thrown the paper away. Or torn out that page."

"What's he going to make, Mother?" I asked.

"Heavens knows," she sighed. "Some men are going to try to get Mars on the radio."

"Mars? You mean the star?"

"It isn't a star, dear, it's a planet. They've arranged to turn off all the big radio stations all over the world for five minutes every hour so the men can listen to Mars. I suppose your father thinks he can listen too."

"Gee," I said, "I'm going down and—"

"You're going to do no such thing," said Mother firmly. "Get yourself all covered with that nasty grease he uses in his soldering, and stay up until all hours! It's almost bedtime. And—Henry—"

"Yes, Mother?"

She put her hands on my shoulders. "Listen to me, darling. People have been—ah—teasing your father." She meant Mr. Bohackus. "Don't ask him any questions about this if he doesn't want to talk, will you, darling? Promise?"

"All right, Mother." She was a wise woman.

Dad bought a big shiny brass padlock for his workshop in the cellar, and every time Mother mentioned the cellar, or the stars, or radio to him in any connection, he would just smile knowingly at her. It drove her wild. She didn't like the key, either. It was a big brass key, and he wore it on a length of rawhide shoelace tied around his neck. He wore it day and night. Mother said it was lumpy. She also said it was dangerous, which he denied, even after the time down at Roton Point when we were running Mr. Bohackus' new gasoline-driven ice cream freezer out on the beach. Dad leaned over to watch it working. He said, "This is the way to get things done, all right. I can't wait to get into that ice cream," and next thing we knew he was face down in the brine and flopping like a banked trout. We got him out before he drowned or froze. He was bleeding freely about the nose and lips, and Mr. Bohackus was displeased because Dad's key had, in passing through the spur-gears in which it had caught, broken off nine teeth. That was six more than Dad lost, but it cost much more to fix Dad's and showed, Mother said, just how narrow-minded Mr. Bohackus was.

Anyway, Dad never would tell us what he was doing down in the cellar. He would arrive home from work with mysterious packages and go below and lock them up before dinner. He would eat abstractedly and disappear for the whole evening. Mother, bless her, bore it with fortitude. As a matter of fact, I think she encouraged it. It was better than the previous fevers, when she had to sit for hours listening to crackling noises and organ music through big, heavy, magnetic earphones—or else. At least she was left to her own devices while all this was going on. As for me, I knew when I wasn't needed, and, as I remember, managed to fill my life quite successfully with clock movements, school, and baseball, and ceased to wonder very much.

About the middle of August Dad began to look frantic. Twice he worked right through the night, and though he went to the office on the days that followed, I doubt that he did much. On August 21—I remember the date because it was the day before my birthday, and I remember that it was a Thursday because Dad took the next day off for a "long weekend," so *it* must have been Friday—the crisis came. My bedtime was nine o'clock. At nine-twenty Dad came storming up from the cellar and demanded that I get my clothes on instantly and go out and get him two hundred feet of No. 27 silk-covered wire. Mother laid down the law and was instantly overridden. "The coil! The one coil I haven't finished!" he shouted hysterically. "Six thousand meters, and I have to run out of it. *Get* your clothes on this instant, Henry, number twenty-seven wire. Just control yourself this once Mother and you can have Henry stop standing there with your silly eyes bulging and get dressed you can have any hat on Fifth Avenue *hurry!*"

I hurried. Dad gave me some money and a list of places to go to, told me not to come back until I'd tried every one of them, and left the house with me. I went east, he went west. Mother stood on the porch and wrung her hands.

I got home about twenty after ten, weary and excited, bearing a large metal spool of wire. I put it down triumphantly while Mother caught me up and felt me all over as if she had picked me up at the foot of a cliff. She looked drawn. Dad wasn't home yet.

After she quieted down a little she took me into the kitchen and fed me some chocolate-covered doughnuts. I forget what we talked about, if we talked, and at the bottom of the steps I could see a ray of yellow light. "Mother," I said, "you know what? Dad ran out and left his workshop open."

She went to the door and looked down the stairs.

"Darling!" she said after a bit, "Uh—wouldn't you like to—I mean, if he—"

I caught on quick. "I'll look. Will you stay up here and bump on the floor if he comes?"

She looked relieved, and nodded. I ran down the steps and cautiously entered the little shop.

Lined up across the bench were no less than six of the one-tube receivers which were the pinnacle of Dad's electronic achievement. The one at the end was turned back-to-front and had its rear shielding off; a naked coil-form dangled unashamedly out.

And I saw what had happened to the two alarm clocks which had disappeared from the bedrooms in the past six weeks. It happened that then, as now, clocks were my passion, and I can remember clearly the way he had set up pieces of the movements.

He had build a frame about four feet long on a shelf at right angles to the bench on which the radios rested. At one end of the frame was a clock mechanism designed to turn a reel on which was an endless band of paper tape about eight inches wide. The tape passed under a hooded camera—Mother's old Brownie—which was on a wall-bracket and aimed downward, on the tape. Next in line, under the tape, were six earphones, so placed that their dia-phragms (the retainers had been removed) just touched the under side of the tape. And at the other end of the frame was the movement from the second alarm clock. The bell-clapper hung downwards, and attached to it was a small container of black powder.

I went to the first clock mechanism and started it by pulling out the toothpick Dad had jammed in the gears. The tape began to move. I pulled the plug on the other movement. The little container of black powder began to shake like mad and, through small holes, laid an even film of the powder over the moving tape. It stopped when it had put down about ten inches of it. The black line moved slowly across until it was over the phones. The magnets smeared the powder, which I recognized thereby as iron fillings. Bending to peer under the tape, I saw that the whole bank of phones was levered to move downward a half an inch away from the tape. The leads from each of the six phones ran to a separate receiver.

I stood back and looked at this goldberg and scratched my head, then shook same and carefully blew away the black powder on the tape, rewound the movements, refilled the containers from a jar which stood on the bench, and put the toothpick back the way I had found it.

I was halfway up the stairs when the scream of burning rubber on the street outside coincided with Mother's sharp thumping on the floor. I got to her side as she reached the front window. Dad was outside paying off a taxi-driver. He never touched the porch steps at all, and came into the house at a dead run. He had a package under his arm.

"Fred!" said Mother.

"Can't stop now," he said, skidding into the hallway. "Couldn't get 27 anywhere. Have to use 25. Probably won't work. Everything happens to me absolutely everything." He headed for the kitchen.

"I got you a whole reel of 27, Dad."

"Don't bother me now. Tomorrow," he said, and thumped downstairs. Mother and I looked at each other. Mother sighed. Dad came bounding back up the stairs. "You *what?*"

"Here." I got the wire off the hall table and gave it to him. He snatched it up, hugged me, swore I'd get a bicycle for my birthday (he made good on that, and on Mother's Fifth Avenue hat, too, by the way) and dove back downstairs.

We waited around for half an hour and then Mother sent me to bed. "You poor baby," she said, but I had the idea it wasn't me she was sorry for.

Now I'd like to be able to come up with a climax to all this, but there wasn't one. Not for years and years. Dad looked, the next morning, as if he had been up all night again—which he had—and as if he were about to close his fingers on the Holy Grail. All that day he would reappear irregularly, pace up and down, compare his watch with the living-room clock and the hall clock, and sprint downstairs again. That even went on during my birthday dinner. He had Mother call up the office and say he had Twonk's disease, a falling of the armpits (to whom do I owe this gem? Not my gag) and kept up his peregrinations all that night and all the following day until midnight. He fell into bed, so Mother told me, at one ayem Sunday morning and slept right through until suppertime. He still maintained a dazzling silence about his activities. For the following four months he walked around looking puzzled. For a year after that he looked resigned. Then he took up stuffing newts and moles. The only thing he ever said about the whole crazy business was that he was born to be disappointed, but at least, this time, no one could rib him about it. Now I'm going to tell you about Cordelia.

This happened the above-mentioned years and years later. The blow-off was only last week, as a matter of fact. I finished school and went into business with Dad and got mixed up in the war and all that. I didn't get married, though. Not yet. That's what I want to tell you about.

I met her at a party at Ferris's. I was stagging it, but I don't think it would have made any difference if I had brought someone; when I saw Cordelia I was, to understate the matter, impressed.

She came in with some guy I didn't notice at the time and, for all I know, haven't seen since. She slipped out of her light wrap with a single graceful movement; the sleeve caught in her bracelet, and she stood there, full profile, in the doorway, both arms straight and her hands together behind her as she worried the coat free, and I remember the small explosion in my throat as my indrawn breath and my gasp collided. Her hair was dark and lustrous, parted widely in a winging curve away from her brow. There were no pins in it; it shadowed the near side of her face as she bent her head and turned it down and toward the room. The cord of her neck showed columnar and clean. Her lips were parted ever so little, and showed an amused chagrin. Her lashes all but lay on her cheek. They stayed there when she was free and turned to face the room, for she threw her head back and up, flinging her hair behind her. She came across to my side of the party and sat down while the Thing who was with her went anonymously away to get her a drink and came unnoticeably back.

I said to myself, "Henry, my boy, stop staring at the lady. You'll embarrass her."

She turned to me just then and gave me a small smile. Her eyes were widely spaced, and the green of deep water. "I don't mind, really," she said, and I realized I had spoken aloud. I took refuge in a grin, which she answered, and then her left eyelid dropped briefly, and she looked away. It was a wink, but such a slight, tasteful one! If she had used both eyelids, it wouldn't have been a wink at all; she would have looked quickly down and up again. It was an understanding, we're-together little wink, a tactful, gracious, wonderful, marvellous, do you begin to see how I felt?

The party progressed. I once heard somebody decline an invitation to one of Ferris's parties on the grounds that he had *been* to one of Ferris's parties. I had to be a little more liberal than that, but tonight I could see the point. It was because of Cordelia. She sat still, her chin on the back of her hand, her fingers curled against her white throat, her eyes shifting lazily from one point in the room to another. She did not belong in this conglomeration of bubbleheads. Look at her—part Sphinx, part Pallas Athene . . .

Ferris was doing his Kasbah act, with the bath towel over his head. He will next imitate Clyde McCoy's trumpet, I thought. He will then inevitably put that lampshade on his head, curl back his upper lip, and be a rickshaw coolie. Following which he will do the adagio dance in which he will be too rough with some girl who will be too polite to protest at his big shiny wet climaxing kiss.

I looked at Cordelia and I looked at Ferris and I thought, no, Henry; that won't do. I drew a deep breath, leaned over to the girl, and said, "If there were a fire in here, do you know the quickest way out?"

She shook her head expectantly.

"I'll show you," I said, and got up. She hesitated a charming moment, rose from her chair as with helium, murmured something polite to her companion, and came to me.

There were French doors opening on to the wide terrace porch which also served the front door. We went through them. The air was fragrant and cool, and there was a moon. She said nothing about escaping from fires. The French doors shut out most of the party noises—enough so that we could hear night sounds. We looked at the sky. I did not touch her.

After a bit she said in a voice of husky silver,

> *"Is the moon tired? she looks so pale*
> *Within her misty veil:*
> *She scales the sky from east to west,*
> *And takes no rest.*
>
> *"Before the coming of the night*
> *The moon shows papery white;*
> *Before the drawing of the day*
> *She fades away."*

It was simple and it was perfect. I looked at her in wonderment. "Who wrote that?"

"Christina Rosset-ti," she said meticulously, looking at the moon. The light lay on her face like dust, and motes of it were caught in the fine down at the side of her jaw.

"I'm Henry Folwell and I know a place where we could talk for about three hours if we hurry," I said, utterly amazed at myself; I don't generally operate like this.

She looked at the moon and me, the slight deep smile playing subtly with her lips. "I'm Cordelia Thorne, and I couldn't think of it," she said. "Do you think you could get my wrap without anyone seeing? It's a—"

"I know what it's," I said, sprinting. I went in through the front door, located her coat, bunched it up small, skinned back outside, shook it out and brought it to her. "You're still here," I said incredulously.

"Did you think I'd go back inside?"

"I thought the wind, or the gods, or my alarm clock would take you away."

"You said that beautifully," she breathed, as I put the coat around her shoulders. I thought I had too. I notched her high up in my estimation as a very discerning girl.

We went to a place called the Stroll Inn where a booth encased us away from all of the world and most of its lights. It was wonderful. I think I did most of the talking. I don't remember all that passed between us but I remember these things, and remember them well.

I was talking about Ferris and the gang he had over there every Saturday night; I checked myself, shrugged, and said, "Oh well. *Chacun à son goût,* as they say, which means—"

And she stopped me. "Please. Don't translate. It couldn't be phrased as well in English."

I had been about to say "—which means Jack's son has the gout." I felt sobered and admiring, and just sat and glowed at her.

And then there was that business with the cigarette. She stared at it as it lay in the ashtray, followed it with her gaze to my lips and back as I talked, until I asked her about it.

She said in a soft, shivery voice, "I feel just like that cigarette."

I, of course, asked her why.

"You pick it up," she whispered, watching it. "You enjoy some of it. You put it down and let it—smolder. You like it, but you hardly notice it. . . ."

I thereupon made some incredibly advanced protestations.

And there was the business about her silence—a long, faintly amused, inward-turning silence. I asked her what she was thinking about.

"I was ruminating," she said, in a self-depreciating, tragic voice, "on the futility of human endeavor," and she smiled. And when I asked her what she meant, she laughed aloud and said, "Don't you know?" And I said, "Oh. That," and worshipped her. She was deep. I'd have dropped dead before I'd have admitted I didn't know what specifically she was driving at.

And books. Music, too. When we were at the stage where I had both her hands and for minutes on end our foreheads were so close together you couldn't have slipped a swizzle stick between them, I murmured, "We seem to think so much alike. . . . Tell me, Cordelia, have you read Cabell?"

She said, "Well, really," in such a tone that, so help me, I apologized. "Lovely stuff." I said, recovering.

She looked reminiscently over my shoulder, smiling her small smile. "So lovely."

"I knew you'd read him," I said, struck with sweet thunder. "And Faulkner— have you read any of Faulkner?"

She gave me a pitying smile. I gulped and said, "Ugly, isn't it?"

She looked reminiscently over my other shoulder, a tiny frown flickering in her flawless brow. "So ugly," she said.

In between times she listened importantly to my opinions on Faulkner and Cabell. And Moussorgsky and Al Jolson. She was wonderful, and we agreed in everything.

And, hours later, when I stood with her at her door, I couldn't do a thing but shuffle my feet and haul on the hem of my jacket. She gave me her hand gravely, and I think she stopped breathing. I said, "Uh, well," and couldn't improve on it. She swept her gaze from my eyes to my mouth, from side to side across my forehead; it was a tortured "No!" her slightly turning head articulated, and her whole body moved minutely with it. She let go my hand, turned slowly toward the door, and then, with a cry which might have been a breath of laughter and which might have been a sob, she pirouetted back to me and kissed me—not on the mouth, but in the hollow at the side of my neck. My fuse blew with a snap and a bright light and, as it were, incapacitated my self-starter. She moved deftly then, and to my blurred vision, apparently changed herself into a closed door. I must have stood lookir₍ at that door for twenty minutes before I turned and walked dazedly home.

I saw her five more times. Once it was a theatre party, and we all went to her house afterward, and she showed great impartiality. Once it was a movie, and who should we run into afterward but her folks. Very nice people. I liked them and I think they liked me. Once it was the circus; we stayed very late, dancing at a pavilion, and yet the street was still crowded outside her home when we arrived there, and a handshake had to do. The fourth time was at a party to which I went alone because she had a date that night. It devolved that the date was the same party. The way she came in did things to me. It wasn't the fact that she was with somebody else; I had no claim on her, and the way she acted with me made me feel pretty confident. It was the way she came in, slipping out of her wrap, which—caught on her—bracelet, freezing her in a profile while framed in the doorway.... I don't want to think about it. Not now.

I did think about it; I left almost immediately so that I could. I went home and slumped down in an easy chair and convinced myself about coincidences, and was almost back to normal when Dad came into the room.

"*Argh!*" he said.

I leapt out of the chair and helped him to pick himself up off the middle of the rug. "Blast it, boy," he growled, "Why don't you turn on a light? What are you doing home? I thought you were out with your goddess. Why can't you pick up your big bony feet, or at least leave them somewhere else besides in the doorway of a dark room?" He dusted off his knees. He wasn't hurt. It's a deep-piled rug with two cushions under it. "You're a howling menace. Kicking your father." Dad had mellowed considerably with the years. "What's the matter with you anyhow? She do you something? Or are you beginning to have doubts?" He wore glasses now, but he saw plenty. He'd ribbed me about Cordelia as can only a man who can't stand ribbing himself.

"It was a lousy party," I said.

He turned on a light, "What's up, Henry?"

"Nothing," I said. "Absolutely nothing. I haven't had a fight with her, if that's what you're digging for."

"All right, then," he said, picking up the paper.

"There's nothing wrong with her. She's one of the most wonderful people I know, that's all."

"Sure she is." He began to read the paper.

"She's deep, too. A real wise head, she is. You wouldn't expect to find that in somebody as young as that. Or as good-looking." I wished he would put his eyebrows down.

"She's read everything worth reading," I added as he turned a page a minute later.

"Marvelous," he said flatly.

I glared at him. "What do you mean by that?" I barked. "What's marvellous?"

He put the paper down on his knee and smoothed it. His voice was gentle. "Why Cordelia, of course. I'm not arguing with you, Henry."

"Yes you—well, anyway, you're not saying what you think."

"You don't want to hear what I think."

"I know what I want!" I flared.

He crackled the paper nervously. "My," he said as if to himself, "this is worse than I thought." Before I could interrupt, he said, "Half of humanity doesn't know what it wants or how to find out. The other half knows what it wants, hasn't got it, and is going crazy trying to convince itself that it already has it."

"Very sound," I said acidly. "Where do you peg me?"

He ignored this. "The radio commercial which annoys me most," he said with apparent irrelevancy, "is the one which begins, 'There are some things so good they don't have to be improved.' That annoys me because there isn't a thing on God's green earth which couldn't stand improvement. By the same token, if you find something which looks to you as if it's unimprovable, then either it's a mirage or you're out of your mind."

"What has that to do with Cordelia?"

"Don't snap at me, son," Dad said quietly. "Let's operate by the rule of reason here. Or must I tear your silly head off and stuff it down your throat?"

I grinned in spite of myself. "Reason prevails, Dad. Go on."

"Now, I've seen the girl, and you're right; she's striking to look at. Extraordinary. In the process of raving about that you've also told me practically every scrap of conversation you've ever had with her."

"I have?"

"You're like your mother; you talk too much," he smiled. "Don't get flustered. It was good to listen to. Shows you're healthy. But I kept noticing one thing in these mouthings—all she's read, all the languages she understands, all the music she likes—and that is that you have never quoted her yet as saying a single declarative sentence. You have never quoted her as opening a conversation, changing the subject, mentioning something you both liked *before* you mentioned it, or having a single idea that you didn't like." He shrugged. "Maybe she is a good listener. They're—"

"Now wait a minute—"

"—They're rare anywhere in the world, especially in this house," he went on smoothly. "Put your hands back in your pockets, Henry, or sit on 'em until I've finished. Now, I'm not making any charges about Cordelia. There aren't any. She's wonderful. That's the trouble. For Pete's sake get her to make a flat statement."

"She has, plenty of times," I said hotly. "You just don't know her! Why, she's the most—"

He put up his hands and turned his head as if I were aiming a bucket of water at him. "Shut up!" he roared. I shut. "Now," he said, "listen to me. If you're right, you're right and there's no use defending anything. If you're wrong you'd better find it out soon before you get hurt. But I don't want to sit here and watch the process. I know how you tick, Henry. By gosh, I ought to. You're like I was. You and I, we get a hot idea and go all out for it, all speed and no control. We spill off at the mouth until we have the whole world watching, and when the idea turns sour the whole world gets in its licks, standing around laughing. Keep your beautiful dreams to yourself. If they don't pan out you can always kick yourself effectively enough, without having every wall-eyed neighbor helping you."

A picture of Mr. Bohackus with the protruding china-blue eyes, our neighbor of along ago, crossed my mind, and I chuckled.

"That's better, Henry," said Dad. "Listen. When a fellow gets to be a big grown-up man, which is likely to happen at my age, or never, he learns to make a pile of his beloved failures and consign them to the flames, and never think of them again. But it ought to be a private bonfire."

It sounded like sense, particularly the part about not having to defend something if it was right enough to be its own defense. I said, "Thanks, Dad. I'll have to think. I don't know if I agree with you. . . . I'll tell you something, though. If Cordelia turned out to be nothing but a phonograph, I'd consider it a pleasure to spend the rest of my life buying new records for her."

"That'd be fine," said Dad, "if it was what you wanted. I seriously doubt that it is just now."

"Of course it isn't. Cordelia's all woman and has a wonderful mind, and that's what I want."

"Bless you, my children," Dad said, and grinned.

I knew I was right, and that Dad was simply expressing a misguided caution. The Foxy Grandpa routine, I thought, was a sign of advancing age. Dad sure was changed since the old days. On the other hand, he hadn't been the same since the mysterious frittering-out of his mysterious down-cellar project. I stopped thinking about Dad, and turned my mind to my own troubles.

I had plenty of time to think; I couldn't get a Saturday date with her for two weeks, and I wanted this session to run until it was finished with no early curfews. Not, as I have said, that I had any doubts. Far from it. All the same, I made a little list . . .

I don't think I said ten words to her until we were three blocks from her house. She quite took my breath away. She was wearing a green suit with surprising lapels that featured her fabulous profile and made me ache inside. I had not known that I was so hungry for a sight of her, and now she was more than a sight, now her warm hand had slipped into mine as we walked. "Cordelia . . ." I whispered.

She turned her face to me, and showed me the tender tuggings in the corners of her mouth. She made an interrogative sound, like a sleepy bird.

"Cordelia," I said thickly. It all came out in a monotone. "I didn't know I could miss anybody so much. There's been a hollow place in my eyes, wherever I looked; it had no color and it was shaped like you. Now you fill it and I can see again."

She dropped her eyes, and her smile was a thing to see. "You said that beautifully," she breathed.

I hadn't thought of that. What I had said was squeezed out of me like toothpaste out of a tube, with the same uniformity between what came out and what was still inside.

"We'll go to the Stroll Inn," I said. It was where we met. We didn't meet at the party. We just saw each other there. We met in that booth.

She nodded gravely and walked with me, her face asleep, its attention turned inward, deeply engaged. It was not until we turned the corner on Winter Street and faced the Inn that I thought of my list; and when I did, I felt a double, sickening impact—first, one of shame that I should dare to examine and experiment with someone like this, second, because item 5 on that list was "You said that beautifully . . ."

The Stroll Inn, as I indicated before, has all its lights, practically, on the outside. Cordelia looked at me thoughtfully as we walked into their worming neon field. "Are you all right?" she asked. "You look pale."

"How can you tell?" I asked, indicating the lights, which flickered and switched, orange and green and blue and red. She smiled appreciatively, and two voices spoke within me. One said joyfully, " 'You look pale' is a declarative statement." The other said angrily, "You're hedging. And by the way, what do you suppose that subtle smile is covering up, if anything?" Both voices spoke forcefully, combining in a jumble which left me badly confused. We went in and found a booth and ordered dinner. Cordelia said with pleasure that she would have what I ordered.

Over the appetizer I said, disliking myself intensely. "Isn't this wonderful? All we need is a moon. Can't you see it, hanging up there over us?"

She laughed and looked up, and sad sensitivity came into her face. I closed my eyes, waiting.

" 'Is the moon tired? She looks so pale—' " she began.

I started to chew again. I think it was marinated herring, and very good too, but at the moment it tasted like cold oatmeal with a dash of warm lard. I called the waiter and ordered a double rum and soda. As he turned away I called him back and asked him to bring a bottle instead. I needed help from somewhere, and pouring it out of a bottle seemed a fine idea at the time.

Over the soup I asked her what she was thinking about. "I was ruminating," she said in a self-depreciating, tragic voice, "on the futility of human endeavor." Oh, brother, me too. I thought. Me too.

Over the dessert we had converse again, the meat course having passed silently. We probably presented a lovely picture, the two of us wordlessly drinking in each other's presence, the girl radiating an understanding tenderness, the young man speechless with admiration. Look how he watches her, how his eyes travel over her face, how he sighs and shakes his head and looks back at his plate.

I looked across the Inn. In a plate-glass window a flashing neon sign said bluely, "nnI llortS. nnI llortS."

"Nnillorts," I murmured.

Cordelia looked up at me expectantly, with her questioning sound. I tensed. I filled the jigger with rum and poured two fingers into my empty highball glass. I took the jigger in one hand and the glass in the other.

I said, "You've read Kremlin von Schtunk, the Hungarian poet?" and drank the jigger.

"Well, really," she said pityingly.

"I was just thinking of his superb line 'Nni llorts, nov shmoz ka smörgasbord,'" I intoned, "which means—" and I drank the glass.

She reached across the table and touched my elbow. "Please. Don't translate. It couldn't be phrased as well in English."

Something within me curled up and died. Small, tight, cold and dense, its corpse settled under my breastbone. I could have raged at her, I supposed. I could have coldly questioned her, pinned her down, stripped from her those layers of schooled conversational reactions, leaving her ignorance in nakedness. But what for? I didn't want it. . . . And I could have talked to her about honesty and ethics and human aims—why did she do it? What did she ever hope to get? Did she think she would ever corral a man and expect him to be blind, for the rest of his life, to the fact that there was nothing behind this false front—nothing at all? Did she think that—did she think? No.

I looked at her, the way she was smiling at me, the deep shifting currents which seemed to be in her eyes. She was a monster. She was some graceful diction backed by a bare half-dozen relays. She was a card-file. She was a bubble, thin-skinned, covered with swirling, puzzling, compelling colors, filled with nothing. I was hurt and angry and, I think, a little frightened. I drank some more rum. I ordered her a drink and then another, and stayed ahead of her four to one. I'd have walked out and gone home if I had been able to summon the strength. I couldn't. I could only sit and stare at her and bathe myself in agonized astonishment. She didn't mind. She sat listening as raptly to my silence as she had to my conversation. Once she said, "We're just *being* together, aren't we?" and I recognized it as another trick from the bag. I wondered idly how many she might come up with if I just waited.

She came up with plenty.

She sat up and leaned forward abruptly. I had the distinct feeling that she was staring at me—her face was positioned right for it—but her eyes were closed. I put my glass down and stared blearily back, thinking, now what?

Her lips parted, twitched, opened wide, pursed. They uttered a glottal gurgling which was most unpleasant. I pushed my chair back, startled. "Are you sick?"

"Are you terrestrial?" she asked me.

"Am I *what?*"

"Making—contact thirty years," she said. Her voice was halting, filled with effort.

"What are you talking about?"

"Terrestrial quickly power going," she said clearly. "Many—uh—much power making contact this way very high frequencies thought. Easy radio. Not again thought. Take radio code quickly."

"Listen, toots," I said nastily, "This old nose no longer has a ring in it. Go play tricks on somebody else." I drank some more rum. An I.Q. of sixty, and crazy besides. "You're a real find, you are," I said.

"Graphic," she said. "Uh—write. Write. Write." She began to claw the table cloth. I looked at her hand. It was making scribbling motions. "Write write."

I flipped a menu over and put it in front of her and gave her my pen.

Now, I read an article once on automatic writing—you know, that spiritualist stuff. Before witnesses, a woman once wrote a long letter in trance in an unfamiliar (to her) hand, at the astonishing rate of four hundred and eight words a minute. Cordelia seemed to be out to break that record. That pen-nib was a blur. She was still leaning forward rigidly, and her eyes were still closed. But instead of a blurred scrawl, what took shape under her flying hand was a neat list or chart. There was an alphabet of sorts, although not arranged in the usual way; it was more a list of sounds. And there were the numbers one to fourteen. Beside each sound and each number was a cluster of regular dots which looked rather like Braille. The whole sheet took her not over forty-five seconds to do. And after she finished she didn't move anything except her eyelids which went up. "I think," she said conversationally, "that I'd better get home, Henry. I feel a little dizzy."

I felt a little more than that. The rum, in rum's inevitable way, had sneaked up on me, and suddenly the room began to spin, diagonally, from the lower left to the upper right. I closed my eyes tight, opened them, fixed my gaze on a beer-tap on the bar at the end of the room, and held it still until the room slowed and stopped. "You're so right," I said, and did a press-up on the table top to assist my legs. I managed to help Cordelia on with her light coat. I put my pen back in my pocket (I found it the next morning with the cap still off and a fine color scheme in the lining of my jacket) and picked up the menu.

"What's that?" asked Cordelia.

"A souvenir," I said glumly. I had no picture, no school ring, no nothing. Only a doodle. I was too tired, twisted, and tanked to wonder much about it, or about the fact that she seemed never to have seen it before. I folded it in two and put it in my hip.

I got her home without leaning on her. I don't know if she was ready to give a repeat performance of that goodnight routine. I didn't wait to find out. I took her to the door and patted her on the cheek and went away from there. It wasn't her fault. . . .

When I got to our house, I dropped my hat on the floor in the hall and went into the dark living-room and fell into the easy-chair by the door. It was a comfortable chair. It was a comfortable room. I felt about as bad as I ever had. I remember wondering smokily whether anyone ever loves a person. People seem to love dreams instead, and for the lucky ones, the person is close to the dream. But it's a dream all the same, a sticky dream. You unload the person, and the dream stays with you.

What was it Dad had said? "When a fellow gets to be a big grown-up man . . . he learns to make a pile of his beloved failures and consign them to the flames." "Hah!" I ejaculated, and gagged. The rum tasted terrible. I had nothing to burn but memories and the lining of my stomach. The latter was flaming merrily. The former stayed where they were. The way she smiled, so deep and secret . . .

Then I remembered the doodle. Her hands had touched it, her mind had—No, her mind hadn't. It could have been anyone's mind, but not hers. The girl operated under a great handicap. No brains. I felt terrible. I got up out of the chair and wove across the room, leaning on the mantel. I put my forehead on the arm which I had put on the mantel, and with my other hand worried the menu out of my pocket. With the one hand and my teeth I tore it into small pieces and dropped the pieces in the grate, all but one. Then I heaved myself upright, braced my shoulder against the mantel, which had suddenly begun to bob and weave, got hold of my lighter, coaxed a flame out of it and lit the piece I'd saved. It burned fine. I let it slip into the grate. It flickered, dimmed, caught on another piece of paper, flared up again. I went down on one knee and carefully fed all the little pieces to the flame. When it finally went out I stirred the ashes around with my finger, got up, wiped my hands on my pants, said, "That was good advice Dad gave me," and went back to the chair. I went back into it, pushed my shoes off my feet, curled my legs under me and, feeling much better, dozed off.

I woke slowly, some time later, and with granulated eyelids and a mouth full of emory and quinine. My head was awake but my legs were asleep and my stomach had its little hands on my backbone and was trying to pull it out by the roots. I sat there groggily looking at the fire.

Fire? What fire? I blinked and winced; I could almost hear my eyelids rasping.

There was a fire in the grate. Dad was kneeling beside it, feeding it small pieces of paper. I didn't say anything; I don't think it occurred to me. I just watched.

He let the fire go out after a while; then he stirred the ashes with his finger and stood up with a sigh, wiping his hands on his pants. "Good advice I gave the boy. Time I took it myself." He loomed across the shadowy room to me, turned around and sat down in my lap. He was relaxed and heavy, but he didn't stay there long enough for me to feel it. "Gah!" he said, crossed the room again in one huge bound, put his back against the mantel and said, "Don't move, you, I've got a gun."

"It's me, Dad."

"Henry! Bythelordharry, you'll be the death of me yet. That was the most inconsiderate thing you have ever done in your entire selfish life. I've a notion to bend this poker over your adam's apple, you snipe." He stamped over to the book case and turned on the light. "This is the last time I'll ever—Henry! What's the matter? You look awful! Are you all right?"

"I'll live," I said regretfully. "What were you burning?"

He grinned sheepishly. "A beloved failure. Remember my preachment a couple weeks ago? It got to working on me. I decided to take my own advice." He breathed deeply. "I feel much better, I think."

"I burned some stuff too," I croaked. "I feel better too. I think," I added.

"Cordelia?" he asked, sitting near me.

"She hasn't got brain one," I said.

"Well," he said. There was more sharing and comfort in the single syllable than in anything I have ever heard. I looked at him. He hadn't changed much over the years. A bit heavier. A bit grayer. Still intensely alive, though. And he'd learned to control those wild projects of his. I thought, quite objectively, "I like this man."

We were quiet for a warm while. Then, "Dad—what was it you burned? The Martian project?"

"Why, you young devil! How did you know?"

"I dunno. You look like I feel. Sort of—well, you've finally unloaded something, and it hurts to lose it, but you're glad you did."

"On the nose," he said, and grinned sheepishly. "Yup, Henry—I really hugged that project to me. Want to hear about it?"

Anything but Cordelia, I thought. "I saw your rig," I said, to break the ice. "The night you sent me out for the wire. You left the workshop open."

"I'll be darned. I thought I'd gotten away with it."

"Mother knew what you were up to, though she didn't know how."

"And you saw how."

"I saw that weird gimmick of yours, but it didn't mean anything to me. Mother told me never to mention it to you. She thought you'd be happier if you were left alone."

He laughed with real delight. "Bless her heart," he said. "She was a most understanding woman."

"I read about the Martian signals in the papers," I said. "Fellow named—what was it?"

"Jenkins," said Dad. "C. Francis Jenkins. He built a film-tape recorder to catch the signals. He tuned to six thousand meters and had a flashing light to record the signals. Primitive, but it worked. Dr. David Todd of Amherst was the man who organized the whole project, and got the big radio people all over the world to cooperate. They had a five-minute silence every hour during Mars' closest proximity—August 1 to 3."

"I remember," I said. "It was my birthday, 1924. What got you so teed off?"

"I got mad," said my father, folding his hands over his stomach. "Just because it had become fashionable to use radio in a certain way on earth, those simple souls had to assume that the Martian signals—if any—would come through the same way. I felt that they'd be different."

"Why should they be?"

"Why should we expect Martians to be the same? Or even think the same? I just took a wild stab at it, that's all. I tuned in on six wavelengths at the same time. I set up my rig so that anything coming through on any one wavelength would actuate a particular phone."

"I remember," I said, trying hard. "The iron filings on the paper tape, over the ear-phones."

"That's right. The phone was positioned far enough below the tape so that the magnetic field would barely contain the filings. When the diaphragm vibrated, the filings tended to cluster. I had six phones on six different wavelengths, arranged like this," and he counted them out on the palm of his hand:

$$
\begin{array}{cc}
1 & 2 \\
3 & 4 \\
5 & 6
\end{array}
$$

"What could you get? I don't figure it, Dad. There'd be no way of separating your dots and dashes."

"Blast!" he exploded. "That's the kind of thinking that made me mad, and makes me mad to this day! No; what I was after was something completely different in transmission. Look; how much would you get out of piano music if all the strings but one were broken? Only when the pianist hit that note in the course of his transmission would you hear anything. See what I mean? Supposing the Martians were sending in notes and chords of an established octave of frequencies? Sure—Jenkins got signals. No one's ever been able to interpret them. Well, supposing I was right—then Jenkins was recording only one of several or many 'notes' of the scale, and of course it was meaningless."

"Well, what did you get?"

"Forty-six photographs, five of which were so badly under-exposed that they were useless to me. I finally got the knack of moving the tape carefully enough and lighting it properly, and they came out pretty well. I got signals on four of the six frequencies. I got the same grouping only three or four times; I mean, sometimes there would be something on phones 1, 2, and 4, and sometimes it would only be on 4, and sometimes it would be on 2 and 6. Three and 5 never did come through; it was just fantastic luck that I picked the right frequencies, I suppose, for the other four."

"What frequencies did you use?"

He grinned. "I don't know. I really don't. It was all by guess and by Golly. I never was an engineer, Henry. I'm in the insurance business. I had no instruments—particularly not in 1924. I wound a 6000-meter coil according to specs they printed in the paper. As for the others, I worked on the knowledge that less turns of heavier wire means shorter wave-lengths. I haven't got the coils now and couldn't duplicate 'em in a million years. All I can say for sure is that they were all different, and stepped down from 6000.

"Anyway, I studied those things until I was blue in the face. It must've been the better part of a year before I called in anyone else. I wrote to Mr. Jenkins and Dr. Todd too, but who am I? A taxidermical broker with a wacky idea. They sent the pictures back with polite letters, and I can't say I blame them . . . anyway, good riddance to the things. But it was a wonderful idea, and I wanted so much to be the man who did the job. . . . Ever want something so badly you couldn't see straight, Henry?"

"Me?" I asked, with bitterness.

"It's all over now, though. I'm through with crazy projects, for life. Never again. But gosh, I did love that project. Know what I mean?"

"No," I said with even more bitterness.

He sat straight. "Hey, I'm sorry, fellow. Those were rhetorical questions. Maybe you'd better spill it."

So I told it to him—all of it. Once I started, I couldn't stop. I told him about the moon poem and the "well, really" gimmick and the "please don't translate" routine, and the more I talked the worse I felt. He sat and listened, and didn't say "I told you so," and the idea was worming its way into the back of my mind as I talked that here sat one of the most understanding people ever created, when he screamed. He screamed as one screams at the intrusion of an ice-cube into the back of one's bathing-suit.

"What's the matter?" I asked, breaking off.

"Go on, go on," he gabbled. "Henry you idiot don't tell me you don't know what you're saying for Pete's sake boy tell it to——"

"Whoa! I don't even remember where I was."

"What she said to you—'Are you a terrestrial?' "

"Oh, don't get so excited, Dad. It doesn't mean anything. Why bother? She was trying to interest me, I suppose. I didn't let it get to me then and I won't now. She—"

"*Blast* her! I'm not talking about her. It was what she said. Go on, Henry! You say she wrote something?"

He wormed it all out of me. He forced me to go over it and over it. The windows paled and the single light by the book case looked yellow and ill in the dawn, but still he pounded at me. And I finally quit. I just quit, out of compounded exhaustion and stubbornness. I lay back in the big chair and glared at him.

He strode up and down the room, trying to beat his left hand to a pulp with a right fist. "Of course, of course," he said excitedly. "That's how they'd do it. The blankest mind in the world. Blank and sensitive, like undeveloped film. *Of course!* 'Making contact thirty years' they said. 'Much power making contact this way—very high frequencies thought.' A radionic means of transmitting thought, and it uses too much power to be practical. 'Easy radio. Not again thought.'"

He stopped in front of me, glaring. "'Not again thought,'" he growled. "You—you *dope!* How could my flesh and blood be so abjectly stupid? There in your hands you held the interplanetary Rosetta Stone, and what did you do with it?"

I glared back at him. "I was quote consigning one of my beloved failures to the flames end quote," I said nastily.

Suddenly he was slumped and tired. "So you were, son. So you were. And it was all there—little Braille, you said. A series of phonetic symbols, and almost certainly a list of the frequency-octave they use. And—and all my pictures. . . . I burned them too." He sat down.

"Henry—"

"Don't take it so hard, Dad," I said. "Your advice was good. You forget your Martians and I'll forget my moron. When a fellow gets to be a grown-up man—"

He didn't hear me. "Henry. You say her folks like you?"

I sprang to my feet. "NO!" I bellowed. "Dad, I will not, repeat, *not* under any circumstances woo that beautiful package of brainless reflexes. I have had mine. I—"

"You really mean it, don't you?"

"That I do," I said positively.

"Well," he said dejectedly, "I guess that's that."

And then that old, old fever came back into his face.

"Dad—"

He slowly straightened up, that hot "Land ho!" expression in his eyes. My father is hale, handsome, and, when he wants to be, extremely persistent.

"Now, Dad," I said. "Let's be reasonable. She's very young, Dad. Now, let's talk this thing over a little more, Dad. You can't go following a girl all over the house with a notebook and pencil. They said they wouldn't use the thought contact again. Dad. Now Dad—"

"Your mother would understand if she were alive," he murmured.

"No! You can't!" I bawled. "Dad, for heaven's sake use your head! Why you—Cordelia—Dad, she'd make me call her *Mummy!*"

Now what am I going to do?

SHADOW, SHADOW ON THE WALL

Good old wicked stepmother; this isn't the first, and certainly not the last of them to supply us with entertainment. Somebody once made a short film of this; the little boy was just great, the rest misunderstood, so it was never seen. There's one line in here I'm really proud of: the fury of the woman who, having banished the child to the bedroom, finds him happy as a little clam. *"Don't you know you're being punished?"* she shouts. Very heavy, that. Nobody can punish you if you can achieve the mindset that says whatever they're doing to you isn't punishment.

It was well after bedtime and Bobby was asleep, dreaming of a place with black butterflies that stayed, and a dog with a wuffly nose and blunt, friendly rubber teeth. It was a dark place, and comfy with all the edges blurred and soft, and he could make them all jump if he wanted to.

But then there was a sharp scythe of light that swept everything away (except in the shaded smoothness of the blank wall beside the door: someone *always* lived there) and Mommy Gwen was coming into the room with a blaze of hallway behind her. She clicked the high-up switch, the one he couldn't reach, and room light came cruelly. Mommy Gwen changed from a flat, black, light-rimmed set of cardboard triangles to a night-lit, daytime sort of Mommy Gwen.

Her hair was wide and her chin was narrow. Her shoulders were wide and her waist was narrow. Her hips were wide and her skirt was narrow, and under it all were her two hard silky sticks of legs. Her arms hung down from the wide tips of her shoulders, straight and elbowless when she walked. She never moved her arms when she walked. She never moved them at all unless she wanted to do something with them.

"You're awake." Her voice was hard, wide, flat, pointy too.

"I was asleep," said Bobby.

"Don't contradict. Get up."

Bobby sat up and fisted his eyes. "Is Daddy—"

"Your father is not in the house. He went away. He won't be back for a whole day—maybe two. So there's no use in yelling for him."

"Wasn't going to yell for him, Mommy Gwen."

"Very well, then. Get up."

Wondering, Bobby got up. His flannel sleeper pulled at his shoulders and at the soles of his snug-covered feet. He felt tousled.

"Get your toys, Bobby."

"What toys, Mommy Gwen?"

Her voice snapped like wet clothes on the line in a big wind. "Your toys—all of them!"

He went to the playbox and lifted the lid. He stopped, turned, stared at her. Her arms hung straight at her sides, as straight as her two level eyes under the straight shelf of brow. He bent to the playbox. Gollywick, Humptydoodle and the blocks came out; the starry-wormy piece of the old phonograph, the cracked sugar egg with the peephole girl in it, the cardboard kaleidoscope and the magic set with the seven silvery rings that made a trick he couldn't do but Daddy could. He took them all out and put them on the floor.

"Here," said Mommy Gwen. She moved one straight-line arm to point to her feet with one straight-line finger. He picked up the toys and brought them to her, one at a time, two at a time, until they were all there. "Neatly, neatly," she muttered. She bent in the middle like a garage door and did brisk things with the toys, so that the scattered pile of them became a square stack. "Get the rest," she said.

He looked into the playbox and took out the old wood-framed slate and the mixed-up box of crayons; the English annual story book and an old candle, and that was all for the playbox. In the closet were some little boxing-gloves and a tennis racket with broken strings, and an old ukulele with no strings at all. And that was all for the closet. He brought them to her, and she stacked them with the others.

"Those things too," she said, and at last bent her elbow to point around. From the dresser came the two squirrels and a monkey that Daddy had made from pipe cleaners, a small square of plate-glass he had found on Henry Street; a clockwork top that sounded like a church talking, and the broken clock Jerry had left on the porch last week. Bobby brought them all to Mommy Gwen, every one. "Are you going to put me in another room?"

"No indeed." Mommy Gwen took up the neat stack of toys. It was tall in her arms. The top fell off and thunked on the floor, bounced, chased around in a tilted circle. "Get it," said Mommy Gwen.

Bobby picked it up and reached it toward her. She stooped until he could put it on the stack, snug between the tennis racket and the box of crayons. Mommy Gwen didn't say thank you, but went away through the door, leaving Bobby standing, staring after her. He heard her hard feet go down the hall, heard the bump as she pressed open the guest-room door with her knee. There was a rattle and click as she set his toys down on the spare bed, the one without a spread, the one with dusty blue ticking on the mattress. Then she came back again.

"Why aren't you in bed?" She clapped her hands. They sounded dry, like sticks breaking. Startled, he popped back into bed and drew the covers up to his chin. There used to be someone who had a warm cheek and a soft word for him when he did that, but that was a long time ago. He lay with his eyes round in the light, looking at Mommy Gwen.

"You've been bad," she said. "You broke a window in the shed and you tracked mud into my kitchen and you've been noisy and rude. So you'll stay right here in this room without your toys until I say you can come out. Do you understand me?"

"Yes," he said. He said quickly, because he remembered in time. "Yes ma'am."

She struck the switch swiftly, without warning, so that the darkness dazzled him, made him blink. But right away it was the room again, with the scythe of light and the shaded something hiding in the top corner of the wall by the door. There was always something shifting about there.

She went away then, thumping the door closed, leaving the darkness and taking away the light, all but a rug-fuzzed yellow streak under the door. Bobby looked away from that, and for a moment, for just a moment, he was inside his shadow-pictures where the rubber-fanged dog and the fleshy black butterflies stayed. Sometimes they stayed ... but mostly they were gone as soon as he moved. Or maybe they changed into something else. Anyway, he liked it there, where they all lived, and he wished he could be with them, in the shadow country.

Just before he fell asleep, he saw them moving and shifting in the blank wall by the door. He smiled at them and went to sleep.

When he awoke, it was early. He couldn't smell the coffee from downstairs yet, even. There was a ruddy-yellow sunswatch on the blank wall, a crooked square, just waiting for him. He jumped out of bed and ran to it. He washed his hands in it, squatted down on the floor with his arms out. "Now!" he said.

He locked his thumbs together and slowly flapped his hands. And there on the wall was a black butterfly, flapping its wings right along with him. "Hello, butterfly," said Bobby.

He made it jump. He made it turn and settle to the bottom of the light patch, and fold its wings up and up until they were together. Suddenly he whipped one hand away, peeled back the sleeve of his sleeper, and presto! there was a long-necked duck. "Quack-ack!" said Bobby, and the duck obligingly opened its bill, threw up its head to quack. Bobby made it curl up its bill until it was an eagle. He didn't know what kind of noise an eagle made, so he said "Eagle-eagle-eagle-eagle," and that sounded fine. He laughed.

When he laughed Mommy Gwen slammed the door open and stood there in a straight-lined white bathrobe and straight flat slippers. "What are you playing with?"

Bobby held up his empty hands.

"I was just—"

She took two steps into the room. "Get up," she said. Her lips were pale. Bobby got up, wondering why she was so angry. "I heard you laugh," she said in a hissy kind of whisper. She looked him up and down, looked at the floor around him. "What were you playing with?"

"A eagle," said Bobby.

"A what? Tell me the truth!"

Bobby waved his empty hands vaguely and looked away from her. She had such an angry face.

She stepped, reached, put a hard hand around his wrist. She lifted his arm so high he went on tiptoes, and with her other hand she felt his body, this side, that side. "You're hiding something. What is it? Where is it? What were you playing with?"

"Nothing. Reely, reely truly nothing," gasped Bobby as she shook and patted. She wasn't spanking. She never spanked. She did other things.

"You're being punished," she said in her shrill angry whisper. "Stupid, stupid, stupid ... too stupid to know you're being punished." She set him down with a thump and went to the door. "Don't let me hear you laugh again. You've been bad, and you're not being kept in this room to enjoy yourself. Now you stay here and think about how bad you are breaking windows. Tracking mud. Lying."

She went out and closed the door with a steadiness that was like slamming, but quiet. Bobby looked at the door and wondered for a moment about that broken window. He'd been terribly sorry; it was just that the golf ball bounced so hard. Daddy had told him he should be more careful, and he had watched sorrowfully while Daddy put in a new pane. Then Daddy had given him a little piece of putty to play with and asked him never to do it again and he'd promised not to. And the whole time Mommy Gwen hadn't said a thing to him about it. She'd just looked at him every once in a while with her eyes and her mouth straight and thin, and she'd waited. She'd waited until Daddy went away.

He went back to his sunbeam and forgot all about Mommy Gwen.

After he'd made another butterfly and a dog's head and an alligator on the wall, the sunbeam got so thin that he couldn't make anything more, except, for a while, little black finger shadows that ran up and down the strip of light like ants on a matchstick. Soon there was no sunbeam at all, so he sat on the edge of his bed and watched the vague flickering of the something that lived in the end wall. It was a *different* kind of something. It wasn't a good something, and it wasn't bad. It just lived there, and the difference between it and the other things, the butterflies and dogs and swans and eagles who lived there, was that the something didn't need his hands to make it be alive. The something— stayed. Some day he was going to make a butterfly or a dog or a horse that would stay after he moved his hands away. Meanwhile, the only one who stayed, the only one who lived all the time in the shadow country, was this something that flickered up there where the two walls met the ceiling. "I'm going right in there and play with you," Bobby told it. "You'll see."

There was a red wagon with three wheels in the yard, and a gnarly tree to be climbed. Jerry came and called for a while, but Mommy Gwen sent him away. *"He's been bad."* So Jerry went away.

Bad bad bad. Funny how the things he did didn't used to be bad before Daddy married Mommy Gwen.

Mommy Gwen didn't want Bobby. That was all right—Bobby didn't want Mommy Gwen either. Daddy sometimes said to grown-up people that Bobby was much better off with someone to care for him. Bobby could remember 'way back when he used to say that with his arm around Mommy Gwen's shoulders and his voice ringing. He could remember when Daddy said it quietly, from the other side of the room, with a voice like an angry "I'm sorry." And now, Daddy hadn't said it at all for a long time.

Bobby sat on the edge of his bed and hummed to himself, thinking these thoughts, and he hummed to himself and didn't think of anything at all. He found a ladybug crawling up the dresser and caught it the careful way, circling it with his thumb and finger so that it crawled up on his hand by itself. Sometimes when you pinched them up they got busted. He stood on the windowsill and hunted until he found the little hole in the screen that the ladybug must have used to come in. He let the bug walk on the screen and guided it to the hole. It flew away, happy.

The room was flooded with warm dull light reflected from the sparkly black shed roof, and he couldn't make any shadow country people at all, so he made them in his head until he felt sleepy. He lay down then and hummed softly to himself until he fell asleep. And through the long afternoon the thing in the wall flickered and shifted and lived.

At dusk Mommy Gwen came back. Bobby may have heard her on the stairs; anyway, when the door opened on the dim room he was sitting up in bed, thumbing his eyes.

The ceiling blazed. "What have you been doing?"

"Was asleep, I guess. Is it night time?"

"Very nearly. I suppose you're hungry." She had a covered dish.

"Mmm."

"What kind of an answer is that?" she snapped.

"Yes ma'am I'm hungry Mommy Gwen," he said rapidly.

"That's a little better. Here." She thrust the dish at him. He took it, removed the top plate and put it under the bowl. Oatmeal. He looked at it, at her.

"Well?"

"Thank you, Mommy Gwen." He began to eat with the teaspoon he had found hilt-deep in the gray-brown mess. There was no sugar on it.

"I suppose you expect me to fetch you some sugar," she said after a time.

"No'm," he said truthfully, and then wondered why her face went all angry and disappointed.

"What have you been doing all day?"

"Nothing. Playin'. Then I was asleep."

"Little sluggard." Suddenly she shouted at him. "What's the matter with you? Are you too stupid to be afraid? Are you too stupid to ask me to let you come downstairs? Are you too stupid to cry? Why don't you cry?"

He stared at her, round-eyed. "You wouldn't let me come down if I ast you," he said wonderingly. "So I didn't ast." He scooped up some oatmeal. "I don't feel like cryin', Mommy Gwen, I don't hurt."

"You're bad and you're being punished and it should hurt," she said furiously. She turned off the light with a vicious swipe of her hard straight hand, and went out, slamming the door.

Bobby sat still in the dark and wished he could go into the shadow country, the way he always dreamed he could. He'd go there and play with the butterflies and the fuzz-edged, blunt-toothed dogs and giraffes, and they'd stay and he'd stay and Mommy Gwen would never be able to get in, ever. Except that Daddy wouldn't be able to come with him, or Jerry either, and that would be a shame.

He scrambled quietly out of bed and stood for a moment looking at the wall by the door. He could almost for-sure see the flickering thing that lived there, even in the dark. When there was light on the wall, it flickered a shade darker than the light. At night it flickered a shade lighter than the black. It was always there, and Bobby knew it was alive. He knew it without question, like "my name is Bobby" and "Mommy Gwen doesn't want me."

Quietly, quietly, he tiptoed to the other side of the room where there was a small table lamp. He took it down and laid it carefully on the floor. He pulled the plug out and brought it down under the lower rung of the table so it led straight across the floor to the wall-receptacle, and plugged it in again. Now he could move the lamp quite far out into the room, almost to the middle.

The lamp had a round shade that was open at the top. Lying on its side, the shade pointed its open top at the blank wall by the door. Bobby, with the sureness of long practice, moved in the darkness to his closet and got his dark-red flannel bathrobe from a low hook. He folded it once and draped it over the large lower end of the lamp shade. He pushed the button.

On the shadow country wall appeared a brilliant disk of light, crossed by just the hints of the four wires that held the shade in place. There was a dark spot in the middle where they met.

Bobby looked at it critically. Then, squatting between the lamp and the wall, he put out his hand.

A duck. "Quackle-ackle," he whispered.

An eagle. "Eagle—eagle—eagle—eagle," he said softly.

An alligator. "Bap bap," the alligator went as it opened and closed its long snout.

He withdrew his hands and studied the round, cross-scarred light on the wall. The blurred center shadow and its radiating lines looked a little like a waterbug, the kind that can run on the surface of a brook. It soon dissatisfied him; it just sat there without doing anything. He put his thumb in his mouth and bit it gently until an idea came to him. Then he scrambled to the bed, underneath which he found his slippers. He put one on the floor in front of the lamp, and propped the other toe-upward against it. He regarded the wall gravely for a time, and then lay flat on his stomach on the floor. Watching the shadow carefully, he put his elbows together on the carpet, twined his forearms together and merged the shadow of his hands with the shadow of the slipper.

The result enchanted him. It was something like a spider, and something like a gorilla. It was a brand-new something that no one had ever seen before. He writhed his fingers and then held them still, and now the thing's knobby head had triangular luminous eyes and a jaw that that swung, gaping. It had long arms for reaching and a delicate whorl of tentacles. He moved the least little bit, and it wagged its great head and blinked at him. Watching it, he felt suddenly that the flickering thing that lived in the high corner had crept out and down toward the beast he had made, closer and closer to it until—whoosh!—it noiselessly merged with the beast, an act as quick and complete as the marriage of raindrops on a windowpane.

Bobby crowed with delight, "Stay, stay," he begged. "Oh, stay there! I'll pet you! I'll give you good things to eat! Please stay, *please!*"

The thing glowered at him. He thought it would stay, but he didn't chance moving his hands away just yet.

The door crashed open, the switch clicked, the room filled with an explosion of light.

"What are you doing?"

Bobby lay frozen, his elbows on the carpet in front of him, his forearms together, his hands twisted oddly. He put his chin on his shoulder so he could look at her standing there stiff and menacing. "I was—was just—"

She swooped down on him. She snatched him up off the floor and plumped him down on the bed. She kicked and scattered his slippers. She snatched up the lamp, pulling the cord out of the wall with the motion. "You were not to have any toys," she said in a hissing voice. "That means you were not to make any toys. For this you'll stay in here for—what are you staring at?"

Bobby spread his hands and brought them together ecstatically, holding tight. His eyes sparkled, and his small white teeth peeped out so that they could see what he was smiling at. "He stayed, he did," said Bobby. "He stayed!"

"I don't know what you're talking about and I will not stay here to find out," snapped Mommy Gwen. "I think you're a mental case." She marched to the door, striking the high switch.

The room went dark—except for that blank wall by the door.

Mommy Gwen screamed.

Bobby covered his eyes.

Mommy Gwen screamed again, hoarsely this time. It was a sound like a dog's bark, but drawn out and out.

There was a long silence. Bobby peeped through his fingers at the dimly glowing wall. He took his hands down, sat up straight, drew his knees up to his chest and put his arms around them. "Well!" he said.

Feet pounded up the stairs. "Gwen! Gwen!"

"Hello, Daddy."

Daddy ran in, turning on the light. "Where's Mommy Gwen, Bob boy? What happened? I heard a—"

Bobby pointed at the wall. "She's in there," he said.

Daddy couldn't have understood him, for he turned and ran out the door calling "Gwen! Gwen!"

Bobby sat still and watched the fading shadow on the wall, quite visible even in the blaze of the overhead light. The shadow was moving, moving. It was a point-down triangle thrust into another point-down triangle which was mounted on a third, and underneath were the two hard sticks of legs. It had its arms up, its shadow-fists clenched, and it pounded and pounded silently on the wall.

"Now I'm never going into the shadow country," said Bobby complacently. "*She's* there."

So he never did.

THE TRAVELING CRAG

For years I have felt that this is one of the worst stories I ever wrote.
A lot of people have said they think otherwise, so here it is.

"I know agents who can get work out of their clients," said the telephone acidly.

"Yes, Nick, but—"

"Matter of fact, I know agents who would be willing to drop everything and go out to that one-shot genius's home town and—"

"I did!"

"I know you did! And what came of it?"

"I got a new story. It came in this morning."

"You just don't know how to handle a real writer. All you have to do is—you what?"

"I got a new story. I have it right here."

A pause. "A new Sig Weiss story? No kidding?"

"No kidding."

The telephone paused a moment again, as if to lick its lips. "I was saying to Joe just yesterday that if there's an agent in town who can pry work out of a primadonna like Weiss, it's good old Crisley Post. Yes, sir. Joe thinks a lot of you, Cris. Says you can take a joke better than—how long is the story?"

"Nine thousand."

"Nine thousand. I've got just the spot for it. By the way, did I tell you I can pay an extra cent a word now? For Weiss, maybe a cent and a half."

"You hadn't told me. Last time we talked rates you were overstocked. You wouldn't pay more than—"

"Aw, now, Cris, I was just—"

"Goodbye, Nick."

"Wait! When will you send—"

"Goodbye, Nick."

It was quiet in the office of Crisley Post, Articles, Fiction, Photographs. Then Naome snickered.

"What's funny?"

"Nothing's funny. You're wonderful. I've been waiting four years to hear you tell an editor off. Particularly that one. Are you going to give him the story?"

"I am not."

"Good! Who gets it? The slicks? What are you going to do: sell it to the highest bidder?"

"Naome, have you read it?"

"No. I gave it to you as soon as it came in. I knew you'd want to—"

"Read it."

"Wh—now?"

"Right now."

She took the manuscript and carried it to her desk by the window. "Corny title," she said.

"Corny title," he agreed.

He sat glumly, watching her. She was too small to be so perfectly proportioned, and her hair was as soft as it looked, which was astonishing. She habitually kept him at arm's length, but her arms were short. She was loyal, arbitrary, and underpaid, and she ran the business, though neither of them would admit it aloud. He thought about Sig Weiss.

Every agent has a Sig Weiss—as a rosy dream. You sit there day after day paddling through oceans of slush, hoping one day to run across a manuscript that means something—sincerity, integrity, high word rates—things like that. You try to understand what editors want in spite of what they say they want, and then you try to tell it to writers who never listen unless they're talking. You lend them money and psychoanalyze them and agree with them when they lie to themselves. When they write stories that don't make it, it's your fault. When they write stories that do make it, they did it by themselves. And when they hit the big time, they get themselves another agent. In the meantime, nobody likes you.

"Real stiff opening," said Naome.

"Real stiff," Cris nodded.

And then it happens. In comes a manuscript with a humble little covering note that says, "This is my first story, so it's probably full of mistakes that I don't know anything about. If you think it has anything in it, I'll be glad to fix it up any way you say." And you start reading it, and the story grabs you by the throat, shakes your bones, puts a heartbeat into your lymph ducts and finally slams you down gasping, weak and oh so happy.

So you send it out and it sells on sight, and the editor calls up to say thanks in an awed voice, and tells an anthologist, who buys reprint rights even before the yarn is published, and rumors get around, and you sell radio rights and TV rights and Portuguese translation rights. And the author writes you another note that claims volubly that if it weren't for you he'd never have been able to do it.

That's the agent's dream, and that was Cris Post's boy Sig Weiss and *The Traveling Crag*. But, like all dream plots, this one contained a sleeper. A rude awakening.

Offers came in and Cris made promises, and waited. He wrote letters. He sent telegrams. He got on the long distance phone (to a neighbor's house, Weiss had no phone).

No more stories.

So he went to see Weiss. He lost six days on the project. It was Naome's idea. "He's in trouble," she announced, as if she knew for sure. "Anyone who can write like that is sensitive. He's humble and he's generous and he's probably real shy and real good-looking. Someone's victimized him, that's what. Someone's taken advantage of him. Cris, go on out there and find out what's the matter."

"All the way out to Turnville? My God, woman, do you know where that is? Besides, who's going to run things around here?" As if he didn't know.

"I'll try, Cris. But you've got to see what's the matter with Sig Weiss. He's the—the greatest thing that ever happened around here."

"I'm jealous," he said, because he was jealous.

"Don't be silly," she said, because he wasn't being silly.

So out he went. He missed connections and spent one night in a depot and had his portable typewriter stolen and found he'd forgotten to pack the brown shoes that went with the brown suit. He brushed his teeth once with shaving cream and took the wrong creaking rural bus and had to creak in to an impossibly authentic small town and creak out again on another bus. Turnville was a general store with gasoline pumps outside and an abandoned milk shed across the road, and Cris wasn't happy when he got there. He went into the general store to ask questions.

The proprietor was a triumph of type-casting. "Whut c'n I dew fr you, young feller? Shay—yer fm the city, ain't cha? Heh!"

Cris fumbled vaguely with his lapels, wondering if someone had pinned a sign on him. "I'm looking for someone called Sig Weiss. Know him?"

"Sure dew. Meanest bastard ever lived. Wouldn't have nought to dew with him, I was you."

"You're not," said Cris, annoyed. "Where does he live?"

"What you want with him?"

"I'm conducting a nation-wide survey of mean bastards," Cris said. "Where does he live?"

"You're on the way to the right place, then. Heh! You show me a man's friends, I'll tell you what he is."

"What about his friends?" Cris asked, startled.

"He ain't got any friends."

Cris closed his eyes and breathed deeply. "Where does he live?"

"Up the road a piece. Two mile, a bit over. That way."

"Thanks."

"He'll shoot you," said the proprietor complacently, "but don't let it worry you none. He loads his shells with rock salt."

Cris walked the two miles and a bit, every uphill inch. He was tired, and his shoes were designed only to carry a high shine and make small smudges on desk tops. It was hot until he reached the top of the mountain, and then the cool wind from the other side made him feel as if he was carrying sacks of crushed ice in his armpits. There was a galvanized tin mailbox on a post by the road with S. WEISS and advanced erosion showing on its ancient sides. In the cutbank near it were some shallow footholds. Cris sighed and started up.

There was a faint path writhing its way through heavy growth. Through the trees he could see a canted shingle roof. He had gone about forty feet when there was a thunderous explosion and shredded greenery settled about his head and shoulders. Sinking his teeth into his tongue, he turned and dove head first into a treebole, and the lights went out.

A fabulous headache was fully conscious before Cris was. He saw it clearly before it moved around behind his eyes. He was lying where he had fallen. A rangy youth with long narrow eyes was squatting ten feet away. He held a ready shotgun under his arm and on his wrist, while he deftly went through Cris's wallet.

"Hey," said Cris.

The man closed the wallet and threw it on the ground by Cris's throbbing head. "So you're Crisley Post," said the man, in a disgusted tone of voice.

Cris sat up and groaned. "You're—you're not Sig Weiss?"

"I'm not?" asked the man pugnaciously.

"Okay, okay," said Cris tiredly. He picked up his wallet and put it away and, with the aid of the tree trunk, got to his feet. Weiss made no move to help him, but watchfully rose with him. Cris asked, "Why the artillery?"

"I got a permit," said Weiss. "This is my land. Why not? Don't go blaming me because you ran into a tree. What do you want?"

"I just wanted to talk to you. I came a long way to do it. If I'd known you'd welcome me like this, I wouldn't've come."

"I didn't ask you to come."

"I'm not going to talk sense if I get sore," said Cris quietly. "Can't we go inside? My head hurts."

Weiss seemed to ponder this for a moment. Then he turned on his heel, grunted, "Come," and strode toward the house. Cris followed painfully.

A gray cat slid across the path and crouched in the long grass. Weiss appeared to ignore it, but as he stepped by, his right leg lashed out sidewise and lifted the yowling animal into the air. It struck a tree trunk and fell, to lie dazed. Cris let out an indignant shout and went to it. The cat cowered away from him, gained its feet and fled into the woods, terrified.

"Your cat?" asked Weiss coldly.

"No, but damn if—"

"If it isn't your cat, why worry?" Weiss walked steadily on toward the house.

Cris stood a moment, shock and fury roiling in and about his headache, and then followed. Standing there or going away would accomplish nothing.

The house was old, small, and solid. It was built of fieldstone, and the ceilings were low and heavy beamed. Overlooking the mountainside was an enormous window, bringing in a breathtaking view of row after row of distant hills. The furniture was rustic and built to be used. There was a fireplace with a crane, also more than ornamental. There were no drapes, no couch covers or flamboyant upholstery. There was comfort, but austerity was the keynote.

"May I sit down?" Cris asked caustically.

"Go ahead," said Weiss. "You can breathe, too, if you want to."

Cris sat in a large split-twig chair that was infinitely more comfortable than it looked. "What's the matter with you, Weiss?"

"Nothing the matter with me."

"What makes you like this? Why the chip on your shoulder? Why this shoot-first-ask-questions-afterward attitude? What's it get you?"

"Gets me a life of my own. Nobody bothers me but once. They don't come back. You won't."

"That's for sure," said Cris fervently, "but I wish I knew what's eating you. No normal human being acts like you do."

"That's enough," said Weiss very gently, and Cris knew how very seriously he meant it. "What I do and why is none of your business. What do you want here, anyhow?"

"I came to find out why you're not writing. That's my business. You're my client, remember?"

"You're my agent," he said. "I like the sound of it better that way."

Cris made an olympian effort and ignored the remark. "*The Traveling Crag* churned up quite a stir. You made yourself a nice piece of change. Write more, you'll make more. Don't you like money?"

"Who doesn't? You got no complaints out of me."

"Fine. Then what about some more copy?"

"You'll get it when I'm good and ready."

"Which is how soon?"

"How do I know?" Weiss barked. "When I feel like it, whenever that is."

Cris talked, then, at some length. He told Weiss some of the ins and outs of publishing. He explained how phenomenal it was that a pulp sale should have created such a turmoil, and pointed out what could be expected in the slicks and Hollywood. "I don't know how you've done it, but you've found a short line to the heavy sugar. But the only way you'll ever touch it is to write more."

"All right, all right," Weiss said at last. "You've sold me. You'll get your story. Is that what you wanted?"

"Not quite." Cris rose. He felt better, and he could allow himself to be angry now that the business was taken care of. "I still want to know how a guy like you could have written a story like *The Traveling Crag* in a place like this."

"Why not?"

Cris looked out at the rolling blue distance. "That story had more sheer humanity in it than anything I've ever read. It was sensitive and—damn it—it was a *kind* story. I can usually visualize who writes the stuff I read; I spend all my time with writing and writers. That story wasn't written in a place like this. And it wasn't written by a man like you."

"Where was it written?" asked Weiss in his very quiet voice. "And who wrote it?"

"Aw, put your dukes down," said Cris tiredly, and with such contempt that he apparently astonished Weiss. "If you're going to jump salty over every little thing that happens, what are you going to do when something big comes along and you've already shot your bolt?"

Weiss did not answer, and Cris went on: "I'm not saying you didn't write it. All I'm saying is that it reads like something dreamed up in some quiet place that smelled like flowers and good clean sweat . . . Some place where everything was right and nothing was sick or off balance. And whoever wrote it suited that kind of a place. It was probably you, but you sure have changed since."

"You know a hell of a lot, don't you?" The soft growl was not completely insulting, and Cris felt that in some obscure way he had scored. Then Weiss said, "Now get the hell out."

"Real glad to," said Cris. At the door, he said, "Thanks for the drink."

When he reached the cutbank, he looked back. Weiss was standing by the corner of the house, staring after him.

Cris trudged back to the crossroads called Turnville and stopped in at the general store. "Shay," said the proprietor. "Looks like a tree reached down and whopped ye. Heh!"

"Heh!" said Cris. "One did. I called it a son of a beech."

The proprietor slapped his knee and wheezed. "Shay, thet's a good 'un. Come out back, young feller, while I put some snake oil on your head. Like some cold beer?"

Cris blessed him noisily. The snake oil turned out to be a benzocaine ointment that took the pain out instantly, and the beer was a transfusion. He looked at the old man with new respect.

"Had a bad time up on the hill?" asked the oldster.

"No worse'n sharing an undershirt with a black widow spider," said Cris. "What's the matter with that character?"

"Nobuddy rightly knows," said the proprietor. "Came up here about eight years ago. Always been thet way. Some say the war did it to him, but I knew him before he went overseas and he was the same. He jest don't like people, is all. Old Tom Sackett, drives the RFD wagon, he says Weiss was weaned off a gallbladder to a bottle of vinegar. Heh!"

"Heh!" said Cris. "How's he live?"

"Gits a check every month. Some trust company. I cash 'em. Not much, but enough. He don't dew nahthin. Hunts a bit, roams these hills a hull lot. Reads. Heh! He's no trouble, though. Stays on his own reservation. Just don't want folks barrelin' in on him. Here comes yer bus."

"My God!" said Naome.

"You're addressing me?" he asked.

She ignored him. "Listen to this:

Jets blasting, Bat Durston came screeching down through the atmosphere of Bbllzznaj, a tiny planet seven billion light years from Sol. He cut out his superhyper-drive for the landing . . . and at that point a tall, lean spaceman stepped out of the tail assembly, proton gun-blaster in a space-tanned hand.

'Get back from those controls, Bat Durston,' the tall stranger lipped thinly. 'You don't know it, but this is your last space trip.' "

She looked up at him dazedly. "That's Sig Weiss?"

"That's Sig Weiss."

"The same Sig Weiss?"

"The very same. Leaf through that thing, Naome. Nine bloody thousand words of it, and it's all like that. Go on—read it."

"No," she said. It was not a refusal, but an exclamation. "Are you going to send it out?"

"Yes. To Sig Weiss. I'm going to tell him to roll it and stuff it up his shotgun. Honey, we have a one-shot on our hands."

"That is—it's impossible!" she blazed. "Cris, you can't give him up just like that. Maybe the next one . . . maybe you can . . . maybe you're right at that," she finished, glancing back at the manuscript.

He said tiredly, "Let's go eat."

"No. You have a lunch."

"I have?"

"With a Miss Tillie Moroney. You're quite safe. She's the Average American Miss. I mean it. She was picked out as such by pollsters last year. She's five-five, has had 2.3 years of college, is 24 years old, brown hair, blue eyes, and so on."

"How much does she weigh?"

"34B," said Naome, with instant understanding, "and presents a united front like a Victorian."

He laughed. "And what have I to do with Miss Tillie Moroney?"

"She's got money. I told you about her—that personals ad in the *Saturday Review*—remember? 'Does basic character ever change? $1000 for authentic case of devil into saint.' "

"Oh my gosh yes. You had this bright idea of calling her in after I told you about getting the Weiss treatment in Turnville." He waved at the manuscript. "Doesn't that change your plans any? You might make a case out of *The Traveling Crag* versus the cat-kicking of Mr. Weiss, if you use that old man's testimony that he's been kicking cats and people for some years. But from my experience," he touched his forehead, which was almost healed, "I'd say it was saint into devil."

"Her ad didn't mention temporary or permanent changes," Naome pointed out. "There may be a buck in it. You can handle her."

"Thanks just the same, but let me see what she looks like before I do any such thing. Personally, I think she's a crank. A mystic maybe. Do you know her?"

"Spoke to her on the phone. Saw her picture last year. The Average American Miss is permitted to be a screwball. That's what makes this country great."

"You and your Machiavellian syndrome. Can't I get out of it?"

"You cannot. What are you making such a fuss about? You've wined and dined uglier chicks than this."

"I know it. Do you think I'd have a chance to see her if I acted eager?"

"I despise you," said Naome. "Straighten your tie and go comb your hair. Oh, Cris, I know it sounds wacky. But what doesn't, in this business? What'll you lose? The price of a lunch!"

"I might lose my honor."

"Authors' agents have no honor."

"As my friend in the general store is wont to remark: Heh! What protects you, little one?"

"My honor," replied Naome.

The brown hair was neat and so was the tailored brown suit that matched it so well. The blue eyes were extremely dark. The rest well befit her Average Miss title, except for her voice, which had the pitch of a husky one while being clear as tropical shoals. Her general air was one of poised shyness. Cris pulled out a restaurant chair for her, which was a tribute; he felt impelled to do that about one time in seven.

"You think I'm a crank," she said when they were settled with a drink.

"Do I?"

"You do," she said positively. He did, too.

"Well," he said, "your ad did make it a little difficult to suspend judgement."

She smiled with him. She had good teeth. "I can't blame you, or the eight hundred-odd other people who answered. Why is it a thousand dollars is so much more appealing than such an incredible thought as a change from basic character?"

"I guess because most people would rather see the change from a thousand dollars."

He was pleased to find she had the rare quality of being able to talk coherently while she laughed. She said, "You are right. One of them wanted to marry me so I could change his character. He assured me that he was a regular devil. But—tell me about this case of yours."

He did, in detail: Sig Weiss's incredible short story, its wide impact, its deep call on everything that is fine and generous in everyone who read it. And then he described the man who had written it.

"In this business, you run into all kinds of flukes," he said. "A superficial, tone-deaf, materialistic character will sit down and write something that positively sings. You read the story, you know the guy, and you say he couldn't have written it. But you know he did. I've seen that time after time, and all it proves is that there are more facets to a man than you see at first—not that there's any real change in him. But Weiss—I'll admit that in his case the theory has got to be stretched to explain it. I'll swear a man like him simply could not contain the emotions and convictions that made *The Traveling Crag* what it is."

"I've read it," she said. He hadn't noticed her lower lip was so full. Perhaps it hadn't been, a moment ago. "It was a beautiful thing."

"Now, tell me about this ad of yours. Have you found such a basic change—devil into saint? Or do you just hope to?"

"I don't know of any such case," she admitted. "But I know it can happen."

"How?"

She paused. She seemed to be listening. Then she said, "I can't tell you. I . . . know something that can have that effect, that's all. I'm trying to find out where it is."

"I don't understand that. You don't think Sig Weiss was under such an influence, do you?"

"I'd like to ask him. I'd like to know if the effect was at all lasting."

"Not so you'd notice it," he said glumly. "He gave me that bouncing around after he wrote *The Traveling Crag,* not before. Not only that . . ." He told her about the latest story.

"Do you suppose he wrote that under the same circumstances as *The Traveling Crag?*"

"I don't see why not. He's a man of pretty regular habits. He probably— wait a minute! Just before I left, I said something to him . . . something about . . ." He drummed on his temples. ". . . Something about the *Crag* reading as if it had been written in a different place, by a different person. And he didn't get sore. He looked at me as if I were a swami. Seems I hit the nail right on the thumb."

The listening expression crossed her smooth face again. She looked up, startled. "Has he got any . . ." She closed her eyes, straining for something. "Has he a radio? I mean—a shortwave set—a transmitter—diathermy—a fever cabinet—any . . . uh . . . RF generator of any kind?"

"What in time made you ask that?"

She opened her eyes and smiled shyly at him. "It just came to me."

"Saving your presence, Miss Moroney, but there are moments when you give me the creeps," he blurted. "I'm sorry. I guess I shouldn't have said that, but—"

"It's all right," she said warmly.

"You hear voices?" he asked.

She smiled. "What about the RF generator?"

"I don't know." He thought hard. "He has electricity. I imagine he has a receiver. About the rest, I really can't say. He didn't take me on a grand tour. Will you tell me what made you ask that?"

"No."

He opened his mouth to protest, but when he saw her expression he closed it again. She asked, "What are you going to do about Weiss?"

"Drop him. What else?"

"Oh, please don't!" she cried. She put a hand on his sleeve. "Please!"

"What else do you expect me to do?" he asked in some annoyance. "A writer who sends in a piece of junk like that as a followup to something like the *Crag* is more than foolish. He's stupid. I can't use a client like that. I'm busy. I got troubles."

"Also, he gave you a bad time."

"That hasn't anyth—well, you're right. If he behaved like a human being, maybe I would take a lot of trouble and analyze his trash and guide and urge and wipe his nose for him. But a guy like that—nah!"

"He has another story like the *Crag* in him."

"You think he has?"

"I know he has."

"You're very positive. Your . . . voices tell you that?"

She nodded, with a small secret smile.

"I have the feeling you're playing with me. You know this Weiss?"

"Oh, no! And I'm not playing with you. Truly. You've got to believe me!" She looked genuinely distressed.

"I don't see why I should. This begins to look real haywire, Tillie Moroney. I think maybe we'd better get down to basics here." She immediately looked so worried that he recognized an advantage. Not knowing exactly what she wanted of him, he knew she wanted something, and now he was prepared to use that to the hilt. "Tell me about it. What's your interest in Weiss? What's this personality-alteration gimmick? What are you after and what gave you your lead? And what do you expect me to do about it? That last question reads, 'What's in it for me?' "

"Y-you're not always very nice, are you?"

He said, more gently, "The last wasn't thrown in to be mean. It was an appeal to your good sense to appeal to my sincerity. You can always judge sincerity—your own or anyone else's—by finding out what's in it for the interested party. Altruism and real sincerity are mutually exclusive. Now, talk. I mean, talk, please."

Again that extraordinary harking expression. Then she drew a deep breath. "I've had an awful time," she said. "Awful. You can't know. I've answered letters and phone calls. I've met cranks and wolves and religious fanatics who have neat little dialectical capsules all packed and ready to make saints out of devils. They all yap about proof—sometimes it's themselves and sometimes it's someone they know—and the proof always turns out to be a reformed drunk or a man who turned to Krishna and no longer beats his wife, not since Tuesday . . ." She stopped for breath and half-smiled at him and, angrily, he felt a warm surge of liking for her. She went on, "And this is the first hint I've had that what I'm looking for really exists."

She leaned forward suddenly. "I need you. You already have a solid contact with Sig Weiss and the way he works. If I had to seek him out myself, I— well, I just wouldn't know how to start. And this is urgent, can't you understand—urgent!"

He looked deep into the dark blue eyes and said, "I understand fine."

She said, "If I tell you a . . . story, will you promise not to ask me any questions about it?"

He fiddled about with his fork for a moment and then said, "I once heard tell of a one-legged man who was pestered by all the kids in the neighborhood about how he lost his leg. They followed him and yelled at him and tagged along after him and made no end of a nuisance of themselves. So one day he stopped and gathered them all around him and asked if they really wanted to know how he lost his leg, and they all chorused YES! And he wanted to know if he told them, would they stop asking him, and they all promised faithfully that they would stop. 'All right,' he said. 'It was bit off.' And he turned and stumped away. As to the promise you want—no."

She laughed ruefully. "All right. I'll tell you the story anyway. But you've got to understand that it isn't the whole story, and that I'm not at liberty to tell the whole story. So please don't pry too hard."

He smiled. He had, he noticed in her eyes, a pretty nice smile. "I'll be good."

"All right. You have a lot of clients who write science fiction, don't you?"

"Not a lot. Just the best," he said modestly.

She smiled again. Two curved dimples put her smile in parenthesis. He liked that. She said, "Let's say this is a science fiction plot. How to begin . . ."

"Once upon a time . . ." he prompted.

She laughed like a child. "Once upon a time," she nodded, "there was a very advanced humanoid race in another galaxy. They had had wars—lots of them. They learned how to control them, but every once in a while things would get out of hand and another, and worse, war would happen. They developed weapon after weapon—things which make the H-bomb like a campfire in comparison. They had planet-smashers. They could explode a sun. They could do things we can only dimly understand. They could put a local warp in time itself, or unify the polarity in the gravitomagnetic field of an entire solar system."

"Does this gobbledegook come easy to you?" he asked.

"It does just now," she answered shyly. "Anyway, they developed the ultimate weapon—one which made all the others obsolete. It was enormously difficult to make, and only a few were manufactured. The secret of making it died out, and the available stocks were used at one time or another. The time to use them is coming again—and I don't mean on Earth. The little fuses we have are flea-hops. This is important business.

"Now, a cargo ship was travelling between galaxies on hyperspatial drive. In a crazy, billion-to-one odds accident, it emerged into normal space smack in the middle of a planetoid. It wasn't a big one; the ship wasn't atomized—just wrecked. It was carrying one of these super-weapons. It took thousands of years to trace it, but it has been traced. The chances are strong that it came down on a planet. It's wanted.

"It gives out no detectable radiation. But in its shielded state, it has a peculiar effect on living tissues which come near it."

"Devils into saints?"

"The effect is . . . peculiar. Now . . ." She held up fingers. "If the nature of this object were known, and if it fell into the wrong hands, the effect here on

Earth could be dreadful. There are megalomaniacs on earth so unbalanced that they would threaten even their own destruction unless their demands were met. Point two: If the weapon were used on Earth, not only would Earth as we know it cease to exist, but the weapon would be unavailable to those who need it importantly."

Cris sat staring at her, waiting for more. There was no more. Finally he licked his lips and said, "You're telling me that Sig Weiss has stumbled across this thing."

"I'm telling you a science fiction plot."

"Where did you get your . . . information?"

"It's a science fiction story."

He grinned suddenly, widely. "I'll be good," he said again. "What do you want me to do?"

Her eyes became very bright. "You aren't like most agents," she said.

"When I was in a British Colony, the English used to say to me, every once in a while, 'You aren't like most Americans.' I always found it slightly insulting. All right; what do you want me to do?"

She patted his hand. "See if you can make Weiss write another *Traveling Crag*. If he can, then find out exactly how and where he wrote it. And let me know."

They rose. He helped her with her light coat. He said, "Know something?" When she smiled up at him he said, "You don't strike me as Miss Average."

"Oh, but I was," she answered softly. "I was."

TELEGRAM

SIG WEISS   JULY 15
TURNVILLE

PLEASE UNDERSTAND THAT WHAT FOLLOWS HAS NOTHING WHATEVER TO DO WITH YOUR GROSS LACK OF HOSPITALITY. I REALIZE THAT YOUR WAY OF LIFE ON YOUR OWN PROPERTY IS JUSTIFIED IN TERMS OF ME, AN INTRUDER. I AM FORGETTING THE EPISODE. I ASSUME YOU ALREADY HAVE. NOW TO BUSINESS: YOUR LAST MANUSCRIPT IS THE MOST UTTERLY INSULTING DOCUMENT I HAVE SEEN IN FOURTEEN PROFESSIONAL YEARS. TO INSULT ONE'S AGENT IS STANDARD OPERATING PROCEDURE: TO INSULT ONESELF IS INEXCUSABLE AND BROTHER YOU'VE DONE IT. SIT DOWN AND READ THE STORY THROUGH, IF YOU CAN, AND THEN REREAD THE TRAVELING CRAG. YOU WILL NOT NEED MY CRITICISM. MY ONLY SUG-GESTION TO YOU IS TO DUPLICATE EXACTLY THE CIRCUMSTANCES UNDER WHICH YOU WROTE YOUR FIRST STORY. UNLESS AND UNTIL YOU DO THIS WE NEED HAVE NO FURTHER COR-RESPONDENCE. I ACCEPT YOUR SINCERE THANKS FOR NOT SUBMITTING YOUR SECOND STORY ANYWHERE.

CRISLEY POST

Naome whistled. "Really—a straight telegram? What about a night letter?"

Cris smiled at the place where the wall met the ceiling. "Straight rate."

"Yes, master." She wielded a busy pencil. "That's costing us $13.75, sir," she said at length, "plus tax. Grand total, $17.46. Cris, you have a hole in your head!"

"If you know of a better 'ole, go to it," he quoted dreamily. She glared at him, reached for the phone, and continued to glare as she put the telegram on the wire.

In the next two weeks Cris had lunch three times with Tillie Moroney, and dinner once. Naome asked for a raise. She got it, and was therefore frightened.

Cris returned from the third of these lunches (which was the day after the dinner) whistling. He found Naome in tears.

"Hey ... what's happening here? You don't do that kind of thing, remember?"

He leaned over her desk. She buried her face in her arms and boohooed lustily. He knelt beside her and put an arm around her shoulders. "There," he said, patting the nape of her neck. "Take a deep breath and tell me about it."

She took a long, quavering breath, tried to speak, and burst into tears again. "F-f-fi-fi ..."

"What?"

"F—" She swallowed with difficulty, then said, *"Fire of Heaven!"* and wailed.

"What?" he yelled. "I thought you said *'Fire of Heaven.'* "

She blew her nose and nodded. "I did," she whispered. "H-here." She dumped a pile of manuscript in front of him and buried her face in her arms again. "L-leave me alone."

In complete bewilderment, he gathered up the typewritten sheets and took them to his desk.

There was a covering letter.

Dear Mr. Post: There will never be a way for me to express my thanks to you, nor my apologies for the way I treated you when you visited me. I am willing to do anything in my power to make amends.

Knowing what I do of you, I think you would be most pleased by another story written the way I did the Crag. Here it is. I hope it measures up. If it doesn't, I earnestly welcome any suggestions you may have to fix it up.

I am looking forward very much indeed to meeting you again under better circumstances. My house is yours when you can find time to come out, and I do hope it will be soon. Sincerely, S. W.

With feelings of awe well mixed with astonishment, Cris turned to the manuscript. *Fire of Heaven,* by Sig Weiss, it was headed. He began to read. For a moment, he was conscious of Naome's difficult and diminishing sniffs, and then he became completely immersed in the story.

Twenty minutes later, his eyes, blurred and smarting, encountered "The End." He propped his forehead on one palm and rummaged clumsily for his handkerchief. Having thoroughly mopped and blown, he looked across at Naome. Her eyes were red-rimmed and still wet. "Yes?" she said.

"Oh my God yes," he answered.

They stared at each other for a breathless moment. Then she said in a soprano near-whisper: *"Fire of . . ."* and began to cry again.

"Cut it out," he said hoarsely.

When he could, he got up and opened the window. Naome came and stood beside him. "You don't read that," he said after a time. "It . . . happens to you."

She said, "What a tragedy. What a beautiful, beautiful tragedy."

"He said in his letter," Cris managed, "that if I had any suggestions to fix it up . . ."

"Fix it up," she said in shaken scorn. "There hasn't been anything like him since—"

"There hasn't been anything like him period." Cris snapped his fingers. "Get on your phone. Call the airlines. Two tickets to the nearest feederfield to Turnville. Call the Drive-Ur-Self service. Have a car waiting at the field. I'm not asking any woman to climb that mountain on foot. Send this telegram to Weiss: Taking up your very kind offer immediately. Bringing a friend. Will wire arrival time. Profound thanks for the privilege of reading *Fire of Heaven.* From a case hardened ten percenter those words come hard and are well earned. Post."

"Two tickets," said Naome breathlessly. "Oh! Who's going to handle the office?"

He thumped her shoulder. "You can do it, kid. You're wonderful. Indispensable. I love you. Get me Tillie Moroney's number, will you?"

She stood frozen, her lips parted, her nostrils slightly distended. He looked at her, looked again. He was aware that she had stopped breathing. "Naome!"

She came to life slowly and turned, not to him, but on him. "You're taking that—that Moron-y creature—"

"Moroney. What's the matter with you?"

"Oh Cris, how could you?"

"What have I done? What's wrong? Listen, this is business. I'm not romancing the girl! Why—"

She curled her lip. "Business! Then it's the first business that's gone on around here that I haven't known about."

"Oh, it isn't office business, Naome. Honestly."

"Then there's only one thing it could be!"

Cris threw up his hands. "Trust me this once. Say! Why should it eat you so much, even if it was monkey-business, which it isn't?"

"I can't bear to see you throw yourself away!"

"You—I didn't know you felt—"

"Shut up!" she roared. "Don't flatter yourself. It's just that she's . . . average. And so are you. And when you add an average to an average, you've produced NOTHING!"

He sat down at his desk with a thump and reached for the phone, very purposefully. But his mind was in such a tangle at the moment, that he didn't know what to do with the phone once it was in his hands, until Naome stormed over and furiously dropped a paper in front of him. It had Tillie's number on it. He grinned at her stupidly and sheepishly and dialled. By this time, Naome was speaking to the airlines office, but he knew perfectly well she could talk and listen at the same time.

"Hello?" said the phone.

"Ull-ull," he said, watching Naome's back stiffen. He spun around in his swivel chair so he could talk facing the wall.

"Hello?" said the phone again.

"Tillie, Weiss found it he wrote another story it's a dream he invited me down and I'm going and you're coming with me," he blurted.

"I beg your—Cris, is anything the matter? You sound so strange."

"Never mind that," he said. He repeated the news more coherently, acutely conscious of Naome's attention to every syllable. Tillie uttered a cry of joy and promised to be right over. He asked her to hang on and forced himself to get the plane departure from Naome. Pleading packing and business odds and ends, he asked her to meet him at the airport. She agreed, for which he was very thankful. The idea of her walking into the office just now was more than he could take.

Naome had done her phoning and was in a flurry of effort involving her files, which had always been a mystery to Cris. She kept bringing things over to him. "Sign these." "You promised to drop Rogers a note about this." "What do you want done about Borilla's scripts?" Until he was snowed under. "Hold it! These things can wait!"

"No they can't," she said icily. "I wouldn't want them on my conscience. You see, this is my last day here."

"Your—Naome! You can't quit! You can't!"

"I can and I am and I do. Check this list."

"Naome, I—"

"I won't listen. My mind's made up."

"All right then. I'll manage. But it's a shame about *Fire of Heaven*. Such a beautiful job. And here it must sit until I get back. I did want you to market it."

"You'd trust me to market that story?" Her eyes were huge.

"No one else. There isn't anyone who knows the market better, or who would make a better deal. I trust you with it absolutely. After you've done that one last big thing for me—go, then, if you'll be happier somewhere else."

"Crisley Post, I hate you and despise you. You're a fiend and a spider. Th-thank you. I'll never forget you for this. I'll type up four originals and sneak them around. Movies, of course. What a TV script! And radio . . . let's see; two, no—three British outfits can bid against each other . . . you're doing this on purpose to keep me from leaving!"

"Sure," he said jovially. "I'm real cute. I wrote the story myself just because I couldn't get anyone to replace you."

At last, she laughed. "There's one thing I'm damn sure you didn't do. An editor is a writer who can't write, and an agent is a writer who can't write as well as an editor."

He laughed with her. He bled too, but it was worth it, to see her laughing again.

The plane trip was pleasant. It lasted a long time. The ship set down every 45 minutes or so all the way across the country. Cris figured it was the best Naome could do on short notice. But it gave them lots of time to talk. And talking to Tillie was a pleasure. She was intelligent and articulate, and had read just as many of his favorite books as he had of hers. He told her enough about *Fire of Heaven* to intrigue her a lot and make her cry a little, without spoiling the plot for her. They found music to disagree about, and shared a view of a wonderful lake down through the clouds, and all in all it was a good trip. Occasionally, Cris glanced at her—most often when she was asleep—with a touch of surmise, like a little curl of smoke, thinking of Naome's suspicions about him and Tillie. He wasn't romancing Tillie. He wasn't. Was he?

They landed at last, and again he blessed Naome; the Drive-Ur-Self car was at the airfield. They got a road map from a field attendant and drove off through the darkest morning hours. Again Cris found himself glancing at the relaxed girl beside him, half asleep in the cold glow of the dash lights. A phrase occurred to him: "undivided front like a Victorian"—Naome's remark. He flushed. It was true. An affectation of Tillie's, probably; but everything she wore was highnecked and full-cut.

The sky had turned from gray to pale pink when they pulled up at the Tunrville store. Cris honked, and in due course the screen door slammed and the old proprietor ambled down the wooden steps and came to peer into his face.

"Heh! If 'taint that city feller. How're ya, son? Didn't know you folks ever got up and about this early."

"We're up late, dad. Got some gas for us?"

"Reckon there's a drop left."

Cris got out and went back with the old man to unlock the gas tank. "Seen Weiss recently?" he asked.

"Same as usual. Put through some big orders. Seen him do that before. Usually means he's holing up for five, six months. Though why he bought so much liquor an' drape material and that, I can't figure."

"How'd he behave?"

"Same as ever. Friendly as a wet wildcat with fleas."

Cris thanked him and paid him and they turned up the rocky hill road. As they reached the crest, they gasped together at the sun-flood valley that lay before them. "Memories are the only thing you ever have that you always keep," said Tillie softly, "and this is one for both of us. I'm . . . glad you're in it for me, Cris."

"I love you, too," he said in the current idiom, and found himself, hot-faced, looking into a face as suffused as his. They recoiled from each other and started to chatter about the weather—stopped and roared together with laughter. He took her hand and helped her up the cutbank. They paused at the top. "Listen," he said in a low voice. "That old character in the store has seen Weiss recently. And he says there's no change. I think we'd better be just a little careful."

He looked at her and again caught that listening expression. "No," she said at length, "it's all right. The store's outside the . . . the influence he's under. He's bound to revert when it's gone. But he'll be all right now. You'll see."

"Will you tell me how you know these things?" he demanded, almost angry.

"Of course," she smiled. Then the smile vanished. "But not now."

"That's more than I've gotten so far," he grumbled. "Well, let's get to it."

Hand in hand, they went up the path. The house seemed the same, and yet . . . there was a difference, an intensification. The leaves were greener, the early sun warmer.

There were three gray kittens on the porch.

"Ahoy the house!" Cris called self-consciously.

The door opened, and Weiss stood there, peering. He looked for a moment exactly as he had when he watched Cris stride off on the earlier visit. Then he moved out into the sun. He scooped up one of the kittens and came swiftly to meet them. "Mr. Post! I got your wire. How very good of you to come."

He was dressed in a soft sport shirt and gray slacks—a startling difference from his grizzled boots-and-khaki appearance before. The kitten snuggled into the crook of his elbow, made a wild grab at his pocket-button, caught its tail instead. He put it down, and it fawned and purred and rubbed against his shoe.

Weiss straightened up and smiled at Tillie. "Hello."

"Tillie, this is Sig Weiss. Miss Moroney."

"Tillie," she said, and gave him her hand.

"Welcome home," Weiss said. He turned to Cris. "This is your home, for as long as you want it, whenever you can come."

Cris stood slack-jawed. "I ought to be more tactful," he said at length, "but I just can't believe it. I should have more sense than to mention my last visit, but this—this—"

Weiss put a hand on his shoulder. "I'm glad you mentioned it. I've been thinking about it, too. Hell—if you'd forgotten all about it, how could you appreciate all this? Come on in. I have some surprises for you."

Tillie held Cris back a moment. "It's here," she whispered. "Here in the house!"

The weapon—here? Somehow, he had visualized it as huge—a great horned mine or a tremendous torpedo shape. He glanced around apprehensively. The ultimate weapon—invented after the planet-smasher, the sun-burster—what incredible thing could it be?

Weiss stood by the door. Tillie stepped through, then Cris.

The straight drapes, the solid sheet of plate glass that replaced the huge sashed window; the heavy skins that softened the wide-planked floor, the gleaming andirons and the copper pots on the fieldstone wall; the record-player and racks of albums—all the other soothing, comforting finishes of the once-bleak room—all these Cris noticed later. His big surprise was not quite a hundred pounds, not quite five feet tall—

"Cris . . ."

"Naome's here," he said inanely, and sat down to goggle at her.

Weiss laughed richly. "Why do you suppose you and Tillie got that pogo-plane cross country, stopping at every ball-park and cornfield? Naome got a non-stop flight to within fifty miles of here, and air-taxi to the bottom of the mountain, and came up by cab."

"I had to," said Naome. "I had to see what you were getting into. You're so—impetuous." She came smiling to Tillie. "I am glad to see you."

"Why, you idiot!" said Cris to Naome. "What could you have done if he—if—"

"I'm prettier than you are, darling," laughed Naome.

"She came pussyfooting up to the house like a kid playing Indian," said Weiss. "I circled through the woods and pussyfooted right along with her. When she was peeping into the side window, I reached out and put a hand on her shoulder."

"You might have scared her into a conniption!"

"Not here," said Weiss gravely.

Surprisingly, Tillie nodded. "You can't be afraid here, Cris. You're saying all those things about what might have happened, but they're not frightening to think about now, are they?"

"No," Cris said thoughtfully. "No." He gazed around him. "This is—crazy. Everybody should be this crazy."

"It would help," said Weiss. "How do you like the place now, Cris?"

"It's-it's grand," said Cris. Naome laughed. She said, "Listen to the vocabulary kid there. 'Grand.' You meant 'Peachy,' didn't you?"

Cris didn't laugh with the others. "Fear," he said. "You can't eliminate fear. Fear is a survival emotion. If you didn't know fear, you'd fall out of windows, cut yourself on rocks, get hunted and killed by mountain lions."

"If I open the window," Weiss asked, "would you be afraid to jump out? Come over here and look."

Cris stepped to the great window. He had not known that the house was built so close to the edge. Crag on crag, fold after billow, the land fell down and away to the distant throat of the valley. Cris stepped back respectfully. "Open it if you like," he said, and swallowed, "and somebody else can jump. Not me, kiddies."

Sig Weiss smiled. "Q.E.D. Survival fear is still with us. What we've lost here is fear of anything that is not so. When you came here before, you saw a very frightened man. Most of my fears were 'might-be' fears. I was afraid people might attack me, so I attacked first. I was afraid of seeming different from people, so I stayed where my imagined difference would not show. I was afraid of being the same as people, so I tried to be different."

"What does it?" Cris asked.

"What makes us all what we are now? Something I found. I won't tell you what it is or where it is. I call it an amulet, a true magic amulet, knowing that it's no more or less magic than flame springing to the end of a wooden stick." He took a kitchen match from his pocket and ran his thumbnail across it. It flared up, and he flipped it into the fireplace. "I won't tell you where or what it is because, although I've lost my fear, I haven't lost my stubbornness. I've lived miserably, a partial, hunted, hunting existence, and now I'm alive. And I mean to stay this way."

"Where did you find it?" Tillie asked. "Mind telling us that?"

"Not at all. A half mile down the mountain there was a tremendous rockfall a couple of years ago. No one owns that land; no one noticed. I climbed down there once looking for hawks' eggs. I found a place . . .

"How can I tell you what that place was like, or what it was like to find it? It was a brush-grown, rocky hillside near the gaping scar of the slide, where the crust of years had sloughed away. Maybe the mountain moved its shoulder in its sleep. There were flowers—ordinary wildflowers—but perfect, vivid, vital. They lived long and hardily, and they were beautiful. The bushes had an extraordinary green and a fine healthy gloss, and it was a place where the birds came close to me as I sat and watched them. It was the birds who taught me that fear never walked in that place.

"How can I tell you—what can I say about the meaning of that place to me? I'd been a psychic cripple all my life, hobbling through the rough country of my own ideas, spending myself in battle against ghosts I had invented to justify my fears, for fear was there first. And when I found that place, my inner self threw away its crutches. More than that—it could fly!

"How can I tell you what it meant to me to leave that place? To walk away from it was to buckle on the braces, pick up the crutches again, to feel my new wings moult and fall away.

"I went there more and more. Once I took my typewriter and worked there, and that was *The Traveling Crag*. Cris never knew how offended I was, how invaded, to find that he had divined the existence of that place through the story. That was why I turned out that other abortion, out of stubbornness—a desire to prove to Cris and to myself that my writing came from me and not from the magic of that place. I know better now. I don't know what another writer would do here. Better than anything he could conceivably do anywhere else. But it wouldn't be the *Crag* or *Fire*, because they could only have been mine."

Cris asked, "Would you let another writer work here?"

"I'd love it! Do you mean to ask if I want to monopolize this place, and the wonders it works? Of course not. One or another fear or combinations of fear are at the base of any monopoly, whether it's in industry, or in politics, or in the area of religious thought. And there's no fear here."

"There should be some sort of a—a shrine here," murmured Naome.

"There is. There will be, as long as I can keep the amulet. I found it, you see. It was lying right out in the sun. I took it and brought it here. The birds wouldn't forgive me for a while, but I've made them happy here since. And here it is and here it will stay, and there's your shrine."

Fear walked in then. It closed gently on Cris's heart, and he turned to look at Tillie. Her eyes were closed. She was listening.

A hell of an agent I turned out to be, he thought. How much I was willing to do for Weiss, how much for all the world through his work! By himself he found himself, the greatest of human achievements. And I have done the one thing that will take that way from him and from us all, leaving only the dwindling memory of this life without fear—and two great short stories.

He looked at Tillie again. His gaze caught hers, and she rose. Her features were rigidly controlled, but through his mounting fear Cris could recognize the thing she was fighting. She surely understood what was about to happen to Weiss and to the world if she succeeded. Her understanding versus her ... orders, was it?

Cris had sat in that incredible aura, listening to the joyous expression of Sig Weiss's delivery from fear, and he had thought of killing. Now, he realized that part of her already thought as he did, and perhaps ... perhaps ...

"Sig, can we look around outside?" Cris had stepped over to Tillie almost before he knew he wanted to.

"You own the place," said Weiss cheerfully. "Naome and I'll stir up some food. You've had a nice leisurely trip. I wonder if you realize that Naome spent fourteen hours on a typewriter before she took that long hop? *Fire of Heaven's* well launched now, thanks to her. Anyway, she deserves food."

"And a golden crown, which I shall include in the next pay envelope. Thank you, Naome. You're out of your mind."

"Thank you," she twinkled.

Cris led Tillie out, and they walked rapidly away from the house. "Not too far," she cautioned. "Let's stay where we can think. We're in a magic circle, you know, and outside we'll be afraid of each other, and of ourselves and of all our ghosts."

He asked her, "What are you going to do?"

"I shouldn't have got you into this. I should have come by myself."

"I'd have stopped you then. Don't you see? Sig would have told me. Even with whatever help you have, you couldn't have succeeded in getting the weapon on the first try. He's too alert, too alive, far too jealous of what the 'amulet' has given him. He'd have told me, and I'd have stopped you, to save him and his work. You made me an ally, and that prevented me."

"Cris, Cris, I didn't think that out!"

"I know you didn't. It was done for you. Who is it, Tillie? Who?"

"A ship," she whispered. "A space ship."

"You've seen it?"

"Oh, yes."

"Where is it?"

"Here."

"Here, in Turnville?"

She nodded.

"And it—they—communicate with you?"

"Yes."

He asked her again. "What are you going to do?"

"If I tell you I'll get the weapon, you'll kill me to save Weiss, and his work, and his birds, and his shrine, and all they can mean to the world. Won't you, Cris?"

"I will certainly try."

"And if I refuse to get it for them—"

"Would they kill you?"

"They could."

"If they did, could they then get the weapon?"

"I don't know. I don't think so. They've never forced me, Cris, never. They've always appealed to my reason. I think if they could control me or anyone else, they'd have done it. They'd have to find another human ally, and start the persuading process all over again. By which time Weiss and everyone else would be warned, and it would be much more difficult for them."

"Nothing's difficult for them," he said suddenly. "They can smash planets."

"Cris, we don't think as well as they do, but we don't think the way they do, either. And from what I can get, I'm sure that they're good—that they will do anything they can to spare this planet and the life on it. That seems to be one of the big reasons for their wanting to get that weapon away from here."

"And what of their other aims, then? Can we take all this away from humanity in favor of some cosmic civilization that we don't know and have never seen, which regards us as a dust-fleck in a minor galaxy? Let's face it, Tilly: they'll get it sooner or later. They're strong enough. But let's keep it while we can. A minute, a day of this aura is a minute or a day in which a human being can know what it's like to live without fear. Look at what it's done for Weiss; think what it can do for others. What are you going to do?"

"I— Kiss me, Cris."

His lips had just touched hers when there was a small giggle behind them. Cris whirled.

"Bless you, my children."

"Naome!"

"I didn't mean to bust anything up. I mean that." She skipped up to them. "You can go right back to it after I've finished interrupting. But I've just got to tell you. You know the fright Sig tried to throw into me when I got here last night? I'm getting even. I found his amulet. I really did. It was stuck to the underside of a shelf in the linen closet. You'd have to be my size to see it. I swiped it."

Tillie's breath hissed in. "Where is it? What did you do with it?"

"Oh, don't worry, it's safe enough. I hid it good, this time. Now we'll make him wonder where it is."

"Where is it?" asked Cris.

"Promise not to tell him?"

"Of course."

"Well, it's smack in the innards of one of his pet new possessions. You haven't been in the west room—the ell he calls a library—have you?"

They shook their heads.

"Well, he's got himself a great big radio. I lifted the lid, see, and down inside among the tubes and condensers and all that macaroni are some wire hoops, sort of. This amulet, it's a tiny thing—maybe four inches long and as wide as my two thumbs. It's sort of—blurry around the edges. Anyway, I stuck it inside one set of those hoops. Cris—you're green! What's the matter?"

"Tillie—the coil—the RF coil. If he turns that set on—"

"Oh, dear God . . ." Tillie breathed.

"What's the matter with you two? I didn't do anything wrong, did I?"

They raced into the house, through the living room. "In here!" bellowed

Cris. They pounded to the west room, getting into each other's way as they went in.

Sig Weiss was there, smiling. "Just in time. I want to show you the best damn transceiver in—"

"Don't! Don't touch it—"

"Oh a little hamming won't hurt," said Sig.

He threw the switch.

There was a loud click and a shower of dust.

And silence.

Naome came all the way in, went like a sleepwalker to the radio and opened the lid. There was a hole in the gray crinkle-finished steel, roughly rectangular. Weiss looked at it curiously, touched it, looked up. There was a similar hole in the ceiling. He bent over the chassis. "Now how do you like that! A coil torn all to hell. Something came down through the roof—see?—and smashed right through my new transmitter."

"It didn't go down," said Cris hoarsely. "It went up."

Naome began to cry.

"What the hell's the matter with you people?" Sig demanded.

Cris suddenly clutched Tillie's arm. "The ship! The space ship! They wouldn't let it go off while they're here!"

"They did," said Tillie in a flat voice.

"Will somebody please tell me what gives here?" asked Sig plaintively.

Through a thick silence, Tillie said, "I'll tell it." She sank down on her knees, slowly sat on the rug. "Cris knows most of this," she said. "Don't stop to wonder if it's all true. It is." She told about the races, the wars, the weapons of greater and greater destructiveness and, finally, the ultimate weapon, and its strange effect on living tissue. "Eight months ago, the ship contacted me. There was a connection made with my nerve-endings. I don't understand it. It wasn't telepathy; they were artificial neural currents. They talked to me. They've been talking ever since."

"My amulet!" Sig suddenly cried. "Sit down," said Tillie flatly. He sat.

Cris said, "I thought you required some physical contact for them to communicate with you. But I've been with you while you were communicating, and you had no contact."

"I hadn't?" She began to unbutton her blouse at the throat. She stopped with the fourth button, and gently drew out a metal object shaped somewhat like a bulbous spearhead with a blunt point. It glittered strangely with a color not quite that of gold and not quite of polished brass. It seemed to be glazed with a thin layer of clear crystal.

"Oh-h-h," breathed Naome, in a revelatory tone.

Tillie smiled suddenly at her. "You minx. You always wondered why I never wore a V-neck. Come here, all of you. Down on the rug."

Mystified, they gathered around. "Put your hands on it." They did so, and stared at each other, and at their hands, waiting like old maids over a Ouija board. "It hurts a tiny bit at first as the probes go in, but it passes quickly. Be very still."

A strange, not unpleasant prickling sensation came and went. There was a slight shock, another, more prickling.

Testing. Testing. Naome Cris Sig Tillie . . .

"Everybody get that?" asked Tillie calmly.

Naome squeaked. "It's like someone talking inside my sinuses!"

"It said our names," said Sig tautly. Cris nodded, fascinated.

The silent voice spoke: *Sig, your amulet is gone and you have lost nothing.*

Tillie, you have been faithful to your own.

Naome, you have been used, and you have done no wrong.

Cris, we have observed that it takes superhuman understanding to guide and direct work you cannot do yourself.

Reorient your thinking, all of you. You insist that what is lethal or cosmically important must be huge. You insist that anything which transcends a horror must be greater horror.

The amulet was indeed the ultimate weapon. Its effect is not to destroy, but to stop useless conflict. At this moment there is a chain reaction occurring throughout this planet's atmosphere affecting only one rare isotope of nitrogen. In times to come, your people will understand its radiochemistry; it is enough for you now to know that its most significant effect is to turn on the full analytical powers of the mind whenever fear is experienced. Panic occurs when analysis is shut off. Embarrassment occurs when fear is not analyzed. Hereafter, no truck-driver will fear to use the word 'exquisite', no propagandist will create the semblance of truth by repeating falsehoods, no human group will be able to instill fears about any other human group which are not common to the respective individuals of the groups. There will be no fear-ridden movements of securities, and no lovers will be with each other and afraid to state their love. In large issues and in small ones, the greater the emergency the greater will be the stimulation of the analytical powers.

That is the meaning and purpose and constitution of the ultimate weapon. To you it is a gift. There are few races in cosmic history with a higher potential than yours, or with a more miserable expression of it. The gift is yours because of this phenomenon.

As for us, our quest is as stated to you. We were to seek out the weapon and bring it back with us. We gave it to you instead, by manipulation of your impulses, Naome, and yours, Sig, with the radio. Earth needs it more than we do.

But we have not failed. The radio-chemistry of the nitrogen-isotope reaction and its catalyses are now widely available to us. It will be simplicity itself for us to recreate the weapon, and the time it will take us is as nothing . . .

. . . For we are a race which commands the fluxes of time, and we can braid a distance about our fingers, and hold Alpha and Omega together in the palms of our hands.

"The probes are gone," said Tillie, after a long silence.

Reluctantly, they removed their hands from the communicator, and flexed them.

Cris said, "Tillie, where is the ship?"

She smiled. "Remember? 'You insist that what is cosmically important must be huge.' " She pointed. "That is the ship."

They stared at the bulbous arrowhead. It rose and drifted toward the door. It paused there, tilted toward them in an obvious salute, and then, like a light extinguished, it was gone.

Naome sprang to her feet. "Is it all true, about the propaganda, the panic, the—the lovers who can speak their minds?"

"All true," smiled Tillie.

Naome said, "Testing. Testing. Sig Weiss, I love you."

Sig picked her up and hugged her. "Come on, all of you. I want to talk clear down to the corners and have a beer with the old man. I want to tell him something I've never said before—that he's my neighbor."

Cris helped Tillie up. "I think he stocks some real V-type halters."

Outside, it was a greener world, and all over it the birds sang.

THE TOUCH OF YOUR HAND

This is from the fertile postwar period, when I was writing the likes of *More Than Human*. It's about love and authoritarianism, as is so much of my work since.

"Dig there," said Osser, pointing.

The black-browed man pulled back. "Why?"

"We must dig deep to build high, and we are going to build high."

"Why?" the man asked again.

"To keep the enemy out."

"There are no enemies."

Osser laughed bitterly. "I'll have enemies."

"Why?"

Osser came to him. "Because I'm going to pick up this village and shake it until it wakes up. And if it won't wake up, I'll keep shaking until I break its back and it dies. Dig."

"I don't see why," said the man doggedly.

Osser looked at the golden backs of his hands, turned them over, watched them closing. He raised his eyes to the other.

"This is why," he said.

His right fist tore the man's cheek. His left turned the man's breath to a bullet which exploded as it left him. He huddled on the ground, unable to exhale, inhaling in small, heavy, tearing sobs. His eyes opened and he looked up at Osser. He could not speak, but his eyes did; and through shock and pain all they said was "Why?"

"You want reasons," Osser said, when he felt the man could hear him. "You want reasons—all of you. You see both sides of every question and you weigh and balance and cancel yourselves out. I want an end to reason. I want things done."

He bent to lift the bearded man to his feet. Osser stood half a head taller and his shoulders were as full and smooth as the bottoms of bowls. Golden hairs shifted and glinted on his forearms as he moved his fingers and the great cords tensed and valleyed. He lifted the man clear of the ground and set him easily on his feet and held him until he was sure of his balance.

"You don't understand me, do you?"

The man shook his head weakly.

"Don't try. You'll dig more if you don't try." He clapped the handle of the shovel into the man's hand and picked up a mattock. "Dig," he said, and the man began to dig.

Osser smiled when the man turned to work, arched his nostrils and drew the warm clean air into his lungs. He liked the sunlight now, the morning smell of the turned soil, the work he had to do and the idea itself of working.

Standing so, with his head raised, he saw a flash of bright yellow, the turn of a tanned face. Just a glimpse, and she was gone.

For a moment he tensed, frowning. If she had seen him he would be off to clatter the story of it to the whole village. Then he smiled. Let her. Let them all know. They must, sooner or later. Let them try to stop him.

He laughed, gripped his mattock, and the sod flew. So Jubilith saw fit to watch him, did she?

He laughed again. Work now, Juby later. In time he would have everything. Everything.

The village street wound and wandered and from time to time divided and rejoined itself, for each house was built on a man's whim—near, far, high, small, separate, turned to or away. What did not harmonize contrasted well, and over all it was a pleasing place to walk.

Before a shop a wood-cobbler sat, gouging out sabots; and he was next door to the old leatherworker who cunningly wove immortal belts of square-knotted rawhide. Then a house, and another, and a cabin; a space of green where children played; and the skeleton of a new building where a man, his apron pockets full of hardwood pegs, worked knowledgeably with a heavy mallet.

The cobbler, the leatherworker, the children and the builder all stopped to watch Jubilith because she was beautiful and because she ran. When she was by, they each saw the others watching, and each smiled and waved and laughed a little, though nothing was said.

A puppy lolloped along after her, three legs deft, the fourth in the way. Had it been frightened, it would not have run, and had Jubilith spoken to it, it would have followed wherever she went. But she ignored it, even when it barked its small soprano bark, so it curved away from her, pretending it had been going somewhere else anyway, and then it sat and puffed and looked after her sadly.

Past the smithy with its shadowed, glowing heart she ran; past the gristmill with its wonderful wheel, taking and yielding with its heavy cupped hands. A boy struck his hoop and it rolled across her path. Without breaking stride, she leaped high over it and ran on, and the glassblower's lips burst away from his pipe, for a man can smile or blow glass, but not both at the same time.

When at last she reached Wrenn's house, she was breathing deeply, but with no difficulty, in the way possible only to those who run beautifully. She stopped by the open door and waited politely, not looking in until Oyva came out and touched her shoulder.

Jubilith faced her, keeping her eyes closed for a long moment, for Oyva was not only very old, she was Wrenn's wife.

"Is it Jubilith?" asked Oyva, smiling.

"It is," said the girl. She opened her eyes.

Oyva, seeing their taut corners, said shrewdly, "A troubled Jubilith as well. I'll not keep you. He's just inside."

Juby found a swift flash of smile to give her and went into the house, leaving the old woman to wonder where, where in her long life she had seen such a brief flash of such great loveliness. A firebird's wing? A green meteor? She put it away in her mind next to the memory of a burst of laughter—Wrenn's, just after he had kissed her first—and sat down on a three-legged stool by the side of the house.

A heavy fiber screen had been set up inside the doorway, to form a sort of meander, and at the third turn it was very dark. Juby paused to let the sunlight drain away from her vision. Somewhere in the dark before her there was music, the hay-clean smell of flower petals dried and freshly rubbed, and a voice humming. The voice and the music were open and free, but choked a listener's throat like the sudden appearance of a field of daffodils.

The voice and the music stopped short, and someone breathed quietly in the darkness.

"Is . . . is it Wrenn?" she faltered.

"It is," said the voice.

"Jubilith here."

"Move the screen," said the voice. "I'd like the light, talking to you, Jubilith."

She felt behind her, touched the screen. It had many hinges and swung easily away to the doorside. Wrenn sat crosslegged in the corner behind a frame which held a glittering complex of stones.

He brushed petal-dust from his hands. "Sit there, child, and tell me what it is you do not understand."

She sat down before him and lowered her eyes, and his widened, as if someone had taken away a great light.

When she had nothing to say, he prompted her gently: "See if you can put it all into a single word, Jubilith."

She said immediately, "Osser."

"Ah," said Wrenn.

"I followed him this morning, out to the foothills beyond the Sky-tree Grove. He—"

Wrenn waited.

Jubilith put up her small hands, clenched, and talked in a rush. "Sussten, with the black brows, he was with Osser. They stopped and Osser shouted at him, and, when I came to where I could look down and see them, Osser took his fists and hammered Sussten, knocked him down. He laughed and picked him up. Sussten was sick; he was shaken and there was blood on his face. Osser told him to dig, and Sussten dug, Osser laughed again, he laughed . . . I think he saw me. I came here."

Slowly she put her fists down. Wrenn said nothing.

Jubilith said, in a voice like a puzzled sigh, "I understand this: when a man hammers something, iron or clay or wood, it is to change what he hammers from what it is to what he wishes it to be." She raised one hand, made a fist, and put it down again. She shook her head slightly and her heavy soft hair moved on her back. "To hammer a man is to change nothing. Sussten remains Sussten."

"It was good to tell me of this," said Wrenn when he was sure she had finished.

"Not good," Jubilith disclaimed. "I want to understand."

Wrenn shook his head. Juby cocked her head on one side like a wondering bright bird. When she realized that his gesture was a refusal, a small paired crease came and went between her brows.

"May I not understand this?"

"You *must* not understand it," Wrenn corrected. "Not yet, anyway. Perhaps after a time. Perhaps never."

"Ah," she said. "I—I didn't know."

"How could you know?" he asked kindly. "Don't follow Osser again, Jubilith."

She parted her lips, then again gave the small headshake. She rose and went out.

Oyva came to her. "Better now, Jubilith?"

Juby turned her head away; then, realizing that this was ill-mannered, met Oyva's gaze. The girl's eyes were full of tears. She closed them respectfully. Oyva touched her shoulder and let her go.

Watching the slim, bright figure trudge away, bowed with thought, drag-footed, unseeing, Oyva grunted and stumped into the house.

"Did she have to be hurt?" she demanded.

"She did," said Wrenn gently. "Osser," he added.

"Oh," she said, in just the tone he had used when Jubilith first mentioned the name. "What has he done now?"

Wrenn told her. Oyva sucked her lips in thoughtfully. "Why was the girl following him?"

"I didn't ask her. But don't you know?"

"I suppose I do," said Oyva, and sighed. "That mustn't happen, Wrenn."

"It won't. I told her not to follow him again."

She looked at him fondly. "I suppose even you can act like a fool once in a while."

He was startled. "Fool?"

"She loves him. You won't keep her from him by a word of advice."

"You judge her by yourself," he said, just as fondly. "She's only a child. In a day, a week, she'll wrap someone else up in her dreams."

"Suppose she doesn't?"

"Don't even think about it." A shudder touched his voice.

"I shall, though," said Oyva with determination. "And you'd do well to think about it, too." When his eyes grew troubled, she touched his cheek gently, "Now play some more for me."

He sat down before the instrument, his hands poised. Then into the tiny bins his fingers went, rubbing this dried-petal powder and that, and the stones glowed, changing the flower-scents into music and shifting colors.

He began to sing softly to the music.

They dug deep, day by day, and they built. Osser did the work of three men, and sometimes six or eight others worked with him, and sometimes one or two. Once he had twelve. But never did he work alone.

When the stone was three tiers above the ground level, Osser climbed the nearest rise and stood looking down at it proudly, at the thickness and strength of the growing walls, at the toiling workers who lifted and strained to make them grow.

"Is it Osser?"

The voice was as faint and shy as a fern uncurling, as promising as spring itself.

He turned.

"Jubilith," she told him.

"What are you doing here?"

"I come here every day," she said. She indicated the copse which crowned the hill. "I hide here and watch you."

"What do you want?"

She laced her fingers. "I would like to dig there and lift stones."

"No," he said, and turned to study the work again.

"Why not?"

"Never ask me why. 'Because I say so'—that's all the answer you'll get from me—you or anyone."

She came to stand beside him. "You build fast."

He nodded. "Faster than any village house was ever built." He could sense the 'why' rising within her, and could feel it being checked.

"I want to build it, too," she pleaded.

"No," he said. His eyes widened as he watched the work. Suddenly he was gone, leaping down the slope in great springy strides. He turned the corner of the new wall and stood, saying nothing. The man who had been idling turned quickly and lifted a stone. Osser smiled a quick, taut smile and went to work beside him. Jubilith stood on the slope, watching, wondering.

She came almost every day as the tower grew. Osser never spoke to her. She watched the sunlight on him, the lithe strength, the rippling gold. He stood like a great tree, squatted like a rock, moved like a thundercloud. His voice was a whip, a bugle, the roar of a bull.

She saw him less and less in the village. Once it was a fearsome thing to see. Early in the morning he appeared suddenly, overtook a man, lifted him and threw him flat on the ground.

"I told you to be out there yesterday," he growled, and strode away.

Friends came and picked the man up, held him softly while he coughed, took him away to be healed.

No one went to Wrenn about it; the word had gone around that Osser and his affairs were not to be understood by anyone. Wrenn's function was to explain those few things which could not be understood. But certain of these few were not to be understood at all. So Osser was left alone to do as he wished—which was a liberty, after all, that was enjoyed by everyone else.

Twilight came when Jubilith waited past her usual time. She waited until by ones and twos the workers left the tower, until Osser himself had climbed the hill, until he had paused to look back and be proud and think of tomorrow's work, until he, too, had turned his face to the town. Then she slipped down to the tower and around it, and carefully climbed the scaffolding on the far side. She looked about her.

The tower was now four stories high and seemed to be shaping toward a roof. Circular in cross-section, the tower had two rooms on each floor, an east-west wall between them on the ground floor, a north-south wall on the next, and so on up.

There was a central well into which was built a spiral staircase—a double spiral, as if one helix had been screwed into the other. This made possible two exits to stairs on each floor at the same level, though they were walled off one from the other. Each of the two rooms on every floor had one connecting doorway. Each room had three windows in it, wide on the inside, tapering through the thick stone wall to form the barest slit outside.

A portion of the castellated roof was already built. It overhung the entrance, and had slots in the overhang through which the whole entrance face of the tower could be covered by one man lying unseen on the roof, looking straight down.

Stones lay in a trough ready for placing, and there was some leftover mortar in the box. Jubilith picked up a trowel and worked it experimentally in the stuff, then lifted some out and tipped it down on the unfinished top of the wall, just as she had seen Osser do so many times. She put down the trowel and chose a stone. It was heavy—much heavier than she had expected—but she made it move, made it lift, made it seat itself to suit her on the fresh mortar. She ticked off the excess from the join and stepped back to admire it in the fading light.

Two great clamps, hard as teeth, strong as a hurricane, caught her right thigh and her left armpit. She was swung into the air and held helpless over the unfinished parapet.

She was utterly silent, shocked past the ability even to gasp.

"I told you you were not to work here," said Osser between his teeth. So tall he was, so long were his arms as he held her high over his head, that it seemed almost as far to the parapet as it was to the ground below.

He leaned close to the edge and shook her. "I'll throw you off. This tower is mine to build, you hear?"

If she had been able to breathe, she might have screamed or pleaded with him. If she had screamed or pleaded, he might have dropped her. But her silence apparently surprised him. He grunted and set her roughly on her feet. She caught at his shoulder to keep her balance, then quickly transferred her hold to the edge of the parapet. She dropped her head between her upper arms. Her long soft hair fell forward over her face, and she moaned.

"I told you," he said, really seeing her at last. His voice shook. He stepped toward her and put out his hand. She screamed. "Be *quiet!*" he roared. A moan shut off in mid-breath. "Ah, I told you, Juby. You shouldn't have tried to build here."

He ran his great hands over the edge of the stonework, found the one she had laid, the one that had cost her such effort to lift. With one hand, he plucked it up and threw it far out into the shadows below.

"I wanted to help you with it," she whispered.

"Don't you understand?" he cried. "No one builds here who *wants* to help!"

She simply shook her head.

She tried to breathe deeply and a long shudder possessed her. When it passed, she turned weakly and stood, her back partly arched over the edge of the parapet, her hands behind her to cushion the stone. She shook the hair out of her face; it fell away on either side like a dawnlit bow-wave. She looked up at him with an expression of such piteous confusion that his dwindling rage vanished altogether.

He dropped his eyes and shuffled one foot like a guilty child. "Juby, leave me alone."

Something almost like a smile touched her lips. She brushed her bruised arm, then walked past him to the place where the scaffolding projected above the parapet.

"Not that way," he called. "Come here."

He took her hand and led her to the spiral staircase at the center of the tower. It was almost totally dark inside. It seemed like an age to her as they descended; she was alone in a black universe consisting of a rhythmic drop and turn, and a warm hard hand in hers, holding and leading her.

When they emerged, he stopped in the strange twilight, a darkness for all the world but a dazzle to them, so soaked with blackness were their eyes. She tugged gently, but he would not release her hand. She moved close to see his face. His eyes were wide and turned unseeing to the far slopes; he was frowning, yet his mouth was not fierce, but irresolute. Whatever his inward struggle was, it left his face gradually and transferred itself to his hand. Its pressure on hers became firm, hard, intense, painful.

"Osser!"

He dropped the hand and stepped back, shamed. "Juby, I will take you to ... Juby, do you want to understand?" He waved at the tower.

She said, "Oh, yes!"

He looked at her closely, and the angry, troubled diffidence came and went. "Half a day there, half a day back again," he said.

She recognized that this was as near as this feral, unhappy man could come to asking a permission. "I'd like to understand," she said.

"If you don't, I'm going to kill you," he blurted. He turned to the west and strode off, not looking back.

Jubilith watched him go, and suddenly there was a sparkle in her wide eyes. She slipped out of her sandals, caught them up in her hand, and ran lightly and silently after him. He planted his feet strongly, like the sure, powerful teeth of the millwheel gears, and he would not look back. She sensed how immensely important it was to him not to look back. She knew that right-handed men look back over their left shoulders, so she drifted along close to him, a little behind him, a little to his right. How long, how long, until he looked to see if she was coming?

Up and up the slope, to its crest, over ... down ... ah! Just here, just at the last second where he could turn and look without stopping and still catch a glimpse of the tower's base, where they had stood. So he turned, and she passed around him like a windblown feather, unseen.

And he stopped, looking back, craning. His shoulders slumped, and slowly he turned to his path again—and there was Jubilith before him.

She laughed.

His jaw dropped, and then his lips came together in a thin, angry seal. For a moment he stared at her; and suddenly, quite against his will, there burst from him a single harsh bark of laughter. She put out her hand and he came to her, took it, and they went their way together.

They came to a village when it was very late and very dark, and Osser circled it. They came to another, and Jubilith thought he would do the same, for he turned south; but when they came abreast of it, he struck north again.

"We'll be seen," he explained gruffly, "but we'll be seen coming from the south and leaving northward."

She would not ask where he was taking her, or why he was making these elaborate arrangements, but already she had an idea. What lay to the west was—not forbidden, exactly, but, say discouraged. It was felt that there was nothing in that country that could be of value. Anyone traveling that way would surely be remembered.

So through the village they went, and they dined quickly at an inn, and went northward, and once in the darkness, veered west again. In a wood so dark that she had taken his hand again, he stopped and built a fire. He threw down springy boughs and a thick heap of ferns, and this was her bed. He slept sitting up, his back to a tree trunk, with Jubilith between him and the fire.

Jubilith awoke twice during the long night, once to see him with his eyes closed, but feeling that he was not asleep; and once to see him with his eyes open and the dying flames flickering in the pupils, and she thought then that he was asleep, or at least not with her, but lost in the pcitures the flames painted.

In the morning they moved on, gathering berries for breakfast, washing in a humorous brook. And during this whole journey, nothing passed between them but the small necessary phrases: "You go first here." "Look out—it drops." "Tired yet?"

For there was that about Jubilith which made explanations unnecessary. Though she did not know where they were going, or why, she understood what must be done to get them there within the framework of his desire: to go immediately, as quickly as possible, undetected by anyone else.

She did only what she could to help and did not plague him with questions which would certainly be answered in good time. So: "Here are berries." "Look, a red bird!" "Can we get through there, or shall we go around?" And nothing more.

They did well, the weather was fine, and by midmorning they had reached the tumbled country of the Crooked Hills. Jubilith had seen them from afar—

great broken mounds and masses against the western sky—but no one ever went there, and she knew nothing about them.

They were in open land now, and Jubilith regretted leaving the color and aliveness of the forest. The grasses here were strange, like yet unlike those near her village. They were taller, sickly, and some had odd ugly flowers. There were bald places, scored with ancient rain-gullies, as if some mighty hand had dashed acid against the soil. There were few insects and no animals that she could see, and no birds sang. It was a place of great sadness rather than terror; there was little to fear, but much to grieve for.

By noon, they faced a huge curved ridge, covered with broken stones. It looked as if the land itself had reared up and pressed back from a hidden something on the other side—something which it would not touch. Osser quickened their pace as they began to climb, although the going was hard. Jubilith realized that they were near the end of their journey, and uncomplainingly struggled along at the cruel pace he set.

At the top, they paused, giving their first attention to their wind, and gradually to the scene before them.

The ridge on which they stood was nearly circular, and perhaps a mile and a half in diameter. In its center was a small round lake with unnaturally bare shores. Mounds of rubble sloped down toward it on all sides, and farther back was broken stone.

But it was the next zone which caught and held the eye. The weed-grown wreckage there was beyond description. Great twisted webs and ribs of gleaming metal wove in and out of the slumped heaps of soil and masonry. Nearby, a half-acre of laminated stone stood on the edge like a dinner plate in a clay bank. What could have been a building taller than any Jubilith had ever heard about lay on its side, smashed and bulging.

Gradually she began to realize the peculiarity of this place—All the larger wreckage lay in lines directly to and from the lake in a monstrous radiation of ruin.

"What is this place?" she asked at last.

"Don't know," he grunted, and went over the edge to slip down the steep slope. When she caught up with him near the bottom, he said, "There's miles of this, west and north of here, much bigger. But this is the one we came to see. Come."

He looked to right and left as if to get his bearings, then plunged into the tough and scrubby underbrush that vainly tried to cover those tortured metal bones. She followed as closely as she could, beating at the branches which he carelessly let whip back.

Just in front of her, he turned the corner of a sharp block of stone, and when she turned it no more than a second later, he was gone.

She stopped, turned, again. Dust, weeds, lonely and sorrowful ruins. No Osser. She shrank back against the stone, her eyes wide.

The bushes nearby trembled, then lashed. Osser's head emerged. "What's the matter? Come on!" he said gruffly.

She checked an impulse to cry out and run to him, and came silently forward. Osser held the bushes briefly, and beside him she saw a black hole with broken steps leading downward.

She hesitated, but he moved his head impatiently, and she passed him and led the way downward. When he followed, his wide flat body blocked out the light. The darkness was so heavy, her eyes ached.

He prodded her in the small of the back. "Go on, go on!"

The foot of the steps came sooner than she expected and her knees buckled as she took the downward step that was not there. She tripped, almost fell, then somehow got to the side wall and braced herself there, trembling.

"Wait," he said, and the irrepressible smile quirked the corners of her mouth. As if she would go anywhere!

She heard him fumbling about somewhere, and then there was a sudden aching blaze of light that made her cry out and clap her hands over her face.

"Look," he said. "I want you to look at this. Hold it."

Into her hands he pressed a cylinder about half the length of her forearm. At one end was a lens from which the blue-white light was streaming.

"See this little thing here," he said, and touched a stud at the side of the cylinder. The light disappeared, came on again.

She laughed delightedly, took the cylinder and played its light around, switching it on and off. "It's wonderful!" she cried. "Oh, wonderful!"

"You take this one," he said, pleased. He handed her another torch and took the first from her. "It isn't as good, but it will help. I'll go first."

She took the second torch and tried it. It worked the same way, but the light was orange and feeble. Osser strode ahead down a slanting passageway. At first there was a great deal of rubble underfoot, but soon the way was clear as they went farther and deeper. Osser walked with confidence, and she knew he had been here before, probably many times.

"Here," he said, stopping to wait for her. His voice echoed strangely, vibrant with controlled excitement.

He turned his torch ahead, swept it back and forth.

They were at the entrance to a room. It was three times the height of a man, and as big as their village green. She stared around, awed.

"Come," Osser said again, and went to the far corner.

A massive, boxlike object stood there. One panel, about eye-level, was of a milky smooth substance, the rest of a black metal. Projecting from the floor in front of it was a lever. Osser grasped it confidently and pulled. It yielded sluggishly, and returned to its original position. Osser tugged again. There was a low growling sound from the box. Osser pulled, released, pulled, released, each time a little faster. The sound rose in pitch, higher and higher.

"Turn off your light," he said.

She did so and blackness snapped in around them. As the dazzle faded from her eyes, she detected a flicker of silver light before her, and realized that it came from the milky pane in the box. As Osser pulled at the lever and the whine rose and rose in pitch, the square got bright enough for her to see her hands when she looked down at them.

And then—the pictures.

Jubilith had never seen pictures like these. They moved, for one thing; for another, they had no color. Everything in them was black and white and shades of gray. Yet everything they showed seemed very real.

Not at first, for there was flickering and stopped motion, and then slow motion as Osser's lever moved faster and faster. But at last the picture steadied, and Osser kept the lever going at the same speed, flicking it with apparent ease about twice a second, while the whine inside the box settled to a steady, soft moan.

The picture showed a ball spinning against a black, light-flecked curtain. It rushed close until it filled the screen, and still closer, and Jubilith suddenly had the feeling that she was falling at tremendous velocity from an unthinkable height. Down and down the scene went, until at last the surface began to take on the qualities of a bird's-eye view. She saw a river and lakes, and a great range of hills—

And, at last, the city.

It was a city beyond fantasy, greater and more elaborate than imagination could cope with. Its towers stretched skyward to pierce the clouds themselves— some actually did. It had wide ramps on which traffic crawled, great bridges across the river, parks over which the buildings hung like mighty cliffs. Closer still the silver eye came to the scene, and she realized that the traffic was not crawling, but moving faster than a bird, faster than the wind. The vehicles were low and sleek and efficient.

And on the walks were people, and the scene wheeled and slowed and showed them. They were elaborately clothed and well-fed; they were hurried and orderly at the same time. There was a square in which perhaps a thousand of them, all dressed alike, were drawn up in lines as straight as stretched string. Even as she watched, they all began to move together, a thousand left legs coming forward, a thousand right arms swinging back.

Higher, then, and more of the city—more and more of it, until the sense of wonder filled her lungs and she hardly breathed; and still more of it, miles of it. And at last a great open space with what looked like sections of road crossing on it—but such unthinkable roads! Each was as wide as her whole village and miles long. And on these roads, great birdlike machines tilted down and touched and rolled, and swung and ran and took the air, dozens of them every minute. The scene swept close again, and it was as if she were in such a machine herself; but it did not land. It raced past the huge busy crossroads and out to a coastline.

And there were ships, ships as long as the tallest buildings were high, and clusters, dozens, hundreds of other vessels working and smoking and milling about in the gray water. Huge machines crouched over ships and lifted out cargoes; small, agile machines scurried about the docks and warehouses.

Then at last the scene dwindled as the magic eye rose higher and higher, faster and faster. Details disappeared, and clouds raced past and downward, and at last the scene was a disc and then a ball floating in starlit space.

Osser let the lever go and it snapped back to its original position. The moan descended quickly in pitch, and the motion on the screen slowed, flickered, faded and went out.

Jubilith let the darkness come. Her mind spun and shook with the impact of what she had seen. Slowly she recovered herself. She became conscious of Osser's hard breathing. She turned on her dim orange torch and looked at him. He was watching her.

"What was it?" she breathed.

"What I came to show you."

She thought hard. She thought about his tower, about his refusal to let her work on it, about his cruelty to those who had. She looked at him, at the blank screen. And this was to supply the reason.

She shook her head.

He lowered himself slowly and squatted like an animal, hunched up tight, his knees in his armpits. This lifted and crooked his heavy arms. He rested their knuckles on the floor. He glowered at her and said nothing. He was waiting.

On the way here, he had said, "I'll kill you if you don't understand." But he wouldn't really, would he? Would he?

If he had towered over her, ranted and shouted, she would not have been afraid. But squatting there, waiting, silent, with his great arms bowed out like that, he was like some patient, preying beast.

She turned off the light to blot out the sight of him, and immediately became speechless with terror at the idea of his sitting there in the dark so close, waiting. She might run; she was so swift . . . but no; crouched like that, he could spring and catch her before she could tense a muscle.

Again she looked at the dead screen. "Will you . . . tell me something?" she quavered.

"I might."

"Tell me, then: When you first saw that picture, did you understand? The very first time?"

His expression did not change. But slowly he relaxed. He rocked sidewise, sat down, extended his legs. He was man again, not monster. She shuddered, then controlled it.

He said, "It took me a long time and many visits. I should not have asked you to understand at once."

She again accepted the timid half-step toward an apology, and was grateful.

He said, "Those were men and women just like us. Did you see that? Just like us."

"Their clothes—"

"Just like us," he insisted. "Of course they dressed differently, lived differently! In a world like that, why not? Ah, how they built, how they built!"

"Yes," she whispered. Those towers, the shining, swift vehicles, the thousand who moved like one . . . "Who were they?" she asked him.

"Don't you know? Think—think!"

"Osser, I want to understand. I truly want to!"

She hunted frantically for the right thing to say, the right way to catch at this elusive thing which was so frighteningly important to him. All her life she had had the answers to the questions she wanted to understand. All she had ever had to do was to close her eyes and think of the problem, and the answers soon came.

But not this problem.

"Osser," she pleaded, "where is it, the city, the great complicated city?"

"Say, 'Where was it?' " he growled.

She caught his thought and gasped. "This? These ruins, Osser?"

"Ah," he said approvingly. "It comes slowly, doesn't it? No, Juby. Not here. What was here was an outpost, a village, compared with the big city. North and west, I told you, didn't I? Miles of it. So big that . . . so big—" He extended his arms, dropped them helplessly. Suddenly he leaned close to her, began to talk fast, feverishly. "Juby, that city—that world—was built by *people*. Why did they build and why do we not? What is the difference between those people and ours?"

"They must have had . . ."

"They had nothing we don't have. They're the same kind of people; they *used* something we haven't been using. Juby, I've got that something. I can build. I can make others build."

A mental picture of the tower glimmered before her. "You built it with hate," she said wonderingly. "Is that what they had—cruelty, brutality, hatred?"

"Yes!"

"I don't believe it! I don't believe anyone could live with that much hate!"

"Perhaps not. Perhaps they didn't. But they *built* with it. They built because some men could flog others into building for them, building higher and faster than all the good neighbors would ever do helping one another."

"They'd hate the man who made them build like that."

Osser's hands crackled as he pressed them together. He laughed, and the echoes took everything that was unpleasant about that laughter and filled the far reaches of the dark room with it.

"They'd hate him," he agreed. "But he's strong, you see. He was strong in the first place, to make them build, and he's stronger afterward with what they built for him. Do you know the only way they can express their hatred, once they find he's too strong for them?"

Jubilith shook her head.

"They'd build," he chuckled. "They'd build higher and faster than he did. They would find the strongest man among them and *ask* him to flog them into it. That's the way a great city goes up. A strong man builds, and strong men follow, and soon the man who's strongest of all makes all the other strong ones do his work. Do you see?"

"And the . . . the others, the weak?"

"What of them?" he asked scornfully. "There are more of them than strong ones—so there are more hands to do the strong man's work. And why shouldn't they? Don't they get the city to live in when it's built? Don't they ride about in swift shining carriers and fly through the air in the bird-machines?"

"Would they be—happy?" she asked.

He looked at her in genuine puzzlement. "Happy?" He smashed a heavy fist into his palm. "They'd have a *city!*" Again the words tumbled from him. "How do you live, you and the rest of the village? What do you do when you want a—well, a garden, food from the ground?"

"I dig up the soil," she said. "I plant and water and weed."

"Suppose you want a plow?"

"I make one. Or I do work for someone who has one."

"Uh," he grunted. "And there you are, hundreds of you in the village, each one planting a little, smithing a little, thatching and cutting and building a little. Everyone does everything except for how many—four, five?—the leatherworker, old Griak who makes wooden pegs for house beams, one or two others."

"They like to do just one work. But anyone can do any of the work. Those few, we take care of. Someone has to keep the skills alive."

He snorted. "Put a strong man in the village and give him strong men to do what he wants. Get ten villagers at once and make them all plant at once. You'll have food then for fifty, not ten!"

"But it would go to waste!"

"It would not, because it would all belong to the head man. He would give it away as he saw fit—a lot to those who obeyed him, nothing to those who didn't. What was left over he could keep for himself, and barter it out to keep building. Soon he would have the biggest house and the best animals and the finest women, and the more he got, the stronger he would be. And a city would grow—a *city!* And the strong man would give everyone better things if they worked hard, and protect them."

"Protect them? Against what?"

"Against the other strong ones. There would be others."

"And you—"

"I shall be the strongest of all," he said proudly. He waved at the box. "We were a great people once. We're ants now—less than ants, for at least the ants work together for a common purpose. I'll make us great again." His head sank onto his hand and he looked somberly into the shadows. "Something happened to this world. Something smashed the cities and the people and drove them down to what they are today. Something was broken within them, and they no longer dared to be great. Well, they will be. *I* have the extra something that was smashed out of them."

"What smashed them, Osser?"

"Who can know? I don't. I don't care, either." He tapped her with a long forefinger to emphasize. "All I care about is this: They were smashed because they were not strong enough. I shall be so strong I can't be smashed."

She said, "A stomach can hold only so much. A man asleep takes just so much space. So much and no more clothing makes one comfortable. Why do you want more than these things, Osser?"

She knew he was annoyed, and knew, too, that he was considering the question as honestly as he could.

"It's because I . . . I want to be strong," he said in a strained voice.

"You *are* strong."

"Who knows that?" he raged, and the echoes giggled and whispered.

"I do. Wrenn. Sussten. The whole village."

"The whole world will know. They will all do things for me."

She thought, But everyone does everything for himself, all over the world. Except, she added, those who aren't able . . .

With that in mind, she looked at him, his oaken shoulders, his powerful, bitter mouth. She touched the bruises his hands had left, and the beginnings of the understanding she had been groping for left her completely.

She said dully, "Your tower . . . you'd better get back there."

"Work goes on," he said, smiling tightly, "whether I'm there or not, as long as they don't know my plans. They are afraid. But—yes, we can go now."

Rising, he flicked the stud of his torch. It flared blue-white, faded to the weak orange of Jubilith's, then died.

"The light . . ."

"It's all right," said Jubilith. "I have mine."

"When they get like that, so dim, you can't tell when they'll go out. Come—hurry! This place is full of corridors; without light, we could be lost here for days."

She glanced around at the crowding shadows. "Make it work again," she suggested.

He looked at the dead torch in his hand. "You," he said flatly. He tossed it. She caught it in her free hand, put her torch on the floor, and held the broken one down so she could see it in the waning orange glow. She turned it over twice, her sensitive hands feeling with every part rather than with fingertips alone. She held it still and closed her eyes; and then it came to her, and she grasped one end with her right hand and the other with her left, and twisted.

There was a faint click and the outer shell of the torch separated. She drew off the butt end of it; it was just a hollow shell. The entire mechanism was attached to the lens end and was now exposed.

She turned it over carefully, keeping her fingers away from the workings. Again she closed her eyes and thought, and at last she bent close and peered. She nodded, fumbled in her hair, and detached a copper clasp. She bent and broke off a narrow strip of it and inserted it carefully into the light mechanism. Very carefully, she pried apart two small strands of wire, dipped a little deeper, hooked onto a tiny white sphere, and drew it out.

"Poor thing," she murmured under her breath.

"Poor what?"

"Spider's egg," she said ruefully. "They fight so to save them; and this one will never hatch out now. It's been burned."

She picked up the butt-end housing, slipped the two parts together, and twisted them until they clicked. She handed the torch to Osser.

"You've wasted time," he complained, surly.

"No, I haven't," she said. "We'll have light now."

He touched the stud on the torch. The brilliant, comforting white light poured from it.

"Yes," he admitted quietly.

Watching his face as he handled the torch, she knew that if she could read what was in his mind in that second, she would have the answer to everything about him. She could not, however, and he said nothing, but led across the room to the dark corridor.

He was silent all the way back to the broken steps.

They stood halfway up, letting their eyes adjust to the daylight which poured down on them, and he said, "You didn't even try the torch to see if it would work, after you took out that egg."

"I knew it would work." She looked at him, amazed. "You're angry."

"Yes," he said.

He took her torch and his and put them away in a niche in the ruined stairwell, and they climbed up into the noon light. It was all but intolerable, as the two suns were all but in syzygy, the blue-white midget shining through the great pale gaseous mass of the giant, so that together they cast only a single shadow.

"It will be hot this afternoon," she said, but he was silent, steeped in some bitterness of his own, so she followed him quietly without attempting conversation.

Old Oyva stirred sleepily in her basking chair, and suddenly sat upright.

Jubilith approached her, pale and straight. "Is it Oyva?"

"It is, Jubilith," said the old woman. "I knew you would be back, my dear. I'm sore in my heart with you."

"Is he here?"

"He is. He has been on a journey. You'll find him tired."

"He should have been here, with all that has happened," said Jubilith.

"He should have done exactly as he has done," Oyva stated bluntly.

Jubilith recognized the enormity of her rudeness, and the taste of it was bad in her mouth. One did not criticize Wrenn's comings and goings.

She faced Oyva and closed her eyes humbly.

Oyva touched her. "It's all right, child. You are distressed. Wrenn!" she called. "She is here!"

"Come, Jubilith," Wrenn's voice called from the house.

"He knows? *No* one knew I was coming here!"

"He knows," said Oyva. "Go to him, child."

Jubilith entered the house. Wrenn sat in his corner. The musical instrument was nowhere in sight. Aside from his cushions, there was nothing in the room.

Wrenn gave her his wise, sweet smile. "Jubilith," he said. "Come close." He looked drawn and pale, but quite untroubled. He put a cushion by him and she crossed slowly and sank down on it.

He was quiet, and when she was sure it was because he waited for her to speak, she said, "Some things may not be understood."

"True," he agreed.

She kneaded her hands. "Is there never a change?"

"Always," he said, "when it's time."

"Osser—"

"Everyone will understand Osser very soon now."

She screwed up her courage. "Soon is not soon enough. I must know him now."

"Before anyone else?" he inquired mildly.

"Let everyone know now," she suggested.

He shook his head and there was no appeal in it.

"Then let me. I shall be a part of you and speak of it only to you."

"Why must you understand?"

She shuddered. It was not cold, or fear, but simply the surgings of a great emotion.

"I love him," she said. "And to love is to guard and protect. He needs me."

"Go to him then." But she sat where she was, her long eyes cast down, weeping. Wrenn said, "There is more, then?"

"I love ..." She threw out an arm in a gesture which enfolded Wrenn, the house, the village. "I love the people, too, the gardens, the little houses; the way we go and come, and sing, and make music, and make our own tools and clothes. To love is to guard and protect ... and I love these things, and I love Osser. I can destroy Osser, because he would not expect it of me; and, if I did, I would protect all of you. But if I protect him, he will destroy you. There is no answer to such a problem, Wrenn; it is a road," she cried, "with a precipice at each end, and no standing still!"

"And understanding him would be an answer?"

"There's no other!" She turned her face up to him, imploring. "Osser is strong, Wrenn, with a—new thing about him, a thing none of the rest of us have. He has told me of it. It is a thing that can change us, make us part of him. He will build cities with our hands, on our broken bodies if we resist him. He wants us to be a great people again—he says we were, once, and have lost it all."

"And do you regard that as greatness, Jubilith—the towers, the bird-machines?"

"How did you know of them? ... Greatness? I don't know, I don't know," she said, and wept. "I love him, and he wants to build a city with a wanting greater than anything I have ever known or heard of before. Could he do it, Wrenn? Could he?"

"He might," said Wrenn calmly.

"He is in the village now. He has about him the ones who built his tower for him. They cringe around him, hating to be near and afraid to leave. He sent them one by one to tell all the people to come out to the foothills tomorrow, to begin work on his city. He wants enough building done in one hundred days to shelter everyone, because then, he says, he is going to burn this village to the ground. Why, Wrenn—why?"

"Perhaps," said Wrenn, "so that we may all face his strength and yield to it. A man who could move a whole village in a hundred days just to show his strength would be a strong man indeed."

"What shall we do?"

"I think we shall go out to the foothills in the morning and begin to build." She rose and went to the door.

"I know what to do now," she whispered. "I won't try to understand any more. I shall just go and help him."

"Yes, go," said Wrenn. "He will need you."

Jubilith stood with Osser on the parapet, and with him stared into the dappled dawn. The whole sky flamed with the loom of the red sun's light, but the white one preceded it up in the sky, laying sharp shadows in the soft blunt ones. Birds called and chattered in the Sky-tree Grove, and deep in the thickets the seven-foot bats grunted as they settled in to sleep.

"Suppose they don't come?" she asked.

"They'll come," he said grimly. "Jubilith, why are you here?"

She said, "I don't know what you are doing, Osser. I don't know whether it's right or whether you will keep on succeeding. I do know there will be pain and difficulty and I—I came to keep you safe, if I could . . . I love you."

He looked down at her, as thick and dark over her as his tower was over the foothills. One side of his mouth twitched.

"Little butterfly," he said softly, "do you think *you* can guard *me?*"

Everything beautiful about her poured out to him through her beautiful face, and for a moment his world had three suns instead of two. He put his arms around her. Then his great voice exploded with two syllables of a mighty laugh. He lifted her and swung her behind him, and leaped to the parapet.

Deeply shaken, she came to follow his gaze.

The red sun's foggy limb was above the townward horizon, and silhouetted against it came the van of a procession. On they came and on, the young men of the village, the fathers. Women were with them, too, and everything on wheels that the village possessed—flatbed wagons, two-wheeled rickshaw carts, children's and vendors' and pleasure vehicles. A snorting team of four tiger oxen clawed along before a heavily laden stoneboat, and men shared packs that swung in the center of long poles.

Osser curled his lip. "You see them," he said, as if to himself, "doing the only thing they can think of. Push them, they yield. The clods!" he spat. "Well, one day, one will push back. And when he does, I'll break him, and after that I'll use him. Meantime—I have a thousand hands and a single mind. We'll see building now," he crooned. "When they've built, they'll know what they don't know now—that they're men."

"They're all come," breathed Jubilith. "All of them. Osser—"

"Be quiet," he said, leaning into the wind to watch, floating. With the feel of his hard hands still on her back, she discovered with a crushing impact that there was no room in his heart for her when he thought of his building. And she knew that there never would be, except perhaps for a stolen moment, a touch in passing. With the pain of that realization came the certainty that she would stay with him always, even for so little.

The procession dipped out of sight, then slowly rose over and down the near hill and approached the tower. It spread and thickened at the foot of the slope, as men cast about, testing the ground with their picks, eyeing the land for its color and vegetation and drainage . . . or was that what they were doing?

Osser leaned his elbows on the parapet and shook his head pityingly at their inefficiency. Look at the way they went about laying out houses! And their own houses. Well, he'd let them mill about until they were completely confused, and then he'd go down and make them do it his way. Confused men are soft men; men working against their inner selves are easy to divert from outside.

Beside him, Jubilith gasped.

"What is it?"

She pointed. "There—sending the men to this side, that side. See, by the stone boat? It's Wrenn!"

"Nonsense!" said Osser. "He'd never leave his house. Not to walk around among people who are sweating. He deals only with people who tell him he's right before he speaks."

"It's Wrenn, it is, it is!" cried Jubilith. She clutched his arm. "Osser, I'm afraid!"

"Afraid? Afraid of what? . . . By the dying Red One, it *is* Wrenn, telling men what to do as if this was *his* city." He laughed. "There are few enough here who are strong, Juby, but he's the strongest there is. And look at him scurry around for me!"

"I'm afraid," Jubilith whimpered.

"They jump when he tells them," said Osser reflectively, shading his eyes. "Perhaps I was wrong to let them tire themselves out before I help them do things right. With a man like him to push them . . . Hm. I think we'll get it done right the first time."

He pushed himself away from the parapet and swung to the stairway.

"Osser, don't, please don't!" she begged.

He stopped just long enough to give her a glance like a stone thrown. "You'll never change my mind, Juby, and you'll be hurt if you try too often." He dropped into the opening, went down three steps, five steps . . .

He grunted, stopped.

Jubilith came slowly over to the stairwell. Osser stood on the sixth step, on tiptoe. Impossibly on tiptoe: the points of his sandals barely touched the step at all.

He set his jaw and placed his massive hands one on each side of the curved wall. He pressed them out and up, forcing himself downward. His sandals touched more firmly; his toes bent, his heels made contact. His face became deep red, and the cords at the sides of his neck ridged like a weathered fallow field.

A strained crackle came from his shoulders, and then the pent breath burst from him. His hands slipped, and he came up again just the height of the single stair-riser, to bob ludicrously like a boat at anchor, his pointed toe touching and lifting from the sixth step.

He gave an inarticulate roar, bent double, and plunged his hands downward as if to dive headfirst down the stairs. His wrists turned under and he yelped with the pain. More cautiously he felt around and down, from wall to wall. It was as if the air in the stairway had solidified, become at once viscous and resilient. Whatever was there was invisible and completely impassable.

He backed slowly up the steps. On his face there was fury and frustration, hurt and a shaking reaction.

Jubilith wrung her hands. "Please, please, Osser, be care—"

The sound of her voice gave him something to strike out at, and he spun about, raising his great bludgeon of a fist. Jubilith stood frozen, too shocked to dodge the blow.

"Osser!"

Osser stopped, tensed high, fist up, like some terrifying monument to vengeance. The voice had been Wrenn's—Wrenn speaking quietly, even conversationally, but magnified beyond belief. The echoes of it rolled off and were lost in the hills.

"Come watch men building, Osser!"

Dazed, Osser lowered his arm and went to the parapet.

Far below, near the base of the hill, Wrenn stood, looking up at the tower. When Osser appeared, Wrenn turned his back and signaled the men by the stone-boat. They twitched away the tarpaulin that covered its load.

Osser's hands gripped the stone as if they would powder it. His eyes slowly widened and his jaw slowly dropped.

At first it seemed like a mound of silver on the rude platform of the ox-drawn stone-boat. Gradually he perceived that it was a machine, a machine so finished, so clean-lined and so businesslike that the pictures he had shown Jubilith were clumsy toys in comparison.

It was Sussten, a man Osser had crushed to the ground with two heavy blows, who sprang lightly up on the machine and settled into it. It backed off the platform, and Osser could hear the faintest of whines from it. The machine rolled and yet it stepped; it kept itself horizon-level as it ran, its long endless treads dipping and rising with the terrain, its sleek body moving smooth as a swan. It stopped and then went forward, out to the first of a field of stakes that a crew had been driving.

The flat, gleaming sides of the machine opened away and forward and locked, and became a single blade twice the width of the machine. It dropped until its sharp lower edge just touched the ground, checked for a moment, and then sank into the soil.

Dirt mounded up before it until flakes fell back over the wide moldboard. The machine slid ahead, and dirt ran off the sides of the blade to make two straight windrows. And behind the machine as it labored, the ground was flat and smooth; and it was done as easily as a smoothing hand in a sandbox. Here it was cut and there it was filled, but everywhere the swath was like planed wood, all done just as fast as a man can run.

Osser made a sick noise far back in his tight throat.

Guided by the stakes, the machine wheeled and returned, one end of the blade now curved forward to catch up the windrow and carry it across the new parallel cut. And now the planed soil was twice as wide.

As it worked, men worked, and Osser saw, that, shockingly, they moved with no less efficiency and certainty than the machine. For Osser, these men had plodded and sweated, drudged, each a single, obstinate unit to be flogged and pressed. But now they sprinted, sprang; they held, drove, measured, and carried as if to swift and intricate music.

A cart clattered up and from it men took metal spikes, as thick as a leg, twice as tall as a man. Four men to a spike, they ran with them to staked positions on the new-cut ground, set them upright. A man flung a metal clamp around the spike. Two men, one on each side, drove down on the clamp with heavy sledges until the spike would stand alone. And already those four were back with another spike.

Twenty-six such spikes were set, but long before they were all out of the wagon, Sussten spun the machine in its own length and stopped. The mold-board rose, hinged, folded back to become the silver sides of the machine again. Sussten drove forward, nosed the machine into the first of the spikes, which fitted into a slot at the front of the machine. There was the sound of a frantic giant ringing a metal triangle, and the spike sank as if the ground had turned to bread.

Leaving perhaps two hands'-breadths of the spike showing, the machine slid to the next and the next, sinking the spikes so quickly that it had almost a whole minute to wait while the spike crew set the very last one. At that a sound rolled out of the crowd, a sound utterly unlike any that had ever been heard during the building of the tower—a friendly, jeering roar of laughter at the crew who had made the machine wait.

Men unrolled heavy cable along the lines of spikes; others followed right behind them, one with a tool which stretched the cable taut, two with a tool that in two swift motions connected the cable to the tops of the sunken spikes. And by the time the cable was connected, two flatbeds, a buckboard and a hay wagon had unloaded a cluster of glistening machine parts. Men and women swarmed over them, wrenches, pliers and special tools in hand, bolting, fitting, clamping, connecting. Three heavy leads from the great ground cable were connected; a great parabolic wire basket was raised and guyed.

Wrenn ran to the structure and pulled a lever. A high-pitched scream of force dropped sickeningly in pitch to a jarring subsonic, and rose immediately high out of the audible range.

A rosy haze enveloped the end of the new machine, opposite the ground array and under the basket. It thickened, shimmered, and steadied, until it was a stable glowing sphere with an off-focus muzziness barely showing all around its profile.

The crowd—not a group now, but a line—cheered and the line moved forward. Every conceivable village conveyance moved in single file toward the shining sphere, and, as each stopped, heavy metal was unloaded. Cast-iron stove legs could be recognized, and long strips of tinning solder, a bell, a kettle, the framing of a bench. The blacksmith's anvil was there, and parts of his forge. Pots and skillets. A ratchet and pawl from the gristmill. The weights and pendulum from the big village clock.

As each scrap was unloaded, exactly the number of hands demanded by its weight were waiting to catch it, swing it from its conveyance into the strange sphere. They went in without resistance and without sound, and they did not come out. Wagon after wagon, pack after handsack were unloaded, and still the sphere took and took.

It took heavy metal and more mass than its own dimensions. Had the metal been melted down into a sphere, it would have been a third again, half again, twice as large as the sphere, and still it took.

But its color was changing. The orange went to burned sienna and then to a strident brown. Imperceptibly this darkened until at last it was black. For a moment, it was a black of impossible glossiness, but this softened. Blacker and blacker it became, and at length it was not a good thing to look into—the blackness seemed to be hungry for something more intimate than metal. And still the metals came and the sphere took.

A great roar came from the crowd; men fell back to look upward. High in the west was a glowing golden spark which showed a long blue tail. It raced across the sky and was gone, and moments later the human roar was answered by thunder from above.

If the work had been swift before, it now became a blur. Men no longer waited for the line of wagons to move, but ran back along it to snatch metal and stagger forward again to the sphere. Women ripped off bracelets and hammered earrings and threw them to the implacable melanosphere. Men threw in their knives, even their buttons. A rain of metal was sucked silently into the dazzling black.

Another cry from the crowd, and now there was hurried anguish in it; again the craning necks, the quick gasp. The golden spark was a speed-blurred ovoid now, the blue tail a banner half a horizon long. The roar, when it came, was a smashing thunder, and the blue band hung where it was long after the thing had gone.

A moan of urgency, caught and maintained by one exhausted throat after another, rose and fell and would not leave. Then it was a happy shout as Sussten drove in, shouldering the beautiful cutting machine through the scattering crowd. Its blade unfolded as it ran, latched high and stayed there like a shining forearm flung across the machine's silver face.

As the last scrambling people dove for safety, Sussten brought the huge blade slashing downward and at the same time threw the machine into its highest speed. It leaped forward as Sussten leaped back. Unmanned, it rushed at the sphere as if to sweep it away, crash the structure that contained it. But at the last microsecond, the blade struck the ground; the nose of the machine snapped upward, and the whole gleaming thing literally vaulted into the sphere.

No words exist for such a black. Some people fell to their knees, their faces covered. Some turned blindly away, unsteady on their feet. Some stood trembling, fixed on it, until friendly hands took and turned them and coaxed them back to reality.

And at last a man staggered close, squinting, and threw in the heavy wrought-iron support for an inn sign—

And the sphere refused it.

Such a cry of joy rose from the village that the sleeping bats in the thickets of Sky-tree Grove, two miles away, stirred and added their porcine grunting to the noise.

A woman ran to Wrenn, screaming, elbowing, unnoticed and unheard in the bedlam. She caught his shoulder roughly, spun him half around, pointed. Pointed up at the tower, at Osser.

Wrenn thumbed a small disc out of a socket in his belt and held it near his lips.

"*Osser!*" The great voice rang and echoed, crushing the ecstatic noises of the people by its sheer weight. "*Osser, come down or you're a dead man!*"

The people, suddenly silent, all stared at the tower. One or two cried, "Yes, come down, come down . . ." but the puniness of their voices was ludicrous after Wrenn's magnified tones, and few tried again.

Osser stood holding the parapet, legs wide apart, eyes wide—too wide—open. His hands curled over the edge, and blood dripped slowly from under the cuticles.

"*Come down, come down . . .*"

He did not move. His eyeballs were nearly dry, and unnoticed saliva lay in a drying streak from one corner of his mouth.

"*Jubilith, bring him down!*"

She was whimpering, begging, murmuring little urgencies to him. His biceps were as hard as the parapet, his face as changeless as the stone.

"*Jubilith, leave him! Leave him and come!*" Wrenn, wise Wrenn, sure, unshakable, imperturbable Wrenn had a sob in his voice; and under such amplification the sob was almost big enough to be voice for the sobs that twisted through Jubilith's tight throat.

She dropped to one knee and put one slim firm shoulder under Osser's wrist. She drove upward against it with all the lithe strength of her panicked body. It came free, leaving a clot of fingertip on the stone. Down she went again, and up again at the other wrist; but this was suddenly flaccid, and her tremendous effort turned to a leap. She clutched at Osser, who tottered forward.

For one endless second they hung there, while their mutual center of gravity made a slow deliberation, and then Jubilith kicked frantically at the parapet, abrading her legs, mingling her blood with his on the masonry. They went together back to the roof. Jubilith twisted like a falling cat and got her feet down, holding Osser's great weight up.

They spun across the roof in an insane staggering dance; then there was the stairway (with its invisible barrier gone) and darkness (with his hand in hers now, holding and leading) and a sprint into daylight and the shattering roar of Wrenn's giant voice: *"Everybody down, down flat!"*

And there was a time of running, pulling Osser after her, and Osser pounding along behind her, docile and wide-eyed as a cat-ox. And then the rebellion and failure of her legs, and the will that refused to let them fail, and the failure of that will; the stunning agony of a cracked patella as she went down on the rocks, and the swift sense of infinite loss as Osser's hand pulled free of hers and he went lumbering blindly along, the only man on his feet in the wide meadow of the fallen.

Jubilith screamed and someone stood up—she thought it was old Oyva—and cried out.

Then the mighty voice again, *"Osser! Down, man!"* Blearily, then, she saw Osser stagger to a halt and peer around him.

"Osser, lie down!"

And then Osser, mad, drooling, turning toward her. His eyes protruded and he slashed about with his heavy fists. He came closer, unseeing, battling some horror he believed in with great cuts and slashes that threatened elbow and shoulder joints by the wrenching of their unimpeded force.

His voice—but not his, rather the voice of an old, wretched crone—squeaking out in a shrill falsetto, "Not down, never down, but up. I'll build, build, build, break to build, kill to build, and all the ones who can do everything, anything, everything, they will build everything for me. I'm strong!" he shrieked, soprano. "All the people who can do anything are less than one strong man . . ."

He jabbered and fought, and suddenly Wrenn rose, quite close by, his left hand enclosed in a round flat box. He moved something on its surface and then waved it at Osser, in a gesture precisely like the command to a guest to be seated.

Down went Osser, close to Jubilith, with his face in the dirt and his eyes open, uncaring. On him and on Jubilith lay the invisible weight of the force that had awaited him in the stairway.

The breath hissed out of Jubilith. Had she not been lying on her side with her face turned skyward in a single convulsive effort toward air, she would never have seen what happened. The golden shape appeared in the west, seen a fraction of a second, but blazoned forever in tangled memories of this day. And simultaneously the earth-shaking cough of the machine as its sphere disappeared.

She could not see it move, but such a blackness is indelible, and she sensed it when it appeared in the high distances as its trajectory and that of the golden flyer intersected.

Then there was—*Nothing*.

The broad blue trail swept from the western horizon to the zenith, and sharply ended. There was no sound, no concussion, no blaze of light. The sphere met the ship and both ceased to exist.

Then there was the wind, from nowhere, from everywhere, all the wind that ever was, tearing in agony from everywhere in the world to the place where the sphere had been, trying to fill the strange space that had contained exactly as much matter as the dead golden ship. Wagons, oxen, trees and stones scraped and flew and crashed together in the center of that monstrous implosion.

The weight Wrenn had laid on Jubilith disappeared, but her sucking lungs could find nothing to draw in. There was air aplenty, but none of it would serve her.

Finally she realized there was unconsciousness waiting for her if she wanted it. She embraced it, sank into it, and left the world to its wailing winds.

Ages later, there was weeping.

She stirred and raised her head.

The sphere machine was gone. There was a heap of something down there, but it supported such a tall and heavy pillar of roiling dust that she could not see what it was. There, and there, and over yonder, in twos and threes, silent, shaken people sat up, some staring about them, some just sitting, waiting for the shock-stopped currents of life to flow back in.

But the weeping . . .

She put her palm on the ground and inched it, heel first, in a weak series of little hops, until she was half sitting.

Osser was weeping.

He sat upright, his feet together and his knees wide apart, like a little child. He rocked. He lifted his hands and let them fall, lifted them and punctuated his crying with weak poundings on the ground. His mouth was an O, his eyes were single squeezed lines, his face was wet, and his crying was the most heartrending sound she had ever heard.

She thought to speak to him, but knew he would not hear. She thought to go to him, but the first shift of weight sent such agony through her broken kneecap that she almost fainted.

Osser wept.

She turned away from him—suppose, later, he should remember that she had seen this?—and then she knew why he was crying. He was crying because his tower was gone. Tower of strength, tower of defiance, tower of hope, tower of rebellion and hatred and an ambition big enough for a whole race of city-builders, gone without a fight, gone without the triumph of taking him with it, gone in an instant, literally in a puff of wind.

"Where does it hurt?"

It was Wrenn, who had approached unseen through the blinding, sick compassion that filled her.

"It hurts there." She pointed briefly at Osser.

"I know," said Wrenn gently. He checked what she was about to say with a gesture. "No, we won't stop him. When he was a little boy, he never cried. He has been hurt more than most people, and nothing ever made him cry, ever. We all have a cup for tears and a reservoir. No childhood is finished until all the tears flow from the reservoir into the cup. Let him cry; perhaps he is going to be a man. It's your knee, isn't it?"

"Yes. Oh, but I can't stand to hear it, my heart will burst!" she cried.

"Hear him out," said Wrenn softly, taking medication from a flat box at his waist. He ran feather-fingers over her knee and nodded. "You have taken Osser as your own. Keep this weeping with you, all of it. It will fit you to him better through the healing time."

"May I understand now?"

"Yes, oh yes . . . and since he has taught you about hate, you will hate me for it."

"I couldn't hate you, Wrenn."

Something stirred within his placid eyes—a smile, a pointed shard of knowledge—she was not sure. "Perhaps you could."

He kept his eyes on his careful bandaging, and as he worked, he spoke.

"Stop a man in his work to tell him that each of his fingers bears a pattern of loops and whorls, and you waste his time. It is a thing he knows, a thing he has seen for himself, a thing which can be checked on the instant—in short, an obvious, unremarkable thing. Yet, if his attention is not called to it, it is impossible to teach him that these patterns are exclusive, original with him, unduplicated anywhere. Sparing him the truism may cost him the fact.

"It is that kind of truism through which I shall pass to reach the things you must understand. So be patient with me through the familiar paths; I promise you a most remarkable turning.

"We are an ancient and resourceful species, and among the many things we have—our happiness, our simplicity, our harmony with each other and with ourselves—some are the products of intelligence, per se, but most of the good things spring from a quality which we possess in greater degree than any other species yet known. That is—logic.

"Now, there is the obvious logic: you may never have broken your knee before, but you knew, in advance, that if you did it would cause you pain. If I hold this pebble so, you may correctly predict that it will drop when I release it, though you have never seen this stone before. This obvious logic strikes deeper levels as well; for example, if I release the stone and it does not fall, logic tells you not only that some unpredicted force is now acting on it, but a great many things about that force: that it equals gravity in the case of this particular pebble; that it is in stasis; that it is phenomenal, since it is out of the statistical order of things.

"The quality of logic, which we (so far as is known) uniquely possess, is this: any of us can do literally anything that anyone else can do. You need ask no one to solve the problems that you face every day, providing they are problems common to all. To cut material so that a sleeve will fit a shoulder, you pause, you close your eyes; the way to cut material then comes to you, and you proceed. You never need do anything twice, because the first way is the most logical. You may finish the garment and put it away without trying it on for fit, because you know you have done it right and it is perfect.

"If I put you before a machine which you had never seen before, which had a function unknown to you, and which operated on principles you had never heard of, and if I told you it was broken and needed repairing, you would look at it carefully, inside, outside, top and bottom, and you would close your eyes, and suddenly you would understand the principles. With these and the machine, function would explain itself. The step from that point to the location of a faulty part is self-evident.

"Now I lay before you parts which are identical in appearance, and ask you to install the correct one. Since you thoroughly understand the requirements now, the specifications for the correct part are self-evident. Logic dictates the correct tests for the parts. You will rapidly reject the tight one, the heavy one, the too soft one, and the too resilient one, and you will repair my machine. And you will walk away without testing it, since you now know it will operate."

Wrenn continued, "You—all of us—live in this way. We build no cities because we don't need cities. We stay in groups because some things need more than two hands, more than one head, or voice, or mood. We eat exactly what we require, we use only what we need.

"And that is the end of the truism, wherein I so meticulously describe to you what you know about how you live. The turning: Whence this familiar phenomenon, this closing of the eyes and mysterious appearance of the answer? There have been many engrossing theories about it, but the truth is the most fascinating of all.

"We have all spoken of telepathy, and many of us have experienced it. We cannot explain it, as yet. But most of us insist on a limited consideration of it; that is, we judge its success or failure by the amount of detail sent and received. We expect *facts* to be transmitted, *words,* idea sequences—or perhaps pictures; the clearer the picture, the better the telepathy.

"Perhaps one day we will learn to do this; it would be diverting. But what we actually *do* is infinitely more useful.

"You see, we *are* telepathic, not in the way of conveying details, but in the much more useful way of conveying a *manner of thinking.*

"Let us try to envisage a man who lacks this quality. Faced with your broken machine, he would be utterly at a loss, unless he had been specially trained in this particular field. Do not overlook the fact that he lacks the conditioning of a whole life of the kind of sequence thinking which is possible to us. He would probably bumble through the whole chore in an interminable time, trying one thing and then another and going forward from whatever seems to work. You can see the tragic series of pitfalls possible for him in a situation in which an alternate three or four or five consecutive steps are possible, forcing step six, which is wrong in terms of the problem.

"Now, take the same man and train him in this one job. Add a talent, so that he learns quickly and well. Add years of experience—terrible, drudging thought!—to his skill. Face him with the repair problem and it is obvious that he will repair it with a minimum of motion.

"Finally, take this skilled man and equip him with a device which constantly sends out the habit-patterns of his thinking. Long practice has made him efficient in the matter; in terms of machine function he knows better than to question whether a part turns this way or that, whether a rod or tube larger than x diameter is to be considered. Furthermore, imagine a receiving device which absorbs these sendings whenever the receiver is faced with an identical problem. The skilled sender controls the unskilled receiver as long as the receiver is engaged in the problem. Anything the receiver does which is counter to the basic patterns of the sender is automatically rejected as illogical.

"And now I have described our species. We have an unmatchable unitary existence. Each of us with a natural bent—the poets, the musicians, the mechanics, the philosophers—each gives of his basic thinking method every time anyone has an application for it. The expert is unaware of being tapped—which is why it has taken hundreds of centuries to recognize the method. Yet, in spite of what amounts to a veritable race intellect, we are all very much individuals. Because each field has many experts, and each of those experts has his individual approach, only that which is closest both to the receiver *and* his problem comes in. The ones without special talents live fully and richly with all the skills of the gifted. The creative ones share with others in their field as soon as it occurs to any expert to review what he knows; the one step forward then instantly presents itself.

"So much for the bulk of our kind. There remain a few specializing *non-*specialists. When you are faced with a problem to which no logical solution presents itself, you come to one of these few for help. The reason no solution presents itself is that this is a new line of thinking, or (which is very likely) the last expert in it has died. The non-specialist hears your problem and applies simple logic to it. Immediately, others of his kind do the same. But, since they come from widely divergent backgrounds and use a vast variety of methods, one of them is almost certain to find the logical solution. This is your answer— and through you, it is available to anyone who ever faces this particular problem.

"In exceptional cases, the non-specializing specialist encounters a problem which, for good reason, is better left out of the racial 'pool'—as, for example, a physical or psychological experiment within the culture, of long duration, which general knowledge might alter. In such cases, a highly specialized hypnotic technique is used on the investigators, which has the effect of cloaking thought on this particular matter.

"And if you began to fear that I was never coming to Osser's unhappy history, you must understand, my dear, I have just given it to you. Osser was just such an experiment.

"It became desirable to study the probable habit patterns of a species like us in every respect except for our unique attribute. The problem was attacked from many angles, but I must confess that using a live specimen was my idea.

"By deep hypnosis, the telepathic receptors in Osser were severed from the rest of his mind. He was then allowed to grow up among us in real and complete freedom.

"You saw the result. Since few people recognize the nature of this unique talent, and even fewer regard it as worth discussion, this strong, proud, highly intelligent boy grew up feeling a hopeless inferior, and never knowing exactly why. Others did things, made things, solved problems, as easily as thinking about them, while Osser had to study and sweat and piece and try out. He had to assert his superiority in some way. He did, but in as slipshod a fashion as he did everything else.

"So he was led to the pictures you saw. He was permitted to make what conclusions he wished—they were that we are a backward people, incapable of building a city. He suddenly saw in the dreams of a mechanized, star-reaching species a justification of himself. He could not understand our lack of desire for possessions, not knowing that our whole cultural existence is based on sharing— that it is not only undesirable, but impossible for us to hoard an advanced idea, a new comfort. He would master us through strength.

"He was just starting when you came to me about him. You could get no key to his problem because we know nothing about sick minds, and there was no expert you could tap. I couldn't help you—you, of all people—because you loved him, and because we dared not risk having him know what he was, especially when he was just about to take action.

"Why he chose this particular site for his tower I do not know. And why he chose the method of the tower I don't know either, though I can deduce an excellent reason. First, he had to use his strength once he became convinced that in it lay his superiority. Second, he had to *try out* this build-with-hate idea—the bugaboo of all other man-species, the trial-and-error, the inability to *know* what will work and what will not.

"And so we learned through Osser precisely what we had learned in other approaches—that a man without our particular ability must not live among us, for, if he does, he will destroy us.

"It is a small step from that to a conclusion about a whole race of them coexisting with us. And now you know what happened here this afternoon."

Jubilith raised her head slowly. "A whole ship full of . . . of what Osser was?"

"Yes. We did the only thing we could. Quick, quite painless. We have been watching them for a long time—years. We saw them start. We computed their orbit—even to the deceleration spiral. We chose a spot to launch our interceptor." He glanced at Osser, who was almost quiet, quite exhausted. "What sheer hell he must have gone through, to see us build like that. How could he know that not one of us needed training, explanation, or any but the simplest orders? How could he rationalize to himself our possession of machines and devices surpassing the wildest dreams of the god-like men he admired so? How could he understand that, having such things, we use them only when we must, and that otherwise we live in ways which will not violate the walking, working animal we are?"

She turned to him a mask so cold, so beautiful, he forgot for a moment to breathe. "Why did you do it? You had other logics, other approaches. Did you have to do *that* to him."

He studiously avoided a glance at Osser. "I said you might hate me," he murmured. "Jubilith, the men in that ship were so like Osser that the experiment could not be passed by. We had astronomical data, historical, cultural—as far as our observations could go—and ethnological. But only by analogy could we get such a psychological study. And it checked too well. As for having him see this thing, today . . . building, Jubilith, is sometimes begun by tearing down."

He looked at her with deep compassion. "This was not the site chosen for the launching of the interceptor. We uprooted the whole installation, brought it here, rebuilt it, just for Osser; just so that he could stand on his tower and see it happen. He had to be broken, leveled to the earth. Ah-h-h . . ." he breathed painfully, "Osser has earned what he will have from now on."

"He can be—well again?"

"With your help."

"So very right, you are," she snarled suddenly. "So sure that this or that species is fit to associate with superiors like us." She leaned toward him and shook a finger in his startled face. The courtly awe habitual to all when speaking to such as Wrenn had completely left her.

"So fine we are, so mighty. And didn't we build cities? Didn't we have giant bird-machines and shiny carts on our streets? Didn't we let our cities be smashed—haven't you seen the ruins in the west? Tell me," she sparked, "did we ruin them ourselves, because one superior city insisted on proving its superiority over another superior city?"

She stopped abruptly to keep herself from growling like an animal, for he was smiling blandly, and his smile got wider as she spoke. She turned furiously, half away from him, cursing the broken knee that held her so helpless.

"Jubilith."

His voice was so warm, so kind and so startling in these surroundings, held such a bubbling overtone of laughter that she couldn't resist it. She turned grudgingly.

In his hand he held a pebble. When her eye fell to it he rolled it, held it between thumb and forefinger, and let it go.

It stayed motionless in mid-air. "Another factor, Jubilith."

She almost smiled. She looked down at his other hand, and saw it aiming the disc-shaped force-field projector at low power.

He lifted it and, with the field, tossed the pebble into the air and batted it away. "We have no written history, Jubilith. We don't need one, but once in a while it would be useful.

"Jubilith, our culture is one of the oldest in the Galaxy. If we ever had such cities, there are not even legends about it."

"But I saw—"

"A ship came here once. We had never seen a humanoid race. We welcomed them and helped them. We gave them land and seeds. Then they called a flotilla, and the ships came by the hundreds.

"They built cities and, at that, we moved away and left them alone, because we don't *need* cities. Then they began to hate us. They couldn't hate us until they had tall buildings to do it in. They hated our quiet; they hated our understanding. They sent missionaries to change our ways. We welcomed the missionaries, fed them and laughed with them, but when they left us glittering tools and humble machines to amuse us, we let them lie where they were until they rotted.

"In time they sent no more missionaries. They joked about us and forgot us. And then they built a city on land we had not given them, and another, and another. They bred well, and their cities became infernally big. And finally they began to build that one city too many, and we turned a river and drowned it. They were pleased. They could now rid themselves of the backward natives."

Jubilith closed her eyes, and saw the tumbled agony of the mounds, radiating outward from a lake with its shores too bare. "All of them?" she asked.

Wrenn nodded. "Even one might be enough to destroy us." He nodded toward Osser, who had begun to cry again.

"They seemed . . . good," she said, reflectively. "Too fast, too big . . . and it must have been noisy, but—"

"Wait," he said. "You mean the people in the picture Osser showed you?"

"Of course. They were the city-builders you—we—destroyed, weren't they?"

"They were not! The ones who built here were thin, hairy, with backward-slanting faces and webs between their fingers. Beautiful, but they hated us . . . The pictures, Jubilith, were made on the third planet of a pale star out near the Rim; a world with one Moon; a world of humans like Osser . . . the world where that golden ship came from."

"How?" she gasped.

"If logic is good enough," Wrenn said, "it need not be checked. Once we were so treated by humanoids, we built the investigators. They are not manned. They draw their power from anything that radiates, and they home on any planet which could conceivably rear humans. They are, as far as we know, undetectable. We've never lost one. They launch tiny flyers to make close searches—one of them made the pictures you saw. The pictures and other data are coded and sent out into space and, where distances warrant it, other investigators catch the signal and add power and send them on.

"Whenever a human or humanoid species builds a ship, we watch it. When they send their ships to this sector, we watch their planet *and* their ship. Unless we are sure that those people have the ability we have, to share all expertness and all creative thinking with all who want it—they don't land here. And no such species ever will land here."

"You're so sure."

"We explore no planets, Jubilith. We like it here. If others like us exist—why should they visit us?"

She thought about it, and slowly she nodded. "I like it here," she breathed.

Wrenn knelt and looked out across the rolling ground. It was late, and most of the villagers had gone home. A few picked at the mounds of splinters at the implosion center. Their limbs were straight and their faces clear. They owned little and they shared their souls.

He rose and went to Osser, and sat down beside him, facing him, his back to Jubilith. "M-m-mum, mum, mum, mum, mum-mum-mum," he intoned.

Osser blinked at him. Wrenn lifted his hand and his ring, green and gold and a shimmering oval of purple, caught the late light. Osser looked at the ring. He reached for it. Wrenn moved it slightly. Osser's hand passed it and hit the ground and lay there neglected. Osser gaped at the ring, his jaws working, his teeth not meeting.

"Mum, mum, *mummy,* where's your mummy, Osser?"

"In the house," said Osser, looking at the ring.

Wrenn said, "You're a good little boy. When we say the word, you won't be able to do anything but what *you* can do. When we say the key, you'll be able to do anything *anybody* can do."

"All right," Osser said.

"Before I give the word, tell me the key. You must remember the key."

"That ring. And 'last 'n' lost.' "

"Good, Osser. Now listen to me. Can you hear me?"

"Sure." He grabbed at the ring.

"I'm going to change the key. It isn't 'last 'n' lost' any more. 'Last 'n' lost' is no good now. Forget it."

"No good?"

"Forget it. What's the key?"

"I—forgot."

"The key," said Wrenn patiently, "is this." He leaned close and whispered rapidly.

Jubilith was peering out past the implosion center to the townward path. Someone was coming, a tiny figure.

"Jubilith," Wrenn said. She looked up at him. "You must understand something." His voice was grave. His hair reached for an awed little twist of wind, come miles to see this place. The wind escaped and ran away down the hill.

Wrenn said, "He's very happy now. He was a happy child when first I heard of him, and how like a spacebound human he could be. Well, he's that child again. He always will be, until the day he dies. I'll see he's cared for. He'll chase the sunbeams, a velvet red one and a needle of blue-white; he'll eat and he'll love and be loved just as is right for him."

They looked at Osser. There was a blue insect on his wrist. He raised it slowly, slowly, close to his eyes, and through its gauze wings he saw the flame-and-silver sunset. He laughed.

"All his life?"

"All his life," said Wrenn. "With the bitterness and the trouble wiped away, and no chance to mature again into the unfinished thing that fought the world with the conviction it had something extra."

Then he dropped the ring into Jubilith's hand. "But if you care to," he said, watching her face, the responsive motion of her sensitive nostrils, the most delicate index of her lower lip, "if you care to, you can give him back everything I took away. In a moment, you can give him more than he has now; but how long would it take you to make him as happy?"

She made no attempt to answer him. He was Wrenn, he was old and wise; he was a member of a unique species whose resources were incalculable; and yet he was asking her to do something he could not do himself. Perhaps he was asking her to correct a wrong. She would never know that.

"Just the ring," he said, "and the touch of your hand."

He went away, straight and tall, quickening his pace as, far away, the patient figure she had been watching earlier rose and came to meet him. It was Oyva.

Jubilith thought, "He needs her."

Jubilith had never been needed by anyone.

She looked at her hand and in it she saw all she was, all she could ever be in her own right; and with it, the music of ages; never the words, but all of the pressures of poetry. And she saw the extraordinary privacy of love in a world which looked out through her eyes, placed all of its skills in her hands, to do with as she alone wished.

With a touch of her hand . . . what a flood of sensation, what a bursting in of voices and knowledge, for a child!

How long a child?

She closed her eyes, and quietly the answer came, full of pictures; the lute picked up and played; the instant familiarity with the most intricate machine; the stars seen otherwise, and yet again otherwise, and every seeing an honest beauty. A thousand discoveries, and manhood with a rush.

She slipped the ring on her finger, and dragged herself over to him. She put her arms around him and his cheek came down to the hollow of her throat and burrowed there.

He said, sleepily, "Is it nighttime, Mummy?"

"For just a little while," said Jubilith.

TWINK

This is the one and only time I used this particular writer's trick in narrative. I wonder if you can divine what it is. Otherwise, I must express pride at the insightful look at society's insensitivities toward the unusual person. The disabled are unusual; special gifts are unusual; too many people don't know the difference. The slow learners are unusual; psychopaths are unusual; too many people think they're suffering from the same thing. These, *among other things,* are what this story's about, so I hope you will forgive the trickery.

Feeling numb, I put the phone down. I've got to get out of here, I thought. I've got to go ask old Frozen Face. I've got to get home.

But there was the old man, just that minute coming out of his office. For the first time, I was glad he'd put my desk out there in front of the golden-oak slab of his door, like a welcome mat. I looked up at him and I guess I looked anxious.

He stopped beside me. "Something wrong?"

I wet my lips, but I couldn't say anything. Stupid! Why shouldn't I be able to say *I've got to get out of here!*

"The kid?"

"Yes," I said. "We have to take her in this afternoon."

"Well, get out of here," he said brusquely.

I stood up, I couldn't look at him. "Thanks."

"Shaddap," he said gruffly. "Call up if you need anything."

"I won't need anything." Except courage. Faith, if you like. And whatever kind of hypocrisy it takes to conceal from a child how scared you are.

I reached for my hat. Old Frozen Face just stood there. I looked back from the outer door and he was still there, staring at the place where I'd been.

I almost yelled at him some explosive, blathering series of syllables that would in some way explain to him that I'm not a freak; look at the creases in my blue pants; look at my shoeshine, just the same as yours; look how my hairline's receding—look, look, I've got heartburn and lumps in my throat!

At the same time, I wanted to yell something else, something about, yes, you were kind to me because you know what's with me, with my kid; but you can't know how it is. With you, I'm once removed from anything you could feel, like the Hundred Neediest Cases in the newspaper at Christmas. You believe it, sure, but you can't know how it is.

So with one inner voice saying I'm what you are and another saying You can't know how it is, I let them crash together and silence one another, and said nothing, but made the frosted glass door swing shut and walked over to the elevators.

I had to wait and that seemed wrong. I looked at the indicators, and saw that all of the cars were running, and that seemed wrong, too. Everything else ought to stop except one car for me and it ought to be here now! I stood there realizing how irrational all this was, but fuming anyway.

Behind me, I heard *thunk*-pat, *thunk*-pat, and from the corner of my eye saw it was Bernie Pitt on his crutches. I turned very slightly so my back was to him. Bernie is a very nice guy, but I just didn't want to talk to anybody. It was as if talking to somebody would slow up the elevator.

I hoped he hadn't noticed my turning away like that. Then I found I could see his reflection in the polished gray-green marble of the wall by the elevator. He was looking at me; I could see his face tilt as he glanced down at the hat I was twisting in my hands. Then it tipped up and back a little as he studied the tops of the doors, the way a man does when he wants to look as if he's absorbed in his own thoughts. So he's seen that hat, at ten in the morning, and that meant I was going out, and he knew all about me and Twink and the accident, and was being considerate.

Old Frozen Face was being considerate, too. Old Frozen Face always did the correctly considerate thing. Like hiring Bernie, who was a cripple.

I hated myself for thinking that.

It made me hate Bernie. I glared at his reflection. Just then, one of the elevator doors across the corridor rolled open and I jumped and spun.

"Up!" said the operator.

Bernie stumped into it without looking at me. The door closed. I wished I had a rock to throw at it.

I tried hard to get hold of myself. I knew what was happening. Scare a man badly enough, and then make the thing he fears diffuse and unreachable, and he'll lash out indiscriminately at everything and everyone. Well, lash away, boy,

I told myself, and get it out of your stinking small-minded system before you get home.

"Down?" the operator asked.

Shouldering into the car, I felt I had a right to be sore at the operator for taking so long. The elevator was full of intruders and the descent took forever, and for a moment I got so mad, I swear I could have hunched my shoulders and sprayed them all with adrenaline. Then the doors opened again and there was the lobby like a part of all outdoors, and the offices upstairs no longer contained or confined me, and their people no longer intruded.

I scurried down the steps and along the concourse to the interurban station, trusting my feet and letting the rest of me fly along with the eager aimlessness of a peace-dove released at a school pageant.

How can there be any unreality in your cosmos? I asked myself. The day Twink goes to the hospital—that's *today;* it's here. It's been a real thing all this time, for all it was in the future; it was more real than most other things in the world. And now it's come and you're walking underwater, seeing through murk.

But the whole world's helping, too. Nothing is so unreal to the commuter as a commuter's station at ten in the morning. The trains, lying in these echoing acres, look like great eviscerated larvae. The funereal train crew, gossiping as if work were done, as if it weren't their job to get me home before the sawbones went to work on my little girl.

I went to them. "Baytown?"

They looked at me, a conductor, a motorman, a platform man. They were different sizes and shapes, but their faces were all the same gray, and contained the same damnable sense of the fitness of things. They were in a place that belonged to them, doing the right thing at the right time in it. They were steady and sober and absolutely at the service of commuters-by-the-ton, but a man outbound at ten in the morning, though tolerable, could hardly be served. He wasn't what they were there for.

I went into the train and sat down and looked at my watch. Four minutes. They were going to make me wait four minutes.

I sat in an empty car and looked at the glare of yellow woven plastic pretending to be, steel panels pretending to be wood, and the advertising signs. There were three kinds of signs: the imperatives, which said Buy and Drink and Use; the comparatives, which said Better, Richer, Finer (and never stated what they were better and richer and finer than); and the nominatives, which stupidly and without explanation proclaimed a name.

I snorted at them all and reached for a paper someone had left on a nearby seat. If its previous owner had been there, I think I'd have punched him right in the mouth. I've always respected books and I've always felt that a paper is a sort of book. This character had put the middle section in upside down, folded some sheets back on themselves and away from the centerline, so that page covers skewed and flopped all around, and he had generally churned up and mutilated the dead white body before discarding it.

Growling, I began to put it back together again.

CHEERFUL TONY WEAKER
Doomed Child Sinking. Gifts
and Cards Pouring In for
Early Birthday

New York, June 25 (AP)—1973's Child of the Year, five-year-old Tony Marshall, has been placed under oxygen at Memorial Hospital, while a staff of top cancer specialists stand a twenty-four-hour watch at his bedside. Hope that he will live to see his sixth birthday in August has faded.

The boy, whose famous smile made him known from coast to coast as Cheerful Tony, is suffering from advanced leukemia.

Angrily I hurled the paper away from me. It came to pieces in midair and fluttered to the floor, to lie there accusingly and stare at me. I swore and got up and gathered it together and crammed it out of sight on the seat ahead of mine.

"Cheerful Tony," I muttered. Some convolution of the face muscles, some accident of the dental arch, a trick of the light and the fortuitous presence of a news photographer as lucky as the guy who got the flag-raising at Iwo—put 'em all together and you've got a national hero. What good did it do to anyone to read about Cheerful Tony or to write about it? What good did it do Tony?

For an ugly moment, I wished I could trade places with Tony's father. All he had to worry about was cancer—nice, certain cancer—and once it was finished, that would be the end of it.

But I didn't envy him the publicity, and for the hundred thousandth time, I thanked the Powers that so few people knew about Twink.

The doors slid shut and the train started. I let go a sigh of relief and hunched back in my seat, wondering how to make the time go faster. Not the time; the train. I pushed my feet uselessly against the legs of the next seat, made a calm and childish calculation of what I was doing (forty pounds foot-pressure forward, forty pounds shoulder-pressure backward—equals zero) and sat up feeling like a fool. I began to look at the ads again.

Imperative, comparative, nominative.

Maybe my technique had been wrong all along. Maybe I should have used nothing but advertising tactics on Twink the whole time. After all, those were tested methods, with more than a century of proof behind them.

"Relax with oxygen," I should have told her. "Live," I should have told her, twelve times a minute, in the best imperative mood. "Live ... live." And, "Don't struggle. Let the doctor work. It will be easier." (Than what?) And, of course, the pervasive, institutional nominative: "Twink. Everybody knows Twink. Everybody loves Twink." Until she believes it all. . . .

The anger, which had changed to hysteria, converted itself now into crawling depression. It descended on me like the shadow of some great reptile, something that moved slowly and implacably and without human understanding. I felt utterly alone. I was different. Apart. More apart than Bernie, who had left half a leg in Formosa. More than Sue Gaskell, who was the only Negro in the copy department—by God, another "kindness" of old Frozen Face.

Why couldn't someone (besides Twink) share this with me? Even Doris couldn't. Doris loved me; she ate with me, slept with me, worried and hoped with me, but this thing with Twink was something she couldn't share. She just wasn't equipped for it. Sometimes I wondered how she held still for that. This might go on for years ... if Twink lived at all ... Twink and I sharing a thing that Doris could never know, even being Twink's mother.

Suddenly I found someone else to be mad at and the depression lifted enough to let it in. You guys, I thought, you helpful people who put welded track on these roadbeds, who designed pneumatic dampers and cushioned wheels for the trains—did it ever occur to you that a man might want something to listen to in a train in 1973? Twenty years ago, I could have listened to the wheels and I could have made up a song to go along with them; *blippety-clak, blippety-clak.*

Blippety-clink, poor little Twink, don't let her die—

All right, fellows—on second thought, you can have your welded rails.

"Baytown," said the annunciator in a cultured voice, and deceleration helped me up out of the seat.

I went to the door and was through it before it had slid all the way open, shot down the platform while fumbling for my commuter's plate, missed the scanner slot with it and skinned my knuckles, dropped the plate, picked it up, got it into the slot, waited forever—well, three seconds—while it scanned, punched and slid out my receipt.

I was just about to blow a fuse because there was no taxi, but there was. I couldn't bark my address because the driver knew it, and I couldn't wave bribes at him because he was paid by the development, and anyway his turbines had a governor to keep him from speeding as fast as I wanted. All I could do was huddle on the cushion and bite the ball of my thumb.

The house was very quiet. For some reason, I had expected to find them in the nursery, but there wasn't a sound from there. I found Doris stretched out on the settee in the den, looking drowsy.

"Doris!"

"Shh. 'Lo. Twink's asleep."

I ran to her. "Is she . . . do you . . . are you . . ."

She rumpled my hair. "Shhh," she said again. "My goodness, it's going to be all right."

I leaned very close and whispered, "Scared. I'm scared."

"I'm scared, too," she said reasonably, "but I'm not going to go all to pieces."

I knelt there, soaking up a kind of strength, a kind of peace from her. "Sorry, darling. I've been——" I shuddered. "On the train, I was reading about Cheerful Tony. I was thinking how they'd do the same thing with us, if they knew."

"Only more." She half-laughed. "All that mail, all those reporters, newsreel men. All that glory. All that——noise."

We listened together to the morning silence. It was the first time since she'd phoned me that I'd noticed how lovely the day was.

"Thank you," she whispered.

"For what?"

"For not telling them. For being—well, for just being; I guess that's what I'm trying to say. And for Twink."

"For *Twink?*"

"Of course. She's my little girl. If it hadn't been for you, I'd never have known her."

"I think the way motherhood makes people crazy is one of the nicest things around," I said.

She answered, but with her eyes. Then she said, "We have to be there at noon."

I looked at my watch, leaped wildly to my feet, turned left, turned right.

Doris openly laughed at me. "How long does it take to get to the hospital?" she asked.

"Well, ten minutes, but we have to . . . don't we have to, uh?"

"No, we don't. We have more than an hour. Sit down and help me be quiet. Want something to eat before we go?"

"No. God, no. Shall I fix——"

"Not for me."

"Oh," Slowly I sat down again.

She giggled. "You're funny."

"Yeah."

"Have any trouble getting away?" She was making talk, I knew, but I went right along with it.

"Matter of fact, no," I said. "Old Frozen Face took one look at me after you called and chased me out."

"He's so wonderful. . . . Honey! Don't call him that!"

I growled something wordless. "He makes me mad."

"After all he's done?"

"Yes, after all he's done," I said irritably.

Because of all he's done, I think. All my life, I'm a misfit for one reason or another; then, in college, they found out this thing about me and I worked my way through being a laboratory curiosity. I got into the papers. Not too much—just enough to keep me from getting any decent job after I graduated. Except with Frozen Face, of course. I didn't apply; he wrote me. He hired all his people that way. People with half a leg. Blind people in Personnel. Ex-cons who couldn't get started.

At first, it looked as if his people had escaped the things that hung over them—thanks to him. Then, after a while, you began to realize that you wouldn't be working there if you didn't have something wrong with you. It was like starving all your life until you found you could be well fed and taken care of till the day you died—in a leprosarium.

But I said, "Sorry, Doris. Just naturally ungrateful, I guess ... Twink's waking up."

"Oh dear! I thought she might sleep until—"

"Shh."

Ever since the accident (I'd turned the car over; they say you can't do that with any car later than 1970, but I'm the guy), Twink had terrified me every time she woke up. She'd come out of the normal sleep of a normal baby and enter a frightening stillness, a cessation of everything but life itself. It was, I suppose, coma; but I'd lived with seven weeks of it once, and even now the momentary passage through it, from sleep to waking, was so loaded with terror and guilt for me that it was all I could take. And when you add to that the fact that I had to hide it, that above all else I had to be strength to her, and comfort, as she awoke—

Then it was over; she was awake, confused, dimly happy.

"Hi, baby. How's my Twink?"

Doris, tense on the couch, not breathing, waiting—

"It's all right. Twink's all right," I said.

"Well, of course!"

I shot Doris a look. There wasn't a hairline crack in that enamel of hers, but it suddenly occurred to me that it was past time for me to stop using her as the pillar of strength around here. I bent and kissed her and said (making it sound like a joke, because I knew she'd prefer it that way), "Okay, honey; from here on, you can scream curses."

"I'll just do that," she said gratefully.

Did the accident have anything directly to do with it or was it just me?

Champlain (yes, the Champlain, who took up where Rhine left off) had a number of theories about it. The most likely one was that when my peculiar equipment got stirred up enough in the crash and for that awful hour afterward, I sent such a surge of empathy at Twink that I created a response. You can call it telepathy if you like—Champlain did—but I don't like the sound of that. Of course, I'm biased. You can take your extrasensoria, all of them, and—well, just take 'em and leave me be.

It may be that I was better equipped than the next guy to adjust to this, having lived for some eight years with the mild notoriety of being the boy who never scored less than 88 on the Rhine cards. But personally, constitutionally, I never was meant to be different from other people. What I mean is that my useless ability (I don't regard it as a talent and I won't call it a gift) didn't have to make any difference to anyone. I could be just as good as a short-order cook, just as bad a ticket-taker, as anyone else. But I was never given the chance of living like a human being.

I could stick around the parapsychology laboratories, earning a living like an ape in the zoo (and not much of a living at that; even in this enlightened era, there isn't a rich parapsychologist), or I could go out and get a job. And the way my dark past followed me, you'd think I was wearing a Flying Saucer for a halo. "Oh, yes—you're the mind-reading fellow." You know what that can do to your prospects?

Usually I didn't get the job. Once I was hired, though, they knew. Twice I landed jobs and they found out later. Each time there was someone who went to the boss, seniority and all, and said, "Look, it's him or me." And guess who got the pink slip.

Would you work every day with somebody who could read your mind? Who hasn't got secrets? Whose life really is an open book? I can tell you, I wouldn't work next to someone like that, yet I'm about as inoffensive as they come. And what was driving me out of my head—and I was two-thirds out when I met Doris and then Frozen Face—was that everyone thought I could read minds and I *can't!*

But Doris, who had heard of me even before she met me, never mentioned it. First she was nice to be with, and then I had to be with her, and then I came to a big, fat, soul-searching decision and confessed All to her one night, and she kissed me on the end of the nose and said she'd known about it all along and it didn't matter; and if I said I couldn't read minds but was only good at guessing Rhine cards, why, she believed me; and if I ever did learn to read minds, she wished I'd hurry up and read hers, because she was getting awfully impatient. After that, I'd have married her if she looked like a gila monster. Actually she looked like the Tenniel Alice-in-Wonderland, only with curly hair.

When I came up for breath from that interchange, I liked people a hell of a lot more than I ever had before. I guess that's another way of saying I liked myself some, at last.

Then along came the letter from Frozen Face, and Twink came up, and the accident happened.

And after the accident, the nightmare ability to dip down into the living silence that was Twink now, an unstirring something that couldn't see or speak or hear, something that was dreadfully hurt and just hovering, barely alive. My kid. And after about seven weeks, a movement, a weak tensing. It was the faintest possible echo of fear, and always a retreat from it that shoved the little thing close to dying again. Then there would be the silence again, and the stirring, and the fear and retreat.

Why I tried, how I thought to try, I don't know, but I did what I could each time to reassure her. I would tense till I ached and say, *It's all right, honey, don't be afraid, it's all over now.* And I hoped it helped her, and then I thought it did, and then one night I knew it did, because I saw the tension coming and stopped it, and there was a different kind of silence, like sleeping, not like coma.

After that, she got better fast, and I took hold of the slim hope that she might one day see and run and climb like other kids, hear music, go to school . . .

She had to, she *had* to, or I was a murderer. I was worse than that. Your out-and-out murderer knows what he's doing. More likely than not, he does it to get something, for profit.

But me—want to know what I did?

We'd been out for a drive in our shiny new car—well, it was second-hand, but the newest one I'd ever owned—and I wanted to get a couple of cartons of cigarettes before we crossed the state line, to save—guess!—a few cents tax. It was a six-lane road, three each way. I was in my middle lane.

Doris pointed at a big neon sign. "There's a place!"

I hauled the wheel over and shot straight across the right-hand lane. The truck just nipped the rear fender and over we went.

For six cents. Come to think of it, I never did buy the cigarettes, so I can't even claim that.

There's your superman, "wild talents" and all. A goddam highway boob.

Doris and Twink went to the hospital, bleeding and bleeding, then lying for days, waxy, doll-like, and came out, back to me, saying it wasn't my fault it wasn't my fault . . . God! And Twink as good as dead.

There was a reception committee waiting for us—two big names in medicine, McClintock and Zein—and, of course, Champlain. Busy boy. He wouldn't miss this for the world. But, thank heavens, no press.

"Come on, I want to talk to you," said Champlain, big breezy as ever, looking like the world's least likely suspect as a parapsychologist. I never did like Champlain, but he was the only person in the world besides Doris I could really talk to. At the moment, I wished I hadn't ever talked to him. Especially about Twink. But he knew and that was that.

He muscled me away from Doris and Twink.

"No!" cried Doris, and Twink was frightened.

"Now don't you worry, little lady; he'll be back with you before we do a thing," he called heartily, and there I was going one way and Doris and Twink the other. What could I do?

He pushed me through a door and I had the choice of sitting in a big armchair or falling down, the way he rushed me. He kicked the door shut.

"Here's some medicine." He got a bottle out of the top desk drawer. "McClintock let me see where he put it, the fool."

"I don't want any."

"Come on now."

"Get away from me," I said, and meant it. Inside myself, I turned to admire that tone, harsh and rough and completely decisive. I'd always thought only movie gangsters could make a speech like that sound so real. And while I was backing off from myself, admiring. I suddenly sobbed and swore and swore and sobbed. It was pretty disgusting.

"Wow," said Champlain. He put the bottle down and got some pills. He filled a paper cup with icewater and came over to me. "Take these."

"I don't want any."

"You'll take'm or I'll hold your nose and ram 'em down your neck with a stick!"

I took them and the water. As I keep saying, I'm no superman. "What are they?"

"Dexamyl. Brighten you up, smooth you down all at once. Now tell me what's the matter."

I said it, said what I hadn't put in words before. "Twink's going to die. I want her to."

"The two best specialists in the world say no."

"Let her die! She's going out of here as a basket case if you don't! I know. I know better'n anybody. Blind. Deaf. Paralyzed. All she can do is sort of flop. Let her die!"

"Don't be so goddamn selfish."

A kick in the face would have shocked me a good deal less. I just gawked at him.

"Sure, selfish," he repeated. "You pulled a little bobble that anybody might have done and your wife won't blame you for it. To you, it's become a big, important bobble because you never were involved in anything important before. The only way you can prove it's important is to suffer an important punishment. The worst thing you can think of is to have Twink dead. The next worse is to have her go through life the way she is now. You want one of those things."

I called him something.

"Sure I am," he agreed. "Absolutely. In the eyes of the guy who's wrong, the guy who's right is always just what you said."

I used another one.

"That, too," he said, and beamed.

I put up my hands and let them fall. "What do you want me to do? What are you picking on me for?"

He came over and sat sideways on the broad arm of the chair. "I want you to get in there and help us. Help Twink."

"I'd be in the way."

He hit me on the shoulderblade. It was done as a sort of friendly gesture, but it was done hard. "You can get through to her, can't you?"

"Yes."

"She's been hurt. Badly. This is going to hurt her, too—a whole lot. She may not want to go through with it."

"She has a choice?"

"Every patient has a choice. Other things being equal, they live or they don't. If they've been hurt and they see more pain coming, they might not want to go through with it."

"I still don't see how I—"

"Would you like to keep wondering whether you could have saved her life?"

"She's going to die, anyway."

He got up and stood in front of me with his big fists on his hips, glaring at me silently until I had to raise my face. He held me with his eyes until I couldn't stand it and then he said, rough and gentle like a tiger purring, "You damn near killed her once and now you want to finish the job. That it?"

"All right, all *right!*" I shouted. "I'll do *anything!*"

"Good!" And suddenly he dropped on one knee and took both of my hands in both of his. It was a very surprising thing for him to do and strangely effective. I could feel currents of his immense vitality from those big hands; it was as if my ego, wrinkled like a prune, was swelling up sleek and healthy.

He said, softly and with deep earnestness, "All you've got to do is make her want to live. You've got to be with her and wait for her and help her along and keep her convinced that no matter what happens, no matter how it hurts, it's worth it because she's going to live."

"All right," I whispered.

"She's only a little girl. She takes things just the way she finds them and she doesn't make allowances. If something looks like fear to her, or anger, it is that. If something looks like love, or wisdom, or strength, that's just how she'll take it. Be strong and wise for her."

"Me?"

He got up. "You." He went to the desk and got the bottle and poured a paper cup full. He held it out to me.

I wiped my eyes with the backs of my hands and stood up. "No thanks. I don't need it," I told him.

He twitched his eyebrows and drank the liquor himself and we went out.

They put me through the scrub room just as if I'd been a surgeon—gloves, mask and all—and then we went into the operating theater. Doris was already there, all fixed up, too. I went and kissed her right through the mask and she smiled.

I said, "You look lovely in white," and wondered where that had come from; and, "Hi-i, Twink."

Somewhere in the blindness, in the confines of paralysis, there was a shadow of fear and, down inside that, a warm little response. And the fear evaporated. I looked up and met Champlain's eyes. That unnatural feeling under my mask was, to my complete astonishment, a grin. I nodded and he winked back and said, "I guess you can go ahead, Mac."

Now listen, Twink, I said with all my heart, I love you and I'm here, I'm right here with you no matter what happens. Something's going to happen, something big, and it's going to change everything for you. Some of it won't be . . . won't be nice. But they have to do it. For you, Twink. Even when it isn't nice, it's for you. You've got to let them. You've got to help them. They love you, but I love you most of all. You mustn't go away. If it hurts you too much, you just tell me and I'll make them stop.

Then something was the matter, very much the matter. Shaken, I crowded close and tried to see what McClintock was doing. "Back off a little," he growled.

"Back off, my eyeball. What the hell are you winding around her head?"

Champlain barked at me, "Cut it out! The one thing you don't get is angry!"

Doris made a little sound. I spun to her. She was smiling. No, she wasn't. Her eyes were all screwed up. A tear came out.

"Doris!"

Her face relaxed instantly, as if the nerves had been cut. Then she opened her eyes and looked at me. "I'm all right," she said.

There was a calling, a calling, a calling.

All right, Twink, I'm here. I didn't go away. I'm right here, honey. If you want them to stop, you just say so.

A pause, then a tremulous questioning.

Yes, yes, I said, I'm here. Every single second. I'm not going away. Again the pause and then, like a flicker of light, a hot, glad little response.

Doris moaned, almost a whisper. I shot a glance at her, then at Champlain.

"You want that stopped?" he asked.

"No," I said. "I promised her she could."

Doris' hand moved. I took it. It was wet. She squeezed mine, hard.

Something from Twink, unlike anything I had ever experienced before. Except the accident. Yes, it was like the accident—and *stop!* STOP!

"Stop!" I gasped. "Stop it!"

McClintock went right on working as if I hadn't made a sound. The other specialist, Zein, said to Champlain as if I couldn't hear, "Do we have to stand for this?"

"You're damn right you do," said Champlain.

Working, McClintock asked, "Stop? What do you mean, stop?"

Zein mumbled something to him. McClintock nodded and a nurse came flying across the room with a tray of hypodermics. McClintock used a number of them.

Twink went quiet. For a moment, I thought I would faint from relief.

All right, honey? All right? I made them stop. Twinkie. Is it all right?

Twink!

Twink!

I made some sort of noise, I don't know what. Champlain's hands were on my shoulders, grinding down like two oversized C-clamps. I shrugged off one, knocked off the other with my wrist. "Twink!" I shouted. Then Doris screamed shrilly and Twink vibrated like a gong.

"That won't do," I snapped, gesturing with my head.

"Want her out?"

"Don't you dare," said Doris.

"Yes. Now."

McClintock began, "Who's—" but Champlain said, "Shut up. Take her out."

After that, it went very quickly.

Just a little more, Twink, and it'll be all over and you'll be warm and comfy and you can sleep. And I'll be near while you sleep and with you when you wake up.

I tried to stop McClintock once more, when he took the little arm that had been immobilized across Twink's chest for so long and twisted it brutally up and back. But this time Champlain was on McClintock's side and he was right; the pain stopped almost instantly.

And then—was it weeks later, hours? The biggest part was over and they did things to her eyes, her mouth, while I found ways and yet new ways to thrust aside fury, ignore fatigue, negate fear, and press on and on and around and inside with I love you, Twink; I'm here; it's all right. Just a little more, a little—there, it's stopped. Are you all right, Twink?

She was all right. She was wonderful. When they were through with her, she was weak and she looked like hell, but she was all right. I stared at her and stared at her and I couldn't believe it; I couldn't contain it, either. I didn't know what to do. So I began to laugh.

"Okay, let's get out of here." Champlain loomed over me like a grounded parachute.

"Yeah, wait." I sidled around him and went to McClintock. "Thanks," I said. "I'm sorry."

"It's okay," he said tonelessly.

Zein just turned his back.

I sat by the bed where they had put Doris, tired, and I waited.

This was a lot different from that other hospital, that other time. Then I'd committed something and I was full of fear. Now I'd accomplished something and I was full of hope—and liquor, but they tasted much the same. Twink was asleep, breathing beautiful even breaths, far too weary to be afraid.

I was glad about so many things and I mentally thumbed through them all, one by one, with a huge and quiet delight. And I think that the one I was happiest about was my saying to Champlain afterward, "She'd have been perfectly all right even if I hadn't been there."

What I was so pleased about was that I said it, I didn't ask it. And he had laughed and filled my cup again.

"You're a mind-reader," he said, and it was the first time I had ever heard that and thought it was funny.

"You wanted a case history of a human being born with little or no birth trauma, you son."

"Well, nobody ever had one before," he admitted. "I'd have had a lot less trouble in my young life if my dad had been able to paddle me down that particular canal in a canoe."

"You're a louse and it was worth it," I told him.

Doris turned her head impatiently.

"I'm here," I whispered.

She looked at me out of the same composed, porcelain face. "Hi. How's your girl friend?"

"My *other* girl friend. Doris, she's beautiful! All pink. She has two eyes. Ten toes. Eight fingers."

"What?"

"And two thumbs. She's all right, darling, really all right. A perfectly normal newborn girl-baby."

"Oh, I'm . . . so glad. Does she . . . can you still—even after the Caesarean?"

I nodded and in that split second, I wished my fool head had rolled right off. Because as I did it, I realized that I could have lied; she *wanted* me to.

She began to cry. She said, "You made them knock me out and you did it all yourself. You've had her to talk to all this time and you always will, as long as you both live. I'll never ever cry about this again, I promise, because it's not your fault and I love you, anyway. But I'm going to cry about it now."

I crouched with my head on her pillow for a long, long time. Then I went away, because she was nowhere near finished.

She's never cried about that since, though.

Never once.

I guess there's some way a man can make up a thing like that to a woman.

If he keeps looking.

I guess.

BRIGHT SEGMENT

Surely one of the most powerful stories I have ever written. This was made into a 58-minute TV film in France, with Gert (Goldfinger) Frobe cast as the old man, and doing an extraordinary piece of acting. Further, the French shot it almost exactly the way I wrote it, and I wrote it despairing that it could not be filmed; American TV could never (1955) handle that much blood and that much skin, I wish you could see it. I own the only print in North America, but can't use it for admission or release it to net or cable. I can, however, use it as a lecture resource: a three-hour performance during which I read the story up to but not including the ending; challenge the students (creative writing, scripting, directing, cinematography, what have you) to suggest what they would include or change or eliminate if this were their film; then I show the film, read my ending, and launch a Q&A. It takes about three hours, and it costs, but I understand it's worth the nut. The French director is Christian de Chalonge; he's unavailable at this writing, but he seems to be, so far, the only one in the industry anywhere who really understands what I am all about. He's also unavailable at this writing. 'Sway, as Lady Jayne says: it means, "That's the way things are" . . . there is, by the way, no important language difficulty; you will see as you read it that it's about 92% visual—virtually without dialogue, by its very nature.

He had never held a girl before. He was not terrified; he had used that up earlier when he had carried her in and kicked the door shut behind him and had heard the steady drip of blood from her soaked skirt, and before that, when he had thought her dead there on the curb, and again when she made that sound, that sigh or whispered moan. He had brought her in and when he saw all that blood he had turned left, turned right, put her down on the floor, his brains all clabbered and churned and his temples athump with the unaccustomed exercise. All he could act on was *Don't get blood on the bedspread.* He turned on the overhead light and stood for a moment blinking and breathing hard; suddenly he leaped for the window to lower the blind against the street light staring in and all other eyes. He saw his hands reach for the blind and checked himself; they were red and ready to paint anything he touched. He made a sound, a detached part of his mind recognizing it as the exact duplicate of that agonized whisper she had uttered out there on the dark, wet street, and leapt to the light switch, seeing the one red smudge already there, knowing as he swept his hand over it he was leaving another. He stumbled to the sink in the corner and washed his hands, washed them again, every few seconds looking over his shoulder at the girl's body and the thick flat finger of blood which crept curling toward him over the linoleum.

He had his breath now, and moved more carefully to the window. He drew down the blind and pulled the curtains and looked at the sides and the bottom to see that there were no crevices. In pitch blackness he felt his way back to the opposite wall, going around the edges of the linoleum, and turned on the light again. The finger of blood was a tentacle now, fumbling toward the soft, stain-starved floorboards. From the enamel table beside the stove he snatched a plastic sponge and dropped it on the tentacle's seeking tip and was pleased, it was a reaching thing no more, it was only something spilled that could be mopped up.

He took off the bedspread and hung it over the brass headrail. From the drawer of the china closet and from the gate leg table he took his two plastic table cloths. He covered the bed with them, leaving plenty of overlap, then stood a moment rocking with worry and pulling out his lower lip with a thumb and forefinger. *Fix it right*, he told himself firmly. So she'll die before you fix it, never mind, fix it, right.

He expelled air from his nostrils and got books from the shelf in the china closet—a six-year-old World Almanac, a half-dozen paperback novels, a heavy catalog of jewelry findings. He pulled the bed away from the wall and put books one by one under two of the legs so that the bed was tilted slightly down to the foot and slightly to one side. He got a blanket and rolled it and slipped it under the plastic so that it formed a sort of fence down the high side. He got a six-quart aluminum pot from under the sink and set it on the floor by the lowest corner of the bed and pushed the trailing end of plastic down into it. *So bleed now*, he told the girl silently, with satisfaction.

He bent over her and grunted, lifting her by the armpits. Her head fell back as if she had no bones in her neck and he almost dropped her. He dragged her to the bed, leaving a wide red swath as her skirt trailed through the scarlet puddle she had lain in. He lifted her clear of the floor, settled his feet, and leaned over the bed with her in his arms. It took an unexpected effort to do it. He realized only then how drained, how tired he was, and how old. He put her down clumsily, almost dropping her in an effort to leave the carefully arranged tablecloths undisturbed, and he very nearly fell into the bed with her. He levered himself away with rubbery arms and stood panting. Around the soggy hem of her skirt blood began to gather, and as he watched, began to find its way lazily to the low corner. *So much, so much blood in a person*, he marveled, and *stop it, how to make it stop if it won't stop?*

He glanced at the locked door, the blinded window, the clock. He listened. It was raining harder now, drumming and hissing in the darkest hours. Otherwise nothing; the house was asleep and the street, dead. He was alone with his problem.

He pulled at his lip, then snatched his hand away as he tasted her blood. He coughed and ran to the sink and spat, and washed his mouth and then his hands.

So all right, go call up. . . .

Call up? Call what, the hospital they should call the cops? Might as well call the cops altogether. *Stupid.* What could I tell them, she's my sister, she's hit by a car, they going to believe me? Tell them the truth, a block away I see somebody push her out of a car, drive off, no lights, I bring her in out of the rain, only inside I find she is bleeding like this, they believe me? *Stupid.* What's the matter with you, mind your own business why don't you.

He thought he would pick her up now and put her back in the rain. Yes and somebody sees you, *stupid.*

He saw that the wide, streaked patch of blood on the linoleum was losing gloss where it lay thin, drying and soaking in. He picked up the sponge, two-thirds red now and the rest its original baby-blue except at one end where it looked like bread drawn with a sharp red pencil. He turned it over so it wouldn't drip while he carried it and took it to the sink and rinsed it, wringing it over and over in the running water. *Stupid*, call up somebody and get help.

Call who?

He thought of the department store where for eighteen years he had waxed floors and vacuumed rugs at night. The neighborhood, where he knew the grocery and the butcher. Closed up, asleep, everybody gone; names, numbers he didn't know and anyway, who to trust? *My God in fifty-three years you haven't got a friend?*

He took the clean sponge and sank to his knees on the linoleum, and just then the band of blood creeping down the bed reached the corner and turned to a sharp streak; *ponk* it went into the pan, and *pitti-pittipitti* in a rush, then drip-drip-drip-drip, three to the second and not stopping. He knew then with absolute and belated certainty that this bleeding was not going to stop by itself. He whimpered softly and then got up and went to the bed. *"Don't be dead,"* he said aloud, and the way his voice sounded, it frightened him. He put out his hand to her chest, but drew it back when he saw her blouse was torn and blood came from there too.

He swallowed hard and then began fumbling with her clothes. Flat ballet slippers, worn, soggy, thin like paper and little silken things he had never seen before, like just the foot of a stocking. More blood on—but no, that was peeled and chipped enamel on her cold white toes. The skirt had a button at the side and a zipper which baffled him for a moment, but he got it down and tugged the skirt off in an interminable series of jerks from the hem, one side and the other, while she rolled slightly and limply to the motion. Small silken pants, completely soaked and so badly cut on the left side that he snapped them apart easily between his fingers; but the other side was surprisingly strong and he had to get his scissors to cut them away. The blouse buttoned up the front and was no problem; under it was a brassiere which was cut right in two near the front. He lifted it away but had to cut one of the straps with his scissors to free it altogether.

He ran to the sink with his sponge, washed it and wrung it out, filled a saucepan with warm water and ran back. He sponged the body down; it looked firm but too thin, with its shadow-ladder of ribs down each side and the sharp protrusion of the hip-bones. Under the left breast was a long cut, starting on the ribs in front and curving upward almost to the nipple. It seemed deep but the blood merely welled out. The other cut, though, in her groin, released blood brightly in regular gouts, one after the other, eager but weakly. He had seen the like before, the time Garber pinched his arm off in the elevator cable-room, but then the blood squirted a foot away. Maybe this did, too, he thought suddenly, but now it's slowing up, now it's going to stop, yes, and you, stupid, you have a dead body you can tell stories to the police.

He wrung out the sponge in the water and mopped the wound. Before it could fill up again he spread the sides of the cut and looked down into it. He could clearly see the femoral artery, looking like an end of spaghetti and cut almost through; and then there was nothing but blood again.

He squatted back on his heels, pulling heedlessly at his lip with his bloody hand and trying to think. *Pinch, shut, squeeze. Squeezers. Tweezers!* He ran to his toolbox and clawed it open. Years ago he had learned to make fine chains out of square silver wire, and he used to pass the time away by making link after tiny link, soldering each one closed with an alcohol torch and a needle-tipped iron. He picked up the tweezers and dropped them in favor of the small spring clamp which he used for holding the link while he worked on it. He ran to the sink and washed the clamp and came back to the bed. Again he sponged away the little lake of blood, and quickly reached down and got the fine jaws of the clamp on the artery near its cut. Immediately there was another gush of blood. Again he sponged it away, and in a blaze of inspiration, released the clamp, moved it to the other side of the cut, and clamped it again.

Blood still oozed from the inside of the wound, but that terrible pulsing gush was gone. He sat back on his heels and painfully released a breath he must have held for two minutes. His eyes ached from the strain, and his brain was still whirling, but with these was a feeling, a new feeling almost like an ache or a pain, but it was nowhere and everywhere inside him; it wanted him to laugh but at the same time his eyes stung and hot salt squeezed out through holes too small for it.

After a time he recovered, blinking away his exhaustion, and sprang up, overwhelmed by urgency. *Got to fix everything.* He went to the medicine cabinet over the sink. Adhesive tape, pack of gauze pads. Maybe not big enough; okay tape together, fix right. New tube this sulfa-thia-dia-whatchamacall-um, fix anything, time I got vacuum-cleaner grit in cut hand, infection. Fixed boils too.

He filled a kettle and his saucepan with clean water and put them on the stove. Sew up, yes. He found needles, white thread, dumped them into the water. He went back to the bed and stood musing for a long time, looking at the oozing gash under the girl's breast. He sponged out the femoral wound again and stared pensively into it until the blood slowly covered the clamped artery. He could not be positive, but he had a vague recollection of something about tourniquets, they should be opened up every once in a while or there is trouble; same for an artery, maybe? Better he should sew up the artery; it was only opened, not cut through. If he could find out how to do it and still let it be like a pipe, not like a darned sock.

So into the pot went the tweezers, a small pair of needle-nose pliers, and, after some more thought, a dozen silver broach-pins out of his jewelry kit. Waiting for the water to boil, he inspected the wounds again. He pulled on his lip, frowning, then got another fine needle, held it with pliers in the gas flame until it was red, and with another of his set of pliers bent it around in a small semi-circle and dropped it into the water. From the sponge he cut a number of small flat slabs and dropped them in too.

He glanced at the clock, and then for ten minutes he scrubbed the white enamel table-top with cleanser. He tipped it into the sink, rinsed it at the faucet, and then slowly poured the contents of the kettle over it. He took it to the stove, held it with one hand while he fished in the boiling saucepan with a silver knife until he had the pliers resting with their handles out of the water. He grasped them gingerly with a clean washcloth and carefully, one by one, transferred everything from saucepan to table. By the time he had found the last of the needles and the elusive silver pins, sweat was running into his eyes and the arm that held the table-top threatened to drop right off. But he set his stumpy yellow teeth and kept at it.

Carrying the table-top, he kicked a wooden chair bit by bit across the room until it rested by the bed, and set his burden down on its seat. *This no hospital*, he thought, *but I fix everything.*

Hospital! Yes, in the movies—

He went to a drawer and got a clean white handkerchief and tried to tie it over his mouth and nose like in the movies. His knobby face and square head were too much for one handkerchief; it took three before he got it right, with a great white tassel hanging down the back like in an airplane picture.

He looked helplessly at his hands, then shrugged; so no rubber gloves, what the hell. *I wash good.* His hands were already pink and wrinkled from his labors, but he went back to the sink and scratched a bar of soap until his horny nails were packed with it, then cleaned them with a file until they hurt, and washed and cleaned them again. And at last he knelt by the bed, holding his shriven hands up in a careful salaam. Almost, he reached for his lip to pull it, but not quite.

He squeezed out two globs of the sulfa ointment onto the table top and, with the pliers, squashed two slabs of sponge until the creamy stuff was through and through them. He mopped out the femoral wound and placed a medicated sponge on each side of the wound, leaving the artery exposed at the bottom. Using tweezers and pliers, he laboriously threaded the curved needle while quelling the urge to stick the end of the thread into his mouth.

He managed to get four tiny stitches into the artery below the break, out of it above the break. Each one he knotted with exquisite care so that the thread would not cut the tissue but still would draw the severed edges together. Then he squatted back on his heels to rest, his shoulders afire with tension, his eyes misted. Then, taking a deep breath, he removed the clamp.

Blood filled the wound and soaked the sponges. But it came slowly, without spurting. He shrugged grimly. So what's to do, use a tire patch? He mopped the blood out once more, and quickly filled the incision with ointment, slapping a piece of gauze over it more to hide it than to help it.

He wiped his eyebrows first with one shoulder, then the other, and fixed his eyes on the opposite wall the way he used to do when he worked on his little silver chains. When the mist went away he turned his attention to the long cut on the underside of the breast. He didn't know how to stitch one this size, but he could cook and he knew how to skewer up a chicken. Biting his tongue, he stuck the first of his silver pins into the flesh at right angles to the cut, pressing it across the wound and out the other side. He started the next pin not quite an inch away, and the same with the third. The fourth grated on something in the wound; it startled him like a door slamming and he bit his tongue painfully. He backed the pin out and probed carefully with his tweezers. Yes, something hard in there. He probed deeper with both points of the tweezers, feeling them enter uncut tissue with a soft crunching that only a fearful fingertip could hear. He conquered a shudder and glanced up at the girl's face. He resolved not to look up there again. It was a very dead face.

Stupid! but the self-insult was lost in concentration even as it was born. The tweezers closed on something hard, slippery and stubborn. He worked it gently back and forth, feeling a puzzled annoyance at this unfamiliar flesh that yielded as he moved. Gradually, very gradually, a sharp angular corner of *something* appeared. He kept at it until there was enough to grasp with his fingers; then he set his tweezers aside and gently worked it loose. Blood began to flow freely before it was half out, but he did not stop until he could draw it free. The light glinted on the strip of hollow-ground steel and its shattered margins; he turned it over twice before it came to him that it was a piece of straight razor. He set it down on his enamel table, thinking of what the police might have said to him if he had turned her over to them with that story about a car accident.

He stanched the blood, pulled the wound as wide apart as he could. The nipple writhed under his fingers, its pink halo shrunken and wrinkled; he grunted, thinking that a bug had crawled under his hand, and then aware that whatever the thing meant, it couldn't mean death, not yet anyway. He had to go back and start over, stanching the cut and spreading it, and quickly squeezing in as much ointment as it would hold. Then he went on with his insertion of the silver pins, until there was a little ladder of twelve of them from one end of the wound to the other. He took his thread, doubled it, put the loop around the topmost pin and drew the two parts of the thread underneath. Holding them both in one hand, he gently pinched the edges of the wound together at the pin. Then he drew the loop tight without cutting, crossed the threads and put them under the next pin, and again closed the wound. He continued this all the way down, lacing the cut closed around the ladder of pins. At the bottom he tied the thread off and cut it. There was blood and ointment all over his handiwork, but when he mopped up it looked good to him.

He stood up and let sensation flow agonizingly into his numb feet. He was sopping wet; he could feel perspiration searching its way down through the hairs of his legs, like a migration of bedbugs. He looked down at himself; wrinkles and water and blood. He looked across at the wavery mirror, and saw a bandaged goblin with brow-ridges like a shelf and sunken eyes with a cast to them, with grizzled hair which could be scrubbed only to the color of grime, and with a great gout of blood where the mouth hid behind the bandage. He snatched it down and looked again. *More better you cover your face, no matter what.* He turned away, not from his face, but with it, in the pained patience of a burro with saddle sores.

Wearily he carried his enameled table-top to the sink. He washed his hands and forearms and took off the handkerchiefs from around his neck and washed his face. Then he got what was left of his sponge and a pan of warm soapy water and came back to the bed.

It took him hours. He sponged the tablecloths on which she lay, shifted her gently so as to put no strain on the wounds, and washed and dried where she had lain. He washed her from head to toe, going back for clean water, and then had to dry the bed again afterward. When he lifted her head he found her hair matted and tacky with rain and drying blood, and fresh blood with it, so he propped up her shoulders with a big pillow under the plastic and tipped her head back and washed and dried her hair, and found an ugly lump and a bleeding contusion on the back of her head. He combed the hair away from it on each side and put cold water on it, and it stopped bleeding, but there was a lump the size of a plum. He separated half a dozen of the gauze pads and packed them around the lump so that it need not take the pressure off her head; he dared not turn her over.

When her hair was wet and fouled it was only a dark mat, but cleaned and combed, it was the darkest of auburns, perfectly straight. There was a broad lustrous band of it on the bed on each side of her face, which was radiant with pallor, cold as a moon. He covered her with the bedspread, and for a long while stood over her, full of that strange nowhere-everywhere almost-pain, not liking it but afraid to turn away from it ... maybe he would never have it again.

He sighed, a thing that came from his marrow and his years, and doggedly set to work scrubbing the floor. When he had finished, and the needles and thread were put away, the bit of tape which he had not used, the wrappers of the gauze pads and the pan of blood from the end of the bed disposed of, and all the tools cleaned and back in their box, the night was over and daylight pressed weakly against the drawn blind. He turned out the light and stood without breathing, listening with all his mind, wanting to know from where he stood if she still lived. To bend close and find out she was gone—oh no. He wanted to know from here.

But a truck went by, and a woman called a child, and someone laughed; so he went and knelt by the bed and closed his eyes and slowly put his hand on her throat. It was cool—please, not cold!—and quiet as a lost glove.

Then the hairs on the back of his hand stirred to her breath, and again, the faintest of motions. The stinging came to his eyes and through and through him came the fiery urge to *do*: make some soup, buy some medicine, maybe, for her, a ribbon or a watch; clean the house, run to the store ... and while doing all these things, all at once, to shout and shout great shaking wordless bellows to tell himself over and over again, so he could hear for sure, that she was alive. At the very peak of this explosion of urges, there was a funny little side-slip and he was fast asleep.

He dreamed someone was sewing his legs together with a big curved sail needle, and at the same time drawing the thread from his belly; he could feel the spool inside spinning and emptying. He groaned and opened his eyes, and knew instantly where he was and what had happened, and hated himself for the noise he made. He lifted his hand and churned his fingers to be sure they could feel, and lowered them gently to her throat. It was warm—no, hot, too hot. He pushed back from the bed and scrabbled half-across the floor on his knuckles and his numb, rubbery legs. Cursing silently he made a long lunge and caught the wooden chair to him, and used it to climb to his feet. He dared not let it go, so clumped softly with it over to the corner, where he twisted and hung gasping to the edge of the sink, while boiling acid ate downward through his legs. When he could, he splashed cold water on his face and neck and, still drying himself on a towel, stumbled across to the bed. He flung the bedspread off and *stupid!* he almost screamed as it plucked at his fingers on the way; it had adhered to the wound in her groin and he was sure he had ripped it to shreds, torn a whole section out of the clumsily patched artery. And he couldn't see; it must be getting dark outside; how long had he crouched there? He ran to the light switch, leaped back. Yes, bleeding, it was bleeding again—

But a little, only a very little. The gauze was turned up perhaps halfway, and though the exposed wound was wet with blood, blood was not running. It had, while he was asleep, but hardly enough to find its way to the mattress. He lifted the loose corner of the gauze very gently, and found it stuck fast. But the sponges, the little sponges to put on the sulfa-whatchama, they were still in the wound. He'd meant to take them out after a couple of hours, not let the whole clot form around them!

He ran for warm water, his big sponge. Soap in it, yes. He squatted beside the bed, though his legs still protested noisily, and began to bathe the gauze with tiny, gentle touches.

Something made him look up. She had her eyes open, and was looking down at him. Her face and her eyes were utterly without expression. He watched them close slowly and slowly open again, lackluster and uninterested. "All right, all right," he said harshly, "I fix everything." She just kept on looking. He nodded violently, it was all that soothes, all that encourages, hope for her and a total promise for her, but it was only a rapid bobbing of his ugly head. Annoyed as he always was at his own speechlessness, he went back to work. He got the gauze off and began soaking the edge of one of the sponges. When he thought it was ready to come, he tugged gently at it.

In a high, whispery soprano, "Ho-o-o-o . . .?" she said; it was like a question and a sob. Slowly she turned her head to the left. "Ho-o-o-o?" She turned her head again and slipped back to unconsciousness.

"I," he said loudly, excitedly, and "I—" and that was all; she wouldn't hear him anyway. He held still until his hands stopped trembling, and went on with the job.

The wound looked wonderfully clean, though the skin all around it was dry and hot.

Down inside the cut he could see the artery in a nest of wet jelly; that was probably right—he didn't know, but it looked all right, he wouldn't disturb it. He packed the opening full of ointment, pressed the edges gently together, and put on a piece of tape. It promptly came unstuck, so he discarded it and dried the flesh all around the wound, put on gauze first, then the tape, and this time it held.

The other cut was quite closed, though more so where the pins were than between them. It too was surrounded by hot, dry, red flesh.

The scrape on the back of her head had not bled, but the lump was bigger than ever. Her face and neck were dry and very warm, though the rest of her body seemed cool. He went for a cold cloth and put it across her eyes and pressed it down on her cheeks, and she sighed. When he took it away she was looking at him again.

"You all right?" he asked her, and inanely, "You all right," he told her. A small frown flickered for a moment and then her eyes closed. He knew somehow that she was asleep. He touched her cheeks with the backs of his fingers. "Very hot," he muttered.

He turned out the light and in the dimness changed his clothes. From the bottom of a drawer he took a child's exercise book, and from it a piece of paper with a telephone number in large black penciled script. "I come back," he said to the darkness. She didn't say anything. He went out, locking the door behind him.

Laboriously he called the office from the big drugstore, referring to his paper for each digit and for each, holding the dial against the stop for a full three or four seconds as if to be sure the number would stick. He got the big boss Mr. Laddie first of all, which was acutely embarrassing; he had not spoken to him in a dozen years. At the top of his bull voice he collided with Laddie's third impatient "Hello?" with "Sick! I—uh, *sick!*" He heard the phone say "—in God's name . . .?" and Mr. Wismer's laughter, and "Gimme the phone, that's got to be that orangutan of mine," and right in his ear, "Hello?"

"Sick tonight," he shouted.

"What's the matter with you?"

He swallowed. "I can't," he yelled.

"That's just old age," said Mr. Wismer. He heard Mr. Laddie laughing too. Mr. Wismer said, "How many nights you had off in the last fifteen years?"

He thought about it. "No!" he roared. Anyway, it was eighteen years.

"You know, that's right," said Mr. Wismer, speaking to Mr. Laddie without trying to cover his phone, "Fifteen years and never asked for a night off before."

"So who needs him? Give him all his nights off."

"Not at those prices," said Mr. Wismer, and to his phone, "Sure, dummy, take off. Don't work no con games." The phone clicked off on laughter, and he waited there in the booth until he was sure nothing else would be said. Then he hung up his receiver and emerged into the big drugstore where everyone all over was looking at him. Well, they always did. That didn't bother him. Only one thing bothered him, and that was Mr. Laddie's voice saying over and over in his head, "So who needs him?" He knew he would have to stop and face those words and let them and all that went with them go through his mind. But not now, please not now.

He kept them away by being busy; he bought tape and gauze and ointment and a canvas cot and three icebags and, after some thought, aspirin, because someone had told him once . . . and then to the supermarket where he bought enough to feed a family of nine for nine days. And for all his bundles, he still had a thick arm and a wide shoulder for a twenty-five-pound cake of ice.

He got the door open and the ice in the box, and went out in the hall and picked up the bundles and brought those in, and then went to her. She was burning up, and her breathing was like the way seabirds fly into the wind, a small beat, a small beat, and a long wait, balancing. He cracked a corner off the ice-cake, wrapped it in a dishtowel and whacked it angrily against the sink. He crowded the crushed ice into one of the bags and put it on her head. She sighed but did not open her eyes. He filled the other bags and put one on her breast and one on her groin. He wrung his hands uselessly over her until it came to him *she has to eat, losing blood like that.*

So he cooked, tremendously, watching her every second minute. He made minestrone and baked cabbage and mashed potatoes and veal cutlets. He cut a pie and warmed cinnamon buns, and he had hot coffee with icecream ready to spoon into it. She didn't eat it, any of it, nor did she drink a drop. She lay there and occasionally let her head fall to the side, so he had to run and pick up the icebag and replace it. Once again she sighed, and once he thought she opened her eyes, but couldn't be sure.

On the second day she ate nothing and drank nothing, and her fever was unbelievable. During the night, crouched on the floor beside her, he awoke once with the echoes of weeping still in the room, but he may have dreamed it.

Once he cut the tenderest, juiciest piece of veal he could find on a cutlet, and put it between her lips. Three hours later he pressed them apart to put in another piece, but the first one was still there. The same thing happened with aspirin, little white crumbs on a dry tongue.

And the time soon came when he had busied himself out of things to do, and fretted himself into a worry-reflex that operated by itself, and the very act of thinking new thoughts trapped him into facing the old ones, and then of course there was nothing to do but let them run on through, with all the ache and humiliation they carried with them. He was trying to think a new thing about what would happen if he called a doctor, and the doctor would want to take her to a hospital; he would say, "She needs treatment, old man, she doesn't need you," and there it was in his mind, ready to run, so:

Be eleven years old, bulky and strong and shy, standing in the kitchen doorway, holding your wooden box by its string and trying to shape your mouth so that the reluctant words can press out properly; and there's Mama hunched over a gin bottle like a cat over a half-eaten bird, peering; watch her lipless wide mouth twitch and say, "Don't stand there clackin' and slurpin'! Speak up, boy! What are you tryin' to say, you're leaving?"

So nod, it's easier, and she'll say "Leave, then, leave, who needs you?" and you go:

And be a squat, powerful sixteen and go to the recruiting station and watch the sergeant with the presses and creases asking "Whadda *you* want?" and you try, you try and you can't say it so you nod your head at the poster with the pointing finger, UNCLE SAM NEEDS YOU; and the sergeant glances at it and at you, and suddenly his pointing finger is half an inch away from your nose; cross-eyed you watch it while he barks, "Well, Uncle don't need *you!*" and you wait, watching the finger that way, not moving until you understand; you understand things real good, it's just that you hear slowly. So there you hang cross-eyed and they all laugh.

Or 'way back, you're eight years old and in school, that Phyllis with the row of springy brown sausage-curls flying when she tosses her head, pink and clean and so pretty; you have the chocolates wrapped in gold paper tied in gold-string mesh; you go up the aisle to her desk and put the chocolates down and run back; she comes down the aisle and throws them so hard the mesh breaks on your desk and she says, loud, "I don't need these and I don't need you, and you know what, you got snot on your face," and you put up your hand and sure enough you have.

That's all. Only every time anyone says "Who needs him?" or the like, you have to go through all of them, every one. Sooner or later, however much you put it off, you've got to do it all.

I get doctor, you don't need me.

You die, you don't need me.

Please . . .

Far back in her throat, a scraping hiss, and her lips moved. She held his eyes with hers, and her lips moved silently, and a little late for the lips, the hiss came again. He didn't know how he guessed right, but he did and brought water, dribbling it slowly on her mouth. She licked at it greedily, lifting her head up. He put a hand under it, being careful of the lump, and helped her. After a while she slumped back and smiled weakly at the cup. Then she looked up into his face and though the smile disappeared, he felt much better. He ran to the icebox and the stove, and got glasses and straws—one each of orange juice, chocolate milk, plain milk, consommé from a can, and ice water. He lined them up on the chair-seat by the bed and watched them and her eagerly, like a circus seal waiting to play "America" on the bulb-horns. She did smile this time, faintly, briefly, but right at him, and he tried the consommé. She drank almost half of it through the straw without stopping and fell asleep.

Later, when he checked to see if there was any bleeding, the plastic sheet was wet, but not with blood. *Stupid!* he raged at himself, and stamped out and bought a bedpan.

She slept a lot now, and ate often but lightly. She began to watch him as he moved about; sometimes when he thought she was asleep, he would turn and meet her eyes. Mostly, it was his hands she watched, those next two days. He washed and ironed her clothes, and sat and mended them with straight small stitches; he hung by his elbows to the edge of the enameled table and worked his silver wire, making her a broach like a flower on a fan, and a pendant on a silver chain, and a bracelet to match them. She watched his hands while he cooked; he made his own spaghetti—tagliatelli, really—rolling and rolling the dough until it was a huge tough sheet, winding it up like a jelly-roll only tight, slicing it in quick, accurate flickers of a paring-knife so it came out like yellow-white flat shoelaces. He had hands which had never learned their limitations, because he had never thought to limit them. Nothing else in life cared for this man but his hands, and since they did everything, they could do anything.

But when he changed her dressings or washed her, or helped with the bedpan, she never looked at his hands. She would lie perfectly still and watch his face.

She was very weak at first and could move nothing but her head. He was glad because her stitches were healing nicely. When he withdrew the pins it must have hurt, but she made not a sound; twelve flickers of her smooth brow, one for each pin as it came out.

"Hurts," he rumbled.

Faintly, she nodded. It was the first communication between them, except for those mute, crowded eyes following him about. She smiled too, as she nodded, and he turned his back and ground his knuckles into his eyes and felt wonderful.

He went back to work on the sixth night, having puttered and fussed over her all day to keep her from sleeping until he was ready to leave, then not leaving until he was sure she was fast asleep. He would lock her in and hurry to work, warm inside and ready to do three men's work; and home again in the dark early hours as fast as his bandy legs would carry him, bringing her a present—a little radio, a scarf, something special to eat—every single day. He would lock the door firmly and then hurry to her, touching her forehead and cheek to see what her temperature was, straightening the bed gently so she wouldn't wake. Then he would go out of her sight, away back by the sink, and undress and change to the long drawers he slept in, and come back and curl up on the camp cot. For perhaps an hour and a half he would sleep like a stone, but after that the slightest rustle of her sheet, the smallest catch of breath, would bring him to her in a bound, croaking, "You all right?" and hanging over her tensely, frantically trying to divine what she might need, what he might do or get for her.

And when the daylight came he would give her warm milk with an egg beaten in it, and then he would bathe her and change her dressings and comb her hair, and when there was nothing left to do for her he would clean the room, scrub the floor, wash clothes and dishes and, interminably, cook. In the afternoon he shopped, moving everywhere at a half-trot, running home again as soon as he could to show her what he had bought, what he had planned for her dinner. All these days, and then these weeks, he glowed inwardly, hugging the glow while he was away from her, fanning it with her presence when they were together.

He found her crying one afternoon late in the second week, staring at the little radio with the tears streaking her face. He made a harsh cooing syllable and wiped her cheeks with a dry washcloth and stood back with torture on his animal face. She patted his hand weakly, and made a series of faint gestures which utterly baffled him. He sat on the bedside chair and put his face close to hers as if he could tear the meaning out of her with his eyes. There was something different about her; she had watched him, up to now, with the fascinated, uncomprehending attention of a kitten watching a tankful of tropical fish; but now there was something more in her gaze, in the way she moved and in what she did.

"You hurt?" he rasped.

She shook her head. Her mouth moved, and she pointed to it and began to cry again.

"Oh, you hungry. I fix, fix good." He rose but she caught his wrist, shaking her head and crying, but smiling too. He sat down, torn apart by his perplexity. Again she moved her mouth, pointing to it, shaking her head.

"No talk," he said. She was breathing so hard it frightened him, but when he said that she gasped and half sat up; he caught her shoulders and put her down, but she was nodding urgently. "You can't talk!" he said.

Yes, yes! she nodded.

He looked at her for a long time. The music on the radio stopped and someone began to sell used cars in a crackling baritone. She glanced at it and her eyes filled with tears again. He leaned across her and shut the set off. After a profound effort he formed his mouth in the right shape and released a disdainful snort: "Ha! What you want talk? Don't talk. I fix everything, no talk.

I—" He ran out of words, so instead slapped himself powerfully on the chest and nodded at her, the stove, the bedpan, the tray of bandages. He said again, "What you want talk?"

She looked up at him, overwhelmed by his violence, and shrank down. He tenderly wiped her cheeks again, mumbling, "I fix everything."

He came home in the dark one morning, and after seeing that she was comfortable according to his iron standards, went to bed. The smell of bacon and fresh coffee was, of course, part of a dream; what else could it be? And the faint sounds of movement around the room had to be his weary imagination.

He opened his eyes on the dream and closed them again, laughing at himself for a crazy stupid. Then he went still inside, and slowly opened his eyes again.

Beside his cot was the bedside chair, and on it was a plate of fried eggs and crisp bacon, a cup of strong black coffee, toast with the gold of butter disappearing into its older gold. He stared at these things in total disbelief, and then looked up.

She was sitting on the end of the bed, where it formed an eight-inch corridor between itself and the cot. She wore her pressed and mended blouse and her skirt. Her shoulders sagged with weariness and she seemed to have some difficulty in holding her head up; her hands hung limply between her knees. But her face was suffused with delight and anticipation as she watched him waking up to his breakfast.

His mouth writhed and he bared his blunt yellow teeth, and ground them together while he uttered a howl of fury. It was a strangled, rasping sound and she scuttled away from it as if it had burned her, and crouched in the middle of the bed with her eyes huge and her mouth slack. He advanced on her with his arms raised and his big fists clenched; she dropped her face on the bed and covered the back of her neck with both hands and lay there trembling. For a long moment he hung over her, then slowly dropped his arms. He tugged at the skirt. "Take off," he grated. He tugged it again, harder.

She peeped up at him and then slowly turned over. She fumbled weakly at the button. He helped her. He pulled the skirt away and tossed it on the cot, and gestured sternly at the blouse. She unbuttoned it and he lifted it from her shoulders. He pulled down the sheet, taking it right out from under her. He took her ankles gently in his powerful hands and pulled them down until she was straightened out on the bed, and then covered her carefully. He was breathing hard. She watched him in terror.

In a frightening quiet he turned back to his cot and the laden chair beside it. Slowly he picked up the cup of coffee and smashed it on the floor. Steadily as the beat of a woodman's axe the saucer followed, the plate of toast, the plate of eggs. China and yolk squirted and sprayed over the floor and on the walls.

When he had finished he turned back to her. "I fix everything," he said hoarsely. He emphasized each syllable with a thick forefinger as he said again, "*I fix everything.*"

She whipped over on her stomach and buried her face in the pillow, and began to sob so hard he could feel the bed shaking the floor through the soles of his feet. He turned angrily away from her and got a pan and a scrub-brush and a broom and dustpan, and laboriously, methodically, cleaned up the mess.

Two hours later he approached her where she lay, still on her stomach, stiff and motionless. He had had a long time to think of what to say: "Look, you see, you *sick* . . . you see?" He said it, as gently as he could. He put his hand on her shoulder but she twitched violently, flinging it away. Hurt and baffled, he backed away and sat down on the couch, watching her miserably.

She wouldn't eat any lunch.

She wouldn't eat any dinner.

As the time approached for him to go to work, she turned over. He still sat on the cot in his long johns, utter misery on his face and in every line of his ugly body. She looked at him and her eyes filled with tears. He met her gaze but did not move. She sighed suddenly and held out her hand. He leaped to it and pulled it to his forehead, knelt, bowed over it and began to cry. She patted his wiry hair until the storm passed, which it did abruptly, at its height. He sprang away from her and clattered pans on the stove, and in a few minutes brought her some bread and gravy and a parboiled artichoke, rich with olive oil and basil. She smiled wanly and took the plate, and slowly ate while he watched each mouthful and radiated what could only be gratitude. Then he changed his clothes and went to work.

He brought her a red housecoat when she began to sit up, though he would not let her out of bed. He brought her a glass globe in which a flower would keep, submerged in water, for a week, and two live turtles in a plastic bowl and a pale-blue toy rabbit with a music box in it that played "Rock-a-bye Baby" and a blinding vermilion lipstick. She remained obedient and more watchful than ever; when his fussing and puttering were over and he took up his crouch on the cot, waiting for whatever need in her he could divine next, their eyes would meet, and increasingly, his would drop. She would hold the blue rabbit tight to her and watch him unblinkingly, or smile suddenly, parting her lips as if something vitally important and deeply happy was about to escape them. Sometimes she seemed inexpressibly sad, and sometimes she was so restless that he would go to her and stroke her hair until she fell asleep, or seemed to. It occurred to him that he had not seen her wounds for almost two days, and that perhaps they were bothering her during one of these restless spells, and so he pressed her gently down and uncovered her. He touched the scar carefully and she suddenly thrust his hand away and grasped her own flesh firmly, kneading it, slapping it stingingly. Shocked, he looked at her face and saw she was smiling, nodding. "Hurt?" She shook her head. He said, proudly, as he covered her, "I fix. I fix good." She nodded and caught his hand briefly between her chin and her shoulder.

It was that night, after he had fallen into that heavy first sleep on his return from the store, that he felt the warm firm length of her tight up against him on the cot. He lay still for a moment, somnolent, uncomprehending, while quick fingers plucked at the buttons of his long johns. He brought his hands up and trapped her wrists. She was immediately still, though her breath came swiftly and her heart pounded his chest like an angry little knuckle. He made a labored, inquisitive syllable, "Wh-wha ...?" and she moved against him and then stopped, trembling. He held her wrists for more than a minute, trying to think this out, and at last sat up. He put one arm around her shoulders and the other under her knees. He stood up. She clung to him and the breath hissed in her nostrils. He moved to the side of her bed and bent slowly and put her down. He had to reach back and detach her arms from around his neck before he could straighten up. "You sleep," he said. He fumbled for the sheet and pulled it over her and tucked it around her. She lay absolutely motionless, and he touched her hair and went back to his cot. He lay down and after a long time fell into a troubled sleep. But something woke him; he lay and listened, hearing nothing. He remembered suddenly and vividly the night she had balanced between life and death, and he had awakened to the echo of a sob which was not repeated; in sudden fright he jumped up and went to her, bent down and touched her head. She was lying face down. "You cry?" he whispered, and she shook her head rapidly. He grunted and went back to bed.

It was the ninth week and it was raining; he plodded homeward through the black, shining streets, and when he turned into his own block and saw the dead, slick river stretching between him and the streetlight in front of his house, he experienced a moment of fantasy, of dreamlike disorientation; it seemed to him for a second that none of this had happened, that in a moment the car would flash by him and dip toward the curb momentarily while a limp body tumbled out, and he must run to it and take it indoors, and it would bleed, it would bleed, it might die.... He shook himself like a big dog and put his head down against the rain, saying *Stupid!* to his inner self. Nothing could be wrong, now. He had found a way to live, and live that way he would, and he would abide no change in it.

But there was a change, and he knew it before he entered the house; his window, facing the street, had a dull orange glow which could not have been given it by the street light alone. But maybe she was reading one of those paperback novels he had inherited with the apartment; maybe she had to use the bedpan or was just looking at the clock ... but the thoughts did not comfort him; he was sick with an unaccountable fear as he unlocked the hall door. His own entrance showed light through the crack at the bottom; he dropped his keys as he fumbled with them, and at last opened the door.

He gasped as if he had been struck in the solar plexus. The bed was made, flat, neat, and she was not in it. He spun around; his frantic gaze saw her and passed her before he could believe his eyes. Tall, queenly in her red housecoat, she stood at the other end of the room, by the sink.

He stared at her in amazement. She came to him, and as he filled his lungs for one of his grating yells, she put a finger on her lips and, lightly, her other hand across his mouth. Neither of these gestures, both even would have been enough to quiet him ordinarily, but there was something else about her, something which did not wait for what he might do and would not quail before him if he did it. He was instantly confused, and silent. He stared after her as, without breaking stride, she passed him and gently closed the door. She took his hand, but the keys were in the way; she drew them from his fingers and tossed them on the table and then took his hand again, firmly. She was sure, decisive; she was one who had thought things out and weighed and discarded, and now knew what to do. But she was triumphant in some way, too; she had the poise of a victor and the radiance of the witness to a miracle. He could cope with her helplessness, of any kind, to any degree, but this—he had to think, and she gave him no time to think.

She led him to the bed and put her hands on his shoulders, turning him and making him sit down. She sat close to him, her face alight, and when again he filled his lungs, "Shh!" she hissed, sharply, and smilingly covered his mouth with her hand. She took his shoulders again and looked straight into his eyes, and said clearly, "I can talk now, I can talk!"

Numbly he gaped at her.

"Three days already, it was a secret, it was a surprise." Her voice was husky, hoarse even, but very clear and deeper than her slight body indicated. "I been practicing, to be sure. I'm all right again, I'm all right. You fix everything!" she said, and laughed.

Hearing that laugh, seeing the pride and joy in her face, he could take nothing away from her. "Ahh . . ." he said, wonderingly.

She laughed again. "I can go, I can go!" she sang. She leapt up suddenly and pirouetted, and leaned over him laughing. He gazed up at her and her flying hair, and squinted his eyes as he would looking into the sun. "Go?" he blared, the pressure of his confusion forcing the syllable out as an explosive shout.

She sobered immediately, and sat down again close to him. "Oh, honey, don't, *don't* look as if you was knifed or something. You know I can't camp on you, live off you, just *forever!*"

"No, no you stay," he blurted, anguish in his face.

"Now look," she said, speaking simply and slowly as to a child. "I'm all well again, I can talk now. It wouldn't be right, me staying, locked up here, that bedpan and all. Now wait, wait," she said quickly before he could form a word, "I don't mean I'm not grateful, you been ... you been, well, I just can't tell you. Look, nobody in my life ever did anything like this, I mean, I had to run away when I was thirteen, I done all sorts of bad things. And I got treated ... I mean, nobody else ... look, here's what I mean, up to now I'd steal, I'd rob anybody, what the hell. What I mean, why not, you see?" She shook him gently to make him see; then, recognizing the blankness and misery of his expression, she wet her lips and started over. "What I'm trying to say is, you been so kind, all this—" She waved her hand at the blue rabbit, the turtle tank, everything in the room— "I can't take any more. I mean, not a thing, not breakfast. If I could pay you back some way, no matter what, I would, you know I would." There was a tinge of bitterness in her husky voice. "Nobody can pay you anything. You don't need anything or anybody. I can't give you anything you need, or do anything for you that needs doing, you do it all yourself. If there was something you wanted from me—" She curled her hands inward and placed her fingertips between her breasts, inclining her head with a strange submissiveness that made him ache. "But no, you fix everything," she mimicked. There was no mockery in it.

"No, no, you don't go," he whispered harshly.

She patted his cheek, and her eyes loved him. "I do go," she said, smiling. Then the smile disappeared. "I got to explain to you, those hoods who cut me, I asked for that. I goofed. I was doing something real bad—well, I'll tell you. I was a runner, know what I mean? I mean dope, I was selling it."

He looked at her blankly. He was not catching one word in ten; he was biting and biting only on emptiness and uselessness, aloneness, and the terrible truth of this room without her or the blue rabbit or anything else but what it had contained all these years—linoleum with the design scrubbed off, six novels he couldn't read, a stove waiting for someone to cook for, grime and regularity and who needs you?

She misunderstood his expression. "Honey, honey, don't look at me like that, I'll never do it again. I only did it because I didn't care, I used to get glad when people hurt themselves; yeah, I mean that. I never knew someone could be kind, like you; I always thought that was sort of a lie, like the movies. Nice but not real, not for me.

"But I have to tell you, I swiped a cache, my God, twenty, twenty-two G's worth. I had it all of forty minutes, they caught up with me." Her eyes widened and saw things not in the room. "With a razor, he went to hit me with it so hard he broke it on top of the car door. He hit me here *down* and here *up*, I guess he was going to gut me but the razor was busted." She expelled air from her nostrils, and her gaze came back into the room. "I guess I got the lump on the head when they threw me out of the car. I guess that's why I couldn't talk, I heard of that. Oh *honey!* Don't look like that, you're tearing me apart!"

He looked at her dolefully and wagged his big head helplessly from side to side. She knelt before him suddenly and took both his hands. "Listen, you *got* to understand. I was going to slide out while you were working but I stayed just so I could make you understand. After all you done. . . . See, I'm well, I can't stay cooped up in one room forever. If I could, I'd get work some place near here and see you all the time, honest I would. But my life isn't worth a rubber dime in this town. I got to leave here and that means I got to leave town. I'll be all right, honey. I'll write to you; I'll never forget you, how could I?"

She was far ahead of him. He had grasped that she wanted to leave him; the next thing he understood was that she wanted to leave town too.

"You don't go," he choked. "You need me."

"You don't need me," she said fondly, "and I don't need you. It comes to that, honey; it's the way you fixed it. It's the right way; can't you see that?"

Right in there was the third thing he understood.

He stood up slowly, feeling her hands slide from his, from his knees to the floor as he stepped away from her. "Oh God!" she cried from the floor where she knelt, "you're killing me, taking it this way! Can't you be happy for me?"

He stumbled across the room and caught himself on the lower shelf of the china closet. He looked back and forward along the dark, echoing corridor of his years, stretching so far and drearily, and he looked at this short bright segment slipping away from him. . . . He heard her quick footsteps behind him and when he turned he had the flatiron in his hand. She never saw it. She came to him bright-faced, pleading, and he put out his arms and she ran inside, and the iron curved around and crashed into the back of her head.

He lowered her gently down on the linoleum and stood for a long time over her, crying quietly.

Then he put the iron away and filled the kettle and a saucepan with water, and in the saucepan he put needles and a clamp and thread and little slabs of sponge and a knife and pliers. From the gateleg table and from a drawer he got his two plastic tablecloths and began arranging them on the bed.

"I fix everything," he murmured as he worked, "Fix it right."

WON'T YOU WALK—

When I was a little boy, my mother used to recite a poem called "The Spider and the Fly," which I remembered as having begun with these words. In the course of a correspondence with a bright lady, hight Shelley Frier, she took it upon herself to research it for me in the public library. It begins with " 'Will you walk into my parlor?' said the spider to the fly," which, oddly enough, means the same thing. This is acknowledgment and thanks to the bright lady.

Joe Fritch walked under the moon, and behind the bridge of his nose something rose and stung him. When he was a little boy, which was better than thirty years ago, this exact sensation was the prelude to tears. There had been no tears for a long time, but the sting came to him, on its occasions, quite unchanged. There was another goad to plague him too, as demanding and insistent as the sting, but at the moment it was absent. They were mutually exclusive.

His mind was a jumble of half-curses, half-wishes, not weak or pale ones by any means, but just unfinished. He need not finish them any of them; his curses and his wishes were his personal clichés, and required only a code, a syllable for each. "He who hesitates—" people say, and that's enough. "Too many cooks—" they say wisely. "What's sauce for the goose—" Valid sagacities, every one, classic as the Parthenon and as widely known.

Such were the damnations and the prayers in the microcosm called Joe Fritch. "Oh, I wish—" he would say to himself, and "If only—" and "Some day, by God—"; and for each of these there was a wish, detailed and dramatic, so thought-out, touched-up, policed and maintained that it had everything but reality to make it real. And in the other area, the curses the code-words expressed wide meticulous matrices: "That Barnes—" dealt not only with his employer, a snide, selfish, sarcastic sadist with a presence like itching powder, but with every social circumstance which produced and permitted a way of life wherein a man like Joe Fritch could work for a man like Barnes. "Lutie—" was his wife's name, but as a code word it was dowdy breakfasts and I-can't-afford, that-old-dress and the finger in her ear, the hand beginning to waggle rapidly when she was annoyed; "Lutie—" said as the overture to this massive curse was that which was wanted and lost ("Joe?" "What, li'l Lutie?" "Nothing, Joe. Just . . . Joe—") and that which was unwanted and owned, like the mortgage which would be paid off in only eighteen more years, and the single setting of expensive flowery sterling which they would never, never be able to add to.

Something had happened after dinner—he could almost not remember it now; what bursts the balloon, the last puff of air, or the air it already contains? Is the final drop the only factor in the spilling-over of a brimming glass? Something about Marie Next Door (Lutie always spoke of her that way, a name like William Jennings Bryan) and a new TV console, and something about Lutie's chances, ten years ago, of marrying no end of TV consoles, with houses free-and-clear and a car and a coat, and all these chances forsworn for the likes of Joe Fritch. It had been an evening like other evenings, through 10:13 p.m. At 10:14 something silent and scalding had burst in the back of Joe's throat; he had risen without haste and had left the house. Another man might have roared an epithet, hurled an ashtray. Some might have slammed the door, and some, more skilled in maliciousness, might have left it open so the angry wife, sooner or later, must get up and close it. Joe had simply shambled out, shrinking away from her in the mindless way an amoeba avoids a hot pin. There were things he might have said. There were things he could have said to Barnes, too, time and time again, and to the elevator-starter who caught him by the elbow one morning and jammed him into a car, laughing at him through the gate before the doors slid shut. But he never said the things, not to anyone. Why not? Why not?

"They wouldn't listen," he said aloud, and again the sting came back of his nose.

He stopped and heeled water out of his left eye with the base of his thumb. This, and the sound of his own voice, brought him his lost sense of presence. He looked around like a child awakening in a strange bed.

It was a curved and sloping street, quite unlike the angled regimentation of his neighborhood. There was a huge elm arched over the street-lamp a block away, and to Joe's disoriented eye it looked like a photographic negative, a shadow-tree lit by darkness looming over a shadow of light. A tailored hedge grew on a neat stone wall beside him; across the street was a white picket fence enclosing a rolling acre and the dark mass of the house he could never own, belonging, no doubt, to someone people listened to. Bitterly he looked at it and its two gates, its rolled white driveway, and, inevitably, the low, long coupé which stood in it. The shape of that car, the compact, obedient, directional eagerness of it, came to him like the welcome answer to some deep question within him, something he had thought too complex to have any solution. For a moment a pure, bright vision overwhelmed and exalted him; his heart, his very bones cried *well, of course!* and he crossed to the driveway, along its quiet grassy margin to the car.

He laid a hand on its cool ivory flank, and had his vision again. At the wheel of this fleetfooted dream-car, he would meet the morning somewhere far from here. There would be a high hill, and a white road winding up it, and over the brow of that hill, there would be the sea. Below, a beach, and rocks; and there would be people. Up the hill he would hurtle, through and over a stone wall at the top, and in the moment he was airborne, he would blow the horn. Louder, *bigger* than the horn would be his one bright burst of laughter. He had never laughed like that, but he would, he could, for all of him would be in it, rejoicing that they listened to him, they'd all be listening, up and down the beach and craning over the cliff. After that he'd fall, but that didn't matter. Nothing would matter, even the fact that his act was criminal and childish. All the "If only—" and "Some day, by God—" wishes, all the "That Barnes—" curses, for all their detail, lacked implementation. But this one, this one—

The window was open on the driver's side. Joe looked around; the street was deserted and the house was dark. He bent and slid his hand along the line of dimly-glowing phosphorescence that was a dashboard. Something tinkled, dangled—the keys, the keys!

He opened the door, got in. He could feel the shift in balance as the splendid machine accepted him like a lover, and they were one together. He pulled the door all but closed, checked it, then pressed it the rest of the way. It closed with a quiet, solid click. Joe grasped the steering wheel in both hands, settled himself, and quelled the great trumpeting of laughter he had envisioned. *Later, later.* He reached for the key, turned it.

There was a soft purring deep under the hood. The window at his left slid up, nudging his elbow out of the way, seated itself in the molding above. The purring stopped. Then silence.

Joe grunted in surprise and turned the key again. Nothing. He fumbled along the dashboard, over the cowling, under its edge. He moved his feet around. Accelerator, brake. No clutch. A headlight dimmer switch. With less and less caution he pushed, turned and pulled at the controls on the instrument panel. No lights came on. The radio did not work. Neither did the cigarette lighter, which startled him when it came out in his hand. There wasn't a starter anywhere.

Joe Fritch, who couldn't weep, very nearly did then. If a man had a car burglar-proofed with some sort of concealed switch, wasn't that enough? Why did he have to amuse himself by leaving the keys in it? Even Barnes never thought of anything quite that sadistic.

For a split second he glanced forlornly at his glorious vision, then forever let it go. Once he sniffed; then he put his hand on the door control and half rose in his seat.

The handle spun easily, uselessly around. Joe stopped it, pulled it upward. It spun just as easily that way. He tried pulling it toward him, pushing it outward. Nothing.

He bit his lower lip and dove for the other door. It had exactly the same kind of handle, which behaved exactly the same way. Suddenly Joe was panting as if from running hard.

Now take it easy. Don't try to do anything. Think. Think, Joe.

The windows!

On his door there were two buttons; on the other, one. He tried them all. "I can't get out," he whispered. "I can't—" Suddenly he spun one of the door handles. He fluttered his hands helplessly and looked out into the welcome, open dark. *"Can't!"* he cried.

"That's right," said a voice. "You sure can't."

The sting at the base of Joe Fritch's nose—that was one of the unexpressed, inexpressible pains which had plagued him ever since he was a boy. Now came the other.

It was a ball of ice, big as a fist, in his solar plexus; and around this ball stretched a membrane; and the ball was fury, and the membrane was fear. The more terrified he became, the tighter the membrane shrank and the more it hurt. If ever he was frightened beyond bearing, the membrane would break and let the fury out, and that must not, must not happen, for the fury was so cold and so uncaring of consequence. This was no churning confusion—there was nothing confused about it. There was only compression and stretching and a breaking point so near it could be felt in advance. There was nothing that could be done about it except to sit quite still and wait until it went away, which it did when whatever caused it went away.

This voice, though, here in the car with him, it didn't go away. Conversationally it said, "Were you thinking of breaking the glass?"

Joe just sat. The voice said, "Look in the glove compartment." It waited five seconds, and said, "Go ahead. Look in the glove compartment."

Trembling, Joe reached over and fumbled the catch of the glove compartment. He felt around inside. It seemed empty, and then something moved under his fingers. It was a rectangle of wood, about six inches by three, extremely light and soft. Balsa. "I used to use a real piece of glass as a sample," said the voice, "but one of you fools got to bashing it around and broke two of his own fingers. Anyway, that piece of wood is exactly as thick as the windshield and windows." It was nearly three quarters of an inch thick. "Bulletproof is an understatement. Which reminds me," said the voice, stifling a yawn, "if you have a gun, for Pete's sake don't use it. The slug'll ricochet. Did you ever see the wound a ricocheted bullet makes?" The yawn again. " 'Scuse me. You woke me up."

Joe licked his lips, which made him shudder. The tongue and lip were so dry they scraped all but audibly. "Where are you?" he whispered.

"In the house. I always take that question as a compliment. You're hearing me on the car radio. Clean, hm-m-m? Flat to twenty-seven thousand cycles. Designed it myself."

Joe said, "Let me out."

"I'll let you out, but I won't let you go. You people are my bread and butter."

"Listen," said Joe, "I'm not a thief, or a . . . or a . . . or anything. I mean, this was just a sort of wild idea. Just let me go, huh? I won't *ever* . . . I mean, I promise." He scraped at his lip with his tongue again and added. "Please. I mean, please."

"Where were you going with my car, Mister I'm-not-a-thief?"

Joe was silent.

A sudden blaze of light made him wince. His eyes adjusted, and he found it was only the light over the porte cochere which bridged the driveway where it passed the house. "Come on inside," said the voice warmly.

Joe looked across the rolling lawn at the light. The car was parked in the drive near the street; the house was nearly two hundred feet away. *Catch ten times as many with it parked way out here*, he thought wildly. And, *I thought Barnes was good at making people squirm.* And, *Two hundred feet, and him in the house. He can outthink me; could he outrun me?* "What do you want me inside for?"

"Would it make any difference how I answered that question?"

Joe saw that it wouldn't. The voice was calling the shots just now, and Joe was hardly in a position to make any demands. Resignedly he asked, "You're going to call the police?"

"Absolutely not."

A wave of relief was overtaken and drowned in a flood of terror. No one knew where he was. No one had seen him get into the car. Being arrested would be unpleasant, but at least it would be a known kind of unpleasantness. But what lay in store for him in this mysterious expensive house?

"You better just call the police," he said. "I mean, have me arrested. I'll wait where I am."

"No," said the voice. It carried a new tone, and only by the change did Joe realize how—how *kind* it had been before. Joe believed that single syllable completely. Again he eyed the two hundred feet. He tensed himself, and said, "All right. I'll come."

"Good boy," said the voice, kind again. "Sleep sweet." Something went *pfffft!* on the dashboard and Joe's head was enveloped in a fine, very cold mist. He fell forward and hit his mouth on the big V emblem in the hub of the steering wheel. A profound astonishment enveloped him because he felt the impact but no pain.

He blacked out.

There was a comfortable forever during which he lay in a dim place, talking lazily, on and on. Something questioned him from time to time, and perhaps he knew he was not questioning himself; he certainly didn't care. He rested in an euphoric cloud, calmly relating things he thought he had forgotten, and while an objective corner of his mind continued to operate, to look around, to feel and judge and report, it was almost completely preoccupied with an astonished delight that he could talk about his job, his marriage, his sister Anna, even about Joey—whom he'd killed when he and Joey were ten years old—without either the self-pitying twinge of unshed tears nor the painful fear which contained his rage.

Someone moved into his range of vision, someone with a stranger's face and a manner somehow familiar. He had something shiny in his hand. He advanced and bent over him, and Joe felt the nip of a needle in his upper arm. He lay quietly then, not talking because he had finished what he had to say, not moving because he was so comfortable, and began to feel warm from the inside out. That lasted for another immeasurable time. Then he detected movement again, and was drawn to it; the stranger crossed in front of him and sat down in an easy chair. Their faces were about at the same level, but Joe was not on an easy chair. Neither was it a couch. It was something in between. He glanced down and saw his knees, his feet. He was in one of those clumsy-looking, superbly comfortable devices known as contour chair. He half-sat, half-reclined in it, looked at the other man and felt just wonderful. He smiled sleepily, and the man smiled back.

The man looked too old to be thirty, though he might be. He looked too young for fifty, though that was possible, too. His hair was dark, his eyebrows flecked with gray—a combination Joe thought he had never seen before. His eyes were light—in this dim room it was hard to see their color. The nose was ridiculous: it belonged to a happy fat man, and not someone with a face as long and lean as this one. The mouth was large and flexible; it was exactly what is meant by the term "generous," yet its lips were thin, the upper one almost nonexistent. He seemed of average height, say five, ten or eleven, but he gave the impression of being somehow too wide and too flat. Joe looked at him and at his smile, and it flashed across his mind that the French call a smile *sourire*, which means literally "under a laugh"; and surely, in any absolute scale of merriment, this smile was just exactly that. "How are you feeling?"

"I feel fine," said Joe. He really meant it.

"I'm Zeitgeist," said the man.

Joe was unquestioningly aware that the man knew him, knew all about him, so he didn't offer his name in return. He accepted the introduction and after a moment let his eyes stray from the friendly face to the wall behind him, to some sort of framed document, around to the side where a massive bookcase stood. He suddenly realized that he was in a strange room. He snapped his gaze back to the man. "Where am I?"

"In my house," said Zeitgeist. He uncrossed his legs and leaned forward. "I'm the man whose car you were stealing. Remember?"

Joe did, with a rush. An echo of his painful panic struck him, made him leap to his feet, a reflex which utterly failed. Something caught him gently and firmly around the midriff and slammed him back into the contour chair. He looked down and saw a piece of webbing like that used in aircraft safety belts, but twice as wide. It was around his waist and had no buckle; or if it had, it was behind and under the back of the chair, well out of his reach.

"It's O.K.," Zeitgeist soothed him. "You didn't actually steal it, and I understand perfectly why you tried. Let's just forget that part of it."

"Who are you? What are you trying to do? Let me out of this thing!" The memory of this man approaching him with a glittering hypodermic returned to him. "What did you do, drug me?"

Zeitgeist crossed his legs again, and leaned back. "Yes, several times, and the nicest part of it is that you can't stay that excited very long just now." He smiled again, warm.

Joe heaved again against the webbing, lay back, opened his mouth to protest, closed it helplessly. Then he met the man's eyes again, and he could feel the indignation and fright draining out of him. He suddenly felt foolish, and found a smile of his own, a timid, foolish one.

"First I anaesthetized you," said Zeitgeist informatively, apparently pursuing exactly the line of thought brought out by Joe's question, "because not for a second would I trust any of you to come across that lawn just because I asked you to. Then I filled you full of what we'd call truth serum if this was a TV play. And when you'd talked enough I gave you another shot to pull you out of it. Yes, I drugged you."

"What for? What do you want from me, anyway?"

"You'll find out when you get my bill."

"Bill?"

"Sure. I have to make a living just like anybody else."

"Bill for what?"

"I'm going to fix you up."

"There's nothing the matter with me!"

Zeitgeist twitched his mobile lips. "Nothing wrong with a man who wants to take an expensive automobile and kill himself with it?"

Joe dropped his eyes. A little less pugnaciously, he demanded, "What are you, a psychiatrist or something?"

"Or something," laughed Zeitgeist. "Now listen to me," he said easily. "There are classic explanations for people doing the things they do, and you have a textbook full. You were an undersized kid who lost his mother early. You were brutalized by a big sister who just wouldn't be a mother to you. When you were ten you threw one of your tantrums and crowded another kid, and he slipped on the ice and was hit by a truck and killed. Your sister lambasted you for it until you ran away from home nine years later. You got married and didn't know how to put your wife into the mother-image; so you treated her like your sister Anna instead; you obeyed, you didn't answer back, you did as little as possible to make her happy because no matter how happy she got you were subconsciously convinced it would do you no good. And by the way, the kid who was killed had the same name as you did." He smiled his kindly smile, wagged his head and *tsk-tsked*. "You should see what the textbooks say about *that* kind of thing. Identification: you are the Joey who was killed when you got mad and hit him. Ergo, don't ever let yourself get mad or you'll be dead. Joe Fritch, you know what you are? You're a mess."

"What am I supposed to say?" asked Joe in a low voice. Had he run off at the mouth that much? He was utterly disarmed. In the face of such penetrating revelation, anger would be ridiculous.

"Don't say anything. That is, don't try to explain—I already understand. How'd you like to get rid of all that garbage? I can do that for you. Will you let me?"

"Why should you?"

"I've already told you. It's my living."

"You say you're a psychiatrist?"

"I said nothing of the kind, and that's beside the point. Well?"

"Well, O.K. I mean . . . O.K."

Zeitgeist rose, smiling, and stepped behind Joe. There was a metallic click and the webbing loosened. Joe looked up at his host, thinking: *Suppose I won't? Suppose I just don't? What could he do?*

"There are lots of things I could do," said Zeitgeist with gentle cheerfulness. "Full of tricks, I am."

In spite of himself, Joe laughed. He got up. Zeitgeist steadied him, then released his elbow. Joe said, "Thanks . . . what are you, I mean, a mind reader?"

"I don't have to be."

Joe thought about it. "I guess you don't," he said.

"Come on." Zeitgeist turned away to the door. Joe reflected that anyone who would turn his back on a prisoner like that was more than just confident—he must have a secret weapon. *But at the moment confidence is enough.* He followed Zeitgeist into the next room.

It, too, was a low room, but much wider than the other, and its dimness was of quite another kind. Pools of brilliance from floating fluorescents mounted over three different laboratory benches made them like three islands in a dark sea. At about eye-level—as he stood—in the shadows over one of the benches, the bright green worm of a cathode-ray oscilloscope writhed in its twelve-inch circular prison. Ranked along the walls were instrument racks and consoles; he was sure he could not have named one in ten of them in broad daylight. The room was almost silent, but it was a living silence of almost undetectable clickings and hummings and the charged, noiseless *presence* of power. It was a waiting, busy sort of room.

"Boo," said Zeitgeist.

"I beg your . . . huh?"

Zeitgeist laughed. "You say it." He pointed. "Boooo."

Joe looked up at the oscilloscope. The worm had changed to a wiggling, scraggly child's scrawl, which, when Zeitgeist's long-drawn syllable was finished, changed into a green worm again. Zeitgeist touched a control knob on one of the benches and the worm became a straight line. "Go ahead."

"Boo," said Joe self-consciously. The line was a squiggle and then a line again. "Come on, a good loud long one," said Zeitgeist. This time Joe produced the same sort of "grass" the other man had. Or at least, it looked the same. "Good," said Zeitgeist. "What do you do for a living?"

"Advertising. You mean I didn't tell you?"

"You were more interested in talking about your boss than your work. What kind of advertising?"

"Well, I mean, it isn't advertising like in an agency. I mean, I work for the advertising section of the public relations division of a big corporation."

"You write ads? Sell them? Art, production, research—what?"

"All that, I mean, a little of all those. We're not very big. The company is, I mean, but not our office. We only advertise in trade magazines. The engineer'll come to me with something he wants to promote and I check with the . . . I mean, that Barnes, and if he O.K.'s it I write copy on it and check back with the engineer and write again and check back with Barnes and write it again; and after that I do the layout, I mean I draft the layout just on a piece of typewriter paper, that's all, I can't draw or anything like that, I mean; and then I see it through Art and go back and check with Barnes, and then I order space, for it in the magazines and—"

"You ever take a vocational analysis?"

"Yes. I mean, sure I did. I'm in the right sort of job, according to the tests. I mean, it was the Kline-Western test."

"Good test," said Zeitgeist approvingly.

"You think I'm not in the right sort of job?" He paused, and then with sudden animation, "You think I should quit that lousy job, I mean, get into something else?"

"That's your business. All right, that's enough."

The man could be as impersonal as a sixpenny nail when he wanted to be. He worked absorbedly at his controls for a while. There was a soft whine from one piece of apparatus, a clicking from another, and before Joe knew what was happening he heard someone saying, "All that. I mean, a little of all those. We're not very big. The company is, I mean, but not our office. We only advertise—" on and on, in his exact words. His exact voice, too, he realized belatedly. He listened to it without enthusiasm. From time to time a light blazed, bright as a photo-flash but scalding red. Patiently, brilliantly, the oscillo- scope traced each syllable, each pulse with each syllable. ". . . and check with Barnes, and then I order sp—" The voice ceased abruptly as Zeitgeist threw a switch.

"I didn't know you were recording," said Joe, "or I would have . . . I mean, said something different maybe."

"I know," said Zeitgeist. "That red light bother you?"

"It was pretty bright," said Joe, not wanting to complain.

"Look here." He opened the top of the recorder. Joe saw reels and more heads than he had ever seen on a recorder before, and a number of other unfamiliar components. "I don't know much about—"

"You don't have to," said Zeitgeist. "See there?" He pointed with one hand, and with the other reached for a button on the bench and pressed it. A little metal arm snapped up against the tape just where it passed over an idler. "That punched a little hole in the tape. Not enough to affect the recording." Zeitgeist turned the reel slowly by hand, moving the tape along an inch or so. Joe saw, on the moving tape, a tiny bright spot of light. When the almost invisible hole moved into it, the red light flared. "I pushed that button every time you said 'I mean.' Let's play it again."

He played it again, and Joe listened—an act of courage, because with all his heart he wanted to cover his ears, shut his eyes against that red blaze. He was consumed with embarrassment. He had never heard anything that sounded so completely idiotic. When at last it was over, Zeitgeist grinned at him. "Learn something?"

"I did," said Joe devoutly.

"O.K.," said Zeitgeist, in a tone which disposed of the matter completely as far as he was concerned, at the same time acting as prelude to something new.

The man's expressiveness was extraordinary; with a single word he had Joe's gratitude and his fullest attention. "Now listen to this." He made some adjustments, threw a switch. Joe's taped voice said, ". . . go back and check it with Ba-a-a-a-a-a-ah—" with the "ah" going on and on like an all-clear signal. "That bother you?" called Zeitgeist over the noise.

"It's awful!" shouted Joe. This time he did cover his ears. It didn't help. Zeitgeist switched off the noise and laughed at him. "That's understandable. Your own voice, and it goes on and on like that. What's bothering you is, it doesn't breathe. I swear you could choke a man half to death, just by making him listen to that. Well, don't let it worry you. That thing over there"—he pointed to a massive cabinet against the wall—"is my analyzer. It breaks up your voice into all the tones and overtones it contains, finds out the energy level of each, and shoots the information to that tone-generator yonder. The generator reproduces each component exactly as received, through seventy-two band-pass filters two hundred cycles apart. All of which means that when I tell it to, it picks out a single vowel sound—in this case your 'a' in 'Barnes'—and hangs it up there on the 'scope like a photograph for as long as I want to look at it."

"All that, to do what I do when I say 'ah'?"

"All that," beamed Zeitgeist. Joe could see he was unashamedly proud of his equipment. He leaned forward and flicked Joe across the Adam's apple. "That's a hell of a compact little machine, that pharynx of yours. Just look at that wave-form."

Joe looked at the screen. "Some mess."

"A little tomato sauce and you could serve it in an Italian restaurant," said Zeitgeist. "Now let's take it apart."

From another bench he carried the cable of a large control box, and plugged it into the analyzer with a many-pronged jack. The box had on it nearly a hundred keys. He fingered a control at the end of each row and the oscilloscope subsided to its single straight line. "Each one of these keys controls one of those narrow two-hundred-cycle bands I was talking about," he told Joe. "Your voice—everybody's voice—has high and low overtones, some loud, some soft. Here's one at the top, one in the middle, one at the bottom." He pressed three widely separated keys. The speaker uttered a faint breathy note, then a flat tone, the same in pitch but totally different in quality; it was a little like hearing the same note played first on a piccolo and then on a viola. The third key produced only a murmuring hiss, hardly louder than the noise of the amplifier itself. With each note, the 'scope showed a single wavy line. With the high it was a steep but even squiggle. In the middle it was a series of shallow waves like a child's drawing of an ocean. Down at the bottom it just shook itself and lay there.

"Just what I thought. I'm not saying you're a soprano, Joe, but there's five times more energy in your high register than there is at the bottom. Ever hear the way a kid's voice climbs the scale when he's upset—whining, crying, demanding? 'Spose I told you that all the protest against life that you're afraid to express in anger, is showing up here?" He slid his fingers across the entire upper register, and the speaker bleated. "Listen to that, the poor little feller."

In abysmal self-hatred, Joe felt the sting of tears. "Cut it out," he blurted.

"Caht eet ow-oot," mimicked Zeitgeist. Joe thought he'd kill him, then and there, but couldn't because he found himself laughing. The imitation was very good. "You know, Joe, the one thing you kept droning on about in the other room was something about 'they won't listen to me. Nobody will listen.' How many times, say, in the office, have you had a really solid idea and kept it to yourself because 'nobody will listen'? How many times have you wanted to do something with your wife, go somewhere, ask her to get something from the cleaners—and then decided not to because she wouldn't listen?" He glanced around at Joe, and charitably turned away from the contorted face. "Don't answer that: you know, and it doesn't matter to me.

"Now get this, Joe. There's something in all animals just about as basic as hunger. It's the urge to attack something that's retreating, and its converse: to be wary of something that won't retreat. Next time a dog comes running up to you, growling, with his ears laid back, turn and run and see if he doesn't take a flank steak out of your southern hemisphere. After you get out of the hospital, go back and when he rushes you, laugh at him and keep going on about your business, and see him decide you're not on his calorie chart for the day. Well, the same thing works with people. No one's going to attack you unless he has you figured out—especially if he figures you'll retreat. Walk around with a big neon sign on your head that says HEY EVERYBODY I WILL RETREAT, and you're just going to get clobbered wherever you go. You've got a sign like that and it lights up every time you open your mouth. Caht eet owoot."

Joe's lower lip protruded childishly. "I can't help what kind of voice I've got."

"Probably you can't. I can, though."

"But how—"

"Shut up." Zeitgeist returned all the keys to a neutral position and listened a moment to the blaring audio. Then he switched it off and began flicking keys, some up, some down. "Mind you, this isn't a matter of changing a tenor into a baritone. New York City once had a mayor with a voice like a Punch and Judy show, and he hadn't an ounce of retreat in him. All I'm going to do is cure a symptom. Some people say that doesn't work, but ask the gimpy guy who finds himself three inches taller and walking like other people, the first time he tries his built-up shoes. Ask the guy who wears a well-made toupee." He stared for a while at the 'scope, and moved some more keys. "You want people to listen to you. All right, they will, whether they want to or not. Of course, *what* they listen to is something else again. It better be something that backs up this voice I'm giving you. That's up to you."

"I don't under——"

"You'll understand a lot quicker if we fix it so you listen and I talk. O.K.?" Zeitgeist demanded truculently, and sent over such an engaging grin that the words did not smart. "Now, like I said, I'm only curing a symptom. What you have to get through your thick head is that the disease doesn't exist. All that stuff about your sister Anna, and Joey, that doesn't exist because it happened and it's finished and it's years ago and doesn't matter any more. Lutie, Barnes . . . well, they bother you mostly because they won't listen to you. *They'll listen to you now.* So that botherment is over with, too; finished, done with, nonexistent. For all practical purposes yesterday is as far beyond recall as twenty years ago; just as finished, just as dead. So the little boy who got punished by his big sister until he thought he deserved being punished—he doesn't exist. The man with the guilty feeling killing a kid called Joey, he doesn't exist either any more, and by the way he wasn't guilty in the first place. The copy man who lets a pipsqueak sadist prick him with petty sarcasms—he's gone too, because now there's a man who won't swallow what he wants to say, what he knows is right. He'll say it, just because *people will listen.* A beer stein is pretty useless to anyone until you put beer in it. The gadget I'm going to give you won't do you a bit of good unless you put yourself, your real self into it." He had finished with the keys while he spoke, had turned and was holding Joe absolutely paralyzed with his strange light eyes.

Inanely, Joe said, "G-gadget?"

"Listen." Zeitgeist hit the master switch and Joe's voice again came from the speaker. "We only advertise in trade magazines. The engineer'll come to me with something he wants to promote and——"

And the voice was his voice, but it was something else, too. Its pitch was the same, inflection, accent; but there was a forceful resonance in it somewhere, somehow. It was a compelling voice, a rich voice; above all it was assertive and sure. (And when the 'I means' came, and the scalding light flashed, it wasn't laughable or embarrassing; it was simply unnecessary.)

"That isn't me."

"You're quite right. It isn't. But it's the way the world will hear you. It's behind the way the world will treat you. And the way the world treats the man is the way the man grows, if he wants to and he's got any growing left in him. Whatever is in that voice you can *be* because I will help and the world will help. But you've got to help, too."

"I'll help," Joe whispered.

"Sometimes I make speeches," said Zeitgeist, and grinned shyly. The next second he was deeply immersed in work.

He drew out a piece of paper with mimeographed rulings on it, and here and there in the ruled squares he jotted down symbols, referring to the keyboard in front of him. He seemed then to be totaling columns; once he reset two or three keys, turned on the audio and listened intently, then erased figures and put down others. At last he nodded approvingly, rose, stretched till his spine cracked, picked up the paper and went over to the third bench.

From drawers and cubbyholes he withdrew components—springs, pads, plugs, rods. He moved with precision and swift familiarity. He rolled out what looked like a file drawer, but instead of papers it contained ranks and rows of black plastic elements, about the size and shape of miniature match boxes, each with two bright brass contacts at top and bottom.

"We're living in a wonderful age, Joe," said Zeitgeist as he worked. "Before long I'll turn the old soldering iron out to stud and let it father waffles. Printed circuits, sub-mini tubes, transistors. These things here are electrets, which I won't attempt to explain to you." He bolted and clipped, bent and formed, and every once in a while, referring to his list, he selected another of the black boxes from the file and added it to his project. When there were four rows of components, each row about one and a half by six inches, he made some connections with test clips and thrust a jack into a receptacle in the bench. He glanced up at the 'scope, grunted, unclipped one of the black rectangles and substituted another from the files.

"These days, Joe, when they can pack a whole radar set—transmitter, receiver, timing and arming mechanisms and a power supply into the nose of a shell, a package no bigger than your fist—these days you can do anything with a machine. Anything, Joe. You just have to figure out how. Most of the parts exist, they make 'em in job lots. You just have to plug 'em together." He plugged in the jack, as if to demonstrate, and glanced up at the 'scope. "Good. The rest won't take long." Working with tin-snips, then with a small sheet-metal brake, he said, "Some day you're going to ask me what I'm doing, what all this is for, and I'll just grin at you. I'm going to tell you now and if you don't remember what I say, well, then forget it.

"They say our technology has surpassed, or bypassed, our souls, Joe. They say if we don't turn from science to the spirit, we're doomed. I agree that we're uncomfortably close to damnation, but I don't think we'll appease any great powers by throwing our gears and gimmicks over the cliff as a sacrifice, a propitiation. Science didn't get us into this mess; we *used* science to get us in.

"So I'm just a guy who's convinced we can use science to get us out. In other words, I'm not for hanging the gunsmith every time someone gets shot. Take off your shirt."

"What?" said Joe, back from a thousand miles. "Oh." Bemused, he took off his jacket and shirt and stood shyly clutching his thin ribs.

Zeitgeist picked up his project from the bench and put it over Joe's head. A flat band of spring steel passed over each shoulder, snugly. The four long flat casings, each filled with components, rested against his collar-bones, pressing upward in the small hollow just below the bones, and against his shoulder blades. Zeitgeist bent and manipulated the bands until they were tight but comfortable. Then he hooked the back pieces to the front pieces with soft strong elastic bands passing under Joe's arms. "O.K.? O.K. Now—say something."

"Say what?" said Joe stupidly, and immediately clapped his hand to his chest. *"Uh!"*

"What happened?"

"It . . . I mean, it buzzed!"

Zeitgeist laughed. "Let me tell you what you've got there. In front, two little speakers, an amplifier to drive them, and a contact microphone that picks up your chest tones. In back, on this side, a band-pass arrangement that suppresses all those dominating high-frequency whimperings of yours and feeds the rest, the stuff you're weak in, up front to be amplified. And over here, in back— that's where the power supply goes. Go over there where you were and record something. And remember what I told you—you have to help this thing. Talk a little slower and you won't have to say 'I mean' while you think of what comes next. You *know* what comes next, anyway. You don't have to be afraid to say it."

Dazed, Joe stepped back to where he had been when the first recording was made, glanced for help up at the green line of the oscilloscope, closed his eyes and said, falteringly at first, then stronger and steadier, " 'Four score and seven years ago, our fathers brought forth upon this contin—' "

"Cut!" cried Zeitgeist. "Joe, see that tone-generator over there? It's big as a spinet piano. I can do a lot but believe me, you haven't got one of those strapped on you. Your amplifier can only blow up what it gets. You don't have much, but for Pete's sake give it what you have. Try talking with your lungs full instead of empty. Push your voice a little, don't just let it fall out of you."

"Nothing happens, though. I sound the same to myself. Is it working? Maybe it doesn't work."

"Like I told you before," said Zeitgeist with exaggerated patience, "people who are talking aren't listening. It's working all right. Don't go looking for failures, Joe. Plenty'll come along that you didn't ask for. Now go ahead and do as I said."

Joe wet his lips, took a deep breath. Zeitgeist barked, "Now slowly!" and he began: " 'Four score and seven years—' " The sonorous words rolled out, his chest vibrated from the buzzing, synchronized to his syllables. And though he was almost totally immersed in his performance, a part of him leaped excitedly, realizing that never in his whole life before had he listened, really listened to that majestic language. When he was finished he opened his eyes and found Zeitgeist standing very near him, his eyes alight.

"Good," the man breathed. "Ah, but . . . good."

"Was it? Was it really?"

In answer, Zeitgeist went to the controls, rewound the tape, and hit the playback button.

And afterwards, he said gently to Joe, "You *can* cry—see?"

"Damn foolishness," said Joe.

"No it isn't," Zeitgeist told him.

Outside, it was morning—what a morning, with all the gold and green, thrust and rustle of a new morning in a new summer. He hadn't been out all night; he had died and was born again! He stood tall, walked tall, he carried his shining new voice sheathed like Excalibur, but for all its concealment, he was armed!

He had tried to thank Zeitgeist, and that strange man had shaken his head soberly and said, "Don't, Joe. You're going to pay me for it."

"Well I will, of course I will! Anything you say . . . how much, anyhow?"

Zeitgeist had shaken his head slightly. "We'll talk about it later. Go on—get in the car. I'll drive you to work." And silently, he had.

Downtown, he reached across Joe and opened the door. For him, the door worked. "Come see me day after tomorrow. After dinner—nine."

"O.K. Why? Got another . . . treatment?"

"Not for you," said Zeitgeist, and his smile made it a fine compliment for both of them. "But no power plant lasts forever. Luck." And before Joe could answer the door was closed and the big car had swung out into traffic. Joe watched it go, grinning and shaking his head.

The corner clock said five minutes to nine. Just time, if he hurried.

He didn't hurry. He went to Harry's and got shaved, while they pressed his suit and sponged his collar in the back room. He kept the bathrobe they gave him pulled snugly over his amplifier, and under a hot towel he reached almost the euphoric state he had been in last night. He thought of Barnes, and the anger stirred in him. With some new internal motion he peeled away its skin of fear and set it free. Nothing happened, except that it lived in him instead of just lying there. It didn't make him tremble. It made him smile.

Clean, pressed, and smelling sweet, he walked into his building at eight minutes before ten. He went down to the express elevator and stepped into the one open door. Then he said, "Wait," and stepped out again. The operator goggled at him.

Joe walked up to the starter, a bushy character in faded brown and raveled gold braid. "Hey . . . you."

The starter pursed a pair of liver-colored lips and glowered at him. "Whaddayeh want?"

Joe filled his lungs and said evenly, "Day before yesterday you took hold of me and shoved me into an elevator like I was a burlap sack."

The starter's eyes flickered. "Not me."

"You calling me a liar, too?"

Suddenly the man's defenses caved. There was a swift pucker which came and went on his chin, and he said, "Look, I got a job to do, mister, rush hours, if I don't get these cars out of here it's *my* neck, I didn't mean nothing by it, I——"

"Don't tell me your troubles," said Joe. He glared at the man for a second. "All right, do your job, but don't do it on me like that again."

He turned his back, knowing he was mimicking Zeitgeist with the gesture and enjoying the knowledge. He went back to the elevator and got in. Through the closing gate he saw the starter, right where he had left him, gaping. The kid running the elevator was gaping, too.

"Eleven," said Joe.

"Yes, *sir*," said the boy. He started the car. "You told *him*."

"Bout time," said Joe modestly.

"Past time," said the kid.

Joe got out on the eleventh floor, feeling wonderful. He walked down the hall thumped a door open, and ambled in. Eleanor Bulmer, the receptionist, looked up. He saw her eyes flick to the clock and back to his face. "Well!"

"Morning," he said expansively, from his inflated lungs. She blinked as if he had fired a cap pistol, then looked confusedly down at her typewriter.

He took a step toward his corner desk when there was a flurry, a botherment up from the left, then an apparition of thinning hair and exophthalmic blue eyes. Barnes, moving at a half-trot as usual, jacket off, suspenders, arm-bands pulling immaculate cuffs high and away from rust-fuzzed scrawny wrists, "Eleanor, get me Apex on the phone. Get me Apex on the——" And then he saw Joe. He stopped. He smiled. He had gleaming pale-yellow incisors like a rodent. He, too, flicked a glance at the clock.

Joe knew exactly what he was going to say, exactly how he was going to say it. He took a deep breath, and if old ghosts were about to rise in him, the friendly pressure of the amplifier just under his collar-bones turned them to mist. *Why, Miss Terr Fritch*, Barnes would say with exaggerated and dramatic politeness, *how ki-i-ind of you to drop in today*. Then the smile would snap off and the long series of not-to-be-answered questions would begin. Didn't he know this was a place of business? Was he aware of the customary starting time? Did it not seem that among fourteen punctual people, he alone—and so on. During it, seven typewriters would stop, a grinning stock boy would stick his head over a filing cabinet to listen, and Miss Bulmer, over whose nape the monologue would stream, would sit with her head bowed waiting for it to pass. Already the typewriters had stopped. And yes, sure enough: behind Barnes he could see the stock boy's head.

"Why, Miss Terr Fritch!" said Barnes happily.

Joe immediately filled his lungs, turned his back on Barnes, and said into the stunned silence, "Better get him Apex on the phone, Eleanor. He has the whole place at a stand-still." He then walked around Barnes as if the man were a pillar and went to his desk and sat down.

Barnes stood with his bony head lowered and his shoulders humped as if he had been bitten on the neck by a fire-ant. Slowly he turned and glared up the office. There was an immediate explosion of typewriter noise, shuffling feet, shuffling papers. "I'll take it in my office," Barnes said to the girl.

He had to pass Joe to get there, and to Joe's great delight he could see how reluctant Barnes was to do it. "I'll see you later," Barnes hissed as he went by, and Joe called cheerfully after him, "You just betcha." Out in the office, somebody whistled appreciatively; somebody snickered. Joe knew Barnes had heard it. He smiled, and picked up the phone. "Outside, Eleanor. Personal."

Eleanor Bulmer knew Barnes didn't allow personal calls except in emergencies, and then preferred to give his permission first. Joe could hear her breathing, hesitating. Then, "Yes, Mr. Fritch." And the dial tone crooned in his ear. *Mr. Fritch*, he thought. *That's the first time she ever called me Mr. Fritch. What do you know. Why . . . why, she never called me anything before! Just "Mr. Barnes wants to see you," or "Cohen of Electrical Marketing on the line."*

Mr. Fritch dialed his home. "Hello—Lutie?"

"Joe! Where were you all night?" The voice was waspish, harrying; he could see her gathering her forces, he could see her mountain of complaints about to be shoveled into the telephone as if it were a hopper.

"I called up to tell you I'm all right because I thought it was a good idea. Maybe it was a bad idea."

"What?" There was a pause, and then in quite a different tone she said, "Joe? Is this . . . Joe, is that you?"

"Sure," he said heartily. "I'm at work and I'm all right and I'll be home for dinner. Hungry," he added.

"You expect me to cook you a dinner after—" she began, but without quite her accustomed vigor.

"All right, then I won't be home for dinner," he said reasonably.

She didn't say anything for a long time, but he knew she was still there. He sat and waited. At last she said faintly, "Will veal cutlets be all right?"

On the second night after this fledging, Mr. Joseph Fritch strode into the porte-cochere and bounded up the steps. He ground the bell-push with his thumb until it hurt, and then knocked. He stood very straight until the door opened.

"Joe, boy! Come on in." Zeitgeist left the door and opened another. Joe had the choice of following or of standing where he was and shouting. He followed. He found himself in a room new to him, low-ceilinged like the others, but with books from floor to ceiling. In a massive fieldstone fireplace flames leaped cheerfully, yet the room was quite cool. Air-conditioned. Well, he guessed Zeitgeist just *liked* a fire. "Look," he said abruptly.

"Sit down. Drink?"

"No. Listen, you've made a mistake."

"I know, I know. The bill. Got it with you?"

"I have."

Zeitgeist nodded approvingly. Joe caught himself wondering why. Zeitgeist glided across to him and pressed a tall glass into his hand. It was frosty, beaded, sparkling. "What's in it?" he snapped.

Zeitgeist burst out laughing, and in Joe fury passed, and shame passed, and he found himself laughing, too. He held out his glass and Zeitgeist clinked with him. "You're a . . . a—Luck."

"Luck," said Zeitgeist. They drank. It was whisky, the old gentle muscular whisky that lines the throat with velvet and instantly heats the ear lobes. "How did you make out?"

Joe drank again and smiled. "I walked into that office almost an hour late," he began, an told what had happened. Then, "And all day it was like that. I didn't know a job . . . people . . . I didn't know things could be like that. Look, I told you I'd pay you. I said I'd pay you anything you—"

"Never mind that just now. What else happened? The suit and all?"

"That. Oh, I guess I was kind of—" Joe looked into the friendly amber in his glass, "well, intoxicated. Lunch time I just walked into King's and got the suit. Two suits. I haven't had a new suit for four years, and then it didn't come from King's. I just signed for 'em," he added, a reflective wonderment creeping into his voice. "They didn't mind. Shirts," he said, closing his eyes.

"It'll pay off."

"It did pay off," said Joe, bouncing on his soft chair to sit upright on the edge, shoulders back, head up. His voice drummed and his eyes were bright. He set his glass down on the carpet and swatted his hands gleefully together. "There was this liaison meeting, they call it, this morning. I don't know what got into me. Well, I do; but anyway, like every other copywriter I have a project tucked away; you know—I like it but maybe no one else will. I had it in my own roughs, up to yesterday. So I got this bee in my bonnet and went in to the Art Department and started in on them, and you know, they caught fire, they worked almost all *night*? And at the meeting this morning, the usual once-a-month kind of thing, the brass from the main office looking over us step-children and wondering why they don't fold us up and go to an outside agency. It was so easy!" he chortled.

"I just sat there, shy like always, and there was old Barnes as usual trying to head off product advertising and go into institutionals, because he likes to write that stuff himself. Thinks it makes the brass think he loves the company. So soon as he said 'institutionals' I jumped up and agreed with him and said let me show you one of Mr. Barnes' ideas. Yeah! I went and got it and you should *see* that presentation; you could eat it! So here's two VP's and a board secretary with their eyes bugging out and old Barnes not daring to deny anything, and everybody in the place knew I was lying and thought what a nice fellow I was to do it that way. And there sat that brass, looking at my haircut and my tie and my suit and me, and *buying* it piece by piece, and Barnes, old Barnes sweating it out."

"What did they offer you?"

"They haven't exactly. I'm supposed to go see the chairman Monday."

"What are you going to do?"

"Say no. Whatever it is, I'll say no. I have lots of ideas piled up—nobody would *listen* before! Word'll get around soon enough; I'll get my big raise the only smart way a man can get a really big one—just before he goes to work for a new company. Meanwhile I'll stay and work hard and be nice to Barnes, who'll die a thousand deaths."

Zeitgeist chuckled. "You're a stinker. What happened when you went home?"

Joe sank back into his chair and turned toward the flames; whatever his thoughts were, they suffused him with firelight and old amber, strength through curing, through waiting. His voice was just that mellow as he murmured, "That wasn't you at all. That was me."

"Oh, sorry. I wasn't prying."

"Don't get me wrong!" said Joe. "I want to tell you." He laughed softly. "We had veal cutlets."

A log fell and Joe watched the sparks shooting upward while Zeitgeist waited. Suddenly Joe looked across at him with a most peculiar expression on his face. "The one thing I never thought of till the time came. I couldn't wear that thing all night, could I now? I don't want her to know. I'll be . . . you said I'd grow to . . . that if I put my back into it, maybe some day I wouldn't need it." He touched his collarbone.

"That's right," said Zeitgeist.

"So I couldn't wear it. And then I couldn't talk. Not a word." Again, the soft laugh. "She wouldn't sleep, not for the longest time. 'Joe?' she'd say, and I'd know she was going to ask where I'd been that night. I'd say, '*Shh.*' and put my hand on her face. She'd hold on to it. Funny. Funny, how you know the difference," he said in a near whisper, looking at the fire again. "She said, 'Joe?'

just like before, and I knew she was going to say she was sorry for being . . . well, all the trouble we've had. But I said '*Shh.*'" He watched the fire silently, and Zeitgeist seemed to know that he was finished.

"I'm glad," said Zeitgeist.

"Yeah."

They shared some quiet. Then Zeitgeist said, waving his glass at the mantel, "Still think the bill's out of line?"

Joe looked at it, at the man. "It's not a question of how much it's worth," he said with some difficulty. "It's how much I can pay. When I left here I wanted to pay you whatever you asked—five dollars or five hundred, I didn't care what I had to sacrifice. But I never thought it would be five *thousand!*" He sat up. "I'll level with you; I don't have that kind of money. I never did have. Maybe I never will have."

"What do you think I fixed you up for?" Zeitgeist's voice cracked like a target-gun. "What do you think I'm in business for? I don't gamble."

Joe stood up slowly. "I guess I just don't understand you," he said coldly. "Well, at those prices I guess I can ask you to service this thing so I can get out of here."

"Sure." Zeitgeist rose and led the way out of the room and down the hall to the laboratory. His face was absolutely expressionless, but not fixed; only relaxed.

Joe shucked out of his jacket, unbuttoned his shirt and took it off. He unclipped the elastics and pulled the amplifier off over his head. Zeitgeist took it and tossed it on the bench. "All right," he said, "get dressed."

Joe went white. "What, you want to haggle? Three thousand then, when I get it," he said shrilly.

Zeitgeist sighed. "Get dressed."

Joe turned and snatched at his shirt. "Blackmail. Lousy blackmail."

Zeitgeist said, "You know better than that."

There is a quality of permanence about the phrase that precedes a silence. It bridges the gap between speech and speech, hanging in midair to be stared at. Joe pulled on his shirt, glaring defiantly at the other man. He buttoned it up, he tucked in the tails, he put on his tie and knotted it, and replaced his tie-clasp. He picked up his coat. And all the while the words hung there.

He said, miserably, "I want to know better than that."

Zeitgeist's breath hissed out; Joe wondered how long he had been holding it. "Come here, Joe," he said gently.

Joe went to the bench. Zeitgeist pulled the amplifier front and center. "Remember what I told you about this thing—a mike here to pick up the chest tones, band-passes to cut down on what you have too much of, and the amplifier here to blow up those low resonances? And this?" he pointed.

"The power supply."

"The power supply," Zeitgeist nodded. "Well, look; there's nothing wrong with the theory. Some day someone will design a rig this compact that will do the job, and it'll work just as I said." He pale gaze flicked across Joe's perplexed face and he laughed. "You're sort of impressed with all this, aren't you?" He indicated the whole lab and its contents.

"Who wouldn't be?"

"That's the mythos of science, Joe. The layman is as willing to believe in the super-powers of science as he once did in witches. Now, I told you once that I believe in the ability of science to save our souls ... our *selves*, if you like that any better. I believe that it's legitimate to use any and all parts of science for this purpose. And I believe the mythos of science is as much one of its parts as Avogadro's Law or the conservation of energy. Any layman who's seen the size of a modern hearing-aid, who knows what it can do, will accept with ease the idea of a band-passing amplifier with five watts output powered by a couple of penlite cells. Well, we just can't do it. We will, but we haven't yet."

"Then what's this thing? What's all this gobbledegook you've been feeding me? You give me something, you take it away. You make it work, you tell me it can't work. I mean, what are you trying to pull?"

"You're squeaking. And you're saying 'I mean,' " said Zeitgeist.

"Cut it out," Joe said desperately.

The pale eyes twinkled at him, but Zeitgeist made a large effort and went back to his subject. "All this is, this thing you've been wearing, is the mike here, which triggers these two diaphragm vibrators here, powered by these little dry cells. No amplifier, no speaker, no nothing but this junk and the mythos."

"But it worked; I heard it right here on your tape machine!"

"With the help of half a ton of components."

"But at the office, the liaison meeting, I ... I—Oh—"

"For the first time in your life you walked around with your chest out. You faced people with your shoulders back and you looked 'em smack in the eye. You dredged up what resonance you had in that flattened-out chest of yours and flung it in people's faces. I didn't lie to you when I said they *had* to listen to you. They had to as long as you believed they had to."

"Did you have to drag out all this junk to make me believe that?"

"I most certainly did! Just picture it: you come to me here all covered with bruises and guilt, suicidal, cowed, and without any realizable ambition. I tell you all you need to do is stand up straight and spit in their eye. How much good would that have done you?"

Joe laughed shakily. "I feel like one of those characters in the old animated cartoons. They'd walk off the edge of a cliff and hang there in midair, and there they'd stay, grinning and twirling their canes, until they looked down. Then—

boom!" He tried another laugh, and failed with it. "I just looked down," he said hoarsely.

"You've got it a little backwards," said Zeitgeist. "Remember how you looked forward to graduating—to the time when you could discard that monkey-puzzle and stand on your own feet? Well, son, you just made it. Come on; this calls for a drink!"

Joe jammed his arms into his jacket. "Thanks, but I just found out I can talk to my wife."

They started up the hall. "What do you do this for, Zeitgeist?"

"It's a living."

"Is that streamlined mousetrap out there the only bait you use?"

Zeitgeist smiled and shook his head.

For the second time in fifteen minutes Joe said, "I guess I just don't understand you," but there was a world of difference. Suddenly he broke away from the old man and went into the room with the fireplace. He came back, jamming the envelope into his pocket. "I can handle this," he said. He went out.

Zeitgeist leaned in the doorway, watching him go. He'd have offered him a ride, but he wanted to see him walk like that, with his head up.

BLUEJAY SPECIAL EDITIONS

1 A MIRROR FOR OBSERVERS
   by Edgar Pangborn $5.95

2 DEATHBIRD STORIES by Harlan Ellison $6.95

3 THE PENULTIMATE TRUTH
   by Philip K. Dick $5.95

4 THE STARS ARE THE STYX
   by Theodore Sturgeon $6.95

5 CLANS OF THE ALPHANE MOON
   by Philip K. Dick $6.95

6 ELLISON WONDERLAND
   by Harlan Ellison $6.95

7 TIME OUT OF JOINT by Philip K. Dick $7.95

8 THE BEAST THAT SHOUTED LOVE AT THE
   HEART OF THE WORLD
   by Harlan Ellison $6.95

9 THE ENGINES OF THE NIGHT
   by Barry N. Malzberg $6.95

10 DR. BLOODMONEY by Philip K. Dick $7.95

11 THE GOLDEN HELIX
    by Theodore Sturgeon $7.95

12 APPROACHING OBLIVION
    by Harlan Ellison $7.95

13 ALIEN CARGO by Theodore Sturgeon $8.95

For ordering information see following page

BECOME A
BLUEJAY WATCHER

If you enjoyed this book and would like to know about some of the nearly one hundred Bluejay Books, write to us for a free list of books, % Dept. CATALOG

Ask your bookseller for other Bluejay books, or call (800) 221-7945 for direct-ordering information.

If you would like information about upcoming Bluejay books, write to Dept. CHASCH with your name and address, and we'll send you The Bluejay Fantastic Flyer, a quarterly informational brochure.

Bluejay Books Inc.
James Frenkel, Publisher
1123 Broadway, Suite 306
New York, New York 10010